The Shrouded Throne

Mages of Asterheim Book 1

The Shrouded Throne

Steven D. Jackson

PRESS

VULPINE

PRESS

Published by Vulpine Press in the United Kingdom in 2023

ISBN: 978-1-83919-499-3
Map image © Rowan Thomas

www.vulpine-press.com

For A and C. The magic in my world.
And for Gan Gan, the original Lady Gloriana. Sadly missed.

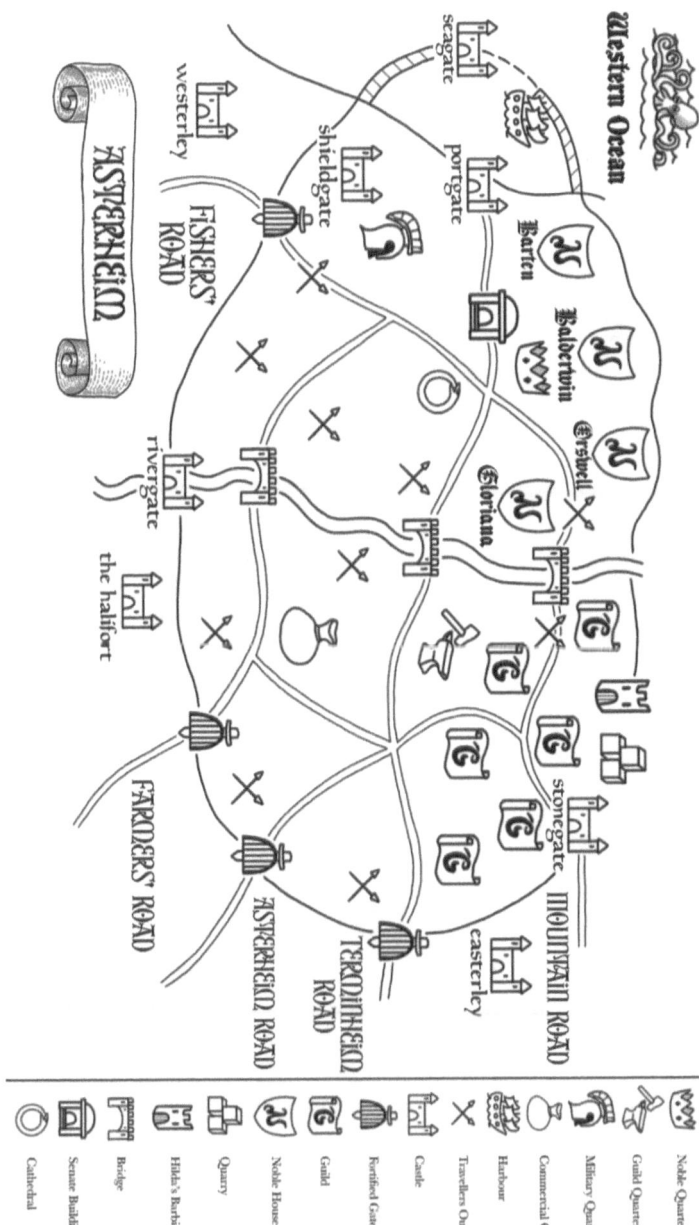

Chapter One

Sprawled and lifeless the limp form lay; prone in the dark, secrets veiled in shadow.

'Here he is, sir,' said the young watchman in a hushed, conspiratorial voice, holding the torch up. The flickering flames cast feeble light on the body that lay half-hidden in the muddy filth of the dark alley. The watchman stepped nimbly aside, muttering a short curse as his feet splashed in something unpleasant, making way for the heavy-set man with the scarred jaw.

Crouching in his golden priest's robe amid the rank puddles, the scarred man poked at the body with one gnarled finger, ignoring the stench rising from the still-warm corpse.

The scarred man wrinkled his nose. It was impossible to tell how much of the smell was the natural odour of the body and how much the general filth of the narrow alleyway. Moonlight and the glow of the watchman's torch glinted on pools of unknown foulness not far away.

'No puncture wounds?' he asked eventually, glancing suspiciously up at the watchman. The young man shook his head earnestly, his eyes wide and hopeful, full of the thrill of the crime. The older man who called himself a priest held the youngster's gaze a moment longer and then looked back at the body.

'And you're sure this one had a disagreement with one of *them?*' he asked, addressing the third conspirator.

The thin man with the grey hair standing behind them sniffed, a meek sound that made the priest's lip curl instinctively. 'I am. I checked the logs twice. He paid for a service, but not all that was agreed.'

'Twice?'

The accountant bristled.

'I'm sure,' he said tightly. 'I'm exceptionally familiar with those logs.'

The priest grunted something between a scornful laugh and a long-suffering sigh. He turned from the cooling body and gave the man a hard glare.

'You had better not be wrong this time.'

'I'm not,' the accountant sniffed.

The priest fished inside his moth-eaten gold-coloured robe and, with his eyes still on the accountant, handed a pouch to the watchman. The young man took it with fevered excitement. It clinked with the promise of gold.

'Go now, my son,' said the scarred priest in a pious tone, though he had never held any holy office. The watchman hefted the pouch and grinned, hurrying away. The shadows danced madly, reaching up to claim the priest and the body as the young man carried the torch and its flickering circle of light further from them.

'Remember, no more than an hour,' the priest called after him.

The watchman half-turned and nodded, his eyes still on the bulging pouch in his hands, more gold than he'd seen in a lifetime.

'Yes sir, an hour, sir. I'll be sure of it.'

'Do. I can retake those coins if I choose.'

2

The watchman looked about to retort, but something in the priest's eyes, dark and glinting in the moonlight beyond the reach of his torch, gave him pause.

'Yes sir,' he said, hurrying away.

'You should go too,' the scarred priest said, turning back to the body in the still darkness. The accountant sniffed and hesitated. 'You'll be paid when I have three. Find me one more.'

He waited until the sound of the thin man's footsteps receded down the alleyway and was lost in the stillness of the night before he pulled out the flask and carefully tipped the contents onto the corpse, standing back as foul mist instantly began to rise from the cadaver. He looked away as the flesh was charred and blackened, grateful for the thick shadow. The dead man's clothes were untouched by the noxious chemical, lending the corpse an unsettling, fearful aspect.

'Burned without flame,' the priest said with reverence. He crouched beside the steaming body and leaned towards the approximate place where its ears should have been.

'Thank you,' he whispered.

***

In her private box overlooking the upper seats in the Senate House, Lady Ariene Gloriana tightened her grip on her cane. Thin, gnarled skin on old, gnarled wood. The pain in her knuckles refused to be ignored however, and redoubled its demands that she make some show of obeisance to its supremacy. She gritted her teeth instead, tightening her grip still further out of spite. Her assistant Darcy, the devoted woman she still couldn't help thinking of as a girl, looked round in alarm, sweeping her mousy hair away from her eyes.

'Everything alright, my lady?'

Ariene sighed and tried to concentrate on the proceedings below. Darcy rose from her seat, a concerned look on her pale face. A face only now starting to thicken and wrinkle as the glow of youth faded and her figure became plump where once it had been voluptuous. Ariene ignored her and focused on the discussions being held beneath them, forcing aside the nagging worry about what would become of Darcy if she did in fact just give up and die.

'You made a strange noise,' Darcy said, fussing around her like a fly headbutting a window.

'Sometimes I make noises, dear,' said Lady Gloriana, 'it's all part of the fun of being a thousand years old. Very rarely do I intend to imbue one with meaning, however. It was probably a knuckle cracking or something. I shouldn't be at all surprised, the way they're carrying on.'

'No, no,' Darcy said, largely ignoring everything Ariene said as she customarily did, 'it was a sort of groan. Are you in pain?'

'Constantly, dear. But not the kind you mean. Although, yes. That kind too. I can be scandalously conventional at times. As can my knuckles.'

Darcy looked at her oddly and made to touch something on Ariene's face. She batted the probing fingers aside, ignoring the hot flare in her own fingers.

'What is it that you're so interested in, my lady?' Darcy asked, sitting back but keeping a watchful gaze on her. Evaluating her, no doubt. And subtle as a hammer to the face. Ariene sighed. The nagging worry crept back into her mind; Asterheim was no place for

4

the discarded former servants of great nobles who passed without heirs. Especially those whose principal talents were companionship and love.

'Look at that,' she said, putting the thought aside and pointing down at the audience chamber of the Senate.

Below her the small amphitheatre stretched, seats in tiered rings leading down to an open circular floor. Red seats on the upper tiers, for those worthies of the city who did not have Senatorial rank; white seats in the lower tiers closest to the floor for the Senators. A central dais was raised in the middle of the open speaking area, upon which sat an ornate throne shrouded beneath purple silk.

'The throne of the Echelarch,' she said with a hint of pride, 'the overlord of Asterheim and of course by extension the country. Covered and humbled for centuries. You know how that happened?'

'The Bloodless Coup,' said Darcy, a flicker of concern crossing her face. Ariene couldn't help but smile.

'The Bloodless Coup,' Ariene agreed with a nod. 'And it was House Gloriana, my dear, back in those dark days. My House. House Chetney, as it was known then. The one that finally persuaded the last of the Echelarchs to find an alternative career at the head of a united army of like-minded reformers. I think he became a tailor, poor boy. What was his name?'

'Reglius Augustus,' said Darcy with a fond smile. 'I remember from school.'

'That's the one,' Lady Gloriana grinned. 'Only fifteen he was. It must have been a glorious time. Such hope for the city, hope for everyone. After the dark days of that terrible purge, it must have seemed like the future had arrived. And House Chetney took the name Gloriana in memory of it.' She sighed and shook her head, staring down at the figures bickering and arguing below. 'Now look at us. Days, weeks, whole lifetimes spent fighting for little scraps of power. Who's up, who's down. Everyone suspicious of everyone. No one forming a true alliance in case someone tries to reach for that blasted chair under the purple silk. So much for glory. I do wonder sometimes.'

'Wonder what, my lady?'

Ariene sighed and turned to the younger woman.

'Whether we wouldn't have been better to strike young Reglius's head from his shoulders and burn his crown, his throne, this whole building to the ground and start again.'

'That's...horrible.'

Ariene laughed and looked back at the Senators.

'Yes. But what we have now is no system. The spectre of that throne haunts everything. A little blood centuries ago might have saved gallons now.'

She glanced at Darcy with a small smile.

'Have I convinced you, dear? Do I still have my marbles?' Darcy laughed and shook her head.

'Not at all. But I won't be turning you in to the Priory Sisters just yet.'

'Well, that's a relief. Let's go, dear.'

Ariene rose to her feet. Quite smartly too, she thought, considering that her knees felt as though they were presently inhabited by a hundred angry bees. She gathered her blue shimmering Senate dress about her, a morbid fear of tripping on it having become more and more prevalent in recent years. The dress was old and tattered, and had apparently earned her the epithet 'The Blue Lady'. Before she'd heard the name whispered in amusement from behind unfurled fans, she hadn't noticed that she'd worn it to so many Senate functions. Ever since her beloved husband had died and every day had become a tedious trudge towards seeing him again, she'd barely given any thought to her wardrobe. But since the name had appeared, she'd worn the tattered dress deliberately each and every time out of spite.

'The Senate recognises the honourable Lady Ariene Gloriana!' someone cried out from the lower tiers. She hesitated. To leave now would either make her seem deaf or rude, only one of which she wanted to seem to the vultures who endlessly circled her. Half of them no doubt wanted her dead so they could get their hands on her guilds, and the other half probably just wanted her dead. She let her dress drop and approached the bar that separated her box from the auditorium and looked out.

The Speaker for the month was standing by the throne, looking pleased with himself.

She didn't recognise him; a younger son of a lesser House she guessed, gaining a bit of exposure by getting himself elected to the facilitator's position. He was looking up at her, smiling warmly.

'Thank you for recognising me,' she said, her voice carrying in strident tones even now in her eighty-fifth year. Of course she did not mean it, but then no one expected her to. She had chosen to sit in her observation booth precisely because it should have accorded her the privilege of watching without participating. The angry bees in her knees buzzed more loudly, and she suppressed a grimace.

'May we ask, my lady,' said someone to the left, 'whether you have a view on these matters?'

The motion before them was one doomed to fail; it was one she would never support and which enough Senators had already shouted down to ensure it could not pass. Half had simply not bothered turning up.

'I had not intended to speak on this matter, my lord. I am patron of The Guild of Mages, it would seem inappropriate for me to speak on an issue relating to their conduct without first having regard to all the facts.'

'The facts are not disputed!' declared a woman in a purple gown who most likely had a considerable horse in whatever race was being played beneath today's words. Ariene couldn't quite place her face and made a mental note to make sure no one realised. 'Three dreadful unexplained deaths that can only be attributed to witchcraft. No normal affliction kills in such a manner, where a fireless flame consumes the body within its very clothing!'

'I consider myself an educated woman,' Lady Gloriana said lightly, 'but I couldn't say I am educated enough to know of all the ways in which a person can be killed and nor, I suspect, are you.'

'You deny that this is the work of malign magic? Even though each victim had a connection to a mage?'

The woman's face was infuriatingly familiar, but the name just wouldn't hold still and let her stab it with her fork. She pressed on.

'Who here does not have a connection to a mage, my lady?'

'You, *my lady*! You've never kept one and don't visit them for treatments which is why–' she caught herself.

'Which is why I'm so old and decrepit?'

She let the woman squirm a moment before returning to the point.

'Of course I deny that these were murders by disgruntled mages. As would anyone else with half a brain. As a society we have trained and used mages, relied on them, for centuries. They're our healers, our crop growers, our animal handlers, our builders. This very building with its pretty spires and pretty speeches would have fallen over long ago but for them. Since the dark days of the great purge, no foolish notion of witchcraft has been permitted to take root in learned people's minds, and I would not see those days return.'

'Even if mages have returned to their devilish practices?' a pompous little man in a garish outfit of pink and yellow silk demanded.

'I remember my history lessons from school, Senator,' she retorted, trying not to grit her teeth as the bees buzzed louder. They were making it very difficult to stay civil in the face of such foolishness. 'And I don't recall any instance of hidden witches killing their customers by setting fire to them from afar, but even so, if modern day mages had access to such powers I am sure we would know of it. Besides which, even if they could do so, it would be supremely counter-productive to murder people in such peculiar ways when perfectly adequate poisons are available on every street in the Commercial Quarter. Poisons that don't make corpses so fascinating that the Senate itself decides to crawl all over them which, I might add, is something hidden assassins might be quite keen to avoid.'

There were some nods of agreement and mild laughter at this. The pompous little fellow sat back down, fuming. His long, oiled moustache quivered.

'In case it wasn't clear,' Ariene said, gathering her dress again and turning away, 'I and all my guilds vote against the motion to censure The Guild of Mages or revoke licences for practising mages.'

'My lady!' someone else called. She cursed bitterly under her breath and dropped the dress again, shuffling her feet to keep them clear of the gauzy material. The bees buzzed.

'What?'

'Is it still your intention to retain sole control of your guilds, or will you permit some of us to assist you and relieve you of some of the heavy burdens you so admirably bear for the benefit of our city?'

A hushed silence fell as she located him. Expensive jacket, dark hair oiled back, a short greying beard oiled and cropped. Lord Orswell was in his mid-fifties, a man who took care of himself physically but never seemed to smile. Worry lines showed permanently on a tight and haunted face that she knew well. He had the look of a man forever on the edge of ruin, suspecting everyone and fearing everything, but with no choice but to continue. She pitied him a little, that his secret should be such a terrible, lonely burden. Perhaps the thought of getting his hands on some of the Gloriana holdings gave him some hope of advancement, something to comfort him in his solitary existence.

Ha, she thought, *not likely*.

She toyed with the idea of throwing his private life in his face for a moment, but decided instead to once again tuck the arrow away in her quiver. She strongly suspected that any number of others in the room also held the same arrow, and all were simply awaiting the moment that House Orswell either became a danger or an opportunity worthy enough to use it. Lord Orswell probably knew it too, hence his perpetual worry and his politically neutral attitude.

His major guild was the Citizenry, for goodness' sake; one could not ask for a less controversial yet benignly influential guild on which to spend one's life. A wise choice on his part.

'My decision remains unchanged, my Lord Orswell,' she replied as lightly as she could, 'but I thank you for your repeated offers of help. I trust you will offer the same to my successor when I appoint one.'

'And when will that be, my lady?' interjected someone else. She did not bother to look for this one.

'When the time is right. I am not dead today, so ask me tomorrow.'

'My lady's piety is an inspiration,' said one of the Priests of the Sacred Circle, sitting in the lowest red tier in his golden robes. She cast a disdainful look at the pompous fool.

'I wasn't referring to your Circle,' she said.

The priest smiled that condescending smile only fully paid-up members of religious orders can manage.

'You don't need to, Lady. Your words carry the meaning regardless and your fearless example to us all has been a wonder to behold. When your destination is your origin, the journey holds no fear. That is the way of the Circle.'

'Cowards walk in circles,' she snapped, 'the brave step forward and do not look back.'

The priest's smile wavered at that, and something in his eyes changed. Lady Gloriana felt a chill. A silence fell in the chamber that dismayed her; had the priests really risen so far in power?

'My lords,' she said, nodding to the assembly as she turned away. Darcy buzzed around trying to help her up the short flight of stairs. She waved her away.

'Enough, enough,' she said, 'I don't need more bees to contend with.'

The look on Darcy's face kept her chuckling all the way up the stairs.

***

The blood oozing from the wound on Rigel's arm had formed a peculiar shape that put him in mind of a pig's head. The red pool caught the light in just such a way that the pig also looked as though it was grinning at him. He grinned back, making a muted pig noise under his breath. He imagined it squealing, with its jaws bouncing up and down and its eyes spinning crazily in their sockets—

'Rigel!' the master shouted. Something bounced off the floor by his chair. A piece of chalk. Rigel looked round; everyone was looking at him.

'Nice to have you back,' Master Thomas said. 'What exactly was so funny? Care to share? Some of us have very dull lives.'

Rigel shifted about on his chair and gestured weakly to his numb arm, lying motionless on his desk as though not even connected to him. All around the drab, stone classroom, other students were sitting in much the same way, their arms slumped dead on the heavy wooden desks with shallow cuts on them. Daylight filtered through large windows, swirling dust motes gleaming in the sun. He could feel heat crawling up his neck and onto his cheeks.

'It, er...well it looks a bit like a pig,' he said with a weak laugh, 'I was thinking about it, you know, squealing. It looks like it's grinning so...'

Master Thomas held his gaze for a moment, then turned away. His grey robes swished about him, far too big for his body, and dragged along the floor. Dust floated lazily upward in his wake. Rigel wrinkled a nose at the sight. There was one thing of which he was very much certain, and that was he would never become a teacher.

Master Thomas was probably not that much older than him but was made to dress and act like an old man and live here in this dusty purgatory amid the ruins of ancient splendour.

No thanks.

'Try again.' With that, Master Thomas slumped down in his chair behind the desk at the front of the class. He put a hand to his forehead and rubbed his temples. Rigel shook his head with something between disgust and pity, and turned back to the pig.

'Heal damn you,' he muttered. Thaniel, to his left, sniggered as he hunched over his arm, poking it with a pencil.

'Squeal at it,' whispered Sophine, to his right. 'Make friends...'

'Har har,' he muttered, giving the slice in his arm an experimental poke. It was an unpleasant sensation, to prod at an arm and feel nothing. The blood trickled down to pool underneath it.

'Do you think that—' he began, glancing over at Sophine. She wasn't listening, her eyes closed, mouth moving as she recited some silent prayer or mantra. Everyone had their way of reaching the mindset needed to do anything as a mage. Sophine's thing was reciting secret words she would never ever divulge, and Thaniel seemed to do alright by holding his breath and making a comically exaggerated 'concentration' face. Rigel was jealous of both of them; at least they had a system.

13

Rigel closed his eyes and tried to visualise the small wound head in his mind.

We don't make things happen, Master Thomas had told them way back in their first classes, *we just link to the energy that everything already has and nudge them along. See in your mind the way everything is connected, then push.*

'I'm already healing,' Rigel whispered, ignoring the tightening of his stomach, the rapid beat of his heart and the growing certainty that he was never, ever going to amount to anything. 'So all I have to do is help it along.'

Stone, fire, water, even the air, Master Thomas had said. *Everything. The entire world is nothing but beautifully ordered energy, some of it aligning in patterns that – if you stand back far enough – look like physical things. But it's only an illusion. Remember that, hold it in your mind. Because your mind, your* will, *is energy too. Feel the connection between it and the outside world, and you can perform wonders.*

Well. The cut in his arm wasn't a wonder. It was an absurd, numb distraction cut in the shape of a mocking grin, sitting on top of a yawning pit of worry and doubt that had been growing inside Rigel for five years now. His body would heal in its own time, and wasn't in the least bit interested in his attempts to speed it up–'I did it,' said Sophine tonelessly, breaking Rigel's concentration or at least giving him something to blame for his own lack of it. He opened his eyes with a frustrated grunt and looked over. The wound in Sophine's arm was healed. It looked odd, like she'd spilled red paint on herself, but it was healed. She was looking at it sadly, her dark eyes troubled. He looked away.

The slice in his arm was still grinning at him, red and wet and numb. He prodded it again with his other arm.

Then he pushed it off the table.

***

Three feet above the damp ground of the disused undercroft below the ancient fortification known as Hilda's Barbican, which housed the academy for young mages, two lumpy grey stones ground against one another. The stones were held aloft by nothing but the concentration of two young students. Tiny cracks and fissures crept along the rocks as they grappled, each trying to push through the other. Every now and then little clouds of dust or crumbling pieces of cracked stone would escape, falling to the ground amidst the cheers of the gathered students. One rock was already about half its size, streams of dust falling from it ever faster as the opposing stone ground it away.

Rigel had seen enough of these contests to be fairly sure which way it was going to end, and he glanced with some satisfaction at the face of the boy standing on the crudely painted green box at one end of the makeshift arena which was little more than a ring of stones about six feet apart. He knew the boy, at least a little. His name was Alakis, and he couldn't have been more than about twelve. One of those annoyingly talented people who take nothing seriously and are therefore popular with the younger kids, but who are also top of any class they happen to be in, thus irritating the older students. Tonight, however, it seemed he'd picked the wrong rock. Rigel fought to keep an unseemly smirk off his face as Alakis grimaced with the effort of maintaining his composure and the carefully clear-headed focus it took to levitate something even a few feet.

'I give it thirty seconds,' Rigel muttered to the boy by his side, who like him was too old to deign to actually compete in the underground extra-curricular hijinks that passed for entertainment amongst the younger kids, but who also like him had nothing better to do.

'Twenty,' the boy chuckled back.

Even that might be a stretch. Alakis was struggling, his face arranged almost painfully into an expression of forced serenity that everyone in the crowded cellar knew he wasn't feeling. The key to any kind of energy manipulation was calmness. Order. Clearing your mind and connecting with the forces at work in the world. When people were shrieking and jeering, hurling insults and making bets, when you wanted to win and were starting to lose, that was when all of a sudden you were just a kid on a box trying not to cry.

Alakis' rock dropped suddenly to the ground with a sad thump, a puff of dust rising slowly from where it landed. The opposing rock, unexpectedly free of any opposing force, flew madly across the room and exploded against one of the ancient brick pillars holding up the ceiling of the abandoned cellar.

Rigel saw a flash of light and felt something hit him hard on his side, and for some reason he couldn't breathe. Everything was turned around; the floor was a vertical line but the people running back and forth along it weren't falling off. He blinked in confusion, the realisation that he was lying on his side coming to him only sluggishly. Something was wet and warm on his forehead.

'Ow,' he said, though he couldn't actually feel anything. He closed his eyes.

Some minutes must have passed because when he opened his eyes again he was sitting against the wall and his head had cleared. The Barbican's vaulted undercroft was empty, the green and red boxes overturned, and the ring of stones knocked out of shape by running feet. Master Thomas was kneeling next to him, peering into his eyes.

'Broke up the party,' Rigel croaked with a weak grin. A ghost of a smile flickered over Master Thomas' tired face. He stood up and offered a hand. Rigel noticed it was smeared with blood, which he assumed was his. He took the hand.

'You shouldn't let them do this,' Thomas said wearily, hauling Rigel to his feet. 'You're lucky it was only you who got hurt.'

Rigel snorted.

'Because I'm so dense it doesn't make a difference if I get pummelled with stones?'

'Because you're not twelve.'

'So my skull's thicker?'

Thomas looked at him in that way adults sometimes did when unsure if Rigel was joking or offended. A sort of half-smile coupled with watchful eyes.

'I'm joking,' Rigel said eventually with a heavy, disappointed sigh.

Thomas turned away and made ushering movements towards the door that would take them through the dark, damp corridors towards the dormitories and onward to the rest of the academy buildings that had over centuries grown within and around the original stone fortress of Hilda's Barbican, named for the great mage who had ended the Great Purge and signed the Charter.

Rigel let himself be led out, gingerly touching his head to see if there was anything left of the injury done by the rogue shard of rock that had smacked him in the head. Thomas had done good work; he seemed fine.

'If you ever see them down here again, Rigel, shut it down please,' Thomas said as he trudged along through the dark. A faint nimbus of pale light sat in his hand, gently illuminating the shadows around them, but it barely reached their feet. Rigel thought about asking his tutor to turn up the light, but thought better of it.

'Why?' he asked, stumbling on a loose flagstone. 'It's harmless enough. Unless, you know, stones to the head…'

Thomas sighed, a pace or two ahead of him, but didn't look around.

'Because they need to learn that the rules are in place for everyone's safety. The world, or at least the city, is not as safe as it was.'

'Safe?' Rigel repeated. Since when was any city "safe"?

'For mages,' said Thomas. 'Things haven't been this dangerous for mages since the time of the Great Purge.'

Rigel frowned.

'You're not serious,' he said, stumbling again and cursing under his breath, 'the Purge was about stopping the crazy mages who used dark magic to raise monsters and conjure fire. We couldn't do that. We couldn't conjure fire if our lives depended on it. These are hardly the days of the Darkling Mages.'

Thomas was quiet for a time, turning the corner to head up the creaking stairs out of the disused cellars.

18

'Come with me,' he eventually said, leading the way across the campus to his office. Rigel followed, intrigued. Masters, particularly Master Thomas, did not tend to actually discuss anything with the students. He'd fully intended to be dismissed and sent to bed once they'd emerged. All at once, the air seemed charged with a strangely thrilling sense of conspiracy as he hurried after Thomas.

They reached the cramped office and Thomas closed the heavy wooden door, crossing to his desk and sinking into an old, threadbare armchair behind it. He looked tired, his dark hair starting to give way to silvery grey. Rigel looked around the office in the uncomfortable silence which followed. The thick carpet and single small window made it look more like a prison cell. Heavy wooden bookcases groaned with the weight of ancient tomes, flickering candles perched perilously close to the dusty pages.

'Are those books from before the Charter?' he asked, wondering what forbidden practices might be in there. Thomas nodded, a smile on his face and a gleam in his eyes that Rigel hadn't seen before.

'Are you even allowed to have them?' Rigel half-whispered. The thought that these could be illegal books both amused and scared him.

Thomas nodded slowly.

'The Charter says we can't use them, but it never said anything about keeping them. Besides, the Darkling Mages were hoping to shape a new world and base it entirely on the powerful sorceries they'd discovered. They put a lot of it in writing, back when it all seemed like a grand time of enlightenment and no one had started calling them "Darkling" Mages. Hilda herself insisted that they be kept, as a warning. So having these around is a reminder that good intentions don't always stay good and that history, and truth, is only what we tell each other it is.'

Rigel eyed the dusty tomes, feeling cold.

'Frightening, isn't it?' said Master Thomas, his smile gone as he studied Rigel. 'If even half the stories about the Purge are true, people were burned to death just for doing whatever is written in those books. Mages almost wiped out, erased from history. Tell me, how do you think it all started?'

Rigel hesitated. How it had *ended* was common knowledge. The great Hilda had signed the Charter, officially forming the Guild of Mages under the supervision of the Senate and ending the dangerous independence that had led to the Darklings. The Barbican had been raised to protect the students, or to protect others from them, depending on which way you looked at it, and had come to be known as "Hilda's Barbican" or sometimes simply "Hilda's".

But how it had started, that was another story.

'Well, the Darklings conjured demons and…'

Thomas made a dismissive grunting sound and sat back heavily in his chair. Rigel fell silent, like a scolded child.

'You use magic, Rigel. Whatever you might think of your abilities,' he gave Rigel a meaningful look, 'you're a mage. One day perhaps you'll be a great mage. Have you ever in all your time learning this craft ever had any inkling that *demons* are real?'

Rigel shook his head.

'No,' agreed Thomas. 'And all the other stories the legends tell us, Darklings hurling fire from their fingers and creating howling portals to monstrous worlds, doesn't it sound a little like the work of imagination? Like the work of people who have no idea how magic actually works?'

It did. It all sounded absurd.

Thomas nodded gravely.

'My suspicion is that it was all invented to justify the violent removal of mages as a political group in the power-games of Asterheim those long centuries ago. These chains placed on us now, confining us to guild supervision within the walls of the Barbican and limiting us to what powers we can access through calm meditation and clear-headed concentration, they're the work of ignorance and politics.' He sighed. 'But they are what they are, and we flout those rules at our peril.'

Master Thomas leaned forward, crossing his arms on his desk.

'Do you see what I'm saying, Rigel? I don't ask you to keep the youngsters from ill-disciplined displays because I'm afraid they'll start conjuring demons in their sleep. It's because certain people would like nothing better than to stoke the same fear of us that resulted in the Purge once before. Politicians love an enemy. And once we've been erased from history for good, what stories would they tell of us?'

Rigel nodded reluctantly, fidgeting his feet. Suddenly he wasn't so sure he wanted to have adult discussions with masters after all.

'But sir, we're no threat. Mages are just another guild now. We're healers, builders, we help the crops grow…'

'True,' allowed Thomas, rising to his feet and brushing a finger over the covers of the heavy forbidden books. 'But the fear of raising our heads politically means we do nothing to stop stories spreading about us. Have you heard of The Mournful Shrine?'

'The *Monastery*?' said Rigel with an amused smile. Thomas nodded, pulling a heavy book bound in black leather from the shelf and weighing it in his hands. He fished a pair of reading glasses out of his pocket as he spoke.

'That's them,' he said.

'Isn't that the place where all the city's losers end up?'

Thomas choked back a sudden laugh and tried to look stern, peering at Rigel over the rims of his glasses.

'The Mournful Shrine is a sanctuary for those to whom life has been…' he broke off. 'Yes, it's where the losers end up. Prisoners, failed guild members and the like.'

Rigel grinned.

'Such pious monks. The Circle priests pretend they don't even exist.'

Thomas made a visible effort not to chuckle, managing to turn it into a short, studious cough.

'Yes, well. They're starting to become a problem for us. They've been scamming people by going around 'lifting curses' that mysteriously vanish when they're paid.'

Rigel blinked.

'Nothing to do with us though, right? People know they're not real mages. It's the Mournful Shrine for goodness' sake.'

'Do they?' said Thomas darkly, leafing through his book. 'I'm not so sure. People have been complaining to the rector, as though we're somehow responsible for what charlatans claiming to be guild mages get up to. That's my worry. We just aren't doing enough to stop it and I worry the mood in the city is turning against us.' He found a particular passage in his book and paused.

'*The people were most afeared,*' he read aloud, '*and did strike at once in righteous fury, in fear of their very souls.*' He closed the book. 'There you have it. Probably the only record of the Purge which rings true.' He placed it carefully back on its shelf. 'They struck at the mages first. Not because of demons or fire-witches, but because they were afraid.'

Rigel shivered.

'Afraid of what?'

'Who knows? The truth of it is long lost to time. The point is, we must not give people any reason to fear us. We must all be good, Charter-abiding mages and not do things like hold raucous stone-smashing events in dark cellars that common people might misunderstand. Keep our heads down.'

'But sir, shouldn't we be trying to stop people being afraid of us? Showing people we aren't dangerous? Maybe we should publicly say something about the Mournful Shrine and–'

Thomas sat back in his chair and waved a dismissive finger.

'You just do your part, Rigel. Keep the youngsters from doing anything silly and get them to learn some discipline. Leave the rest to the masters. Besides,' Thomas's voice brightened. 'You need to concentrate on finding yourself a patron.'

Rigel resisted the urge to groan, but couldn't help his eyes rolling.

'The last patronage fair is a few days off–'

'You think I don't know that?' Rigel said hotly. 'I'll be the only one to graduate without a patron and with nowhere to go. Believe me, I know.'

'You've got as much of a chance as anyone,' said Thomas gently.

Rigel instantly thought of Alakis. The kid already had a patron. A rich guild officer had spotted him at the last patronage fair carefully growing a flower from a seed in minutes, and had immediately chosen him. So when Alakis eventually graduated, he would have a job ready and waiting for him in the Farmers' Guild. And he was only twelve. The only person ever to have secured a patron at a younger age was Sophine, though the man who'd chosen her, it was widely suspected, had not done so for her magical talent.

'I really don't,' Rigel muttered.

'I mean it, Rigel. If I'm right, then secure employment with a good guild is the best protection any of you can have if things get harder. The focus will be on us, here at Hilda's, not on individuals with other guilds to protect them.'

'What if I can't?' Rigel blurted out. 'What if I'm just the waste of space my parents thought I was?'

Thomas hesitated, just a moment, but to Rigel even that was like a kick in the stomach.

'Your parents didn't think that...' Thomas said, unconvincingly. 'They wanted you to be a mage, that's why they sent you here.'

'Ha,' Rigel said mirthlessly. 'At that age? No. They wanted one less mouth to feed, that's all. Even you know it.'

Master Thomas sighed and leaned forward. His hair flopped over his eyes briefly and he flicked it away, absently staring at the books on the shelf before fixing Rigel with a look he'd never seen before. Something between pity and fear.

'You must try to be positive, Rigel, even if you don't feel it. Reach above yourself, hold on to that serenity and I *know* you can master healing, building, crop growth, forecasting, all sorts. But the opposite of that, these dark feelings,' he paused for a minute, searching for the right words. 'They are...they do not find young men lucrative careers in Asterheim or anywhere else. And I want

24

you to have a career, Rigel. I really do. You could be a great mage some day.'

Master Thomas's eyes flicked to the heavy books on his shelf, a strange look on his face. Rigel had the distinct impression he was holding something back.

Rigel forced a laugh. 'So what you're saying is…you want me to smile for the patrons in a few days' time?'

Thomas leaned back and smiled tiredly. 'If you wouldn't mind.'

***

Lord Amir Barten made Lady Gloriana's teeth ache. A one-time ally, and a full-time rival, he was one of the most powerful men in the Senate owing to his name, his family and his guild holdings. He was also roundly suspected of being a murderer, an embezzler, a man to make and break alliances on a whim to suit his own purposes. Of course, the same could be said of at least half of the Senate, and what could be said of the rest was every bit as unsavoury. Even the Blue Lady herself had been implicated in multiple intrigues, assassinations, rebellions and takeovers throughout her long life, and some accusations were even true. She was old enough to know such things were merely politics, and didn't hold them against her rivals. Besides which, as Steward of the enormous Labourers' Union and Castellan of Asterheim's major military force, the Battlemasons, Amir was supremely and rightly indifferent to anyone's whinging about his methods.

It was Barten's recent alliance with the priests of the Sacred Circle and their mysterious unseen leader, His Benevolence Lyoris Mountebank, that really upset her. As she shuffled down the richly carpeted and heavily tapestried corridor, followed by a quietly concerned Darcy, Ariene caught sight of the imposing figure of the man towards whom, bizarrely, she now felt more disappointment than hostility. She sucked her teeth and tilted her head; this would not be a fun conversation.

'My lady,' he said as she approached, swooping down into a low bow, one arm outstretched in a manner that made her think of an irate goose and the other across his ruby-studded chest. His hat, trimmed in something that less enlightened people might assume to be mink, somehow stayed on top of his bald head. She waited for him to come back up for air before fixing him with her least animated stare.

'Lord Barten,' she replied with a sigh. Her long-time colleague tried a weak smile, though it sat poorly on his clearly troubled face. Amir was no longer a young man, but still handsome. His dark skin seemed almost to gleam in the candlelit corridor and his build, though thicker now than in his youth, still spoke of strength. She regarded him a moment, then allowed a small smile back.

'I have been sent word from the priesthood,' he said, taking his hat off and running a hand over his smooth head, 'they want you to know that no insult was taken at your spat with the priest in the chamber.'

'Curious,' she said flatly, 'that sounds a little like it means the exact opposite. Darcy, dear, what was the term for that?'

'For what, my lady?' asked Darcy, darting forward as though shaken from a daydream and worried she'd missed half the conversation. Which she plainly had.

'For when a band of self-important fanatics think a mild put-down is a declaration of war, and that I should care two figs for their opinions.'

Amir nodded with a sigh, glancing away as Darcy floundered for an answer.

'No matter, dear. The moment's passed. You didn't come here to pass on passive-aggressive notes from your friends in golden robes, Amir, so why not say what you came to say? My knee bees are buzzing.'

Darcy gave her a concerned look and turned to Lord Barten, trying to usher him aside with hushed words like 'senile' and 'tired'.

Barten ignored Darcy, his pleasant features marred by the tightness to his jaw. 'To business then. You won't talk about it publicly Ariene, and I understand that, but the matter of your successor does need to be addressed. All those guilds. All those people working for them. The city needs a smooth transition of ownership and you owe it to us all to ensure that. With the tragic death of your sons—'

If he saw her stiffen at that, he gave no sign.

'—it falls to me and my associates to insist that—'

She snarled and stepped past him, somehow finding the energy and strength to shove him aside as she went. She turned as Darcy hurried after her, waving the girl away.

'You will insist on nothing,' she barked. 'What I do with my guilds is my concern and I will not be hounded out of this world by the likes of you.'

He stepped after her, reaching out unconsciously.

'Come on Ariene, I didn't mean any disrespect. We've worked together in the past, why not now?'

'Because now you run around the Senate handing out messages from your circular-minded friends like some lapdog, not like the Lord I took you to be.'

He ignored the insult and pressed on; she had to admire him for that.

'You have the Customs Alliance and the Factors' Guild,' he said. 'That covers all of the trade through the Western Ocean and the accounting across the whole of Asterheim. What happens when they're leaderless and the Senate devolves into squabbles and factions? This isn't a game.'

'It's always been a game, Barten,' she sniffed. 'The fact that I'm no longer playing doesn't change that.'

'Enough jokes. You even hold the Travellers. What happens if they suddenly decide that they hold the balance of power?'

'They won't, they have their own officers.'

'I mean the military wing, Ariene. For now, the Overseer is happy policing the city gates and manning the bridges, but they could just as easily deploy their forces wherever else they chose.'

'They wouldn't. And aren't you Castellan of the Battlemasons? The overlord of the castles at the gates and the soldiers within? You have the military power to oppose the Travellers five to one. It wouldn't happen.'

'It could!'

She made a short sniffing noise somewhere between a laugh and a sigh and shook her head.

'And yet through them I have had the luxury of a private paid security service, which I could not only deploy on the streets of Asterheim itself, but could do so legally anytime I chose. Unlike you as Castellan of the actual military. Must be frustrating.' She

28

gave her rival an arch glare. 'You might as well make your peace with that though, Amir, because I promise you will *never* have that guild as long as you associate with those close-minded relics of the Sacred Circle.'

'Never is not a long time for you, Ariene,' he said cuttingly. 'I can wait.'

'I am not dead today. Tomorrow perhaps, I'll decide what to do with my guilds.'

He glared at her. 'You said that yesterday.'

'She said it in the chamber too,' added Darcy in a hushed voice. 'I think she's getting forgetful.'

'I did not forget,' said Ariene, holding Barten's gaze. 'And indeed we did discuss it. So you see, my word is good. Goodnight, Lord Barten.'

She shuffled away, once more an eccentric elderly lady in an old-fashioned blue gown, glittering with gaudy sapphires and trimmed in frond-like lace frills. Barten watched her go. Anyone else daring to speak to him in such a way would find themselves waking up without a face, but House Barten and House Gloriana had a long history.

He turned and trudged slowly back towards the Senate chamber, casting a glance into the shadowed recess to his left. He scowled at the figure observing him.

'I just need more time,' he said, and strode away.

Chapter Two

The stone hovered a few metres above the water, glistening with tiny bursts of light. Rigel flicked his fingers, and the stone flipped heavily into the artificial lake with a splosh.

'See, I can do it *here*,' he griped. 'How come whenever Thomas is staring at me I make such a mess of everything?'

'Because you fancy him,' said Sophine, effortlessly flinging a stone with a twitch of an elegant finger.

'Shut up,' he said automatically, sifting through the rubble he sat on for another stone. '*You* fancy him.'

'No thanks,' she replied, lifting another stone with only mild concentration. 'I'm spoken for, remember?' She flung the stone, hard, her pale face grim. It hit the murky water with a splash and vanished from sight. She pushed her long black hair behind her shoulder with an angry shove.

'I wouldn't say no,' put in Thaniel, standing with his back to them by the edge of the water, throwing stones manually with his shirt off. His athletic body gleamed with sweat in the afternoon sun, as he so very obviously intended it to.

'Put a shirt on Than,' sighed Sophine.

Thaniel hefted a large stone and turned around, pouting. 'Why?' he said. 'I'm just relaxing here.'

'Please,' she scoffed, 'you flex those muscles any harder and *my* arms will start to ache.'

'Fine, whatever. But you're making the quarry ugly.'

Rigel looked around. The quarry was always ugly. It was one of the first and oldest quarries just outside the city walls where the ground started to give way to the northern mountains. Long since exhausted and abandoned, the quarry was now a poorly fenced-off wasteland. Rigel, Thaniel and Sophine had started coming here in their first year at The Barbican, ever since they'd stumbled across a disused accessway behind their dormitory that led down into the tunnels beneath the city. The tunnel took a twisting route through the walls and came out just a short distance from the quarry fence. There were many such passages and gates, old sewers and suchlike, that had been abandoned or forgotten as the city walls were moved, expanded or renovated over the centuries. No one, except possibly some high up members of the Architects' Guild, really knew them all. It was every citizen's duty to report any such find so the city could brick them up or defend them, but how many of those citizens actually did so was another question.

The quarry extended maybe half a mile all round, a landscape of huge cliffs, ugly grey stone and piles of rubble. Much of it was now underwater, after centuries of rainfall and run-off from the mountains. It was on the shores of one of these man-made lakes that they now sat, hurling stones under the fading daylight.

'So what did Thomas want with you?' Thaniel asked, dropping down next to them and pulling on his shirt. Rigel eyed him with some annoyance. Even with his body hidden and his face grimy with quarry dust, Thaniel was still unreasonably good looking. It just wasn't fair.

'He wanted me to keep the kids in line,' he said, and told them about the stone competition in the cellar, and his talk with Master Thomas about the Mournful Shrine.

'That makes sense,' Thaniel said, staring intently at the ground and drawing faces in the dust with his finger. 'I've heard a few things about the monks there, actually this guy was telling me about this protest—'

'Stuff like this would never happen if we had an Echelarch,' Sophine said, cutting across him. She stood up, raising her right hand. Five stones rose smartly into the air and spun in lazy circles around her fingers. She stared across the lake at the mountains.

'Someone to take charge of the city. Even the country. Someone to put an end to the stupid.'

'The stupid?' Rigel laughed. 'That's a big job.'

'Not stupid *people*,' she said, not laughing. 'Just the big pile of stupid surrounding everything. People looking out for themselves and no one else. People interested in how much money they can make. People being bought and sold like—' Her right hand closed into a fist like a vice. The stones were each crushed instantly to dust and drifted away on the wind. Rigel's mouth fell open.

'A strong leader would deal with that,' she finished weakly, staring down at her hand like she'd never noticed it before. She flexed her fingers and then hurriedly crossed her arms, looking pointedly out over the water as though she hadn't just somehow smashed rocks with no more than an angry gesture.

'Er, Soph?' Rigel said tentatively, thinking back to Master Thomas's lecture earlier, about the Charter and forbidden powers. 'How did you just do that?'

Sophine didn't turn around. Rigel and Thaniel shared a silent look as the moments stretched uncomfortably.

'People who want to be leaders are people who look out for themselves,' Thaniel eventually said, resuming the previous conversation with a tone of wry levity that sounded distinctly hollow. 'Name one Echelarch in history who genuinely wanted to make things better for people.' He offered an attempt at a rueful chuckle that fell horribly flat and gave Rigel an expectant glare. Rigel forced a laugh.

'I can't name any at all,' he said, which was almost true. 'Except old Reglius.'

'Exactly,' said Thaniel with a grateful nod. 'We don't need them. The way things are, the nobles have to work together so they tend to be more moderate.'

'They tend to be more useless,' Sophine said, finally turning around and sitting back down.

Rigel started to speak but a glance from Thaniel made him think better of it.

'Nothing ever changes,' she added, 'because they all have their own interests and little exclusive kingdoms to run. A leader would mean they had a single direction to move in and a single purpose, so there would be more room for people like us to move more freely between them.'

'But we're going to be mages,' Thaniel said, confused. 'We don't need that to move freely. Mages are the freest people in Astregoth.'

'Are they?' said Sophine darkly. 'In our class, how many of us have been promised to nobles or lesser noble houses or guild officers? Most of us. And for what? As builders, creators, artists? No. Healers. Most of our classes this year are about healing.'

'Which I am terrible at,' added Rigel. She nodded.

'Which Rigel is terrible at. So what happens when the mages are all healers? The rich stay alive forever and the young are trained as mages to keep them alive? What kind of system is that? And anyone who isn't good at healing just doesn't get a patron? Rigel ends the year as an apprentice, no one pays for him to stay, so he goes back to his village somewhere near Ceresheim to be a farmer.'

'And won't my parents be pleased to see me,' Rigel sighed bitterly.

'The last patron fair is in two days,' Thaniel said brightly, 'I'm sure someone will pick you then. It's not like there are many of us seniors left without a patron so they should be fighting over you.'

Sophine looked at him with a strange smile. 'You don't have a patron either, Than.'

'No, but I'm pretty sure I will. I'll flutter my eyelashes and the old boys will be fighting over who gets me.'

Sophine sighed exasperatedly.

'One day that'll get you in trouble, Than. What if one of the Circle priests heard you?'

'Let them,' Thaniel said with uncharacteristic bitterness. 'It's not like I can change.' Sophine looked at him.

'Sorry. I'm just saying.'

'I know, I know,' he said, picking at the stones by his feet.

Rigel snorted. 'Wish I had his optimism. Everything looks bad for me; the game's rigged and I'm losing. If someone had wanted

34

me, they'd have picked me last year or the year before. I haven't improved much.' Thaniel groped for an answer to that, but eventually gave up and fell silent.

Something stirred beneath Rigel as he sat on the rubble. A faint tremor. He looked at his companions in alarm, but they hadn't noticed anything. Sophine was looking away to the mountains again, thinking her thoughts, and Thaniel was continuing his pictures in the dust, his brow furrowed in concentration. The tremor came again, vibrating through the ground.

Rigel put his hand on the rocky floor, trying to sense the vibration that seemingly only he could feel. Like the world was shaking in time with his frustrated thoughts. An image arose in his mind, Master Thomas warning him about his bleak outlook and how he needed to avoid emotions...

The vibrations weren't in the ground. Rigel lifted his hand slowly from the ground and stared at it. He could still feel it, the thrumming of power within him. Inside him. For a moment, just a moment, he could feel it. A connection with the ground, with the water beyond, with the mountains and the sky they touched. Everything. But it was within, against a backdrop of pain and sadness, not in some serene passivity. A swell of impossible energy was just there beneath his skin, just lapping on the shores of—

'Don't they realise mages don't curse people? Haven't they heard of the Charter?' Sophine was asking Thaniel as Rigel's focus swam back to the here and now. His legs were cold and his backside ached. The powerful feeling was gone.

'They're going after the monks, not mages.'

'Monks who they think *are* mages,' she said. 'that's bad enough. They think these monks are mages and that they curse people. That means they think *we* curse people and they'll be coming for us next.'

'That's what Master Thomas was saying,' said Rigel sadly.

'I don't think it means that,' Thaniel mumbled uncertainly.

'Now I get why there's a curfew tonight,' Sophine added.

'There is?' asked Rigel, shifting his legs about on the stone.

'Thomas announced it whilst you were sulking in your room. No one out after dark tonight.'

'So Hilda's won't be getting involved in this protest?'

'Why should it? The monks brought this on themselves. Besides, the protest is going to march in front of their building and make a nuisance of itself, that's all.

Rigel thought of his discussion with Thomas, and his fear that mages hadn't done enough to protect themselves from the monastery's false association with them.

'I think we should go,' he said. 'We should join the protest, to show them that mages are just as opposed to what those monks get up to as anyone, and that we aren't like them.'

'That's crazy,' Sophine snorted.

'Is it? If we don't do something, they'll be protesting at us next.'

'I meant that there's a curfew. Breaking it would be crazy. And you shouldn't be doing anything that could damage your chances of getting a patron.'

'No one will have a patron if The Barbican is in ashes.'

'That's a bit dramatic.'

'Fine, stay home then. I'll go.'

Thaniel nodded enthusiastically. 'Me too. Sounds like fun.' Rigel hesitated. 'You sure?'

Thaniel smiled an unusually sad smile.

36

'I don't have a patron either, and even I'm not that pretty. I can't see Hilda's patronising me to stay, so I think this is my last year here too. Might as well enjoy it.'

***

The sounds of protest could be heard even now, some miles away over the other side of the river. Sophine felt a stab of guilt, knowing that Thaniel and Rigel were both there. From the sound of it, the protest had turned nasty. Occasionally she heard something like glass breaking or a dim explosion, and from where she was on the hill upon which perched the modest Balderwin Estate in the noble quarter, she could see the glow from what had to be fire in the vague direction of the monastery. Too far away to do anything and too committed to turn back, Sophine drew her dark hood up over her head and looked up at the mansion.

Small, by the imposing standards of the great houses elsewhere in this lavish section of the city, the Balderwin house was nevertheless impressive. Three floors, some of the facade finished in stone, a tiled roof. Stables to the west and expansive grounds surrounded by a high wall. The Balderwins were no longer a powerful force in the city, but they had been once. They held their Senate seat by historical means, controlling only minor interests amongst the guilds. She was reasonably sure she'd seen their seal on ink bottles before, glass blowers perhaps?

So this was to be her fate, to be a plaything for a forgotten lord of glass blowers whose only reputation was as a cruel bully of people smaller than him. Sophine gritted her teeth and cast a last glance at the fiery glow across the river before stretching her hand towards the wall before her. She'd chosen a spot at the back of the house, a fairly solid-looking wall in cut stone which seemed a safe bet.

Sophine had been horrified earlier at the quarry, when impotent anger had risen to the surface of her mind and shattered those rocks. She shouldn't have been able to do that, hadn't even meant to do it either. It was the kind of magic the stories said that Darkling Mages had used, the uncontrolled power that had sparked the purge. For Sophine and the boys, who had spent years learning to suppress emotion to reach the serenity needed to gently manipulate the energy around them, such power had always seemed like a fairy tale. But now she wasn't so sure.

Patronage day was approaching as it did each year. Everyone was looking forward to it; the younger kids eager to demonstrate their new-found abilities, the older students like Rigel and Thaniel preparing to graduate as qualified mages and hoping to secure employment on their last day. Even for those who did not find a patron immediately, the final fair was a chance to be seen by anyone who might want to hire a licensed mage at some point. Putting on a good show would go a long way to persuading the masters to let a student stay on as a fee-earning mage. It was, for everyone else, an exciting opportunity.

Sophine was not excited. She had been chosen years ago and every year the festivities were overshadowed by the suspicion over why. The unspoken fear that she'd been chosen by a monster, one who enjoyed hurting his servants, gradually becoming impossible to ignore and getting in the way of her serenity, robbing her of concentration. This year though, something had changed. This time, those emotions seemed to be *fuelling* her abilities. Something had opened a door somewhere within her through which pain and anger seeped out to contaminate everything else, threatening her whole career. And so she had decided once and for all to do something about it.

The feeling rose slowly, hot and sharp, tempered by her uncertainty and fear. The same feeling that had shattered those rocks back at the quarry. She concentrated, letting it fill her, doing the complete opposite of everything she'd been taught to do in her years as a mage apprentice.

'I am a *person*,' she hissed, allowing the anger to become rage, letting it flood her senses, 'I am a *mage*. I will not be reduced to a plaything for *anyone's* amusement. I will—'

There. The swell of power was like a tangible force within her, swirling through and around her. She opened her eyes. She could see the stones of the wall, but the red-tinged energy within her sharpened her senses. She could perceive the fragile order of the stones. The tiny bonds between imperceptible particles just begging to be set free, returned to the random chaos from which they had been made.

She looked at her hands as she had in the quarry and, in an almost dreamlike state, closed her fist. A section of the wall some four feet high imploded and fell instantly into a heap of dust and gravel. Sophine jumped back with a yelp, the energy vanishing and her senses instantly returning to normal. She waited, hoping the entire wall wasn't about to collapse.

When it did not, she released a long-held breath and, after a moment's hesitation, stepped carefully through the hole, wrapping a shawl around her face as she went.

***

39

Rigel ran as fast as he could through the raging streets. The great monastery of the Mournful Shrine was ablaze, the citizens nearby panicking. Behind him came the yells and screams of his pursuers, shrieking at their fellow citizens to grab the young men running through their ranks. Their cries were lost in the roar of the crowd, the crash of windows and crack of timber, and the horrific crackle of burning buildings.

It had all gone so very, very wrong.

Rigel spotted an alleyway up ahead, half hidden behind a burning wagon which jerked violently as its fear-maddened horse pulled and reared on its harness. He grabbed Thaniel and pulled him towards it, the horse's hooves missing his head by inches as it reeled and whinnied. They fell and tumbled into the relative peace of the dark alley, little more than a recess between two oddly spaced houses. They waited, tense and breathless, watching the madness into which the world had descended. People were running past, but Rigel couldn't tell who was a protester or a rioter or a citizen caught up in the chaotic swirl.

'What happened?' Thaniel was repeating like a mantra. 'I mean…what just *happened*?'

Rigel shook his head. He had no answer.

They'd arrived a few hours past dark, after slipping out of The Barbican the way they had countless times before. The monastery wasn't far, within the same quarter of the city as the other guilds and The Barbican, so they'd made good time. A large crowd had gathered by the time they'd arrived, but seemed largely peaceful. Some people held torches and others weapons of various kinds, but not in an overtly hostile manner. A man was at the front, addressing the crowd. He wore a gold cassock, which marked him out as a

40

member of The Sacred Circle, a priest. No surprises there, since the priesthood had long considered the monks to be apostates at best, if not outright heretics. He was standing on a box, shouting at the crowd about the excesses and abuses of the monks. His face was marred by a long scar across his jawline which cut savagely into his left cheek, and his eyes were fierce in the torchlight. Something about him didn't ring true; the robe was old and torn, the emblems faded, his eyes maniacal.

Thaniel and Rigel had each worn their student robes, distinctive blue with the badge of Hilda's Barbican on the breast. They'd wanted to make sure the protesters got the message; that mages stood with them against these charlatans and frauds. They'd pushed their way to the front of the crowd to hear the priest's speech.

'These unnatural practices defy the order of all things,' he was saying, with much hand waving and clenched fists, 'foul magic and sorcery, disrupting nature and corrupting the soul!'

Rigel shared an uneasy glance with Thaniel. He hadn't mentioned the Charter, but he was certainly very close to it.

'The so-called monks of this place believe in nothing. They lie, they cheat, they deceive you all. A collection of failed priests and unscrupulous mages, hiding beneath new robes and preaching piety. You! Madam! Tell us your tale!' He pointed to a woman who stepped forward on cue and turned to face the crowd.

'I lost my husband and my home to these monsters,' she said tearfully as the crowd listened. 'He died of a curse, a terrible affliction that killed him in but a day. It could only have been the work of magic...'

'Or poison,' muttered Thaniel. 'Wouldn't put it past her.'

'Or anything else,' agreed Rigel quietly. 'You ever heard of a curse that works, let alone kills? It would be way too complex. Just stab the guy.'

'Exactly. Only the Darklings did magic like that. So they say.'

The crowd was muttering now, people making signs to ward off evil. The woman continued in what seemed increasingly like a re-hearsed speech. 'The vile sorcerers in this monastery then charged me more than I could afford to lift the curse from me before I too suffered the same fate!'

'Shame on them!' screamed someone else. A brick cracked against the gate of the monastery, thrown by someone in the crowd.

'We have to do something,' said Rigel, 'they've got this com-pletely wrong. She's lying—'

'Don't be an idiot,' hissed Thaniel, putting his hand on Rigel's shoulder to hold him back. 'This crowd is here for blood. Look.' He nodded at the man to their side. Rigel turned to look. The man was clad in heavy leather, with a large club held loosely in one hand.

Another a few paces away had a crossbow. Rigel blinked. Who would bring a crossbow to a protest?

'They're going to kill people, Than. Innocent people—'

'They're not innocent! For all we know they really do poison people to make money, and then blame us for it! It was a mistake to come here.'

Rigel shook off the hand.

'If we don't say something to tell these people that we're not like these monks then they'll turn up at Hilda's next and...'

It was only then that they'd realised the crowd had gone quiet. Rigel looked around.

The priest was staring right at him, as was the woman and a hundred other eyes. 'Mages,' said the priest with a smile. Rigel started to speak.

'Mages!' the priest shouted at the crowd, pointing at them. 'Come to cast spells on us, wretches? Come to save your friends? Perhaps you were the ones who killed this woman's husband and have come to atone for your sins?'

Rigel stepped forward, eyes on the priest, anger lending him the strength to ignore the braying crowd.

'We came to stand with you,' he said, loud enough to let the crowd hear him. 'We wanted you to know we aren't like the monks. What they did was wrong...'

'Scoundrel!' shouted the priest, brandishing a book at him. 'We will not hear your lies! Down with the Mournful Shrine!' At this, the crowd erupted into a frenzy, hundreds of people storming the monastery gates and tearing them down with alarming ease. Bursts of flame erupted along the grey stone walls and leapt up inside as oil-and-rag bottle missiles found the windows. A group of men seized Rigel and Thaniel by the arms and threw them to the floor, unsheathing blades and hefting mallets and other implements they'd brought with them.

'Vermin,' said one of them, a man with a black beard and laughing eyes. A large, double-handed hammer was held over one shoulder, and as he took hold of the handle in both hands and swung it, Thaniel screamed.

Time seemed to slow. The hammer moved through the air as though it was water, the sounds of the crowd suddenly dulled and echoing as though from far away. Rigel saw his outstretched hand, felt the peculiar sensation of time rippling through him, his to halt

43

at a whim. The primal constant of time, the ultimate symbol of order, now a plaything.

'What...? How are you doing this?' Thaniel was breathless by his side, staring up in disbelief as the hammer moved inch by inch up from the bearded man's shoulder. He got to his feet and looked the thug up and down with an uncertain smile. He prodded the man's arms.

'I don't know,' Rigel replied. Something slipped then, the conversation cracking the perfect alignment of his mind and purpose. The hammer rose faster, the screaming of the crowd intensified.

'Run Thaniel!' Rigel shouted as he scrambled to his feet and ran for his life. Barely a pace behind him, the hammer smashed into the ground with a sickening crunch. The bearded man snarled in anger.

'Stop them!' he cried.

And so they ran blindly, crashing into protesters as they went, shrugging off their robes and leaving them where they dropped. The alley was smoky now, other buildings catching fire as the riot spun out of control.

'We need to get out of here,' Thaniel was saying. 'We need to get back to The Barbican. Can you do that time thing again?'

'No. I don't know how I did it the first time.'

Thaniel peered at the building to the rear of the alley. It was old, crooked and made of timber. 'Think we can climb up there? We can go across the rooftops.'

'Sure. The burning rooftops.'

'They're not all burning.'

Rigel snorted a short laugh. He watched the chaos a moment longer and then nodded.

Without any other option, they headed to the gnarled wood of the building and started to climb.

***

Sophine was edging her way through what seemed to be a very large and deserted kitchen. Wooden work surfaces edged the room around a central table laden with implements, and a smell of baked bread hung in the air. She was just turning to open a door when she caught sight of a young girl. Nine years old, maybe ten, she was clad in a dirty tunic and her arms appeared to be covered in flour. She was cowering at the back of the room, trying not to be seen.

'It's ok,' whispered Sophine, 'I'm not here to hurt you.' The girl sniffed and whimpered something. She had bruises on her arms.

'What did you say?'

'Are you here to save us?' the girl whimpered again.

'Save you…?' Sophine trailed off, peering again at the girl. 'Are you a servant?' The girl hesitated, like she didn't know how to answer. Something in Sophine's chest turned cold and hard.

'A maid?'

The girl said nothing and looked at the floor.

'Listen,' said Sophine, 'how many of you are there?' The girl shrugged. 'I want you to find the eldest, and tell her to meet me outside, alright? Quietly. I'll be there soon. There's a hole in the wall at the back of the house, it leads into a serving corridor. Use that.' The girl stared at her, but nodded and disappeared through another door.

Sophine left the kitchen and climbed a short flight of stairs to the first floor, then up again to the second. Light could be seen

45

beneath a closed door a short way along the corridor, which she was fairly sure had to lead to the master bedroom. She paused, listening. Someone was in there, someone heavy from the sounds of it, stomping across the floor and making the floorboards creak.

Riding a flush of sudden anger, Sophine slammed opened the door and strode in. At the far end of the room, a man turned sharply to face her, grabbing a short sword from where it had been resting by the foot of a richly upholstered bed. Lord Balderwin stood before her, shirtless, in unbuttoned yellow breeches and high black boots. He was a fat man of fifty or so years, pale and pasty, and utterly apoplectic with rage.

'Who the hell are you?' he boomed, brandishing his sword in a flabby hand.

'Don't you recognise me?' she snarled, feeling her hatred for this man welling up inside her. The shame and embarrassment he'd caused her. The doubt. The self-loathing. 'It's only been five years.'

'How did you get in here?' he raged. 'Get out at once! Where are my guards? Guards!'

'Everyone's outside,' she said, coming forward and taking in the surroundings. Satin sheets, mirrors. Thick carpets. A roaring fire in the hearth behind her. It was a plush room. She removed her hood so he could see her face. 'I saw a few guards on my journey around the house but they didn't seem interested in me. Used to kids around here I think, though maybe not as old as me.' She glared at him.

Balderwin seemed to get the idea that he might be in some trouble, his piggy eyes widened a little and he stepped back. 'What do you want?'

'I want your promise,' she said, 'that after you confirm my patronage and pay the funds, I will be treated appropriately as befits a qualified mage.'

'Patronage? What in Astregoth are you talking about?'

Sophine blinked. 'It's me, Sophine. You picked me out years ago to be your mage. The patronage fair is in a few days and it's my last one, so I'll graduate and…' She trailed off.

Balderwin stared at her a moment. Then he laughed and sat down heavily on the bed.

He regarded her with a cruel smile. 'Ah yes. I remember. I wanted you then; a pathetic little thing. You'd have fitted in well around here, the girls like to have company. But they told me I couldn't have you until you'd graduated and it would be *years*. After that I never gave it another thought. I had no use for a mage, still don't. Now get out.'

The words rang in her ears. He'd never meant it, and they'd all assumed she was spoken for. It was all lies. She'd never had a patron at all. And if he'd been permitted to, he'd have taken her back then, and she'd be another little mouse in a filthy tunic scurrying around the kitchen or worse. Far worse. She held out a hand, closed, palm up. She wasn't sure why but it felt *so right*.

'You will fulfil your agreement and pay for the years of damage you've done to me,' she said softly, feeling a rush of heady adrenaline as her hatred and anger combined with the sight of the man who was the centre of it all. She felt his presence swirling, connecting with her mind, with her fist.

'I will do no such thing,' he said, oblivious, still smiling that cruel smile. 'You will go back to your witches, and tell them they have a new enemy to add to the rest. You've accomplished nothing by coming here, girl.'

'Oh,' she whispered as though seeing herself from afar, feeling his essence aligning perfectly with the shape of her hand, 'I think I have.'

She opened her fist.

Lord Balderwin fell apart and collapsed in five pieces to the floor, heavy chunks of him unfolding like the petals of a flower mirroring the motion of her fingers. She gasped and leapt back as a body's worth of blood splashed to the floor and ran in all directions. She wanted to cry, wanted to laugh, wanted to shriek and scream at the monster she'd unthinkingly vanquished. Instead she stood silently and trembled, watching the steaming pieces oozing their last onto the expensive rug.

After a few moments Sophine was able to lift her gaze as other thoughts pressed in. Those poor kids. What would become of them? She looked around the room, her panicked gaze refusing to alight on anything for more than a moment. She blinked and breathed, trying to calm herself as she backed into a corner and stood with her back to the wooden wall.

Her breathing began to return to normal, the light-headedness receding. She didn't know how long she'd stood there gasping, but it felt like a while. She shook her head, straightened up and took in her surroundings, deliberately ignoring the cooling puddle of red on the floor. On a table by the window sat some quills and parchment, and the seal of House Balderwin.

Interesting…

A short while later Sophine emerged from the house through the same hole in the wall bearing four letters, signed and sealed by

Lord Balderwin as far as anyone else was concerned. A group of small children and one older girl were waiting for her on the grass outside. She approached the older girl and smiled.

'I'm Sophine,' she said. The girl, a tall blond girl with haunted eyes, smiled uncertainly. 'Are you in charge here?'

'I'm Misty,' the girl replied, 'I'm the head servant.'

'How old are you, Misty?'

'Twelve.'

Sophine felt sick. What became of the servants when they got too old?

'Listen Misty, I've taken care of Lord Balderwin. He won't be bothering you or anyone else again.' The guarded look on the girl's face told Sophine she was clever enough to make this work.

'He's left instructions,' she said. 'The guards are to take orders from you, as mistress of the house, while he's gone.' She handed her one of the letters. 'The letter to the guards is this one. Can you read?'

Misty nodded.

'Good. Keep that to yourself, no one will expect you to be able to read or write so they won't suspect this is a forgery. This letter is for anyone else if you need to prove your position. It gives you full power to conduct his affairs whilst he is away, for as long as that might be. This last document is a will. It leaves you the estate. Every now and then I will write letters to you from Lord Balderwin, and then they'll stop suddenly. When that happens, I want you to wait a while, then lodge this document and those letters with the Lawyers' Guild saying you don't think he's coming back. They'll do the rest.'

'We can keep the house?'

'Yes, but you will need to clean it up. The bedroom is…a terrible mess. If you have any trouble, you come and find me. Sophine, of The Mages' Guild.'

Misty looked at her in awe. 'Thank you mistress Sophine.'

'Look after the girls, Misty. They're your responsibility now.'

Misty nodded. Sophine gave them all a last look and turned away, pulling her hood over her head and making her way back towards The Barbican on shaking legs.

Chapter Three

'You went to the protest,' Master Thomas's voice was heavy with disappointment. He sat back, rubbing his eyes. The pale light through the window behind him cast shadows on his face, making him seem gaunt and ageing him far beyond his years. Rigel and Thaniel kept silent, sitting on the other side of the master's heavy desk, eyes down, hearts pounding.

'You're wondering how I know,' bitterness crept into the hollow voice. Slowly, Thomas lifted something soft and dirty and flopped it onto the desk. Rigel knew what it was without even looking.

'A helpful, concerned citizen of our enlightened city dropped this off this morning. Together with a demand that those responsible for last night's unrest should be suitably punished. It took all the guild's diplomatic levers to let us handle it internally here at the Barbican, otherwise you might have ended up at the Senate on trial.'

'On trial?' Thaniel repeated in disbelief. 'On trial for what?'

Thomas smiled thinly. It looked more like a snarl. 'For starting fires, inciting riots, murder. Who knows? All I do know is that the people who really did start it vanished like smoke. Not one arrest has been made.'

'I'd recognise the priest,' said Rigel. 'I can still see him when I close my eyes.'

'He won't be found. None of them will. There's a powerful political influence behind this, directing things for its own ends. Someone wanted those protests to happen, I'm sure of it. I'm increasingly feeling like a fly in a web, and I can't yet see the spider.'

Thaniel looked at Rigel with fearful eyes as the moment stretched. He still had ash on his face and Rigel supposed he did too. Rigel looked at the bookshelf, just as a way to avoid those disappointed eyes. Something was strange, something different to the last time he'd looked there...

'One more day, boys. Just one,' Master Thomas interrupted his thoughts. 'That's all you needed. Then patronage, with a bit of luck, and a future. Now...' Thomas's voice cracked and he broke off, shaking his head.

'Now what, sir?' Thaniel leaned forward, looking confused. Rigel knew what the master meant, and felt hollowness seep into his stomach as his limbs turned to ice. Thomas looked at them.

'I'm sorry. I truly am. It's out of my hands. The masters met in session an hour ago to decide what to do, and the association of Hilda's with last night's violence together with the politics at play right now...Their decision was unanimous. Whoever it was, we agreed, would leave The Barbican and return home. I'm so sorry. If I'd known it was you two at the time maybe I'd have argued differently. Messengers have been dispatched to your families that you will be returning, and to the guild office at House Gloriana's estate.'

Thaniel was on his feet, pleading, begging. Shouting and railing and gesturing. Rigel sat in frozen silence, not hearing it. Not really seeing it. He looked at the robe on the desk, dusty and ashy from the road where it had fallen.

Thomas sat silently and let Thaniel rage, meeting Rigel's gaze when he raised it. 'I'm sorry,' he mouthed. Rigel nodded.

Behind them the door opened, and a familiar voice spoke softly to Thaniel. Rigel looked up as Sophine gently took Thaniel by the arm and steered him out of the room. Once through the door, Thaniel's incoherent pleading became sobs of despair. Rigel felt Sophine's hand on his shoulder and rose to leave, but sank back into his chair as she began to speak.

'You haven't informed the other masters or House Gloriana that it was Rigel and Thaniel yet, have you sir?'

'Not yet,' replied Thomas. 'We meet again in session tonight.'

Rigel paused, looking around to peer at Thaniel through the doorway.

'Do me a favour then,' said Sophine. 'When you do, say they're still missing and you haven't found them yet.'

'I don't think that would make a difference,' said Thomas cautiously. 'If they were the only students missing then it would be fairly clear that...'

'Yes but you wouldn't just expel them before you had a chance to talk to them would you? You'd suspend them first, right?' She paused meaningfully.

Master Thomas smiled faintly.

'And if they didn't appear until the patronage fair, they could still potentially graduate, whereas someone who had been dismissed could not.' He nodded. 'Very clever.'

Rigel blinked at that. He glanced at Sophine, who was holding Thomas's gaze.

The master's smile faded.

'I'm sorry Sophine. These boys are lucky to have a friend as fiercely loyal as you. But I had no choice but to expel them the moment I found out. I couldn't wait for the session of the masters, for ethical reasons. The messengers have already left and now I have the paperwork to do.'

Sophine's gaze didn't waver.

'Just agree,' she said softly. 'I can deal with the messengers. Forget the paperwork.'

'What do you mean…'

'I mean, just agree. Do you really want to ruin their careers days from graduation? How is that ethical?'

Thomas hesitated, watching her.

'And if I agree, what then?'

'Better you don't know. Are you in? Or are you going to let whoever is behind all this destroy the lives of your students?'

Thomas stood up from his desk slowly, looking suddenly tired and old. He peered down at his papers for some time. The papers, Rigel presumed, that would either expel or suspend him. He swallowed hard.

As the silence lengthened, Rigel stared at Sophine as though seeing her for the first time. This was not the irritatingly competent student with the troubled eyes and awkward demeanour he'd been friends with for years. She seemed somehow different; she drew his gaze like the only candle in a dim room. Then she was turning, striding towards the door. Rigel got up from his seat as fast as he could and hurried after her. As the door closed behind him, he caught a last glance of Master Thomas. He was smiling.

Sophine marched ahead down the wood panelled corridor, her black boots crunching the faded brown carpet. Rigel and Thaniel hurried after her, each trying haltingly to get her attention but too awed to reach out and grab her.

Thaniel almost ran into her when she stopped abruptly by a door.

'You two get going,' she said distractedly. 'Head for the noble quarter. The mansion of House Balderwin.'

'Balderwin? Never heard of—' Thaniel began. Rigel shushed him and looked at Sophine. He knew who that was. The vile slug of a man who had chosen her so long ago.

'Sophine, if your plan is to turn up at that creep's house and ask him to—'

'Just do what I say Rigel,' she said, turning dark eyes on him that sent a shiver of excitement through his body. He shut his mouth. 'I'll meet you there.'

'Where will you be?'

'I have something to take care of first.'

She turned and exited through the door, slamming it closed behind her. Rigel and Thaniel headed the other way, as what Sophine had said to Master Thomas echoed hauntingly in Rigel's ears.

I'll take care of the messengers…

***

The leaves were turning golden on the trees as Sir Raife and Paul headed down the Farmers' Road. Sunlight dappled between the branches overhanging the road, lending their journey an air of peace and tranquillity. The road led from one of the three minor gates of Asterheim, stretching away into Tynheim in the south through stretches of the agricultural farm country everyone called the Grain Belt. At some point, Paul would need to break off west to Ceresgoth bearing his message and Sir Raife would continue to the larger town down near the coast. It would be a long journey. It would be lengthened still further, Sir Raife suspected, by the fact that Paul was just Paul. No Sir, no Esquire. Just a *Paul*. He wrinkled his nose at the thought.

It had not taken long for the subject to come up, of course. Simply ask a fellow his name and you learn plenty. Often, Sir Raife had found, that was the point at which a man could make a polite exit from extended discussion with the lowborn. Alas, he could not do so this time.

Paul was sitting silently on his horse, pouting over an insult which, Sir Raife felt, he had taken far too much to heart. He had not intended any offence, far from it. But there was such a thing in the world as lowborn and highborn, and Paul was not the latter.

'You ought not to take offence,' said Sir Raife again, determined to make the point sink through the poor peasant's brain. He couldn't be blamed for not having the right stock to understand the finer points of conversation in one go, so Sir Raife was happy to help enlighten him during the long journey they had to take together. If any of his former associates could see him now, they would have approved and toasted his benevolence. Of that, he was sure.

'I only meant that we are born of two different worlds, but look! Here we are on the same path together. The same mission. Wandering the world like itinerant minstrels. Is that not jolly?'

'Very,' Paul muttered. 'But if this is a job for jongleurs why are *you* doing it?'

'Oh it's not *just* a job for peasants, Paul,' said Sir Raife brightly. 'It is a job for anyone who enjoys the open road and isn't afraid of the odd bandit. There's many a man who would fear a blade in the dark doing this kind of thing.'

'You should be more afraid of blades in the *light*,' Paul muttered, looking up at the sunlit leaves overhead.

'Nonsense!' said Sir Raife, laughing. 'The bandits come in the night, my poor ill-educated companion. Nothing to fear in the daytime. Not when I'm here!'

Paul eyed his companion with distaste. He knew all about this pompous fool; Paul took pride in saving his own skin and made a point of finding out about his fellow messengers just in case he happened to end up alongside one on a tedious mission to the Grain Belt, for example. Sir Raife had been kicked unceremoniously out of the Battlemasons for gross dereliction of duty and indecent conduct. The reason he was so cheerful, Paul imagined, was due to his having avoided the hangman's noose through the ancient legal loophole of being absolutely loaded with gold.

'Woah there!' Sir Raife cried, pompously. Paul reined in his own horse at the sight of a hooded figure standing in the road. The figure was slender, female, in a dark hood of homespun cloth and black boots. Something about the demeanour of this stranger made Paul slowly reach down to his belt. The stranger turned her hooded head towards him as his fingers closed around his dagger.

'No need for that,' she said, 'I just want to talk.' The hooded stranger pushed her hood back, showing a young face and thick black hair.

'Stand aside, lady,' said Sir Raife. 'We are on guild business.'

'I have a proposition for you,' the girl said, paying no attention to the mounted knight, her eyes on Paul. He could feel a strange sensation, like someone softly caressing the inside of his skull. It wasn't altogether unpleasant.

The knight laughed. 'We aren't interested in proposals from anyone save our guild masters, young lady, let alone vagabonds like you. Now stand aside or I shall run you down. Interference with guild messengers is a crime, you know.'

'I know,' she said, her eyes still on Paul. 'But I can't let you deliver those messages.' She drew back her cloak and pulled out a pouch of gold. 'I can pay you for your trouble.'

'You what?' the knight spluttered. 'How dare you! I would never accept a bribe!'

The girl barked a short, scornful laugh and turned her gaze to the knight. Paul shuddered as he was released; the girl's eyes had become black, like dark pools of night in an innocent face. 'Your friend here knows a lot about you. You're just the kind of man to take a bribe. Take a life. Take innocence—'

Sir Raife spurred his horse and charged at the girl, drawing his long sword as he did so in one well-practised motion. Paul saw her raise a closed fist, a pale light emanating from it between tightly clenched fingers, and then Sir Raife was in pieces. Paul shrieked and his horse leapt, maddened, the sudden stink of blood flooding its nostrils and driving it momentarily into panic. He flung his message at the witch and managed to wheel the horse, racing back to the city as fast as he could.

***

Thaniel was pacing and it was driving Rigel mad. He sat with his legs outstretched on the grass, staring across the river at the distant shape of the guild quarter. Somewhere there, amidst the spires and dark rooftops, was The Barbican, where he had spent the last ten years of his life. Master Thomas, the other masters, and the other apprentices were all he knew. The chipped stone of Hilda's Barbican, its cracked flagstones and vine-covered pillars were his home. And now, one stupid night of bad judgment had ruined it all.

He picked a handful of grass and flicked it in Thaniel's direction. 'Please stop,' he said tiredly.

Thaniel did not stop.

'You know what's weird?' he said, ignoring Rigel and pacing on. 'I didn't even have a patron. I'm not that great at anything, so I doubt I would have impressed anyone. I haven't so far, why should this year be any different?'

'People mature differently,' Rigel said half-heartedly. 'Maybe you're about to switch on.'

'Not likely. I think this was always going to be the end of the road for me.'

'Except they'd probably let you stay on at Hilda's and teach—'

'Teach?' Thaniel laughed.

'Well, stay anyway. Work there. Be a bookkeeper or something.'

Thaniel sighed frustratedly.

'I am trying to make myself feel better about being thrown out, Rigel. I don't want to hear about how everything might have worked out if we hadn't gone to that stupid protest.' Rigel was silent.

'I'm going to be a farmer,' Thaniel said. He repeated it a few times, as though trying to make it sound more positive. 'One thing's true, I can make things grow. Always been pretty good at crops.' He stretched his hand out towards a daisy near Rigel's foot and made his concentration face.

Rigel got to his feet and stepped on the daisy.

'We're not going to be farmers,' he growled. Thaniel looked at him sadly.

Just then, a shadow seemed to pass over them, except there were no clouds in the sky. Something dark was growing just down the hill from where they stood in the grounds of the Balderwin mansion. A small ball of darkness, like smoke wrapped around a shard of midnight, had appeared and was rapidly expanding. The dark within it was almost impossible to look at, as though it drew in all light and left the eye aching as it searched for a hint of something amongst the absence. The spectral orb unfolded, dark mists peeling back like a lightless flower opening in the air. Black lightning flickered and flashed inside it, and a powerful wind tugged at their clothes, howling out of nowhere. Then it was gone.

Sophine stumbled towards them, the last tendrils of dark mist evaporating from her body as she came. She took two steps and fell to the ground, and an envelope, marked with the seal of The Guild of Mages, skittered away to land by Rigel's feet. Sophine's black hair floated on an unseen current above her head for a moment before settling in a mess onto the grass.

'What the…?' Rigel's voice was choked as he hesitated, caught somewhere between running to help and running away. He'd never seen anything like the magic that had brought Sophine to this place, and everything about it looked *wrong*. Rigel had a sudden image of Master Thomas's office and some dim corner of his brain registered what had been different about it. He shoved the thought aside as Thaniel ran to Sophine's side and helped her up. She was shaking, pale.

'I killed him,' she was repeating in a horrified whisper, her eyes wild and unseeing. 'I killed him, I killed him. I did it *again*! What's *wrong* with me...?'

'Killed? You killed someone?' Rigel gasped. Thaniel shot him a reproachful look. 'You're ok, Soph. You're alright. You're with us now.'

'You took one of the books,' Rigel said. 'One of Thomas's old books from before the Charter.' Sophine looked at him, still leaning heavily against Thaniel.

'Yes,' she said simply.

'So that's how...' he gestured at the dissipating mist. She nodded and stood up straight, smiling weakly at Thaniel as she went to pick up the message she'd dropped. She thrust it at Rigel.

'Here, you weren't expelled after all. You're suspended as long as you keep out of sight.'

Rigel took the envelope and felt a stab of anger. It was addressed to his parents.

'You too, Than,' Sophine said.

Thaniel nodded, watching her intently. 'And the messengers...' he said softly. Sophine looked away.

'Let's get inside,' she said.

'Inside?' said Rigel.

'Inside there,' she gestured at the Balderwin mansion. 'It's mine now. We'll be safe here.'

'Safe?' Rigel said.

'Yours?' Thaniel said at the same time.

Sophine didn't answer, just trudged off heavily through the gardens. Rigel shared a look with Thaniel.

***

'After that happened, I knew I had to figure out what I'd done and how to stop it happening again,' Sophine was saying over a cup of hot tea. The cup was extremely expensive, that much was obvious from the delicate images and the wafer-thin pottery. But then, so was everything else in the room.

They were sitting at the top end of a long table that could have easily seated thirty.

The chairs were heavy carved gold-painted wood with plush red cushions, the candelabra was silver. Above them hung a stupendously heavy looking chandelier that Thaniel kept looking up at, with some apprehension. Tapestries hung on three walls, the fourth taken up with enormous windows edged with thick curtains of green material that looked as though it had gold in it somewhere. Rigel had never been in a room that even approached this level of opulence. Sophine seemed oblivious to its splendour though, as she poured more tea from a ridiculously ornate pot, acting with a nonchalance that chilled Rigel as much as it impressed him. She'd just described how she'd come looking to bargain with her patron, only to find he wasn't her patron at all. She'd released something terrible, and the man had died.

'You can't imagine how horrifying it was. I kept seeing that moment when he…died. I couldn't get it out of my head. So I went to Thomas's office, and found a book that talked about old magic. The kind people used, back before…'

'Before the city started burning mages to death for sorcery,' said Thaniel flatly. 'Soph, seriously if anyone ever finds out…'

Sophine sniffed and nodded. 'I spent the rest of the night reading it. I thought if I could learn more about what I'd done I could stop it happening again…' She trailed off, a tear running down one pale cheek. She swiped it away.

'But then you went after the messengers,' Rigel said, looking pointedly at the letter on the table.

'Not to hurt them! I only wanted to pay them off. I-I took gold. Balderwin has loads in the vault downstairs so I thought I'd offer the messengers more than they can make in a year. Who wouldn't take that?'

'That portal you conjured,' Thaniel said. 'That was one of those old spells wasn't it? From the book.'

Sophine nodded and pushed her hair back behind her ears.

'It was hard, but not as hard as you'd think. It works off emotion. Anger, mainly, for me. It helps you channel how you feel and connect it to who made you feel that way and, boom. Portal. It's the same old thing about feeling the connections, but not in the detached way we've been taught. It opens up so many possibilities.'

'Dangerous ones,' Rigel said. Sophine looked at him for a moment and then nodded.

'Without a doubt. I think maybe it was performing that spell that made me…that made it so easy for me to do what I did to that knight.'

Rigel looked up at the chandelier, trying to picture what Sophine had described. To do that to a person…to kill them with a thought…

He remembered the vibration in the ground under the quarry, when he'd felt that bleakness and despair. And then the man with the hammer.

'Could've been me,' he muttered. Sophine looked at him strangely.

'At the protest,' he said, glancing at Thaniel, 'someone attacked us. A man with a double handed hammer. He swung it at my head and I...' he made a gesture with his hand.

'Froze him,' finished Thaniel.

Sophine snorted in disbelief. 'Froze him? As in, like a block of ice?'

'No not *froze*, froze. Time sort of slowed down. Almost stopped, for everyone else. And then it sped back up again but it gave us enough time to escape.'

'How did you do that?'

'I have no idea. But you said you'd done things using emotion, right? Well I had plenty of those that day. With patronage coming up and everything, I've been so stressed out. And then the priest accusing us of being witches and the crowd wanting to kill us...it just got too much and I lost control.'

Sophine smiled weakly. 'Nice to know it's not just me.'

Rigel snorted. 'I haven't turned anyone inside out.'

'Not yet,' she said.

'That's not funny.'

'It's a bit funny.'

'So what now?' put in Thaniel. 'You're going to just live here and hope no one notices old Balderwin is gone?'

Sophine stood up, gesturing around the richly appointed room. 'Not just me. We can all live here. This can be ours.'

64

'You're not serious.'

'I am. At the patronage fair, I'll provide the money and documents, all signed by Lord Balderwin, and we'll be licensed mages of the guild.'

'No one ever takes more than one mage, Soph.'

'Well, now they will.'

'People will talk.'

'People always talk. It'll all be entirely legal. We will be the Lords Balderwin and no one will ever know any different.' Sophine grinned.

Thaniel started to laugh, and after a moment Rigel joined in. The emotions of the last few hours unbottled themselves in Lord Balderwin's absurdly expensive dining room and they laughed at the sheer madness of it all.

'Lord Thaniel!' shouted Thaniel, twirling around. 'Suck it, farming!'

***

House Gloriana held a grand manse in the south-eastern edge of the noble quarter of Asterheim, a particularly beautiful spot overlooking the river and within easy walking distance of the Northern Bridge, the first of three bridges spanning the River Ceres. The Ceres flowed through the city, dividing it more-or-less in half; the 'noble' quarter, a colloquial term for the oldest and richest area made desirable long ago by the proximity to the port, with the military quarter to its south, sat on the western side edged by the harbour and the great Western Ocean. This was where the beating heart of Asterheim politics sat, the Senate Building, the courts, the private estates of the old families. The guild and commercial quarters sat on the other side, far larger areas than the western side of the river, having been expanded many times since the founding of the original city walls. Here dwelt the majority of the population, and here were the factories and forges of the industries that kept the city alive. To many, the Eastern City was the true Asterheim.

Lady Ariene sat by the window of her eastern reception room overlooking the Northern Bridge and the True City beyond, a large but sparsely decorated chamber where she entertained less important visitors. The view outside, with the river glittering in the afternoon sun, was just about pleasant enough to stop her gritting her teeth as her guest droned on.

'Lord Barten is a threat to Asterheim,' said the pompous little man. The noble Ormond Orswell, younger brother of Lord Orswell, puffed his chest out and adopted a serious mien that made Lady Gloriana want to laugh in his face. She kept her eyes on the river and covered the twitch at the corner of her mouth by raising her glass. She took a sip of the fine wine her guest had so graciously brought her. It was a deep, rich red with a full-bodied flavour and hints of various fruits, or so her guest had gushed when he'd presented it. To Ariene, any wine younger than herself was hardly anything to get excited about.

She became aware of the heavy silence as she contemplated the flavour, trying to identify anything that Ormond had mentioned. She looked around.

'I would have thought your brother would be pleased by Lord Barten's ascent,' she said, leaning over to put the glass on the short wooden table by her knees. 'He holds the Blacksmiths' Guild as well as being the Steward for the Labourers' Union, after all. You're natural allies.'

The younger Orswell bristled at this, puffing his pompous chest out even further.

Ariene wondered if she could make him pop with a few more well-chosen words.

'Lord Barten was handed the Stewardship before the Committee could cast their votes,' Orswell spluttered. She nodded sympathetically.

'And after all that gold you spent on them too,' she said. Orswell glared at her. She laughed lightly, a well-practised tinkle of condescension she'd honed over many years, and picked up her glass. He watched the motion; she wondered if he considered her drinking to be distasteful.

'Barten was always going to get the Stewardship, Ormond. He has the Blacksmiths and the Armourers, not to mention being Castellan of the Battlemasons. Your brother has, what…the Cobblers?'

'He also controls the Citizenry Guild, madam,' he said stiffly. He smoothed his ruffled shirt, peering again at her glass and glancing outside.

'He does,' she allowed. Citizenry was a huge, vital guild and running it was no small task. The elder Orswell had done an excellent job over the years, none could deny. 'The point is, Barten is in the ascendant just now. He has an unwholesome alliance with The Sacred Circle too, I understand.'

Orswell wrinkled his nose at this, rising a notch or two in her estimation purely by that unguarded revelation.

The priesthood of the Sacred Circle were an increasingly irrelevant band of ragged fanatics. In its glory days the priesthood had been vital to the spiritual health of the City, a powerful political force and rich beyond imagination. Unfortunately for them, their power had been inextricably intertwined with that of the royal house of the Echelarch so the Bloodless Coup had left them with nothing but rivals and enemies. Most priests had undergone a spiritual conversion around that point, with only true believers and zealots finding their way to the embrace of the derelict Cathedral and its reclusive High Priest Lyoris these days.

'I'm pleased to see we agree on that at least,' said Ariene lightly.

'Alliances outside the Senate are unpatriotic, my lady,' sniffed Orswell.

Ariene raised an eyebrow at that but nodded.

'One of them came to see me, you know,' she remarked, looking out of the window. 'Wanted to ask me about donating a share of my estate to The Circle. They really are desperate if they're resorting to that. Vultures.'

'Returning to business,' Orswell said, brusquely cutting across her. She sighed, instantly reminded of why she disliked him so. 'I came to ask for your allegiance, my lady.'

'My allegiance. For what?'

'For opposing Barten's recent proposals.'

She frowned. Nothing Lord Barten had proposed recently was particularly interesting, certainly nothing that would inconvenience Orswell unduly. She placed her glass back on the table, blinking away a sudden rush of nausea. She could have sworn she saw a hint of satisfaction on her guest's unpleasant face as she winced.

'You don't need my allegiance for that. I oppose Barten's proposals on principle.' She studied Orswell's face. He didn't seem surprised by her response, didn't seem to even care.

He fidgeted distractedly in his chair. Something wasn't right; she glanced back at the half empty glass of wine and felt suddenly cold. She raised her eyes slowly to find Orswell watching her. He smiled thinly and lowered his gaze to the glass.

'Probably enough,' he said, rising to his feet and smirking down at her. 'You should be careful,' he gloated, 'at your age you should watch what you drink.' She stared back at him.

'If you want to reach my age,' she said, eyeing his waistline, 'you *certainly* should.' Orswell snarled and walked to the door, adjusting his shirt as he went, which pleased her a little. When he was gone, she turned her eyes back to the glass.

'Well well,' she said quietly, 'so this is how it ends.' She felt another wave of nausea, her stomach clenching in response to whatever vile thing the toad had slipped into the wine. She wondered how much time she had left. He hadn't elected to kill her fast, it seemed, as he certainly could have.

'Darcy!' she called, turning to the window and watching the sun on the river.

Somehow it had never looked so dazzling, the motes of light glittering like gold, like sparkles on a winding crystal pathway.

She was aware of Darcy's flustered presence behind her.

'I suppose everything looks more beautiful the last time you see it,' she said softly.

'My lady?'

Ariene winced as a stab of pain lanced through her head. She put a hand on the window and rode a wave of light-headedness.

'Get my blue dress, would you dear?' she said. 'I have a trip to make.'

69

Chapter Four

The clamour in the Senate Chamber was surprisingly loud as Ariene made her halting way up the steps to the main doors. Her limbs ached too much to climb the stairs to her private box, and in any case she wouldn't be entitled to speak from there unless called upon. Today, she simply intended to march through the main doors and right down to the central floor to make her final speech. She might even rest her screaming bones on the damned throne. Quite what she wanted to say, she wasn't sure. Just that she needed to say *something*.

'My lady, you're too ill,' Darcy fussed for the fiftieth time since they'd left the Gloriana estate. 'Let's go back so you can rest.'

'Oh I will rest, dear,' said Ariene through gritted teeth, willing her left leg to take another step against its perfectly reasonable protestations. 'But not just yet. Why don't you go and hail me a carriage and I'll meet you outside in a few minutes?'

Darcy flapped around for a moment or two before finally leaving.

Loyalty, Ariene reflected, was an underrated virtue. Darcy deserved so much more than to be left abandoned when she died. Nausea bubbled up again, robbing her of strength and stealing her breath. She marched on.

'Not yet,' she said. 'Not just yet. A few more things to do.'

The heavy wooden doors of the Senate Chamber were open, three times taller than she stood, and ornately carved with reliefs of heroes from Asterheim's less democratic past. She held a hand out to touch the heavy wood, feeling the rough textures of ancient history beneath her fingers. She felt cheated that this was the first time she'd ever appreciated the artistry, and now could never do so again.

'Lady Ariene Gloriana!' someone shouted from within the chamber. She laughed softly and shook her head, ignoring the ache in her neck; why was it that someone always noticed her before she was ready?

The chamber quietened as she shuffled her way past the doors and onto the highest tier of seats. She leaned heavily on her cane and tugged her dress away from her feet as she contemplated the steps down to the dais. The flappy material seemed to be clinging to her shoes and she yanked it irritably away, thoughts of an ignoble fall hovering at the back of her mind. She gave it one last tug and let it drop. She stood straighter.

'My lords and ladies,' she said, summoning the strength she had once taken for granted to make herself heard across the echoing chamber. It made her chest hurt.

'I have come to bid you all farewell. After so many years of service, for which I hope I will be remembered if not fondly then at least with some respect, I do not believe I will be returning to this chamber. Something in my bones, or possibly my blood,' her eyes managed to pick out the elder Lord Orswell amongst the Senators, 'tells me this is my last evening in this world.' Orswell met her gaze with what looked like such heartfelt pity that she was taken aback. Surely the younger brother hadn't acted alone…

She held the look for a moment, and Orwell's expression folded into a frown.

'My lady,' called the young Viscount Roach, an earnest man with blonde hair and a pleasant demeanour, recently elevated to Senatorial rank by an unlikely combination of fates. An old family struck low by plague, some whispered witchcraft, leaving the youngest daughter as sole heir. Said sole heir having only just married the son of a moderately successful fisherman meant a sudden and bewildering change of fortune for the young man who all of a sudden found himself titled Viscount. However, Viscount or no, his name was still "Roach" which, being a type of fish, had led to many cruel and unusual nicknames being given to the poor fellow in the snootier parts of the Senate.

He was, sadly, the kind of man who would never, ever survive amongst the monsters in rich silk seated around him who no doubt even now wove their webs around him.

'My lady, will you not receive my mage? I will send her to you,' the Fishlord offered earnestly.

She smiled.

'Thank you, Lord Roach for your generous offer. I do appreciate your concern for my health which, contrary to the great traditions of this gloried institution, I believe to be genuine. And I return it in equal measure, truly, for you sit in a nest of vipers in silken robes. Poisonous vipers.' The blonde young man blinked at her and looked around uncertainly.

'So I thank you,' she repeated, 'but I decline. My husband awaits me on the other side, if there is one, or rest if there is not. At my age, those are the only two things I want.'

Are they? asked a voice inside her, with surprising vehemence. She wondered whether she quite believed what she'd just said anymore. She imagined her guilds stolen, those guild officers loyal to her replaced, or worse. Workers forced to change allegiance or forced out of their jobs. She caught the eye of a junior officer of the Travellers' Guild, standing in shock on the third tier. The Overseer had been a close ally of hers for many years; the Travellers would soon be the target of a mad scramble for control. Everyone would want to influence the civilian control of the roads and great gates, not to mention the Ordo Militant, the Travellers' private security force tasked with policing those accessways. The Overseer and the other officers were sure to be replaced if not banished or simply made to vanish, much like the previous Steward of the Labourers' Union. She smiled sadly at the young man and nodded. He bowed his head hurriedly to her, before turning and making his way out of the chamber, calling to his colleagues in the other House Gloriana affiliated guilds. She only hoped he would get the message to the Overseer in time; they had discussed this day many times, but no one had truly thought it was almost upon them.

Least of all me, she thought bitterly. She saw Orswell notice the departure of her guild officers and took some satisfaction from the panic on his face as he motioned to his own aides and began to give orders she couldn't hear.

The commotion in the chamber had intensified, with relatively few of the assembled nobles and almost none of the guild-worthies and officers paying any attention to anyone beyond the fevered discussions in their own groups. Certainly no one was looking at her anymore.

She gripped her cane and limped away, forgotten, her mind ablaze with bitterness and the pounding ache of whatever the poison had been.

'Should have chosen something stronger,' she muttered of Lord Orswell, or his brother, as she made her way outside. At least she'd given them a chance to prepare themselves, something the wretch had obviously not expected her to do.

'Are you well, my lady?' Darcy asked, jumping out of the carriage she'd found to help her mistress. The question struck her as absurd, and Ariene Gloriana laughed giddily through the mounting pain as she was carried away to die.

***

As the night closed in on the hilltop mansion of the late Lord Balderwin, Rigel sat on the grass outside, watching the last rays of sunlight vanishing behind the sliver of the Western Ocean that he could just see over the distant walls of Asterheim's Great Harbour. The sky was aflame with red, making the ships into black shadows on a glaring steel-grey sea.

'Quite a view,' Thaniel said, dropping down next to him. He wore a richly embroidered shirt that was many times too large for him, and a pair of boots that were similarly ill-fitting. His blonde hair stuck out under a gaudy velvet hat.

'You look like a scarecrow,' Rigel said, glancing at him.

'I'm a lord,' Thaniel replied wryly, watching the darkening sky. 'Lord Thaniel has nice clothes.'

'You could fit three Lord Thaniels in those clothes. Walk around in those and people will know.'

Thaniel was quiet.

'People will know anyway, Rige. You can't make a noble vanish and hope people don't find out. We'll be caught eventually, no matter how careful Sophine is.'

'I know.'

'We can't stay. It puts her in danger.'

'I know.'

'Where will we go?'

'I don't know.'

Thaniel was silent again. Rigel looked at him. He'd never see his friend so down, so depleted of the joyous exuberance he normally had in such irritating abundance.

'Get some sleep Than. We can figure this out tomorrow.' Thaniel nodded. 'Where are you going?'

'I'm going for a walk.'

***

The Blue Lady shuffled along the Northern Bridge, watching the moonlight on the water as she gripped the handrail tightly. She no longer had the strength to walk unaided at all, and lurched along in short bursts, leaning bodily against the rail. It was cold and hard under her ribs, which she was sure she'd managed to crack in her determination to make it to the bench halfway across. She intended to be found there in the morning, a dignified corpse witnessing the dawn in her famous Senate dress. The trouble was that the dress was also incredibly unhelpful, its various frills and trails getting in her way with every halting step she took as though determined to ruin her final farewell. The handfuls of material she'd snatched up to keep it away from her feet kept slipping through her failing fingers but Lady Gloriana, last scion of the great House formerly known as Chetney, pushed on with gritted teeth.

The night air was cool and still, and smelt only faintly of smoke and sewage, unlike most of the city. The Northern Bridge was, as its name suggested, situated not far from the northern boundaries of Asterheim, where the mountains stood and the river first entered through the great water gate. As it flowed beneath the bridge, the water hadn't yet gathered so many of the various impurities that would choke it by the time it exited. The Southern Gate, which flowed through Rivergate Castle in the walls, was famously garrisoned by soldiers who were paid extra to put up with the stench. Stenchgate, it was sometimes called. And many far more colourful names.

Tonight, however, it was tranquil up here. The stars looked down upon Lady Ariene as she finally struggled to the bench and collapsed onto it, breathing so heavily she thought she might expire then and there. She had lost both her shoes in her laborious trek, and her feet sang with a hundred aches and agonies now that she could relieve them of their burden.

Heaving herself upright, the Lady of House Gloriana looked out over the river through a haze of darkening eyesight. It was still beautiful, even against the backdrop of her pounding head and screaming nerves. So far, the poison had not been a messy one, content to kill her without fountains of blood or other fluids as some others did; this one was a quiet, industrious murderer working slowly away at her. The better, she supposed, to make it look like the kind of natural death people of her age were expected to enjoy. She doubled over as a particularly vicious cramp took hold in her stomach. In a strange way, she almost took heart that the poison was taking so long to finish her; if her final defiant act was to stay grimly alive as long as possible, then so be it.

'I thought I was ready,' she muttered as the cramp passed and she settled back on the bench, darkly amused at how urgently her body was screaming at her with its aches and pains as though there was anything she could do about them. It apparently shared her refusal to go quietly into the night. She laughed softly.

Over to the right, away across the river, lay the part of town often known as the guild district. The hub of the various unions and assemblies and academies that represented the industries and castes of the people of Asterheim and beyond. She could see the glow of lights, hear the faint murmur of a living city at night. A melancholy feeling descended as her thoughts turned again to the fate of her guilds. After a lifetime of relative peace and self-determination, of faithful representation and support in the Senate, her allies and interests would suddenly be left alone to fend for themselves. Would they remain in a bloc, as she'd instructed, mutually supporting one another despite the lack of a steady hand steering them? Or would they one by one be seduced by the offers of her rivals, or forced to accept their lordship at sword point? To not know, that was the worst.

Darcy had been stunned into uncharacteristic silence when Ariene had sealed the last parchment and handed it to her. She had left the girl as sole holder of her personal property, to use and direct it as she felt appropriate. If she was wise, she would sell it immediately to one of the guilds and move quietly to a nice estate of her own somewhere in the Commercial quarter or even outside of Asterheim. There were beautiful places in the Grain Belt, even in its capital Ceresheim, where Darcy's loyalty could finally be rewarded. Ariene smiled at the thought.

'Lady Darcy of Ceresheim,' she wheezed, soft laughter sending her into an agonising coughing fit. When it had passed, Ariene rested her head against the bench and closed her eyes, as a single tear ran down a wrinkled cheek. 'I wish I could have seen that.'

***

Rigel's hand glowed with a clear blue light, illuminating the bridge around him. The torches were lit, of course, the Lamp Lighters being famous for their diligence and organisation, but conjuring light was one of the first things they'd learned all those years ago. A pure expression of order and harmony, connecting himself with the world around him through the illumination.

Rigel snorted and shook his head. It was all such nonsense. Order at night was *darkness*. To conjure light was breaking that order. To conjure anything at any time was breaking the natural order of the nothing that was there to start with. He gazed at the light and willed it to shift into green, into gold, into the silver of a full moon.

'Uh-oh,' he muttered, 'Looks like someone's drawing attention. Better expel him. Oh wait…'

Something shifted in the gloom just beyond the reach of his light. He lowered his hand and let it fade, realising the glare had been ruining his night-vision. The moon and stars were providing plenty of light, as were the braziers spaced evenly along the bridge. The gloomy shape resolved itself as his eyes adjusted. It was a woman, sitting on the mid-way bench, although 'sitting' was a generous word. As he drew closer he took in the dishevelled blue dress, glittering in the moonlight with a hundred tiny stones, the shoeless feet ghost-white and paper thin. Wisps of white hair unbound and floating in the light breeze from a skull-like face that looked more like that of a long dead corpse than a living woman. Rigel backed up a step and felt a stab of horror, before he saw her thin chest rise, only slightly, a rattling sound coming from the woman's throat as she drew in a thin gasp of breath. The living-corpse's hands were curled into talons, lying by her sides on the bench palms up, as though they'd fallen after clawing at the sky.

'Circle save us,' Rigel breathed, unable to tear his eyes from the cadaverous being before him. Something beneath him vibrated slightly, rippling up through his foot, but he ignored it.

'Hello,' he said, stepping closer and reaching a hesitant hand out to the dying woman. A smell was rising from her, something foul that instinctively made him back away again. The sickly-sweet smell of decay was on her foetid breath, like death itself was within her. The vibration came again, just as it had in the quarry.

Something within him was reacting to the sight he beheld, he knew that. The same way something had reacted to the despair he'd felt at the quarry. His disgust, his horror, his terrible pity for this creature before him all churned and broiled inside him, and the vibration beneath was rising in time with it. In spite of himself, he was excited by it.

'This is wrong,' he said aloud, deliberately stoking the misery as the peculiar sensation gathered intensity. 'You don't deserve this. No one deserves this.'

A voice within him, the one so long nurtured and encouraged by Master Thomas, protested. This was *right*; death is part of life. There is no purer expression of order than the natural return of bodies to the dust from which they are made.

And yet. And *yet*.

Rigel looked at the woman. The pain on her face. The misery, the lost hope. His heart broke for her, in her fine dress so gaudily out of fashion, a memory of a different time when she no doubt lived and loved with the best. Why was she out here on a cold bridge beneath the indifferent stars? No one deserved to die so forgotten, so tragically alone.

The vibration had become a warmth, spreading up his legs, tingling and growing. He let it swell up inside him, enfolding his heart and stomach with heat. He felt light, strong, filled with an energy the like of which he'd never felt before, an energy that gripped him utterly and demanded to be released. He shuddered, trying to hang on to his thoughts but losing them as they were swept away, drowned in the intensity of the feeling.

Rigel looked at the woman again and gasped at what he saw: silvery lines, thousands of them, clustered and intertwined in the vague shape of a human being, against the blackness into which the rest of the world had faded. Pale white light, soft and fragile, pulsed slowly at the centre, where the woman's heart should have been, and clustered again at the head. The light was fading. The silvery lines at the extremities were dull, gleaming only softly like steel in candlelight.

Rigel moved closer, drifting slowly as though in a dream, his gaze fixed on the glittering outlines of the woman's life force as it drained away. Throughout the wisps of silver were vines of sickly green, wrapped around the gleaming sparks and slowly choking the light from the clusters around the heart and head. The tendrils had snaked their way throughout the whole form and pulsed slowly like a vile parasite, gleefully being carried on its destructive route by the body's own network of faint light.

He knew what this was. A body incapable of healing itself. One that had passed so far along the road to death that recovery was impossible. It no longer had the energy to fight for its own life. Such a body could not normally be saved by mages; they enhanced and strengthened a body's own healing and pulled off what appeared to be miracles, but in the end they could not save the unsavable. He reached out sadly, only meaning to touch the woman gently in pity.

The corruption shifted as he held his hand out to it, as though apprehensive of his approach. Rigel snatched his hand back, his amazement threatening for a moment to disrupt the flow of energy within him. He concentrated and moved closer, intoxicated by the thrill of the power flooding through him. He extended the heat within him outwards, wrapping a corner of the foul pestilence in its embrace. He laughed as he closed his fist, feeling the peculiar sensation of holding something, something that writhed and twisted and yet had no form or substance. He pulled.

In the real world beyond Rigel's enhanced senses, the Blue Lady's eyes and mouth opened in a silent scream as the poison within her was ripped unceremoniously from her body. She bucked and heaved as it receded from the cells and organs it had infested, banished by a golden light that burned all traces of it away. She sat bolt upright and spewed the foulness from her stomach onto the bridge, before collapsing once more into unconsciousness.

To Rigel, it had looked as though the green tendrils were a mist carried by a strong wind, flowing and draining away, unravelling reluctantly but unable to resist the force behind it. He moved his hand, directing the pestilence away, and then commanded it to disburse. The ghostly threads seemed to writhe, and almost to scream, but then they were gone. He looked back to the spirit-form of the woman, lying slumped on the bench. The silvery lines of the body were still dulled, the pale light now even fainter. Rigel's incorporeal being drifted closer.

Throughout the body were traces of damage. Silver threads were broken, some twisted and some missing. Damage so extensive he was amazed the light continued to pulse at all. The power within him was cooler now, no longer pulsing, no longer pulling at his mind demanding release. He focused his will and directed the remaining energy into those silver threads. His mind travelled the broken pathways, mapping and tracing, forging connections and bridging gaps. Rigel gasped as the body seemed to push back, its own willpower forcing him up and away, but he held on. He poured the last of his strength into the silvery pathways, binding his will into them.

'You will live,' he insisted mentally, exerting the last of his power. 'You will live.' It seemed that those words burned themselves into the weaving latticework of webs, now gleaming a pure white and becoming too bright to look upon. Rigel pulled back, retreating back inside his head and realising only then that he had been outside of it.

Stumbling back, he fell hard on his backside and yelped. He blinked and looked around. All was quiet; the bridge was serene, dark, bathed in starlight and the dim glow of burning braziers. The air was still, even the low clamour of the districts over the bridge seemed quieter now. He guessed the hour was late. Rigel stood up slowly, rubbing his tingling arms. The memory of the intense heat he'd felt seemed strange, ephemeral, like it had happened in a dream. He held a hand to his head and tried to recall what had just happened.

'Who are you, mage?' someone asked to his right. A strong, commanding female voice that couldn't possibly be coming from the near-dead wraith on the bench. He turned to answer, and fell silent instead.

The woman in the blue dress stood by the handrail, straight-backed and stern, looking at him, absently tugging the folds of material away from her feet. Her hair was thick and dark, greying but only in places, her eyes glittering and intelligent in a handsome face showing only the first hints of old age. She didn't seem to be more than sixty years old, and had the figure of a woman far younger.

Rigel found his voice. 'I'm Rigel,' he said, giving her a weak smile.

The woman stared at him a moment longer and then held out an arm and stared at that instead. She flexed her hand, smiling.

'Astounding,' she said. 'Truly astounding.' She stood on her tip-toes and turned in a slow circle, arms held out to her sides. Now it was Rigel's turn to stare.

'You try that when you're near ninety,' she said once she'd turned back around. She closed her eyes, standing perfectly motionless with a strange expression on her face. 'Nothing,' she said, a smile tugging at the corner of her mouth. 'I feel nothing. *Nothing*. No aches, no throbs, nothing clicking. It's just...an absence of pain. The bees are all gone!'

Rigel hesitated.

'If you say so, ma'am,' he said awkwardly.

'Oh I do, dear. I do. This is the very definition of youth, Rigel. The gift of feeling nothing.'

Rigel frowned.

'Oh I'm sure it isn't to you,' she said, coming forward and taking his arm in hers, 'and you can tell me all about your youthful, tortured existence when we get back to your house. Where is your house?'

'My house?'

'Yes dear, your house. I was murdered tonight you see, and I have no doubt that there are spies out looking for my corpse to confirm I did my duty and died. Which is of course why I didn't do it at home.'

'You were murdered...' Rigel was struggling to process the many, many things happening in his head.

'Yes, dear, do try to keep up. Now, shall we?' She gestured towards the eastern side of the river. Rigel shook his head and pointed the other way.

'I live this way actually,' he said awkwardly. She followed his gaze and peered at him closely.

'You don't look familiar,' she said, 'and I'm sure I know most of the boys in service as mages to the nobles—'

'I'm not a mage.' She frowned.

'I mean, not yet. I'm an apprentice. I *was* an apprentice. I'm going to be patronised, that is I was going to be. Might be. I—' he trailed off and looked at his feet, utterly unsure what he was supposed to say.

'Rigel,' she said softly, 'you have just saved me from a very painful death and apparently restored me to my comparative youth.' He couldn't stop his eyebrow rising; she saw it.

'*Comparative*, I said. And I'm glad of it. The last thing I would have wanted would be to be taken back to those years when appearance counted for more than competence. No, this is perfect. Unexpected, and unwanted,' she gave him a hard look, 'but not unwelcome. I have so much I want to do now. So tell me, where are you living, if you aren't at The Barbican and you aren't anyone's mage?'

Rigel felt his stomach cramp up. So quickly, so very quickly, their little cover story had been blown apart.

'At Lord Balderwin's estate,' he muttered, looking at his feet.

'Balderwin,' she said with distaste. She gave him another hard look. 'I wouldn't have thought you were to his taste, Rigel.'

'No, ma'am.'

She cocked an eyebrow. 'Interesting. And is the good Lord Balderwin alive?'

He hesitated. 'No ma'am.'

'Good,' she said without missing a beat. 'Then we can make this work. Let's go, Rigel. I'm sure you have a fascinating tale to tell and I can't wait to hear it.'

'Yes ma'am.'

'And stop calling me ma'am. If you're to be my mage you will need to learn some proper court etiquette. I am Lady Gloriana.'

'Court?'

'Yes dear, court. Oh dear me, we have a lot to learn, don't we?'

'Yes m—' Rigel stopped himself. 'Lady Gloriana? As in Lady Gloriana the guild patron?'

'I do happen to be the patron of The Guild of Mages, yes.'

Rigel was struck dumb. Only then did what she'd said seep into the mushy mess his brain had become. 'Your mage? You want me to be—'

Lady Gloriana sighed and steered him around, gently walking him along the bridge as the young man burst into tears.

Chapter Five

Ariene dismissed the girl, Misty, with a curt nod as the door to Lord Balderwin's hideously opulent dining room opened. The waif glanced at the door and stepped quietly away, merging almost effortlessly with the shadows. Ariene sucked her teeth and shook her head. The girl put her in mind of a spider waiting in a crevice; blank-eyed and still with the promise of death. Just what had she been through in this place?

The morning light was bright and cool through the windows, gleaming on the tea she stirred with a silver spoon in an exquisite cup. She breathed deeply of the aroma, still finding it hard to believe she was alive. She chuckled to herself and gave silent thanks to whatever strange fates had delivered her unexpected saviour to that bridge.

The saviour himself wandered sleepily through the gilded door and plonked himself heavily in a chair on the other side of the table. He yawned.

'Good morning, Rigel,' said Ariene, peering at him. He didn't look as though he'd slept much. His short brown hair was messy and standing up at the back, his face puffy. He rubbed his eyes. He was wearing what looked like a very expensive shirt that was many times too big for him.

'Morning, my lady,' he said, with a half-smile.

She nodded. 'That's better than *ma'am*.'

The door banged open and another young man walked in, a little taller and broader, and strikingly handsome with thick blonde hair. This one, who she presumed was the other mage apprentice, Thaniel, wore what had to be one of Lord Balderwin's jackets. It was encrusted with green gems, and he wore it open and without a shirt. She felt a momentary twinge of regret that Rigel hadn't made her twenty instead of sixty after all, before she remembered what Rigel had mentioned about Thaniel's preferences. She studied him; yes, she could use this one.

Thaniel paused in the act of reaching for a cup, and blinked at her.

'Hello,' he said, glancing at Rigel. When Rigel just looked back at him, Thaniel straightened up and addressed her. 'Sorry, who are you?'

The voice that answered him belonged to a girl who had appeared in the doorway. Tall, with long dark hair, pale skin, haunting eyes. Sophine. She wore a simple white shirt and dark trousers, with long black boots. She was staring.

'That's Lady Ariene Gloriana,' Sophine said in a guarded tone, those dark eyes measuring her with a penetrating stare, 'the patron of The Mages' Guild and half the other guilds in the city. If she's here, then she knows what happened to Balderwin.'

'I do,' Ariene replied neutrally.

'Then what do you want?' Sophine asked flatly, not moving from the doorway. Thaniel poured himself a cup of tea, apparently unconcerned.

'She's with me,' Rigel said. 'We met last night.'

'You did?' Thaniel asked, sipping his tea and sitting down. 'That's weird. Most Senators don't just wander around talking to random mage apprentices.'

'Yes well. There's a story.'

'Ok, so let's hear it.' Thaniel put his feet up on the table. Ariene suppressed a wince. She dreaded to think how expensive the heavy, beautifully carved wood had been; it was almost certainly a single piece of a very large and very ancient tree. She sighed inwardly at the sight of Thaniel's socks propped up on such a perfect slice of living history.

Rigel began the story of what had happened last night, including the grisly detail about what had happened to Balderwin, and Ariene listened intently to the tale. This was magic of a kind she'd not encountered before, the kind that existed only in tales about the Darklings before the Purge. Purely instinctive and emotional, but evidently extremely dangerous. She thought of the mages she'd briefly employed over her lifetime for various jobs; builders, artists. All so emotionless and studious, striving always to reach a mental harmony that, whilst useful, tended to eventually make them into the most frightful bores. Older mages were, to a man, humourless and sanctimonious creatures. Not so these youngsters who had stumbled upon such uncanny abilities. She shuddered at the thought of what the Priesthood of the Sacred Circle would do if any of it came to light.

'So we came back here,' finished Rigel, falling into a contemplative silence. Sophine had moved to the table through the course of the tale and sat with one hand on Rigel's shoulder, rubbing it affectionately.

'You did brilliantly, Rige,' Sophine was saying. 'You saved someone's life and made her younger all within a few minutes. Most healers take hours to perform even the simplest procedures...'

'You didn't,' he replied. 'Remember your arm?'

'That doesn't count, it was school.'

'It does,' put in Thaniel. 'I couldn't heal mine, remember?'

Rigel sighed and stood up from the table. 'I did this in public though, and then blurted out the whole thing about us living here to a total stranger.'

Sophine nodded. 'Yes that was stupid.'

'Inevitable, I think you mean,' said Thaniel. 'It was always going to come out eventually.'

'And so,' Ariene said loudly, cutting across their chatter. 'I have a plan for you all and you will all accept it. All of you.' She looked at Sophine, those dark eyes glittering for a moment with defiance. 'I am by far the eldest here, and unless you want to have killed two nobles in one house you had better be prepared to take my advice. I am on your side, or else you'd be in a dungeon beneath the Senate building already.' Sophine held her gaze.

'Soph,' Thaniel said softly. The girl lowered her eyes. Ariene nodded. 'Alright then. Now, the patronage fair is tomorrow, yes?'

'Yes,' said Rigel, when it became clear she was actually expecting a response.

'This is what we shall do. Sophine will give me a letter from Lord Balderwin directing me to purchase his chosen mage's patronage.' Sophine looked at her, confusion on her young face. 'If I do it, dear, no one will question it. I will also plant the notion of Balderwin's long term absence in the minds of everyone I meet. You will advance from apprentice and return here to act as Lord

Balderwin's mage, at my direction and under my supervision until he returns. That is a plausible scenario that people will accept.'

She paused, taking a sip of her tea.

'Except for those who know I despise the man, of course. But even then, their suspicion will be directed at me rather than you, dear. You were once, after all, the type he collected. And I am a Senator of Asterheim, if I'm not being suspected of crimes then I'm not doing my job.'

Sophine smiled at that, and Ariene gave her a conspiratorial grin.

'Rigel will simply come with me, and I will patronise him myself. I have clearly been restored by a mage, so people will simply believe that I sought out the kind of magical intervention I have avoided for so long and now have a taste for it. That part of the plan is easy.' She looked at Thaniel contemplatively.

'Yours however, young man, is less simple.'

'It is?'

'I'm afraid so. There is a noble named Orswell. He tried to kill me last night.'

'Oh,' said Thaniel, looking bewildered. 'I'm...sorry to hear that.' Rigel's eyes widened and he stifled a grin.

'Thank you dear,' Ariene said drily. 'It so happens that this lord is actually a younger brother of the real Lord Orswell, who is a reclusive man. Patron of the Citizenry Guild, you know; births, deaths, marriages and so on.' She sipped her tea thoughtfully. 'This Orswell is a political rival of mine, as you have probably gathered, and tragically, his younger brother is about to have a very unfortunate accident.'

'He is?'

'I'm quite sure of it. One gets a nose for such things at my age. And when he does, that is the opportunity we will use to get you patronised. But you need to promise me that you will do as I ask, yes?'

Thaniel nodded without hesitation. 'Yes, ma'am.'

'It might mean compromising your principles.'

'Not a problem, ma'am.'

She searched his face. He was so young, and the city was not exactly welcoming for those of less conventional proclivities; Orswell himself being an example of the price one paid to be accepted. It would be dangerous if it went wrong.

'He's like you, Thaniel,' she said gently. 'Do you see what I mean? You're an attractive young man…'

Thaniel's eyes narrowed, and his accusatory glance at Rigel told Ariene he understood her. He looked away for a moment, staring out of the window with a contemplative expression that looked far too serious on his young face. A muscle danced in his cheek.

'Alright,' he said at last, still looking away.

Ariene hesitated. 'What I mean to say is, you might need to—'

'I get it, ma'am,' he said with a wave of the hand. 'And you needn't worry. It's not like I'm some innocent virgin.'

Ariene blinked, momentarily lost for words. Rigel made a strangled sound somewhere between a cough and a laugh.

'I hope it won't come to that, Thaniel, but I see my concerns were misplaced.'

He smiled faintly, though it didn't seem to meet his eyes. 'Yes ma'am.'

***

Having lived her whole life in fear, enduring cruelty of every flavour at the hands of a bloated monster in fine silks, Misty was a thin, pale creature with lank brown hair. Most of the time. Since the demise of her grotesque overlord, she'd permitted herself to let go of some of the deceptions she'd relied on to survive. Older girls under Balderwin eventually found themselves thrown out or worse, and so she'd made sure she knew how to appear smaller, meeker, younger than she really was. Shapeless tunics, badly tied plaits, a voice so soft and pathetic that it conveyed nothing but submission and fear. But even that had not been enough to survive the cut-throat world of desperate victims known as the House Balderwin: a rats nest of squabbling, frightened girls all fearing for their own lives. So she had learned other skills, and by using them had protected both her life and her precarious position in the house. As the eldest, she was the most vulnerable; she'd quickly learned to become the most ruthless.

This, Lady Gloriana had guessed immediately upon seeing her.

'Such a fragile creature,' the Lady had said when they'd first been introduced, but her eyes did not suggest pity. Most people looked at the girls of the house as though they weren't really there, just phantoms worth a passing glance and nothing more, and for the most part that suited them just fine. This Gloriana lady's eyes were searching, measuring. Unsettling. Misty had simply lowered her eyes and made a clumsy curtsey as Sophine moved on to introduce the other girls to the newcomer. Ariene however had not moved on, keeping those intelligent eyes on her. Eventually, Misty had straightened and returned the look. 'There she is,' Ariene had whispered with a satisfied half-smile, 'I thought so. We'll talk later, Misty.'

93

And so they had. Here, at last, was an ally. A woman who understood her, and who had vowed to protect her and the life they had made following the death of Balderwin. And what she had asked in return was, while frightening and definitely dangerous, a price worth paying.

Something shifted in the shadows to her left and Misty tensed, hand moving to the knife hidden under her clothes before she realised it was just the three girls she'd brought with her. No more than eleven years old, they'd been every bit as invisible as Misty on their trip into the commercial district. She waved at them to be silent and turned to look up the alleyway to the tavern.

She'd watched Lord Orswell's younger brother carefully for the last few hours, keeping him in sight as much as possible just in case he did anything unexpected. Lady Gloriana was supposed to be going to the Senate for midday, she'd said, at the same time that the elder Orswell tended to take his place in the Senate and the younger tended to roll his way towards his favourite brothel, handily situated near the riverbank. Misty glanced at the sky, tracking the position of the sun. Midday was about an hour or so away.

Misty nibbled the sugared bread fancy she'd bought on the way here; something she'd never have been able to afford or ever dared ask for whilst Lord Balderwin had been alive. It had felt glorious to actually pay for it, handing the coin over triumphantly to the suspicious merchant, who clearly wondered how a waif like her could afford to spend money on such things. Each bite sent a rush of warm pleasure through her head, reducing her whole world to her tongue and her brain, both of which tingled and danced with delight for a few intoxicating seconds. It was so enthralling she almost didn't notice the shape of the man stumbling down the alleyway.

94

Misty held an arm out to the girls in the shadows, motioning them to be ready. She dropped the fancy and waited for the stumbling figure to pass her, fishing the knife out from under the tunic. She waited another second and then turned in a smooth movement and drove the knife into his back, aiming roughly for his heart. It was hard; the rich clothes were thick but the blade was sharp and she was stronger than she looked. She rammed it in up to the hilt, her free hand on the shoulder for leverage. Ormond Orswell shuddered and gasped, making no other sound as he collapsed in a heap. She bent down to check the twitching body, then signalled to the girls standing in the shadows.

'The river,' she hissed.

***

The carved wooden heroes once again looked down on Ariene with melodramatic gravity. She let them look, her eyes lingering over their hard faces and theatrical poses. Try as she might, she couldn't recall that razor edged focus she'd had the night before, when she truly felt the hand of death upon her shoulder. There had been a clarity then, a powerful sense of truth; as though she had been experiencing things for the very first time or with senses heightened far beyond the human. Everything had held a significance; everything had meant something. Touch, smell, sight. Something powerful.

It was to be expected, she supposed, that she couldn't recall it now.

'Perhaps lives are like candles,' she said aloud to Darcy, who stood in rapt awe behind her as she had since the moment she'd turned up at the Lawyers' Guild to stop her delivering the documents. 'Only truly valued when threatened by the shadows. We tell ourselves we love them for their beauty, but then the sun rises and they're just old sticks again. Cherish your candle dear, it's no fun in the dark.'

'Yes my lady,' said Darcy quietly, her tone still muted and hushed as though to be in her presence was to be in the presence of the divine. Ariene turned to glance at her.

'Darcy, dear, mages have been around a long time. I can't be the first person you've seen reinvigorated by one of them.'

'No my lady,' her faithful handmaid replied with a rare smile, 'but you didn't see yourself when you left. You were dying, actually *dying*…'

'I know dear, I was there.'

'…and I've never heard of anyone so close to death being cured and brought back young and strong…'

'*Young* might be a stretch, dear.' Darcy was undeterred.

'It's a *miracle,* my lady. The Circle has brought you back, returned you to life for a great purpose…'

'The Circle has nothing to do with it.'

'Maybe it does. The priests always talk about how things naturally return to their beginning.'

'They mean death, Darcy. They preach fatalism and call it enlightened. I assure you, they won't be happy that I'm back to a younger, healthier self. They might even call it an abomination if they don't mind a little hypocrisy with their morning outrage.'

Darcy had nothing to say to that, just nodded in dutiful agreement. If she'd minded being stopped at the very moment of becoming sole owner of all House Gloriana's considerable wealth, she had given no sign of it. The moment she'd seen Ariene in the guild house, she'd dropped all her papers and flung herself at her mistress, sobbing loudly and wetly into her dress as she wrapped her in a powerful hug. Ariene had smiled at the clerk Darcy had been talking to.

'Just lost a fortune,' she'd said, rolling her eyes, 'and the silly girl's happy about it.' The clerk had just looked confused. They had then spent a very pleasant afternoon buying outrageously expensive jewellery and a fabulously overpriced new blue dress for her reappearance at the Senate. Ariene had laughed as she handed over coin after coin, revelling in the giddy freedom that came with finally knowing the value of gold was nothing compared to enjoying her life.

'What do you gentlemen think?' Ariene asked now of the ancient heroes battling eternally on the Senate doors. She twirled for them in her dress, gleaming with cut stones and snugly fitting over her reinvigorated figure. The mighty warriors didn't reply. She pouted at them.

'Just as I suspected,' she said, 'not a brain between you.'

She gazed at them a moment longer, ignoring Darcy's confused look, and turned to the Senate chamber and tugged the dress away from her feet.

The chamber was full today, a loud commotion of voices battling to be heard, small groups huddled together and talking fervently or yelling at one another, individuals standing unheeded on the dais whilst the Speaker tried in vain to call order. Ariene allowed herself a smile; it was a little like attending one's own funeral.

She stood on the threshold and waited, making no effort to announce herself but very much enjoying how the light framed her as she stood in the doorway. It amused her that this time, no one called to her before she was ready. Three seats down, a junior guild officer was turning away from whoever it was he'd been arguing with, rubbing the back of his neck and frowning deeply. His eyes flicked over her as he turned, and he paused. His eyes returned. Someone else saw his open-mouthed face and looked over too. Gradually, hush began to fall as the Senators all looked away from their squabbles to see what was silencing their fellows. For a few moments, no one moved. Then chaos erupted.

Senators shouted over one another, some yelling her name, others denying it could be her as loudly as possible. She saw aspirations and hopes become ashes in the mouths of some, hope and relief blossom on the faces of others. Bargains and agreements fell apart, alliances crumbled, threats evaporated.

She ignored them all and walked slowly down the steps towards the dais, where the Speaker was gaping at her in silence. She waved him aside and stood facing the assemblage, just in front of the throne shrouded in its purple veil. It smelled vaguely musty.

'Senators,' she cried, raising her hands as her voice carried beautifully across the chamber. She grinned broadly, revelling in how pain-free and strong she felt. She surreptitiously stepped to the right, the better to let the light from the window reflect on her many, many jewels. A reverent hush fell over the assembled Senate.

'My apologies for last night's drama,' she smiled, 'but I now feel much better.' There were some nervous laughs amongst the seated senators.

'I know many of you were deeply concerned for my health,' she said, at once sincere and deeply, deeply sarcastic. Her eyes sought out and found Viscount Roach, who was staring with an expression of rapt adoration she rather liked. 'And I assure you that I will be taking steps to ensure you need not be again.'

Senators squirmed and looked at one another, as though trying to decide if that had been a threat and if so, whether it was directed at them. She surveyed the room, looking for anyone particularly agitated by her survival and noting any potential enemies in the back of her mind. Then she gathered her dress and marched away, intending to walk proudly out.

'Stop!' someone called. She paused, looking for the speaker. Her heart sank as she recognised him.

'How do we know you are the Lady Gloriana?' called the Chief Officer of the Lawyers' Guild. A man she'd known for many years.

'You know, Samael,' she said, 'you rather ruined my dramatic exit.' She gave him a wry smile that was every inch Lady Gloriana. His mouth twitched as he suppressed a smile of his own.

'We need some proof, Lady,' he admonished softly, glancing around at the assembly.

'As you wish. How about this then, Samael. Don't say you weren't warned.'

The Chief Officer's brow flickered in sudden concern. She smiled.

'I know of the dagger buried beneath a certain tree within a certain province of Astregoth,' she said with utter self-assurance. 'The dagger was used to—'

'I move that the Senate recognises the speaker on the floor as Lady Gloriana,' Samael blurted, eyes a little wild. His large grey wig wobbled on his head. 'There is no doubt in my mind as Chief Justice that this is the Lady Gloriana.'

'Tell us about the dagger!' someone called. There were some titters of nervous laughter.

'I can vouch for the lady,' wheezed an elderly man in a wheeled chair by the dais, who was in fact the patron of the Lawyers' Guild. 'It has been many years since I have seen her as she is now, but I remember her face. This is beyond doubt the Lady Gloriana. I second the motion.'

'Thank you, Lord Aresbrook,' she laughed, turning to him. 'Perhaps you should find yourself a mage too, we could relive those days together.'

'I fear I am beyond their talents, my lady,' bowed Aresbrook. 'There is only so much you can ask of a healer.'

'You would think,' she allowed, glancing at the gold-cassocked priests in the red-seat upper tier. Their eyes were unfriendly. That gave her pause; had they known about the poison or did they just not like the fact that she was alive?

'What of you, Lord Orswell? Lord Barten?' She called to her two prime suspects in the attempt on her life, enemies on the white tiers. 'Will you not make some farce of a challenge?'

Neither of them spoke, but she didn't fail to notice the murderous look Barten gave Orswell just as an aide appeared to whisper into his ear. Orswell looked suitably shaken, and stood up to make his way from the chamber amidst jeers and calls from her allies. Misty had evidently done her work well.

Good, she thought, filing away the peculiar interaction between Barten and Orswell.

Off you go…

***

100

The crunch of the carriage wheels on the worn path sent spikes of adrenaline through Thaniel's cold, wet body, as well as relief. He'd been waiting for some time, half immersed in the freezing Ceres River, wondering why he'd agreed to this decidedly risky plan.

'This is it,' he muttered, sweeping his lank wet hair back away from his face before quickly brushing it back over his eyes again, totally unsure of which was the better look for the part he was playing. He started to clamber out of the river, stumbling more than once in the thick mud of the riverbank. He cursed through chattering teeth, pausing to clean the muck off as the carriage drew nearer.

'This is it,' he said again, like saying it would somehow make him better prepared. 'This is it, this is it…'

Rigel had been his characteristically awkward self as he set out Lady Gloriana's plan after she'd finally settled on the specifics. 'You're not actually going to be…you know. A prostitute,' he'd fervently insisted more than once, as if that made it all better. 'The story should be enough. You're just…nudging him along.'

'No, I just get to *feel* like a prostitute,' he'd said, a little bitterly. 'What I actually am is a spy in a rival Lord's household, all on my own, with only your lame backstory to protect me. Which is *so much better.*'

Thaniel briefly entertained the notion of running away and becoming a prostitute after all as the carriage approached, wondering if it might be preferable to being a pawn in whatever game Ariene was playing.

It's now or never…

He sighed and hoisted himself out of the river, running through the underbrush towards the road as best he could on bare feet. The

101

carriage, now coming head on, slowed to a halt as the driver stared with wide eyes at the sight of the young man emerging near-naked from the water. Thaniel waved his arms frantically and, when the carriage stopped, wrapped them around his freezing body. All he was wearing was a soaked pair of thin undergarments that clung to his body; the supposed story being that the assassins who'd got Ormond Orswell had stolen everything quite literally down to the shirt on his back. A little on the nose, Thaniel had thought, but Ariene had insisted.

'What's going on?' asked a gruff, irate voice. A man's head poked out of the window and looked up at the driver, demanding an explanation for the interruption of his journey. The man, who Thaniel sincerely hoped was the right one, was an older gentleman, with a short greying beard and a stern look. Not quite how Lord Orswell had been described to him; Lady Gloriana had made him sound weak and withdrawn, which now seemed a tad prejudiced on her part. Thaniel forced a smile as the man's gaze switched to him.

'Thank The Circle you've come my lord!' he said, meaning almost every word; his legs were cramping from the cold water, and he was tired and hungry. He hopped from foot to foot, shaking the ache out and vaguely aware that he was supposed to be trying to look enticing rather than like a landed fish. He didn't feel enticing. He felt moronic.

The man in the carriage got out and walked closer. He was a slim man, richly dressed in a tailored jacket of blue silk studded with gems. A long sword hung by his side.

'Are you alright young man?' he asked, his eyes not leaving Thaniel's face. Thaniel felt another flicker of fear. What if this charade was based purely on Lady Gloriana's misplaced assumptions about men like them? Things could get nasty very quickly.

'I was attacked sir,' Thaniel said, recalling the general gist of the story Ariene had cooked up. 'Upriver, assassins attacked my master and me on our way to—'

'Assassins,' the lord repeated with a snarl, dropping his hand to his sword hilt. He looked away through the trees towards the river, and Thaniel felt the plan slipping away like bare feet on a muddy riverbank. He took another step closer, gesturing in the hope of keeping the man's attention which now appeared to be firmly fixed on the imminent danger Thaniel had stupidly suggested he was in. The man, quite understandably, ignored him.

'My master was killed,' he said, trying to get the story out before it was too late. 'He was thrown in, and they stripped me of all I had before they threw me in too.' He groped for a clever way to drop the name into his rambling account. The nobleman did not seem in the least bit interested in him, which either meant it was the wrong man or that Ariene was just very wrong about him. He fought a sudden mad urge to start jumping and waving his arms.

'Poor Lord Orswell,' he tried lamely.

'What did you say?' said the richly dressed lord, his eyes wide. He blinked, as though waking from some inner diversion. Thaniel's heart fluttered; a faint hope flickering. He plunged in.

'My master, Lord Ormond Orswell. He'd just agreed to buy my patronage at Hilda's at the fair tomorrow and I was to be his mage,' he paused, mentally checking he'd got that right.

'It's just too tragic,' he added, hoping it didn't sound like an afterthought.

Lord Orswell took a step back and blinked again, before looking at Thaniel with sudden intensity. Now Thaniel felt his eyes roving over him, as though seeing him for the first time, and Thaniel's heart jumped. He felt none of the disgust he'd expected when he first agreed to be the bait for Lady Gloriana's slightly grubby plan; somehow having come so close to failure, a glimmer of attention from this man was welcome. Hope flared bright within him and he turned his back; his heart was thrashing frantically in his chest like a caged beast and he didn't trust his face not to give him away.

The moment stretched; the longest of Thaniel's life. He fought and won a brief battle against the urge to flee in panic and find a nice street corner to work on of an evening.

'It seems The Circle has brought us to this place,' said Orswell eventually. Thaniel turned his head slightly, realising the man was still watching him from behind. All of a sudden he was keenly aware of the wet underwear hugging his freezing backside.

About time, he thought with a rush of unexpected relief. He deliberately shifted his weight in a way he was sure Lord Orswell couldn't have failed to notice and tried not to laugh at the absurdity of the situation.

'My brother was a fool,' the lord continued, stepping up behind him, 'but he had his moments.' He clapped a hand on Thaniel's shoulder and gave it a soft squeeze.

'I am Lord *Orlond* Orswell. Ormond was my younger brother.' Thaniel turned sharply in what he hoped looked like shock. 'I never much cared for him, but family is family. If you were his chosen mage, then I will honour his choice.'

'Thank you, my lord,' Thaniel replied with vehemence, realising he actually meant it. After all, he now had a patron and a future, and a patron who didn't seem nearly as lascivious or creepy as he'd been led to believe.

For the cost of a pair of wet pants and some dignity, it wasn't bad at all.

Chapter Six

The next day was the patronage fair, the annual occasion where interested parties could attend The Barbican and pick out any particularly impressive young apprentices they might want to sponsor and eventually employ. Rigel had endured many of these dreaded rituals in his time at Hilda's, and much like his parents so many years before, none of the prospective patrons had ever decided he was worth keeping around. Every year was another reminder of how thoroughly unimpressive he was as a mage. As a son. As a person. He kept his head down as they walked towards the imposing form of The Barbican, concentrating on putting one foot in front of the other and trying not to think about his parents.

'Are you alright, dear?' asked Ariene, tugging slightly on the arm she held. He nodded, not looking up. He felt her eyes on his face, and hated the heat he could feel building up in his eyes; the prickle of tears at their corners. Ariene, to her credit, looked away towards the hulking stone building and left him to his thoughts.

Hilda's Barbican was a huge complex, with housing blocks and kitchens, studios and practice areas all surrounding the central teaching block and library. It had grown from the relatively simple stronghold that Hilda had built centuries ago to house the students of the closely watched, newly created Guild of Mages. Its grounds now rivalled that of the Finance Guild with its famously labyrinthian corridors, chambers and enormous vaults. Sadly, however, it was mostly derelict. There hadn't been many new recruits in years, and only a handful of students were ever in attendance.

The Barbican was encircled by a stone wall, some ten feet tall and at least three thick and accessible only from within. It had been built very much with defence in mind; at the time, fresh from the dark days of the great purge, trust in mages was low and danger to them was high. Now the wall served to lend a sense of grandeur and permanence to Hilda's, and allowed Patronage Day to take place in the grand courtyard beyond the heavy doors. With the portcullis raised and the doors flung wide and hung with bunting, the day promised to be festive and welcoming.

Almost. One small problem marred the occasion on this fine Autumn morning. A group of people stood just beyond the walls, waving signs and shouting at those visitors who turned up at the doors. As they approached, Rigel recognised the man in charge instantly. All thoughts of his parents were instantly banished.

'Ariene,' he said softly. She glanced at him, and he motioned with his head at the priest in the filthy golden robe standing on a box holding a crude sign which read: 'All Mages Are Darklings'. She clicked her tongue.

'No points for originality,' she muttered. 'Does he really think anyone believes that rubbish in this day and age?'

Rigel thought back to the protest from which he'd barely escaped with his life less than a week ago.

'They do, my lady.'

'No,' she turned to him and held up a finger. 'Never forget, Rigel. People don't have to *believe* to be dangerous.' She looked at the scruffy gang of shouting protesters and their ragged signs. 'I look at these people and you know what I see?'

Rigel shook his head. They looked like angry zealots to him.

'I see the poor. The hurt. The abused. People whose lives have been wrecked or marred by something. And this fellow,' she indicated the scarred priest with the angry eyes, 'is there to tell them it's all someone else's fault, and they love him for it. They need him like parasites need a host, poor devils.'

'So I should pity them?'

'Maybe,' she said, gathering up her dress with some irritation. It was a new one, blue again of course, but not as elaborate as her new Senate attire and less stone encrusted. She still found herself tugging it away from her feet, however, and wasn't entirely happy about it.

She sighed and adjusted the small tiara she'd picked out to balance on the mound of hair Darcy had created on her head. 'This damn thing falls off and I'll be a laughing stock,' she muttered.

'Pity them perhaps,' she continued, linking her free arm through his, 'but be wary. Those are people who *need* to believe, and there is nothing more dangerous than that. True believers don't need anything else. They just believe. But *needful* believers need to think they're *right* to believe. That's the difference that makes them dangerous; anything that tells them they're wrong is a threat. And they're desperate enough in the first place.'

Rigel looked at the moth-eaten priest again. The man had paused in his tirade and was watching them, the gleam of recognition in his fierce eyes. Rigel felt his stomach clench.

'Which is he, my lady?' he asked. 'True believer or needful?'

Ariene looked at the man for a long moment as they walked past through the great stone aperture into the courtyard.

'Neither,' she said darkly. 'That one is the puppeteer. Believes in nothing, I'd wager.'

They made their way into the courtyard and Rigel grinned at the sight of the banners and cake stalls, set against the familiar sights of the grounds that he hadn't realised he'd missed in his brief absence. The ornate fountain with its carved dolphins which, over the centuries, had worn down to look more like crude blobs of stone. The old dead tree that had half-fallen over in a storm decades ago and now stood at a peculiar angle, its roots protruding from the ruptured flagstones, which no one had ever fixed. Everywhere, young novices and apprentices tried to attract the attention of the visitors milling around, introducing themselves and demonstrating their skills. A young girl levitated a small wooden ball above her hand, eyes closed and breathing shallowly, and Rigel sighed sadly at the intense concentration on her face. How many times had he been here, desperately trying to stand out and just somehow never managing it as the crippling feeling that he would never amount to anything gnawed away at his insides. In recent years, Hilda's had been struggling to fill its halls, taking on fewer and fewer students each year as mistrust of mages grew. In Rigel's class, there had been no more than six. Six kids sent away to the one place that would, these days, take literally anyone. But seeing them all together, demonstrating their skills, made Hilda's seem to come alive.

'There's Thaniel,' Rigel said happily, pointing past a young man studiously struggling to make a plant grow and getting nowhere. Thaniel was by one of the cake stalls, laughing with a greying man in his forties or fifties wearing a red jacket and high leather boots.

'Is that Orswell?' At his side, Lady Gloriana nodded slowly. She pulled him close and whispered.

'Remember, you don't know one another. Orswell mustn't suspect.' Rigel nodded. He made his way towards his friend, noting with some surprise the way the older man's hand lingered just a moment too long on Thaniel's shoulder as they shared a joke. He was sure Ariene's plan hadn't included friendship. Rigel reached the cake stall and made a show of peering at the goods on sale, waiting for the inevitable conversation to begin.

'Ariene,' Lord Orswell said in some surprise as Lady Gloriana came up behind them.

Rigel's new patron smiled thinly and returned the welcome, 'Orlond.'

'I'm surprised to see you here,' Orswell said. 'Although come to think of it, your aversion to mages seems to have waned recently.' He smiled, with a respectful nod at Rigel.

'I was never averse to them,' Lady Gloriana said, picking up a scone and fishing for a coin to hand the boy behind the counter. 'I'm patron of the guild after all. I just didn't intend to use them to prolong my life.'

'May I ask what changed?'

Ariene handed the coin to the boy, who was fruitlessly trying to point out how he'd made the cakes without an oven. 'If my lady might do me the honour of patronage I could bake all sorts...' he gave up as she turned back to Orswell. Rigel gave him an encouraging smile, which the boy did not return.

'What changed, my dear Orlond, is that someone decided to move things along a little faster than I'd intended.' She gave him

110

an icy look. 'As a man recently bereaved I'm sure you can appreciate the inconvenience of an unplanned demise.'

Orswell narrowed his eyes at that, but Ariene pretended not to notice. She turned to Rigel.

'May I introduce Rigel Wheatley?'

'Your choice?'

'In a manner of speaking, yes. If I were a religious dolt, I'd say it was fate or circles or some such that brought us together but certainly there was a lot more chance than choice in the matter.'

'I see,' said Orswell, looking Rigel up and down and not seeming terribly impressed.

'There's more to him than meets the eye,' Ariene said with a smile.

'There would almost have to be,' replied Orswell. Rigel dropped his gaze and shuffled his feet, that familiar feeling of worthlessness erupting from nowhere at the man's careless words. He struggled to maintain his composure.

'And this one is?' Ariene turned her gaze at Thaniel.

'Thaniel. My brother's choice, as it happens.' Orswell looked at Rigel again. 'You two must be of a similar age, don't you know each other?'

'Not really,' said Thaniel brightly, coming forward to grab Rigel's hand before he could speak. 'He always seemed so quiet and alone, just sat there sadly in the corner.' Rigel glared at him.

'But maybe we could be friends?' Thaniel continued. 'Now that we're going to be working for two of the greatest nobles in the city,' he dipped his head courteously to Lady Gloriana, 'we should at least get to know one another.'

'Not too well, though,' said Orswell quickly, glancing at Thaniel. Rigel couldn't tell if he was being possessive or political. 'Although I daresay from the looks of him, there isn't much to know.'

Thaniel pressed on, ignoring his new master.

'Perhaps we could have a drink later, Rigel?'

Rigel nodded and dropped his gaze again, finding the role Thaniel had carved for him fitted perfectly and hating his friend for knowing him so well.

'I'll come by the Gloriana estate later then,' Thaniel rambled on, with another half-bow to the Lady Gloriana. 'For now, my master and I are going to see the other stalls.'

Orswell nodded a stiff goodbye and steered his new mage away, muttering in his ear.

'I think we underestimated your friend Thaniel,' said Ariene when they were safely out of earshot. 'He's a very clever young man.'

Rigel just scowled, hating himself for the emotional turmoil eating away at his guts. A few words, that's all it had been. A stranger's dismissive words.

A sudden crash and a roar of commotion split the tranquillity of the afternoon festivities; the protesters had evidently taken exception to something and charged through the gates under the portcullis and into the courtyard, where the scar-jawed priest was remonstrating a figure with long black hair wearing an ill-fitting green dress. His band of needful believers had thrown their placards away and were shaking fists and pointing, but so far they stayed in a ragged gang behind their leader as he yelled at the girl, who was backing away slowly.

'Sophine,' Rigel breathed, darting forward. Ariene grabbed him and pulled him back.

'I will deal with this; we don't want any more attention on you.' Rigel stepped aside reluctantly as his new mistress marched past. After a moment's hesitation, he followed.

As he drew nearer he discerned the general gist of what the angry priest was shouting about. Words like 'honest folk' and 'right to protest' were being thrown about. Sophine was making concilia-tory gestures, shaking her head, her dark eyes wide. Her gown was lined in gold trim, the neckline low; glittering gems sewn in the lining danced and glinted in the light. She looked like a servant who'd be caught in her mistress' gown.

'I wasn't trying to stop you,' Sophine was imploring, looking slightly frantic. 'I was just saying there are *children* here, innocent people who don't deserve to be yelled at for being...'

'Being witches!' screamed the priest, virtually frothing at the mouth, his golden robes spattered with mud and dust from the road. 'My followers are faithful devotees of The Sacred Circle and they are justly outraged by the witchcraft practised within these filthy walls!'

Sophine paused at that. She glared at the man and half-turned, as though to storm away in fury, but then stopped. She straight-ened, glancing at Rigel with a curious expression somewhere be-tween fear and determination as the moment lengthened. Then she turned back, head up, hands clasped before her. Suddenly the gown didn't look so ill-fitting.

'Witchcraft,' she snarled. 'Is it witchcraft when someone helps the crops grow? Or heals the sick? Calms a panicked horse? Coaxes iron from stone?'

113

'Don't presume to lecture me!' he shrieked back. 'We know what really goes on here. Spells. Curses...'

Sophine laughed. 'You don't,' she spat. 'You really don't. But I know *you*. A lost little man in a golden robe, so terrified that you've wasted your life for a fantasy that you have to convince everyone else to waste theirs too.'

The priest sneered at this and drew a short blade. 'I'll show you a wasted life!' Sophine bared her teeth in a feral expression and raised a hand. Just then, Ariene reached them.

'A priest of The Sacred Circle, filthy robes, distinctive jawline scar and a penchant for stirring up trouble,' she drawled laconically. 'When I give that description to my Travellers and their Ordo Militant, how long do you think until they find you?' The priest drew himself up, putting his blade away and straightening his clothes. He cast furious glances at Sophine as she stalked angrily away, her oversized gown trailing behind her.

'Lady Gloriana,' he said through gritted teeth.

'I suggest you take your...followers,' she lingered over the word as though it tasted bad in her mouth, 'and go somewhere else. I'd say you've made your point here and caused enough disruption.'

'Don't think this will be forgotten Lady,' he retorted. 'Those who associate with witches are enemies of the church.'

'Well that's good to know, except that no one here is a witch. I remind you of the Charter.'

'Your Charter...' he spat the word, but trailed off when he saw Rigel. 'You,' he breathed. He drew his blade again, thrusting it in Rigel's direction.

'You tell that one of the Charter! There stands a witch if ever there was one!'

114

Silence had fallen across the courtyard. People were staring. A small child had begun to cry.

'I suggest you leave, Priest,' said Ariene. 'And leave now.'

The priest looked around, snarling. His eyes locked on Rigel again for a few agonising heartbeats, before he turned and stalked away, followed by his band of faithful devotees.

Ariene turned slowly to Rigel. 'I told you to stay back.'

'I'm sorry.'

She smiled wryly.

'I think we both might be, before this is over. That one came here looking for enemies, and I think he found some.'

*** *

The way the barman looked at Thaniel made Rigel grimace. He sighed deeply and took a large swig of his near-empty flagon. Thaniel returned to the table with three more, plonking them down on the twisted, gnarled wooden table and sitting heavily down on his stool. He looked pleased with himself.

'Still got it,' he announced smugly. Rigel ignored him and reached for his new drink.

'Of course you've still got it, Than,' said Sophine, still toying with her first flagon. 'You're what, seventeen?'

'Eighteen soon,' he replied with a pained look. 'Practically a crone.'

'Is that what the good Lord Orswell thinks?' put in Rigel with unexpected bitterness. He forced a big smile in an attempt to lighten the comment. Thaniel didn't seem to notice, or chose to ignore it.

'No, thank the abundant curves of the great fat Circle. He likes me.'

'I bet he does.'

'Not like that. Or at least, not just like that. He's not made any move to…you know, do anything.'

'Not yet.'

'Look he isn't that bad, ok? He agreed to patronise me on the day his brother was murdered, I'd say that means he's got heart.'

'Or none.'

Thaniel glared at him with sudden annoyance. 'Can you back off?'

Rigel's false smile faltered. 'Sorry,' he said. 'I'm not sure what's up with me.'

Sophine reached out and rubbed his arm. She'd changed into her more traditional dark clothes, black boots and jacket, grey trousers and shirt. Simple, but she made them look good. Rigel found himself darting glances at her over his drink when she wasn't looking.

'We should be celebrating,' Thaniel said. 'We're all mages now. Can you believe it? I thought I'd end up working at The Barbican forever or being sent back home but here I am, mage to a lord of Asterheim. And my two best friends are too!'

Sophine grinned. 'Sort of,' she agreed.

Thaniel leaned across the table, conspiratorially.

'No one ever said they had to be *living* lords, my good lady Sophine, Mage of House Balderwin.'

Sophine gave a half-smile and looked around the tavern. It was packed with people, some young erstwhile apprentices with their new patrons and others commiserating without. The *Seven Buckets* was the closest tavern to The Barbican and had a long tradition of serving the youngsters who snuck in without leave of their masters. Tonight, everyone had leave. It was a large wooden building, easily capable of holding sixty or more people, with a simple bar along the back wall and a set of stairs leading to the rooms above; nothing else but stools and crude tables. A fire burned in the corner, wholly inadequate for heating the place; it relied mostly on the combined body heat of the evening revellers to keep everyone from freezing to death.

'To us,' declared Thaniel, holding up a flagon. Rigel clanked his against it and drank deeply.

'Doesn't it bother you?' Sophine said incredulously, giving Thaniel a disbelieving glare.

'What?'

'What do you mean what? That we all got our patronage through…you know…Murder and lies—'

'And my frozen backside.'

She ignored that. 'In the space of a few days, we've gone from throwing stones in the quarry to performing illegal magic and *killing* people. You're telling me that doesn't upset you? And now we're toasting our achievements in a tavern full of people who managed to get patronised without putting everyone else in danger.'

'How did it put anyone else in danger?' Rigel asked. 'I mean aside from the murder. Which to be fair, you didn't mean to do.'

'Lady Gloriana did.'

'Well, yes. Maybe she did.'

'She absolutely did.'

'Alright, alright! But *you* didn't.'

117

'There was the priest today,' Thaniel added softly, taking a sip of his drink. 'The same one from the protest. He saw you Rige. He must suspect something. He knows we escaped the protest, when we really shouldn't have. And then here you are with the miraculously restored Lady Gloriana, who shouldn't have survived what she did. Dread to think what a maniac like him thinks, and that's even if they never find out about Balderwin. He's a troublemaker.'

As if conjured by Thaniel's uncharacteristically sober comments, the now-familiar tones of the perpetually outraged scarred priest cut through the hubbub of early evening tavern conversation. Heads turned, smiles wavered, drinks were gulped down as people stood up to leave.

'No way,' breathed Thaniel. 'It can't be.'

A mob of some twenty people was forcing its way into the crowded alehouse, yelling and pointing. At the front, the scarred priest was sermonising, his arms held up above his head, the index fingers and thumbs of each hand touching in the sign of The Circle.

'We need to leave,' Sophine said, looking behind her. Rigel glanced around; there was no way out but the front door.

'Go round,' he said, gesturing to Thaniel, 'round the sides. We'll slip out that way...'

'He followed us,' Sophine muttered in disbelief.

'He didn't follow us,' Rigel replied under his breath, shoving his way through a group of much younger apprentices. 'He just knew where everyone would be. The fact that we're here is—'

'Abomination!' the priest was screaming, angrily jabbing his finger at random people. 'Your filthy fortress is a cancer on Asterheim, a monstrous boil filled with pestilence!'

'Right,' the handsome bartender who had flirted with Thaniel had shoved his way to the front of the crowd, 'I'd like you all to leave please. I don't want any trouble here.'

'You've let trouble in by the front door, poor fool,' thundered the priest as drinkers shared bemused glances. There were some nervous giggles. 'But it will not depart that way.'

'What does that even mean?' the barman asked, looking confused.

'Nothing,' someone shouted from the back, 'like everything else priests say!' There were laughs and murmurs in the crowd.

'Go home!' someone else shouted back. 'Unless you're buying, no one wants you here!'

All it took was one shove. A man Rigel had never seen before, someone who was neither a mage nor a patron from the looks of his labourer's overalls, gave one of the zealots a push. 'Go on, go!' he said.

The zealot pushed back, and the room erupted into madness. Fists flew, blood sprayed, bodies crashed heavily into tables as the crowd went feral. Someone flung a flagon as they fell, smashing a window. Amidst the swirling chaos, Rigel's eyes met those of the dishevelled priest.

He had been standing untouched, watching the unfolding brawl in his tattered golden robe. Now he snarled and unsheathed a short ugly blade from a scabbard at his waist. Rigel's eyes widened in alarm and he tried to shove his way through the mass of struggling bodies, but they were pressed too tight; there was nowhere to go. The priest smiled unpleasantly, but made no move towards him. Rigel frowned, then his eyes widened in dawning horror as the priest turned and slashed the throat of the nearest zealot, then drove his blade into the back of another. Rigel screamed, shoving harder at the men wrestling in front of him, as the priest killed yet another of his followers before throwing the knife high over the heads of the embattled tavern-goers and pushing his way towards the door.

'Stop him,' shrieked Rigel, mad with frustrated anger. 'Stop him!' Energy bubbled up inside him, intensely hot, irresistible…

At his side, Sophine thrust one pale hand out with a scream just as something intangible exploded from inside him. Time slowed, a thrown flagon drifted lazily to a stop and hung weightless in the air, droplets of blood and ale floating delicately in the gleam of firelight. Rigel turned his head; Sophine was still silently screaming, her mouth open and her eyes black. Her hand was curled into a fist, a cold pale light glowing softly around it. He turned to look on his other side, where Thaniel had his eyes closed, a look of intense concentration on his face. In spite of himself, Rigel felt a corner of his mouth twitch in a smile; Than would have loved to see himself as he looked right now. A shabbily dressed zealot, wearing a silver chain around his neck, was floating before him, arms and feet outstretched, in the process of being thrown back by an impressive telekinetic blast.

The feeling of hot energy pouring out of him was waning. He tried to hold onto it, to sustain it, even as he felt it draining away like water through cupped hands. He looked around, catching sight of the scarred priest, frozen between two zealots just by the front door. He tried to push past the man in front of him, but it was like pushing a statue; the man was as hard and unyielding as stone. Rigel grunted in frustration, and then hesitated as he noticed something else.

The man in front of the priest, the one he was trying to push past on his way to the door, was coming apart. Slowly, hideously, he was splitting down the middle. The man's expression was gradually, muscle by muscle, contorting into one of extreme agony as the sorcerous tear gradually bisected him, a red line deepening in his forehead and starting to bleed at the edges as it worked its way down his face.

'No!' Rigel cried, grabbing hold of Sophine's outstretched arm. Her fist was opening, tiny bit by tiny bit, the fingers moving achingly slowly and pulling the man further apart with every millimetre. Rigel tugged, but Sophine was like iron. He screamed as the hot power snapped away from him, spent, and time returned instantly to normal. The man Thaniel had levitated crashed heavily into a wooden beam and slumped unmoving to the floor. Sophine's arm was whipped down and she stumbled, crashing into the man who moments before Rigel had tried to move. She shouted a curse that Rigel didn't hear as a hideous screeching filled the room and drowned out all else. Brawlers, zealots and drinkers alike, paused and turned to the awful sound, the fight forgotten by most.

The zealot who had been splitting in half was shrieking a terrible, animal howl of agony. His face was in ruins, a dreadful slash cutting it neatly in two; skin flapped wetly on either side of a deep gash, within which the gleam of bone could be seen. Blood stained his clothes from head to groin, suggesting the awful wound continued the whole way down his body. The keening wail rose to a fevered pitch and then died away as the man collapsed to the ground, blood spreading in a pool around him.

For a few moments nobody moved. No one breathed. Then chaos again erupted as zealots and drinkers alike surged for the door, knocking tables over in their desperate scramble for safety. Bodies were trampled, screams unheeded. Rigel reached out and grabbed Thaniel, pulling him back against the wall where he and Sophine huddled, breathing hard and whimpering at the horror they'd just witnessed.

When the room had emptied, the young bartender sat alone on an upturned barrel, staring at the ruin of his tavern and the bodies strewn across the floor. Thaniel stepped tentatively towards him.

'Can we…? Is there anything we can…?' he faltered.

The bartender looked at him with an expressionless face.

'Just leave,' he said emotionlessly. 'Just go.' He turned back to look at the carnage. 'Better you aren't here when the Watch arrives.'

Thaniel hesitated.

Rigel put his hand on his friend's shoulder. 'Come on, Than, we need to get out of here.'

Thaniel said nothing but allowed himself to be steered out of the tavern, picking his way over the bodies sprawled everywhere.

Sophine met them outside.

'It was the same group,' she said eventually, after they'd walked in silence for some time. 'The same protesters from the patronage fair.'

Rigel grunted in agreement. 'And the monastery.'

'We need to tell Ariene,' Sophine said. 'This wasn't random chance. Something bigger is happening here. We're being targeted.'

Rigel thought back to what Lady Gloriana had said earlier. *That one is a puppeteer.*

'He was killing his own men,' Rigel said. 'I don't think anyone else saw, but I saw.'

'Why would he kill his own men?' asked Thaniel, floating two stones off the floor and making them click together as they spun in lazy circles above his palm.

'Think about it. The Watch turns up at the tavern that everyone knows mages go to, and it's a massacre. Sacred Circle believers dead. Wouldn't be hard to spin it as an attack on the faithful.'

'No one would believe that.'

'Wouldn't they? After the strange deaths of those people, the debate in the Senate about whether mages were to blame, the protests that happened after, now this. Suddenly the stuff the Church has been saying about us starts to look believable.'

'No way. Not now. Mages have been legal for centuries.'

'They were *legal* before the great purge too.'

Thaniel let the stones drop and turned fearful eyes to Rigel.

'You're scaring me Rige.'

He kicked one of the dropped stones and watched it skitter away into the dark. 'I think we should all be scared.'

Chapter Seven

Thaniel floated a few metres off the floor, arms outstretched. His eyes were closed. He was muttering to himself so intently that he didn't hear the voice until it started to shout.

'Hey! You alright up there?' The voice was just about loud enough to crack his concentration. Thaniel opened one eye and peered down at the young man looking up at him.

'Go away,' he whispered urgently, flapping a hand at the newcomer. He wobbled, even though a detached part of his mind insisted he didn't need to hold his arms steady to remain focused. He looked down at the pile of cushions beneath him, some two or three metres below.

Suddenly he felt a rush of terror and fell to the floor, his legs jarring painfully even with the cushions. 'Dammit!' he exclaimed.

'Sorry,' said the other youth. 'Was that me?'

'Yes it was you,' Thaniel picked himself up and peered at the crack in the wall. It was a huge ugly rend, stretching the whole length of one of the forgotten dining rooms of Lord Orswell's sprawling estate. It was less a crack and more a hole, more suited to a derelict ruin than a noble's estate. He'd been given the task of fixing it, along with the rest of the crumbling walls of the Eastern wing that had been damaged by fire some years ago. He could feel the right mindset hovering just above his consciousness, waiting for him to rise into it. He'd procrastinated by electing to actually rise into the air as though physically embodying the higher level of consciousness he was trying to reach, which had allowed him to fuss with cushions and mattresses for a while before attempting the daunting task.

'I don't think I can do this,' he muttered, peering again at the ruined wall. It was surely beyond repair, the forces of nature were pulling apart the building materials and besides, he just couldn't rise into the passive mindset needed to truly see the extent of the job.

'Why don't you use a ladder?' Thaniel ignored this.

'I could get you a—'

'I don't want a ladder,' Thaniel said. 'It's not about being *high up*, it's more about...' He groped for the words, gesturing loosely with his hands. 'It's more about feeling connected to the forces I'm trying to control.' He laughed at how much like Master Thomas he sounded. Like an actual mage.

He sighed. 'I'll get it in the end.'

He looked around finally. The newcomer was about his age. Short, with dark hair, a round face and big brown eyes. Thaniel smiled; it was a nice face. The youth smiled back. Thaniel felt a jolt of something leap through his stomach and laughed nervously. 'I'll...get the hang of it, I mean. Not a ladder. I don't want the ladder. Like I said.'

'Right,' said the brown eyed boy. 'No ladder.'

Thaniel was suddenly aware of his heart beating harder and his legs going strangely numb. He wondered if he looked as flushed as he felt, and had an overwhelming certainty that his hair was sticking up. He smoothed it down with one hand, struggling to think of something to say. The youth spoke first.

'You're Thaniel?'

'Yes! Yes I am,' Thaniel enthused, with a rush of what felt bizarrely like relief. His heart beat even faster; adrenaline thumping madly through his veins and making his chest tingle.

'The new mage, right? Lord Orswell said we had one.'

'We?'

'Well, yeah. Us. All…all of us?'

'Oh. Good. That's…good.'

What's good, you cretin? an inner voice seethed at him.

He looked away, back at the crack in the wall, and nearly jumped in alarm. He could see it!

A faded web glinted faintly through the substance of what was left of the wall, beautiful silver threads broken and torn amongst the old bricks. Some of them blackened by the fire that had undone them.

'I can see it,' he breathed.

'See what?' the other boy asked in a hushed, watchful tone.

'The way the wall was built,' Thaniel said reverently. 'I can see where the stones were bound, how they used to fit together. How they *want* to fit together. It's beautiful…and broken.'

What remained of the latticework of weakening strength was beyond repair by any ordinary standard. A mage could take an existing network, one forged by cement and stone, and strengthen its bonds, but once a wall was like this and little better than a crumbled ruin, its ethereal threads burned and torn, it was beyond help. Far better to knock it down and rebuild. And yet…Thaniel felt the

126

silvery wisps responding to him in a way he couldn't explain. They seemed to gleam and shiver as his attention passed over them. The realisation fed his elation, and the warm feeling within him became a hot torrent.

He exclaimed happily and held his hands up towards the wall, letting the warm jolty feeling inside his stomach flow through him into the web. The network seemed to glimmer and contract, revitalised by the energy he was feeding it. Threads reached up, across the gap, reached down, reached into the pile of rubble and bricks strewn about the room. Thaniel was dimly aware that his mouth was open in a childish smile of wonder but ignored the thought, gently passing more and more energy into the reforging latticework as it lifted, contracted, pulled the cracking wall back together. Beyond, in the real world, stone and plaster flowed like liquid, reforming and healing like an organic material in seconds. Black soot and ash rearranged itself, regaining the colour and form of the bricks from which it had arisen. Thaniel, however, was only dimly aware of this, his concentration purely on the web. Eventually, the silvery gleam faded and the network vanished from sight as his mind returned to normal.

'Well, would you look at that?' he said with some satisfaction, a pleasant buzz coursing through his body. The wall was perfect. 'What's your name?'

The other boy had been staring at him with amazement. He jumped at the question. 'Eric. Eric Allen. I'm one of the apprentices.'

'Apprentices of what?'

Eric looked down and shuffled his feet. 'Just apprentices.' His hair fell over his face adorably.

Thaniel looked away fast, willing his heart to stop thumping so loudly. His mind had become a mushy blank filled with nothing but this newcomer's face, his well-fitting dark trousers and boots, the light shirt of good material with the top two buttons undone...

Stop it...

Thoughts like that could be dangerous in Asterheim. Although officially everyone was free to be who or what they were, reality wasn't always quite that clear cut. Emotions might be great for healing walls, apparently, but they could get you into a lot of trouble if the wrong person noticed them at the wrong time.

Thaniel cleared his throat, about to make some excuse to walk out and find a dark quiet place to master his raging hormones, when the other boy stepped hesitantly closer.

'Thaniel? Can I ask you something?'

Here it comes, guess I didn't hide it after all...

He could feel the rush of indignant anger before Eric even spoke.

'Yes I prefer boys and no you don't have to worry about it.' He couldn't help himself, the words just tumbled out in a defensive snarl.

Eric stepped back, his hands rising in a gesture of contrition.

'It's ok. I mean, I'm sorry. I didn't mean...'

'Forget it,' Thaniel said hotly, striding across the room as fast as he dared and desperately hoping he wasn't about to cry.

'Wait! I mean, I do too,' called Eric after him. 'We all do. That's why we're here.'

Thaniel stopped, blinking for a moment as his thoughts abruptly shifted gears. He turned slowly.

'You *all* do?'

Eric gave a sad smile.

'So these apprentices…' Thaniel's thoughts flitted to the unpleasant Lord Balderwin. His lip curled with distaste. 'And just how many *apprentices* does Lord Orsell have?'

'Five of us, not including the actual apprentices with proper duties. We're just pages really. Help out at the Citizenry Guild sometimes, fetching files and stamping licences.' He sniffed. 'Worst guild ever,' he added. 'It's all dust and paper and people with no personality.'

Thaniel waited a moment, expecting some horrible confession and a plea for help. When the boy just gave another shrug, Thaniel hesitated.

'Sounds thrilling,' he said finally.

Eric gave a short, uncertain laugh. 'Yeah.'

'So he doesn't…'

Eric raised an eyebrow. 'Did he…with you?'

'No.'

'There you are then.'

'But he just…keeps you around?'

Eric gave another of his sad, heart-melting smiles and went to sit on the windowsill of one of the large floor length windows overlooking the grounds. Outside were carefully cut hedges and well-tended lawns, little pools of water with stones lovingly laid around them. A haven of beauty. Eric looked out, his eyes distant.

'I think our master is…sad. I think he keeps us around because he's alone. It's not a fair world for people like him. Like us.'

'He's not married?'

Eric looked at him flatly. Thaniel looked away.

'Look out there,' Eric said. Thaniel went to sit by him. 'He keeps things nice. Decorates. Buys art and employs…look over there.' He pointed to a corner of the window. Thaniel followed his gaze. A young man with impressive biceps was hacking away at a hedge, making something vaguely the shape of an animal. 'That's why he collects lost souls I think.'

'Because lost souls look nice in gardener's outfits? Or the lack of them?' He eyed the gardener.

'Because they appreciate the beauty in things. Being saved gives you a perspective.'

'Did he save you?'

Eric nodded. Thaniel waited but Eric didn't elaborate. He studied the young man's face, his jawline, the pale gleam of the sunlight on his skin…

'Did you mean what you said?' Eric was looking at him with knowing eyes.

'About?'

'About me "not having to worry".'

'Ah, that.' Thaniel gave him a sheepish smile. 'Nope. Not at all. The opposite, in fact.' He laughed weakly.

Eric grinned.

'So I should worry?'

Thaniel held his gaze, for once enjoying the near-frantic pounding of his heart.

'Oh, definitely,' he said.

***

The formerly great cathedral of The Sacred Circle was named the Heart of Asterheim by its more earnest supporters, but few others. A relic from the darker days of the city's troubled past, it stood now as a gothic spectacle in the centre of the Western side of the city. Once it had greeted travellers from the harbour and Sea Gate with its imposing magnificence.

To most, it now served as a reminder of the fading power of the priesthood; a wounded bear dying in its cave, still snarling as fiercely as it could.

Within the great turrets and battlements of the cathedral, designed long ago to be as much a fortress as a house of worship, hundreds of the devotees of The Sacred Circle scurried back and forth in their threadbare golden robes. An army of them existed solely to ensure the candles remained lit and the windows polished, while still more laboured tirelessly to copy old documents from one pile and add them to another, which in time would need to be copied again. What they said, what secrets they held, was unknown to most and access was not easily granted.

To Lord Amir Barten, the cathedral was both a reminder of how potentially powerful an alliance with The Sacred Circle could be, and how disappointing an ally it had made so far. Not to mention from a democratic point of view, what a waste of public money it had become. He stood in the long public gallery of the central building, watching the flickering shadows cast by the hundreds of candles ensconced in shrines lining the building's high stone walls. The cost of such pointless lighting would be astronomical, all at the expense of the city's people who no doubt had better things to spend money on. The shadows danced across the carpet he knew to be red but which tonight, despite the feeble but expensive light, was simply a dull brown. They glided over heavy wooden pews lovingly maintained but rarely used, slithered around statues of gold and icons studded with dusty gemstones. If ever there was a potent analogy for the state of his allies, it was this pitiful place of lost splendour clinging to the last vestiges of its pride and dignity.

The chamber had been silent since Barten had arrived, granting him a rare moment to stop and reflect without a thousand worries pressing against his troubled mind. The great Ouroboros, a heavy solid silver representation of a serpent eternally devouring its own tail, hung suspended over an altar by no mechanical means. He stared at it, drifting slightly as tiny currents of wind circulating around the room breathed past it. A mage had raised this, of course, in times past. Probably the same one who had lifted the great chains of the chandeliers and possibly even bound the very bricks of the cathedral itself. What had become of the man? He must have lived in a time before the great purge; had he suffered through it? What terrible irony it must have been, to be led bound by ropes to a stake in the courtyard of this very building, to burn staring at his own work, the hypocritical edifice which had condemned him.

Barten shuddered as though a ghost had passed through him; a sudden chill that had nothing to do with the temperature of the inadequately heated cathedral.

'You seem contemplative, my lord.' A rasping voice, one he knew well, imposed itself unbidden upon his thoughts. He turned and nodded a curt greeting to the man he knew as Kassi Kahin, a name he suspected was both fake and loaded with hidden meaning. He wore the golden robe of a priest, but this was no priest. Even if he hadn't known the truth already, Barten was sure the evil scar across his jawline and unpleasant smile would give it away in short order. Tonight, Kahin's robe was spattered with what could only be blood, together with the accumulated dust and grime of weeks' worth of toil; indicating, if the smell were not enough to do so, that he had not taken it off for some time.

Lord Barten stepped back, ostensibly to make a final bow in the direction of the Ouroboros, but in fact to put a little more space between his nose and the stench rising thickly off the man who called himself a priest for reasons known only to him. He looked back.

'I'm here to see His Benevolence,' he said. This was true, as far as it went. He had come to see his ally, but had done so unannounced. The High Priest of the Sacred Circle, Lyoris Mountebank, was a difficult man to see in many senses. He hid his motivations and thoughts behind a mask of jovial good humour, out of which cold eyes stared like ice, refusing any attempt at true camaraderie. Barten had wondered if perhaps taking the man unawares might help him understand the horse he had tied his saddle to, although recently he had become increasingly suspicious that he himself was the horse and Lyoris the rider.

'His Benevolence has retired,' Kahin smirked. 'I was the last to see him.'

'Is that right?' said Barten, staring at the scarred priest and wondering just what the dark gleam in his eyes was all about. 'Well then perhaps you can tell me what he said.'

'He's pleased.'

'Is he? About what?'

'A new way to take care of House Gloriana has presented itself.'

Barten looked up at the chandelier, as nonchalantly as he could. He nodded softly, masking his emotions with some effort.

'I had hoped to convince His Benevolence to allow me a little more time to persuade her. I am sure her recent brush with death must have made her more amenable to my suggestions.'

'Mountebank feels it no longer matters.' Lord Barten forced a smile.

'Enlighten me.'

'She's made a mistake,' the priest grinned. 'I've seen her in the company of a mage—'

Barten rolled his eyes and turned away with what he hoped did not sound like a sigh of relief. The priest raised his voice as he continued.

'One who was involved in a tavern massacre against the faithful!'

Barten paused and turned back.

'Massacre?'

The priest's leering grin told Barten all he needed to know. He felt sick.

'Not only that, but one of those poor souls was murdered in particularly grizzly fashion, my lord. Peeled, almost. Like an orange.'

'What?'

'Oh yes. No denying it was the work of a mage.'

'You would know,' Barten replied, suddenly struck with a hunch.

The priest's smile vanished, his eyes burning with a zealous anger so fierce that for a moment Lord Barten felt a stab of alarm. He only managed not to step back with a force of will.

This one is unhinged, he thought.

'And Gloriana's new mage was there,' the priest added finally. 'You see? She's tied to it. There was a rumour of a similar death not long ago…'

'A rumour only. You can't possibly—'

'His Benevolence has decreed it. She is attainted…'

'*His Benevolence*,' Barten snarled back, making a mockery of the title in his anger, 'can decree all he likes. It takes a vote of the Senate to attaint anyone of her rank for anything. If we do this my way, I can convince Ariene to hand over her guilds and I'll have the votes to put your master where he wants to be. Then he can decree things for real.'

The so-called priest took a sudden step forward, teeth bared in an animal snarl. Barten stepped back, hand falling to the hilt of his sword.

'Easy now, I meant no offence,' he said, not entirely truthfully.

'You're blind, Barten,' the priest said eventually. His eyes lost their manic gleam and he stepped away. 'If she's allying herself with dangerous witches, she needs to die and you said you could take over when she did.'

'It has to be at the right time. Otherwise it would cause chaos. You never should have tried to kill her without my approval before, and you should listen to me now.'

'You said you needed more time. We didn't have time. So it was my turn.'

'You shouldn't have gone to Orswell's brother. I could have told you that; politics is my arena and I'd have told you the man was a fool. Look what happened: he tangled with her and now he's dead and she's more powerful than ever.'

'Witchcraft.'

Barten bit back a stinging retort.

'You don't believe that,' he said instead.

The priest did not reply, pacing now, passing in and out of pools of shadow. His stinking robe gleamed in the glimpses of candlelight. Barten wondered where he'd got it.

Sensing an opening, he took a step towards his supposed ally's head henchman. 'When Mountebank is Echelarch, off the back of my votes in the Senate, you will be High Priest of the Sacred Circle and I will control the Senate.' The priest did not reply. 'We will rule this city and the country together. Kassi, don't put the whole plan in danger. You can't start a war without laying the groundwork, and the fact that Ariene has a new mage who happened to be at a tavern brawl isn't enough to barge into her house and kill her. You need to discredit her. You need to give me time to undermine her. Otherwise I won't be able to take those guilds and we need them for the votes.'

Kahin was quiet for a moment, his hands clenching and unclenching at his sides. 'What do you suggest?'

'Don't do anything without Senate approval.' Barten sighed with relief as the priest seemed to digest this rather than explode into a zealous diatribe. 'Investigate the death of that messenger people have been talking about. Go to the Mortuary Guild and demand to see their records; I can have a demand drawn up that will look official enough to get you in the door. Bring proof to the Senate of the connection between those murders and Ariene's new mage. I'll see to it that she is called to account for herself. It will also stoke the fires of the mage debate that your...corpses...began.'

Kahin shook his head in frustration. 'It's too slow. If she dies, you can make a grab for The Barbican and they'll have to fight back...'

'Fight back?'

'Yes! And then we can have the Senate begin a second purge!'

Barten laughed in spite of himself, ignoring the priest's rapidly colouring face and the evident rage within.

'You're a simpleton if you think that's how it would happen, Kahin. The Guild of Mages aren't stupid enough to do anything of the kind. They'd file suit in the courts. They'd appeal to the Senate. And they'd be right to. I have no rights over them unless it is done legally. And I'm afraid the death of a single woman in a blue dress isn't going to cause chaos enough to change that.'

Kahin stared at him for a furious moment before turning and stalking away back in the direction he'd come from.

'Tell him everything is going to plan,' Barten called after him. 'Tell him that by the time I'm finished with her, Ariene will be begging me to make a deal.'

The scarred priest stopped and inclined his head slightly without looking round.

'Curious,' he said with a soft malice. 'To His Benevolence and myself, the old witch is only ever Lady Gloriana.' He looked around now, his eyes catching the firelight and gleaming in the dark of the cathedral. 'But not to you, Lord Barten. To you, she's always *Ariene*.'

He walked away, leaving Barten alone in the empty hall, staring after him.

***

137

Lord Orswell was in his private study when Thaniel found him. The young mage hesitated by the door; peering in seemed like a violation after his discussion with Eric. The room was surprisingly small; a desk with a lamp, bookshelves full of dusty tomes. It was strangely reminiscent of Master Thomas' private sanctum; a small and simple space for a man with great and complex cares.

Lord Orswell was holding a piece of paper, but did not appear to be reading it. He was staring at it, as if perplexed by it. Or angered by it.

'Come in Thaniel,' his new master said. Thaniel stepped in and gestured at the door. Orlond nodded, so Thaniel closed it and went to sit on the small wooden stool propped up by a bookcase. There seemed to be nowhere else to sit.

'I heard you met Eric.'

Thaniel nodded. Orswell smiled and glanced at him. 'That's good. He's a good boy.'

'Yes sir. He said he was one of the apprentices.'

'And so he is.'

'I was wondering sir,' Thaniel hesitated, pulling back from the blunt question before it got away from him, 'how did Eric come to be in your service? He didn't say.'

'*Wouldn't* say, I suspect,' Lord Orswell said sternly, giving Thaniel a look. 'Well perhaps he doesn't want you to know. Or perhaps not all of us want to remember where we were before we were saved. But you look like the kind of person who won't give up until he knows something, am I right? Something about being a mage, I suspect.'

Thaniel smiled uncertainly. Orswell's analysis had sounded an awful lot like a description of a spy. Did he know? His master didn't seem to notice his sudden flash of fear.

'Eric's story is his to tell, but what I can say is that he came to me through certain…channels I have set up in the city.' Orlond leaned back, letting the letter he'd been holding drop to the desk. 'Channels that direct those who find them to a place where they'll be safe. Suffice to say, those who find them tend to have very sad tales to tell and those stories belong to them alone. We are not our past, Thaniel, but our past is *ours*.'

Thaniel nodded silently, a hundred questions jostling for position in his head.

'Once Eric was here,' said Orswell with a faint, sad smile, 'I did as I always do. I informed his father that either he could face my justice or I could take Eric into my service. His father made the right choice.' He chuckled softly, though his eyes were troubled as they stared into the distance. 'So I brought him here and raised him with the other boys I've taken in over the years. My apprentices, I call them. Some have moved on by now of course; because they've been fostered by a name like Orswell, they eventually get positions in other noble houses or the church, or become true apprentices in a guild. Citizenry is always willing to take them if they want to go, since it's mine. They write to me, sometimes…' he lapsed into a contemplative silence, staring off into memories only he could see, his eyes glinting with unshed tears. 'Sometimes not,' he added softly.

'It would be better not to press Eric on his story,' Orswell said eventually, sitting up again and grabbing the letter off the table. 'Like I said, it belongs to him alone. Now then, this letter.'

'Yes sir.'

'I want you to do something for me, Thaniel. This letter is from a political ally of mine, and it is most peculiar. I want you to tell me what you can about it. Did you learn truth-seeing at Hilda's?'

'I-We were taught that, yes sir.' That much was true. Technically.

'Good. Now, concentrate. I want to know everything you can tell me about it.'

Thaniel had never been good at the more subtle use of energy and willpower. He could raise stones and knock things about with blasts of energy with the best of them, but calming his mind to such a state of serenity that he could follow the paths left by a physical thing as it moved through the world, floating along the ripples caused by its every action, was something beyond his ability. Rigel had never mastered it either, and even Sophine had found it impossible to track something more than a few hours into its past.

He took the letter gingerly, as though it might bite him. His hand trembled slightly.

'Is there anything you can tell me, sir? Something that might help me identify which threads to follow?' he gave Orswell what he hoped was a studiously professional look, hoping he'd sounded convincing enough. His master looked a bit surprised, but nodded affably enough.

'Yes of course, the name's Balderwin.'

Thaniel felt like his heart had stopped. He glanced at the letter. It was one of Sophine's letters to Balderwin's acquaintances explaining his disappearance. He knew had to play this very, very carefully. Too defensive, and Orswell would sense a deception.

Thaniel closed his eyes and calmed his mind, just as he would if he was planning to really attempt truth-seeing.

'The letter was written by a woman. A girl. I can smell her.'

'A woman...' Orswell repeated softly. 'Go on...'

'She was frightened, young...'

'Stop Thaniel,' his master said. Thaniel opened his eyes. Orswell looked pained. 'Don't look at her any further,' he said. 'Terrible things happen in that man's house, to young girls. I know what kind of a man he is, in fact most of us do. The man's untouchable of course on account of the influence he has over...' he trailed off. 'It doesn't matter. Try to look beyond her, Thaniel. Seeing more about her would only upset you.'

Thaniel closed his eyes again.

'The letter...she's writing it because she's being told to. By a man. A fat man...'

'Lord Balderwin?'

'That's his name, yes sir.'

'Interesting. Why isn't he writing his own letters?'

Because he got split into four steaming chunks and now he's buried in his own garden...

'Because he has a condition. Something medical that makes him shake. He picked it up from—'

'No, no. I don't want to know that. Stop Thaniel.'

Thaniel tried not to grin and opened his eyes. Orswell peered again at the letter, holding it up to the dim lamplight.

'He doesn't say why he's going away, only that he doesn't intend to come back for some time. The old letch must be heading to the provinces in search of folk cures for whatever vile disease his life-style has brought him. Well good riddance. I hope it kills him. And

141

this mage of his, might even be a classmate of yours, is to conduct his affairs whilst he's gone.'

Thaniel feigned polite disinterest and stood up to go.

'I'm glad I found you, Thaniel,' Orswell said warmly.

'Thank you, sir, I'm glad too.' He found he really meant it, and guilt began to gnaw at him.

***

The Mortuary Guild's main headquarters was enormous, a sprawling ramshackle estate added to many times by the officers of the guild over the years. The poor construction and cheap labour meant unpleasant draughts in the higher rooms and floors that creaked with every step. The stench was slightly fainter in the records offices on the second floor. Kahin wrinkled his nose and turned over another page, pulling his robe tight around him against the chill.

As their business was eternal, the Death Merchants, as they were commonly known, were an essential guild. But as death rarely paid well, its revenues were meagre. When money was spent on their headquarters, it was often simply for more space: to store corpses, house coffins, and to keep the huge stores of information that went with the business of identification, examination, or inheritance. Within its walls were even rudimentary coroner's court rooms, since Lord Aresbrook's Lawyers' Guild had never dealt with the business of determining causes of death. The whole place had a charnel house smell to it, as the corpses below rotted and mouldered for want of the attention of the overworked pathologists and coroners. In a city as large as this, death was a constant and demanding customer, and the corpse halls were always full.

Up on the second floor, a tired-looking clerk shouldered his way through the door to the study room Kahin was using, carrying another disintegrating box. Flecks of dust and torn parchment drifted into the air as he set it down heavily on the table. Kahin eyed it in the candlelight, mounting frustration lending his voice an even more pronounced rasp.

'That isn't what I asked for.'

The clerk crossed his arms. 'These are the records for the road deaths over the last six months.'

'Then why are they so dusty?'

The clerk frowned and hesitated. He peered into the box again.

'Ah. Yes. They must have misheard me, looks like these are from six *years ago.*'

'They?'

'The sub-clerks for the secondary records rooms.'

Kahin bent his head and forced his clenched fists to relax. He had no wish to consider the tedious administrative networks of clerks and sub-clerks in this detestable place; a bleak labyrinth populated by ghouls who seemed half-dead themselves and morbidly happy about it.

'Take it back,' he said. The clerk nodded without expression and heaved the box into his arms again. As he left the room, Kahin turned back to the description of the messenger death in the large book he'd been given. As it had only been a few days, the right book had only taken an hour or so to locate. With another half hour to find the as-yet preliminary report on the death of Kahin's associate, he'd managed to get what he needed relatively fast, all things considered.

Kahin looked back at the report from the roadside corpse.

Corpse: Male

Age: 30 – 50

Location: Recovered on Fishers Road, half a day's ride from the gate.

Description: Body divided in four, as though sliced in half from crown to groin, and then a second slice dividing the halves perpendicular to the first cut. No tearing of skin or cracked bone, no clotting at edges of wound.

Preliminary Conclusion: Cuts made by an instrument of extreme sharpness passing at extreme speed through the body?

Other: The man was wearing armour. The armour is not sliced. It's not possible.

The similarities to the death in the tavern were clear.

Corpse: Male

Age: 20 – 30

Location: Seven Buckets Tavern, River Street, Guild Quarter

Description: Body bled to death through two wounds. One running crown to groin down the front of the face and one identical to the rear. No tearing of skin.

Preliminary Conclusion: Blades of surpassing sharpness wielded by separate assassins and striking at the same moment.

Other: Conclusion seems unlikely. Victim clothes uncut?

Neither report seemed willing to conclude the obvious: that this was the work of foul sorcery and forbidden magic. Not that he had heard of such power in all his time studying forbidden things, but how else could such a phenomenon have occurred?

144

The clerk came back into the room, the motion of the door threatening to blow the candles out. Shadows flickered over the pages Kahin that stared into. The clerk didn't seem to notice, heavily setting down another box, this time of fresher-looking documents.

'These two reports,' Kahin said, 'I assume the coroners are planning to investigate them.'

The clerk peered over, scanning the various notations and stamps on the pages. He nodded.

'So they've been copied?' The clerk smiled coldly.

'The coroners won't be looking at these for some time, sir. The documents won't be copied until the investigations are scheduled and that won't be for many months yet due to the processes that must first be followed.'

'Months? That's absurd. The corpses will be nothing but mush by then.'

'Which is why we keep such meticulous records.'

Kahin stared at the man's empty eyes. He clearly did not see the irony that the very act of insisting on such bureaucracy was all that made it necessary in the first place.

'In that case, I want copies of these drawn up tonight.'

'I'm afraid that won't be—'

'Tonight.' Kahin held the man's gaze. Something within the clerk's passive stare suddenly flickered. Despite so many years buried here with his books and records, he could apparently still recognise a threat.

'Very well,' he muttered, and shuffled to the desk, skeletal hands reaching for the documents in question. 'These will need stamps from the certifying officer,' he mumbled, scanning the entries, 'and then I'll need to have them sealed as authentic by—'

Kahin leaned towards him, bringing his face close to the pale man's own.

'Words cannot express how little I care for your tiresome paper-shuffling. Just get me those copies by dawn.'

'By dawn? Sir! That's not—'

'It *is* possible. Write the words, find the man who stamps them and stamp them. I am here with the High Priest's authority and I will *not* be fobbed off with your fussing and hand-wringing.'

'Mountebank has no authority here,' the clerk said petulantly. Kahin's knife was out of his belt and buried two inches deep in the table by the man's hand before he realised he'd drawn it. Part of him was vaguely relieved he hadn't rammed it into the fool's head.

'This says he does,' he growled.

The clerk swallowed. 'Yes sir.'

Chapter Eight

Ariene poured tea from a delicate teapot that she'd liberated from Lord Balderwin's house the last time she'd been there. She handed a cup to Thaniel, who took it gratefully. He looked flushed, uncomfortable, shoving his blond hair carelessly past his ears whenever it fell over his face. He was dressed in a good quality white shirt and dark trousers, looking every inch a respectable servant to a great lord, if not the valued mage he really was. She peered at him critically.

'Orswell treating you well?'

'Yes, yes, very well thank you my lady.'

She sipped her tea, watching him. It had been well known to both of them just what her intent had been in placing Thaniel in the service of one of her greatest rivals, yet now he seemed reluctant to speak.

'I hope it wasn't too difficult to come here,' she said finally. 'Did you need an excuse? Anything I need to authenticate somehow?'

Thaniel shook his head and offered a toothy, false smile that made her very concerned indeed.

'No. No, I just said I was going out. He doesn't seem to mind what we do, so long as we come back.' He grinned, more genuinely this time.

'We?'

He looked at her with what she saw clearly as mild alarm, covered again by a smile and a nonchalant laugh.

'The other servants.'

'I see.'

She sipped her tea, her mind running through all kinds of possible explanations and wondering just what to do about them. A thought struck her.

'Any in particular?' she asked. She was rewarded with an instant reaction; Thaniel dipped his head to hide a sudden flash of a smile, covered his face with a hand which then swept his hair back again. She said nothing, allowing the dance of teenage awkwardness to play out as it must whilst enjoying a rush of relief. Young love she could cope with, betrayal less so.

'You don't have to tell me,' she added disingenuously.

'Eric,' Thaniel said quickly. 'His name is Eric. He's an apprentice.'

'An apprentice what?'

'Just an apprentice. A ward really. Lord Orswell has lots of wards.'

'Does he now?'

Thaniel shook his head. 'It's not like that.'

'No?'

'No. Not really. He collects what Eric calls lost souls. Puts them to work at the Citizenry Guild sometimes.'

Ariene peered at Thaniel. There seemed to be no lie in his voice, and his face showed nothing but a kind of sad distance. Interesting.

'Why do you think he does that, Thaniel?'

'Makes them work at Citizenry?'

'No. Collects lost souls.' Thaniel shook his head.

'I think...I think maybe because he was one too. Maybe still is.'

'And you feel a connection to him, don't you? A guilty pity for the man who saves lost boys and who you're being asked to spy on.'

Thaniel looked at her sadly. He nodded and took a sip of his tea.

'I can understand that. But remember who this man really is, Thaniel. This is the man who tried to kill me and who holds enormous power in the Senate. He's not some benevolent orphan-saver. I take it none of these apprentices and lost souls are female?'

Thaniel looked away, his jaw tight. He gave a curt shake of the head.

'And none over, let's say, twenty or so?'

He did not respond. She sat back, sipping her tea.

'Don't make angels out of wounded beasts,' she said. 'Not until they're dead anyway.'

The silence stretched before being rudely sundered by the sudden appearance of a servant, barging through the doorway and screeching an incoherent introduction seconds before Viscount Roach pushed his way past with a face that made her blood run cold.

'My Lady Ariene!' he called, unnecessarily. He fell to one knee, just as unnecessarily.

He was breathing heavily and his clothes were dusty and mud-splattered from the road.

Ariene stood up from her chair, the tea forgotten. 'What's happened?'

'It's the Senate, my lady,' Roach gasped, getting himself under control. She gestured impatiently for him to rise. 'The Sacred Circle has introduced a motion for your censure.'

She let out a short, startled laugh. 'Censure?'

'They say they have proof of witchcraft, my lady. They're planning to call witnesses.'

Ariene glanced in Thaniel's direction. He was standing awkwardly by the chair, his eyes wide and fearful.

'How far have they got?' she asked, running the calculations in her head. Half an hour to reach the Senate building, fifteen minutes to dress first. But only a matter of minutes to damn her in a vote and authorise the Bailiffs' Guild or even the Battlemasons to come for her.

'Lady, I was able to stall them,' said Roach, putting a hand to his chest. 'I told them such matters of import needed a full session of the Senate and summons needed to be sent to the absent members before it could begin.'

Lady Gloriana laughed appreciatively. 'I imagine the priests didn't think much of that,' she said.

'There are still a few Senators who dislike the priests enough to insist on protocol,' Roach smiled. 'They supported the motion and they've suspended the debate for now. But it won't take long to find the other members.'

She was already moving, calling for Darcy and giving orders for her carriage to be made ready. She picked up a quill and parchment from the side desk and began to scribble a note.

'Go back to the Senate, my lord,' she said over her shoulder to Roach. 'Tell them I am coming. Though I do note that I have not myself received a summons.'

'No lady, I suspected you wouldn't.'

She held his gaze for a moment. 'Thank you, my lord. I will not forget this.'

He bowed and swept, somewhat theatrically, from the room. She smiled faintly. He still smelled a bit like fish.

'Thaniel,' she said, beckoning him over, 'I need you to do something for me.'

Thaniel's face was white. 'Yes, yes of course.'

She held up the note. 'Have Darcy seal this, and then get it to the Travellers' Guild as fast as you can. Take Rigel, he's downstairs somewhere. Ask for Overseer Skylock.'

'Skylock. Right.'

'You're to give it to no one else, you understand? Use your abilities if you must.'

'I'm not very good at—'

'You're a lord's mage, Thaniel. Act like one. You get this to Overseer Skylock, no excuses.'

'Yes, my lady.'

'Good. Go.'

Ariene watched him stumble his way out of the door, feeling a cold detachment settling over her. Finally, her opponents had made their first serious power play in this long and deadly Senate dance.

Well, aside from murdering me, she thought.

She smiled grimly.

***

An hour or so later, Ariene sat as proudly as she could on the basic wooden chair she had been given, perched by the dais at the centre of the Senate Building. She sat in the speaking area, ringed by the white Senatorial seats which were presently occupied by a heaving crowd of supporters, enemies and as-yet undeclared opportunists. The throne sat to her left, up on its dais, and before her sat another chair in which her latest accuser mumbled and sniffed his way through his supposed testimony.

The elderly Lord Aresbrook had demanded to have his wheeled chair moved forward to sit by hers, where he was acting as her representative. It was fitting, given that he was patron of the Lawyers' Guild and, though it was not his only guild, it was one to which he had made a long and deep commitment over many decades.

The girl presenting evidence against her was named Elmira Valette, an earnest young woman with a head of long blonde hair pulled back into a savage ponytail who seemed convinced that she was presenting a genuinely damning case. Ariene had to admire her for that; she had to be the only person in the room who was.

Valette was in the process of pacing back and forth between Ariene's side and that of the man being questioned, who sat sniffing pathetically in a chair opposite hers. Valette's hands were clasped together as she paced, and her bespectacled face was a study in composed deliberation.

'And what connection did you find between the bodies, Mr Rodomontade?'

'All the victims owed sums of money to mages, ma'am.'

'You are sure?'

'I had entries in my logs for transactions paid by credit, standard repayment terms applied and the guild took interest at a standard rate...'

'Please just answer the question.'

'Yes ma'am. They all owed money to mages.'

Lord Aresbrook wheeled forward a little way.

'If I may,' he wheezed, 'owing money under a credit arrangement is not quite the same as owing it to the service provider. Would it not be more accurate to say the victims owed money to the Factors' Guild?'

Valette glared at him.

'Partly, yes,' said the accountant, sniffing again, 'but the credit only covered part of the debt. The victims both owed substantially more, and the rest would have been owed to the original service provider instead of us.'

Aresbrook wheeled himself back as Valette gave him a cold smile. 'Lady Gloriana is the patron of your guild is she not?' she asked.

'I protest at the question,' Aresbrook said blandly, to some amused titters. 'Mistress Valette is leading the witness.'

Valette did not deign to look at him. 'Who is the patron of your guild?' she asked through gritted teeth.

'Lady Gloriana,' the man replied. Valette glanced at Aresbrook, as though expecting him to say something. He merely smiled at her. She turned away.

'We've heard from previous witnesses that the bodies of the victims were burned by a flame that consumed only human flesh,' Valette declared. 'A cause of death that the coroners recorded as unknown, and which can only be explained by sorcery…'

'I think I should probably protest,' Aresbrook wheezed. 'Is this a question or is Miss Valette a witness now?'

'I was recounting the words of previous witnesses,' she snarled.

'You said it can only be explained by sorcery,' Aresbrook pointed out with a smile, 'I disagree.'

'You are not a witness.'

'Neither are you, Mistress Valette.'

She turned away again, cracking her knuckles as she went. 'Mr Rodomontade,' she said, 'is Lady Gloriana patron of any other guilds?'

'Yes ma'am.'

'Is she patron of The Mages' Guild?'

'Yes ma'am.'

'Is it possible then that Lady Gloriana knew both the victims and the mages they owed money to, and was therefore able to in some way assist the murder of the...?'

'Enough!' a familiar voice shouted from the white tiers. Lord Barten rose to his feet as all eyes turned to look at him. 'Many of us here have patronage of any number of guilds. That does not mean any of us are liable for the details of their day-to-day business. This line of questioning is unreasonable. I motion that the witness be dismissed; he has nothing to offer against Lady Gloriana but rumour and circumstance.'

There were murmurs of outrage, agreement and surprise. Ariene looked up at her long-time political opponent and found him looking back at her with an unreadable expression she nevertheless read very well.

I control this circus, that look said. I can push it either way.

'I concur,' wheezed Lord Aresbrook.

'You would,' hissed Valette, waving a hand at her witness. 'Get out,' she muttered at him.

'Perhaps we should adjourn,' said Barten, still on his feet.

'I have more witnesses, my lord,' Valette called up to him, her eyes wide with appeal. 'I have witnesses to two bizarre murders who can place the Lady's own mage at the—'

'Perhaps,' repeated Barten, more loudly this time, 'we should adjourn.'

'I concur,' smiled Aresbrook mildly.

'Motion has been placed,' someone said in the white tiers. 'I second, before I kill myself through sheer boredom. All in favour?'

There was a general clamour of ascent. Valette threw a venomous glare at Aresbrook and stalked away, up the tiers towards the door. Ariene rose to her feet.

'Thank you, my old friend,' she said to Aresbrook. 'I think I had better not leave though.'

The old man shook his head sadly. 'I'm sorry my dear. I think you had. I advise you to pack a bag and leave. The city that is.'

'What?'

'They have witnesses which will be hard to discredit. I know, I have my spies in the other camp.'

'That doesn't sound very lawyerly,' she admonished distractedly.

'Only because you do not work in the law, my dear. One must be prepared. I had hoped to keep her talking to the accountant for as long as possible and then demand an adjournment on account of my health.' He gave a weak smile. 'But to have it come from there,' he flicked his eyes up towards Lord Barten, 'that I didn't expect.'

'I can't leave,' she said softly. 'I won't.'

'Then go and make arrangements,' the old man said. 'Don't be here when this concludes.'

155

'If I'm not here it will conclude the wrong way.'

'The conclusion is already written, my dear. Being here won't make any difference except to shorten the distance between you and your enemies.'

'But Amir's intervention...'

'I don't know what to make of that either. But it does prove that the outcome of this sham will be whatever he wants it to be.'

'So much for my allies,' Ariene said bitterly, looking around.

'He's the Castellan of the Battlemasons, Ariene,' he said. 'He controls Asterheim's military. And he's Steward of the Labourers' Union and Patron of the Messengers. Those two are woven throughout every other guild and—'

'I know I know,' she bared her teeth in Barten's direction. 'He might be able to intimidate the others, but he still doesn't have the votes to force anything...'

'Not to be an insufferable poltroon, but he won't need them. Valette's witness can put your young mage at the scene of a murder that genuinely defies explanation, Ariene. And another just like it. And he was the one who...saved you...wasn't he?'

Ariene looked at her old friend.

'I thought so. You see how it looks.'

She nodded.

'Go, my lady.'

Ariene laid a hand on the old man's shoulder and then headed out, feeling eyes on her the whole way.

***

Rigel and Thaniel were led into the audience chamber of the Travellers' Guild by an unsmiling, black-robed man, who closed the door firmly behind them. They stood alone, gazing around the windowless wooden room. The smell of charred wood and smoke permeated everything.

A fire burned in the hearth to their right, beneath a mantlepiece over which hung an enormous piece of parchment detailing a map of the city, with all the roads and gates highlighted prominently along with curious markings like crossed swords at various intersections. Rigel closed his eyes, letting his mind rise into the state of tranquillity Master Thomas had tried to help him develop over so many years. He began to see the lines of energy glistening behind the veil of corporeal reality, and looked up at the parchment. He smiled to see familiar twists and shapes of will binding the fragments of the paper together, holding it firm against the heat of the fire.

'Someone fireproofed this,' he said to Thaniel, admiring the work. 'Nice job too.'

Thaniel came to stand by his side and made a similar inspection. 'Very nice,' he agreed. 'See, this is the sort of thing we should be doing for our lords, not messing around with politics.'

'I'm not sure we're here for politics,' Rigel said uncertainly.

'We are. Ariene's in trouble, and for her, trouble is usually political.'

'Fair point.'

Rigel turned to survey the rest of the room and gasped in awed amazement at the enormous weapon hanging on the wall behind the large desk of the Overseer. It was a huge pole, essentially, with a massive blunt hammer head at the end, a large and very pointed counterweight sticking out the other side. A war hammer. The steel head was carved and shaped to look like a snarling lion, its mane wrapping majestically around the haft of the weapon. The haft itself was decorated in gold writing he couldn't quite make out, tightly wound and written in a delicate looping hand.

'Wow,' Thaniel breathed. 'What is that doing here?'

Rigel glanced at him.

'Travellers have their military wing, remember. That's what the crossed swords are on the map, I think. Their armed response outposts for handling civil unrest on public highways.'

Thaniel looked back at the parchment. 'There's hundreds of them!'

'Ariene says the Travellers are the most important guild for that reason,' Rigel mused, admiring the snarling lion's head as it glinted in the firelight. 'It's probably why we're here.'

The door opened behind them and someone very large stomped their way into the room. Rigel and Thaniel turned to greet their host and words of greeting died away at the sight of the person who trudged heavily to the desk. The newcomer sat down behind the table with a curious grace and economy of movement for one so large.

Overseer Skylock, for it could be none other, was a huge man – bull shouldered and powerful, with a shaved head and a barrel-chested frame like an oxen. His face was worn and weathered, with a faint scar on his bald head. He was draped in the skin of a large animal, possibly a lion, though it was so old and faded it was hard to tell what it was. The pelt rested upon a shirt of chainmail over a leather jerkin, all of which added to his bulk even further. He was quite the largest man either of them had ever seen.

'They tell me you have papers from our patron,' he said. Rigel blinked. The Overseer had a curiously smooth and moderately pitched voice; he'd expected a gruff growl at most. At the Overseer's gesture, they took seats on the other side of the desk. Rigel began to rummage in the bag they'd brought for the papers. By his side, Thaniel was staring.

'See something you like?' Skylock challenged, his chin jutting up. Thaniel shook his head.

'Sorry. I'm spoken for, ma'am. And don't tell anyone,' his voice dropped to a comical whisper, 'but I prefer *men*.' There was a pause. Rigel stopped rummaging, feeling a horrible tension descend.

Thaniel smiled brightly as the moment stretched. Rigel looked at the Overseer with wide terrified eyes.

'Shame,' Skylock said eventually, returning the smile. 'You have sharp eyes, boy.' Rigel sagged with relief and tried not to stare; woman or no he was quite sure the Overseer could have snapped both of them in half without breaking a sweat. Thaniel shrugged.

'Sharp nose, ma'am. Men usually smell worse.'

Skylock snorted. 'That why you like them?'

'The kind I like don't smell.'

'The kind you like don't wear chainmail either, I'm guessing.'

'You guess right, Overseer.'

'Then you're welcome to them, pretty boy.'

The Overseer turned her eyes to Rigel, who was still staring, and casually raised her eyebrows.

'Sorry, sorry,' he said, jolted back into motion by the massive woman's powerful gaze. He found the sealed letter from Lady Gloriana and put it down on the desk. The Overseer's absurdly huge hand managed to pick it up delicately and open it in one smooth movement. She read it within seconds.

'Right,' she said, smacking the letter down on the desk with a dull thud. She rose to her feet and plucked the enormous hammer from the wall as though it weighed nothing and rested it across her shoulder. Thaniel's jaw dropped open.

'Go back to your mistress, boys,' the Overseer said. 'We'll be along shortly.'

***

'Ariene,' a familiar voice said behind her. Lady Gloriana paused in the act of getting into her carriage. Waving Darcy away, she turned around. Amir had the grace at least to look contrite as he nodded a polite bow.

'Lord Barten,' she sneered. 'Are you here to tell me what the purpose of this pantomime is, or do I get three guesses?'

'I'm here to talk, not fight, Ariene. There are things you–' he looked away, as though considering his words. 'There are things you don't know about. Things you are going to be caught up in if you don't let me help you.'

She laughed.

'Help me? Why would you of all people—?'

'Because you are in my way and I am trying to help you get out of it. You need to hand over control of your guilds.'

Ariene sighed and rolled her eyes. 'This again. And why would I do that?'

He didn't answer, merely looked at her. His eyes were surprisingly pleasing when he wasn't sneering.

160

'I see,' she said. 'Because if I don't, I might find myself wishing I had, is that it?'

'Perhaps, but...'

She gave a dismissive wave and turned to her carriage. He caught her arm.

'Do you think I'm some caricature of a villain from a half-penny play,' he hissed, 'wanting power for power's sake? You know me better than that.' She studied him a moment, before looking pointedly at his hand on her arm. He released her.

'What are you then, Amir?'

He hesitated, looking like he was on the verge of telling her something.

'I'm...someone who doesn't want to see Asterheim burn, Ariene.'

She scowled and clambered into the carriage, irritably grabbing fistfuls of her gown away from her feet as she went. She arranged her skirts before looking back at her oldest and bitterest rival.

'I don't know what you're referring to, Amir. But I do know this. If the city's at risk of burning, I certainly wouldn't trust *you* with any more candles.' She reached out and pulled the carriage door shut.

He threw his hands in the air and stomped away. Darcy climbed in the opposite side and gave a reassuring smile.

'You showed him, my lady.'

She tried to smile back, but as she watched Barten stalk away angrily, a cold feeling slithered around her heart.

She shivered.

***

The filthy priest Kahin was waiting for him as he came back into the Senate Building.

The golden robe was more a dirty yellow by now, the stink almost unbearable.

'Adjournment?' demanded Kahin, his scarred face contorted in rage. He was visibly shaking, his hands held stiffly by his sides as though through conscious effort not to reach for his blade.

Barten looked at him with cool disdain. 'I'm the politician, Kahin, not you. Not Mountebank. This is my arena, so I would appreciate it if you—'

'You were told!' Kahin spat. 'You were told to tie her to the mages, to the murders! And you tried to let her just walk away!'

Barten was just about to push past the reprobate when he paused. 'Tried to?' Kahin straightened up, a nasty smile spreading across his unshaven face.

'She won't survive this,' he promised. 'She will be attainted for witchcraft, and the outrage will consume the city.'

'You fool,' Barten growled, stepping closer and instantly regretting it. 'That's not how the real world works. Look around you,' he gestured to the surrounding city; the quiet, the calm. People going about their lives. 'You think these people will suddenly become mindless zealots the moment you execute one of their most beloved nobles?'

Kahin's fiery gaze dimmed a little. 'Of course, it depends on your part…' he conceded.

'Exactly. My part. The political part. Whether *His Benevolence* hopes to capitalise on a high-profile execution or to sweep to power on the back of an outpouring of religious fury, the political work has to be done first.'

Kahin stared at him for long moments. Barten did not drop his gaze. 'I don't trust you,' the foul-smelling priest said softly.

'You don't need to,' Amir replied. 'You just need to stay out of my way. Now if you'll excuse me, I have to rescue this situation from whatever stirring you've been doing behind my back.'

He stalked away, striding into the Senate Building without looking back.

Kahin stared at his departing ally through narrow eyes, fingers lingering over the hilt of his knife.

Chapter Nine

'Motion carries,' the Speaker was saying from the dais as Amir Barten walked back into the Senate Building. There was an uneasy murmur from the assembly.

'What motion?' Barten called, turning heads as he strode down to the floor.

'Out of order!' someone yelled from a red tier. Amir turned his head and located the man: one of a number of gold-robed priests sitting in a large mob around the side of the room.

'I have a right to know what motion this body has managed to pass in the three minutes I was outside, during an adjournment,' he declared angrily, staring the man down. 'I am a member of this Senate and patron of seven guilds. A vote without *me* is out of order, I suggest.'

'A vote without Lady Gloriana is out of order in that case,' someone else in the opposite red tier shouted. One of the lower ranking guild officers, Amir suspected. He ignored the man and the cries of 'hear hear' from tiers red and white, loudest of all from the young Viscount Roach, the Pungent Lord of Fish.

'The motion was posed, seconded and passed, my lord,' said the Speaker apologetically, wringing his hands. 'It was only an order that we proceed *in absentia*.' The man who had spoken up for Lady Gloriana started shouting again.

'The motion has been passed!' the Speaker near-shrieked, hopping from foot to foot and plainly wanting to be just about anywhere else. Roach got to his feet, shaking his fists in what looked like apoplectic rage.

Barten hesitated as the noise grew and shouts became threats, and eyes looked to him for input and leadership. He noticed Kahin taking a seat in the upper red tiers, and averted his eyes before he grimaced at the sight.

'Very well!' Amir shouted, and waited whilst the noise died away and heads turned to him. 'Very well, we shall proceed *in absentia*.' Muttering and rumbling started up again and he held his hands out for silence. 'However! The Lady Gloriana not being here to defend herself will be taken into account at the conclusion of the proceedings.' He glanced up at Kahin, who was staring at him in sullen fury. He smiled and gestured grandly to the Speaker.

'Proceed.'

The next hour was a sham, even by Lord Barten's standards. The wasp-like Elmira Valette was back, grandiosely guiding her witnesses through their evidence with no Lord Aresbrook there to stop her grandstanding. The old man had not returned following the adjournment, which spoke as much for the legality of the proceedings as anything he might have said in person.

'You have heard the evidence!' Elmira cried. Barten cringed a little. She was a good officer, a rising star of the Labourers' Union and fiercely loyal to him as her Patron, but she had no head for politics. He didn't mind, the thicker she laid it on the easier it would be to rescue this mess and stop it becoming a catastrophe.

'Not only was Lady Gloriana's mage at the scene of a tavern brawl that claimed the innocent lives of many devout servants of The Sacred Circle, but also at the scene of the terrible attack on the Monastery of the Mournful Shrine!'

'Maybe he prefers triangles,' someone drawled. There were laughs from the white tiers. Valette ignored them.

'This foul witch has tainted the Lady Gloriana and restored her to unnatural life even after the very brink of death!'

There were some uncomfortable glances amongst the Senators, many of whom had been using mages to stay healthy for many years.

Valette looked around, apparently exasperated.

'Very well,' she said, nodding, 'perhaps it's hard to confront the fact that we have all become too reliant on mages. On their own word of honour that they do not breach the great Charter. Which of us would not turn a blind eye if we could continue to reap the benefits? Crops that give a good harvest. Buildings that don't burn. Cures for illnesses that should lay us low.'

The room had fallen silent. Barten felt a prickle of unease.

'And all the while these breaches are mounting,' Valette said, pacing slowly, as though musing to herself. 'I don't think any one of us could doubt that the deaths these witnesses spoke of could have been caused by anything but sorcery. Men split apart within their clothes? Floods of blood but no rips or tears? This is not natural. And mages able to do this not just here, but beyond the walls on the road, to an innocent messenger. Much like the mysterious deaths we discussed earlier, murders from afar.'

There was no response.

166

'The Guild of Mages is allowing these unseen mages to breach the Charter unimpeded,' she said.

'The Guild of Mages is not on trial here,' Viscount Roach declared. Valette smiled coldly.

'No, it is not. Then are we powerless? Can we not defend ourselves as mages hand themselves the power of life and death over us all?'

There were mutters and whispers of concern. Barten began to rise to his feet but Valette spoke again.

'Or shall we draw a line in the sand and say no more?' she shouted. There were roars of approval. 'Shall we say to the one amongst us who has wilfully allowed this under her watch to go free?' The roars were denials.

'Or shall we say no? Lady Gloriana! You are attainted!'

The roaring was deafening, but Amir couldn't tell if it was for or against. 'Enough!' he bellowed, cutting across the excited frenzy of the Senators and the shouts from the red tiers. 'Enough!'

Gradually the noise died down and he was able to make himself heard.

'I remind you all that Lady Gloriana is not here to defend herself, and that we have not heard from her or her supposed mage about the events of that single—' he looked pointedly at Valette, who stood looking at him in some confusion, 'incident at the tavern he supposedly attended along with, I might add, half of the students at Hilda's and twenty or so other people. Nothing links him or her to the incident on the road, except for a similarity in the cause of death. If we keep our heads, this is not so very much. We must not allow fear to overcome just cause, however expertly the web is spun.'

The room was quiet now, Senators were looking at one another with confused expressions and shakes of the head. Barten flicked his eyes to Kahin again. The priest had gone white and even at this distance Barten could see he was visibly shaking, practically frothing at the mouth. He felt another flicker of concern.

'There may be questions for the Lady Gloriana to face,' Amir said, playing the statesman and conciliator, 'but let us put aside the issues of her involvement in these mysterious deaths or in witchcraft. Merely having a mage does not make us culpable for their actions in taverns, I think we can all agree. The Lady must submit to questioning, with all honour afforded her, so that we can explore the matters brought before us today and any link they may have to her.'

'And her mage?' someone asked.

'What about all the other mages?' someone else shouted.

Barten felt a flush of panic; the door was open now. He avoided Kahin's eyes as he tried to push through.

'She can speak for him. We have heard no direct testimony against him, I would remind you. If she cannot account for her mage, then we will ask her to yield him for questioning.' He looked quickly up at the scarred priest; Kahin was watching him with the black, empty gaze of a shark watching a fish.

'His Benevolence Lyoris Mountebank is a Senator of this august body,' Amir said loudly in a moment of sudden inspiration, 'yet was not able to present himself here today or to take part in these proceedings.' The fact that the High Priest of the Sacred Circle never did take his seat and was also never seen in public was largely irrelevant; this would be his olive branch to the quite clearly unhinged Kahin and a way to keep him in sight. 'As an impartial party, I feel it appropriate that we empower the priests of The Sacred Circle to take the Senate's decision to Lady Gloriana and escort her back here for questioning. Let our colleagues on the red tiers assemble a small delegation to present our decision with all the dignity due to her station.'

'Seconded,' shouted one of the red-tier priests. Some of the Senators laughed. The priest looked murderously at them.

'With respect, sirs,' Barten said, 'you cannot second a motion unless you are a Senator.'

'I will second the motion,' said Lord Orswell, though his tone made it clear he wasn't happy with how the proceedings had played out.

The Speaker got to his feet and made his way from the witness chair he'd been using to the dais.

'Motion has been seconded,' he called. 'All in favour?'

'A moment, Speaker,' Barten said, his instincts for timing honed over many years of experience. The Speaker hesitated, looking panicked.

'I will be the one to question the Lady. In private.'

The Speaker nodded effusively and called the question before anyone could comment. The rumble of assent was slow at first, but at the Speaker's urging grew to sufficient cries of 'aye' to pass the motion. Barten allowed himself a thin smile.

Some Senators were still frowning and rubbing their heads at the last-minute addition as Barten turned and strode to the door, gesturing at an aide as soon as he was out of Kahin's line of sight.

'Get word to Portgate,' he said.

***

The blue dress was the first thing into the box. Trip hazard though it was, having spent so long cultivating the image she felt it appropriate that she should have it for when she made her glorious comeback. Ariene grabbed half a dozen other dresses and threw them in after it; the box was now looking quite full.

'Are you ready, my lady?' asked Darcy, hovering in the doorway. 'I've arranged the carriage.'

'You know, dear,' she replied, pulling a pair of gem-studded shoes she had not seen in many years from the back of the closet, 'when I was dying I hoped you would sell this place and live like a noblewoman in Ceresheim. When I leave, I want you to do that for me. You still have the documents I gave you?'

'Yes my lady,' Darcy sniffed.

'Chin up dear, I'm not dead yet. But tomorrow…tomorrow, I won't be in the city and I won't be coming back.'

'You said something similar last time my lady,' Darcy smiled, wiping away a tear.

Ariene smiled back. 'So I did.'

'If you don't mind, my lady, I'm going to keep believing you'll be here a long time. Right up until the moment you aren't.'

Ariene tried to respond but couldn't. She cleared her throat and tried again. 'Oh Darcy, what did I ever do to deserve you, dear?'

Whatever Darcy was about to say was lost in the crash as the door swung hard on its hinges and slammed into the wall. Rigel and Thaniel burst in, each of them flushed with exertion, their hair drenched in sweat and their clothes filthy with mud from the road.

'Lady Gloriana,' Thaniel wheezed, doubled over and gasping. 'The Travellers…Travellers…are on their way.'

170

She frowned. This was hardly news worth half-killing oneself to deliver. Rigel was also gasping, waving his hand as he tried to form a sentence.

'Outside,' he managed to say, pointing at the window, 'outside!'

Darcy went to the window and shrieked, turning to grab the half-full box and fumbling with it whilst herding Ariene towards the door.

'My lady! My lady, we have to get you out!'

'What, what's happening, what?'

'A mob, Ariene,' said Rigel, getting himself under control. 'There's a mob on its way here. The lunatic priest from the tavern is leading them. They've got torches.'

'Sacred Circle...' Ariene breathed. 'They can't be coming to...to execute me can they? I mean, I haven't had a trial! This is nonsense! It's crazy!'

'That *priest* is crazy my lady,' Thaniel said. 'If he's leading them here he's not coming to chat.'

Ariene nodded, glancing around. She gestured at Darcy to drop the box, which she did with a yelp. Clothes and bits of jewellery spilled everywhere.

'How many are there?' Ariene asked, as she pulled on the gem-encrusted shoes that had rolled within grabbing distance.

'Those aren't really very practical...' Rigel trailed off at her glare. Darcy went back to the window, her plump frame quivering with fear.

'It has to be hundreds, my lady, they're clustering at the gate but they're everywhere.'

Ariene went to see for herself and took a short, sharp breath at the sight. From the window she could see the gardens of her estate, little trees and shrubs nestled between rocky roads and pretty streams looking so calm in the fading light of the evening sunset. It wasn't a huge house so its grounds were modest, all ringed by a high fence. The braying mob surrounded the fence as far round as she could see, shouting and pushing and waving torches. They looked to be mostly normal folk, factory workers or labourers, shop keepers or miners from their clothes. All screaming with such mindless rage that she was terrified just to make eye contact. And down below, at the centre of it all, stood a man in a moth-eaten golden robe, gazing up at her.

She backed away from the window.

'They can't have us surrounded,' said Rigel, 'there can't possibly be enough of them.'

'We can make a run for the back gate, my lady,' said Darcy urgently, pulling on Ariene's sleeves.

'They'll catch us,' she said with a peculiar dispassion. She could see in her mind the way they heaved on the gate, how the posts would snap and fall, bodies tumbling through, screaming for her blood...

'Thaniel and I will go down there,' Rigel said, peering out at the crowd. 'We'll hold them back. You go out the back gate and run for it, or hide in the grounds until the Travellers arrive.'

Ariene nodded and allowed herself to be led by the arm towards the door. Rigel and Thaniel ran through first.

Thaniel turned and looked back for a moment. 'How did you know, my lady?'

'Know what?'

'That we needed the Travellers?' She gave a wan smile.

'I've always felt safer with Skylock nearby,' she said. Thaniel had nothing to say to that, and turned to run after Rigel.

***

The scarred priest smiled unpleasantly as the two mages approached the gate. He dipped his head in mock greeting.

'What are you doing here?' Rigel called, over the shouts of the crowd. The priest's smile became a leer.

'I wanted to make sure,' he said simply.

'Make sure of what?'

'That you were here, of course. And now that you are, well, we can begin.'

Thaniel and Rigel exchanged glances. The priest pulled his hood over his head and stepped back, vanishing into the crowd.

'I think we should—' Whatever Rigel had been about to say was lost in the sudden shriek of the crowd as the shouting took on a new fervour. Individuals were throwing themselves bodily at the gates, clawing at them in frenzied rage. The thin metal bars began to make a groaning sound of protest.

'Get back!' shouted Thaniel.

'That's what I was trying to say!' Rigel shouted. They scrambled back from the fence as it gave another ominous groan.

'Hold it up!' yelled Rigel, as the frantic zealots slammed their bodies against the shuddering bars. Sections of the fence were bending now, the frenzied mob screaming all the louder.

'How?!'

'I don't know! Just try!'

They both tried to compose themselves, controlling their breathing, trying to reach that state of calm they knew was the key to a mage's abilities, but their hearts pounded and their eyes refused to close. Thaniel shook his head.

'It's no use, run!' he cried, grabbing Rigel and dragging him away. Rigel tried to shake him off.

'We have to get back to the back of the house,' Thaniel shouted. 'We can't do anything here!'

Rigel let out a bark of frustration and turned to run just as the metal gave a final shriek and crashed to the ground under the weight of the bodies pressed against it.

They ran, pelting blindly across the gardens, leaping trimmed hedges and winding streams as they went.

Behind them, the roar of voices was joined by the sound of running feet.

***

Ariene tripped as they stumbled away from the servant's entrance of the sprawling house, unfamiliar shoes and unseemly haste combining to make the stony path treacherous underfoot. Darcy caught her.

'We're nearly there my lady, just a few more…'

Darcy trailed off as they beheld the sight before them. The other servants, who had fled like rats on a ship, were milling around in frightened confusion before the locked back gate. Beyond them, pressing heavily against the bars, was a line of braying men and women. Hundreds of them, it seemed, waving torches in the dark and shrieking a terrible bloodthirsty cry. Screams were also emanating from the other side of the house; Ariene turned her head and saw two figures racing through the garden, silhouetted by the blazing torches carried by the mob shrieking after them.

'Rigel!' she shouted, waving, trying desperately to think of a plan.

'Get back inside!' Rigel called, gesturing frantically at the door. Ariene grabbed Darcy and shoved her towards the house.

'Back, back!' She shouted. 'We can't get out, we need to get inside. You!' she screamed at the panicking servants. 'Everyone inside now!'

The servants broke and ran, some bizarrely still clutching mops and buckets. The horse boy from the stable was holding onto a set of reins, his knuckles white from the grip. He looked at her in dazed confusion.

'My lady?' he said, as though waking from a dream.

'Get inside you—'

She stopped as the droning sound of the angry mob changed pitch and became something else. Cries of fear and screams of outrage pierced the wailing, mingled with the battle cry of men in formation and the clash of steel. She shoved the boy towards the house and stared at the gate, the corners of her mouth daring to twitch in the beginnings of a desperate smile.

A bearded man was banging an industrial implement of some kind against the gate and snarling his angry cries when he was abruptly and brutally thrown aside by a swing of an enormous hammer that also knocked aside three others. They lay still and did not rise again. A second swing smashed the gate off its hinges and sent it flying in a mangled heap to crash heavily onto the stony path.

Armoured men began to flood through the gate, charging with spears and swords levelled at the oncoming torch-wielding mob. Their war shout was like music to Ariene's ears and she laughed aloud as the massive form of Overseer Skylock shouldered its way through the ruined gate and stood barking orders with her gargantuan weapon held casually across one bull-like shoulder. She looked at Ariene, the fading sunlight dancing on her shaved head, and gave a small smile.

'My lady,' she said, walking over with a fluid grace that belied her frame. She swung the hammer to the other shoulder and dipped her head. 'I'm sorry we didn't get here sooner.' She inclined her head at Rigel and Thaniel, who stood staring in amazement by Lady Gloriana's side. 'Boys,' she said.

The warriors of the Travellers' Guild's Ordo Militant had formed a blockade and were forcing the mob of howling citizens back when, as one, the mob stopped roaring. An eerie silence fell. A few gold-robed individuals turned and ran, vaulting the fence or leaping the downed sections, racing into the city. Some slunk away into the shadows and slipped out of the gate. Most of the citizens stood in a daze, staring at their surroundings before turning to flee as they realised armed soldiers were standing with weapons levelled at them. The crowd evaporated within moments, before Ariene could think to yell orders to have some captured. She glanced at the prone bodies lying by the gates in the gathering shadows. One was stirring. Further up the road, she could hear the approach of horses and the heavy tread of men in armour. Someone else had finally taken an interest, it seemed.

'Rigel,' she said softly, beckoning him over. She indicated the fallen man, who was now moaning and trying to rise. 'Take Thaniel

176

and get that man to Balderwin's estate. Do not show yourself to anyone until you hear from me.' She gave him a meaningful look and he nodded, hurrying to the man's side with a gesture to Thaniel.

'Form up!' shouted Overseer Skylock at her band of warriors. The fifty or sixty men had been standing around laughing and bantering as the last vestiges of the mob had vanished. They came to attention now, forming three ranks and following their leader to the ruins of the back gate. A familiar figure on a horse had almost reached them, followed by a large number of armed and armoured soldiers of the Battlemasons. The huge woman barred his approach, her eyes flinty. Ariene went to stand by her side.

'By what right have you come here, Castellan?' Skylock asked. 'Need I remind you that the Battlemasons have no jurisdiction over the internal conflicts of the city and—?'

'Unless that conflict threatens the constitution of Asterheim itself,' drawled Lord Barten, atop his horse. Ariene noted that he wore his Senatorial dress rather than his armoured panoply as Castellan of the Battlemasons; he clearly hadn't had long to prepare. 'In which case they are permitted to deploy to maintain order and to restore peace.' He raised his eyebrows blandly. 'Do you disagree, Overseer?'

Skylock made a low sound in her throat and heaved her hammer onto another shoulder. 'No I don't disagree. But as you see, the constitution is not threatened. A mob descended on Lady Gloriana's estate and has been driven off.'

Barten raised his eyebrows again. 'Disturbing,' he said, looking at Ariene. 'It seems I have come too late to lend you my assistance, Lady Gloriana. I offer you my apologies.' He looked out across the estate, a contemplative expression on his face. Ariene was wrong-footed; this wasn't the gloating enemy she'd expected.

'How is it you knew to come, Lord Barten?' she asked. 'The soldiers you have there must have come up from the Shieldgate?' If she was right, then Barten's men would have had to be making their way out of the great castle set in the walls to the south of the city at least an hour ago, long before the mob had arrived.

'Portgate, actually,' Barten replied. 'I had word sent to them the moment the Senate concluded its hearing in absentia. Portgate castle is on the harbour, so I knew they could get here fast.' He gestured to his fine Senatorial clothes. 'As you see, I had to meet them from the Senate on the way.'

'The Senate concluded *in absentia*?' Ariene was outraged, quite forgetting for the moment that she'd had no intention of returning to the hearing anyway.

Barten looked uncomfortable. 'It was not my doing, Ariene,' he said. 'They decided to carry on whilst we were talking outside. It was all I could do to remind them that you weren't there to defend yourself.'

Lady Gloriana felt sick. She clutched at the Overseer's muscled arm for support.

'And their conclusion?' she managed to ask with some measure of dignity.

Barten regarded her for a moment from atop his horse.

'A formality, really. You are to submit to questioning on the subject of your mage,' he looked around the grounds. 'Where is he, by the way?'

'That is none of your concern. It is quite improper to detain a noble's servants without prior—'

178

Barten held his hand up in mock-surrender. 'I know, I know. I was only curious. He isn't the one on trial, peculiarly enough. Though he may soon be.' A shadow of a troubled frown flitted over his face. 'It rather depends on your answers. You are to present yourself at the Senate and the questioning will take place there. In private. With me. It will be a quiet end to an unpleasant matter.'

'And the howling monsters that arrived here were what? My escort?' she snorted and glared up at her rival.

'All I can think was that word got out that you had been accused by the Senate and it started a panic. People are on edge in this city already, perhaps it isn't surprising they got whipped into a frenzy.' His eyes held hers for a steady moment. He was holding something back, and he knew she knew it. He shook his head slightly, a tiny motion, his face taut.

'Whipped by whom I wonder,' she said eventually. 'And how lucky for me that you anticipated the mood of the city with such accuracy.' His jaw relaxed as he saw she wasn't going to press the issue in public.

'You anticipated it yourself it seems,' he said, glancing at the Overseer.

'Long before you,' she smiled. 'I suspected I might need an escort when the Senate hearing was concluded.'

'You planned to run.' Barten's voice held no accusation; it was almost gentle.

'I believe in contingencies.'

He nodded and looked away into the now dark and quiet city and straightened, rolling his shoulders back. Ariene watched him carefully. She had the distinct impression of a man walking a gradually narrowing path but no longer able to turn back.

'Lady Gloriana, if you will agree to accompany me, it would be my pleasure to escort you with my entirely superfluous but very brave and capable soldiers back to the Senate Building, there to discuss with me the matters the Senate has authorised me to put to you.'

Skylock was about to retort when Ariene put a hand on her shoulder. The huge warrior held her tongue, staring with open hostility at the Castellan of the Battlemasons. Ariene considered a moment longer, then made her decision for better or ill.

'I accept your invitation, Lord Barten. It would be a shame to let these young men waste their trip. My dear Overseer, thank you again for your loyalty and timely intervention. Without you I honestly think I might have been torn to pieces by those…people.'

The Overseer leaned in and spoke in a low voice. 'Ariene, are you sure you can trust…' Skylock glanced at Barten.

'I don't think I have a choice, my dear,' she replied.

'You have a choice,' the Overseer growled, tightening her grip on her hammer meaningfully. Ariene smiled.

'Then let's say the game has turned deadly,' she said quietly, 'but I'm suddenly not sure it's Barten playing against me. I think I have to take this opportunity to find out what I can.'

'*They'll* be questioning *you*, Ariene.' Skylock warned.

'Yes dear. They'll certainly think so.'

Chapter Ten

Sophine sat alone in Master Thomas' office, staring into the shadows cast by the single flickering candle she'd allowed herself. She wasn't here by invitation, so she'd blocked the small window with her cloak to prevent the glow from giving her away. The night was still, the apprentices and novices in their chambers would be fast asleep. The tutors probably too. She felt a kind of peace here, a melancholic yearning for the innocence and simplicity of life as it had been only a week or so ago. Since leaving Hilda's she had suffered some terrible revelations and done some terrible things; she wondered now whether she would undo them if she could.

Sophine sighed and closed her eyes. Balderwin's face was waiting for her, as it always was. A flash of guilt and a pang of horror, served up by her subconscious, followed by the usual wave of justification and protest from her rational mind. Emotions fought a short but savage war within her, and as always, anger emerged victorious.

Balderwin had lied to her. Had humiliated her. Reduced her within her own mind to nothing but an object for years, and then finally rejected her. She had spent so long working to accept the humiliating truth that her patron had chosen her because of his cruelty and corruption of spirit rather than her talents, only to find she'd done so for nothing. He'd stolen her innocence without even touching her.

The anger was warm and powerful, as it had been all those other times. Sophine opened her eyes, holding on to the rage she felt when Balderwin's face floated before her inner-sight. She glanced at the candle and fed it some of the energy she could feel pulsing through her body. It flared brightly, far more brightly than it should, the light becoming a cold white that filled the room. She wondered if the cloak would be enough on the window.

'Now to work,' she whispered softly to herself, turning her gaze upon the shelf of forbidden knowledge Master Thomas had accumulated. She'd already taken one of the books; now she wanted more. Asterheim was on the brink of riots, and the wind was blowing against mages. Sophine intended to be ready.

She reached out and touched one of the heavy tomes, letting her heightened consciousness drift the way she'd been taught, but with a precision and purpose she could never have achieved without the fuel of the rage. Her mind ghosted through the pages, feeling the ideas within like tiny scraps of conversation, as though she was moving slowly through a crowded room. Complex uses of energy and delicate designs of the will, ways to create effects over time and distance. She gasped at the knowledge within the books; these were *spells*. Curses, even. Hexes.

A silken voice spoke in chilling tones, barely discernible against the background noise, but promising something cold, something powerful and *wrong*. She moved quickly away, feeling the undertone of darkness and malice pulsing through certain chapters of the oldest book. She pulled back, and opened her eyes.

'Conjuring,' she breathed. 'Necromancy…' She eyed the book with suspicion. No wonder the purge had taken hold and ripped through Asterheim all those centuries ago. Mages dabbling with the dead, raising spectres and monsters from the outer darkness…

'What were they thinking?' she whispered aloud, pretending she didn't feel the nugget of curiosity that had settled unwanted into the back of her mind.

She touched the first book again, letting it fill her with half-formed thoughts and specks of knowledge. She dug deeper, not sure what she was looking for…

There! She stopped; something familiar had leapt out at her. A passage dedicated to more complex portals than those covered in the first book she'd stolen, but still similar. She opened the book and flipped to the page, smiling as she recognised some of the principles.

'Guess I'm a mage after all,' she said, allowing herself a small smile. She read on, the book explaining how to enhance doorways and portals with diligent use of carefully controlled emotions. Extended distance, carrying more than one person, doorways to other places not strictly of the material world…

She frowned as the topic took a darker turn. She scanned a few more paragraphs and paused, her stomach clenching in a sudden horror at the stark warning someone had hand-written in the margin.

'Mages who lose control of the flow of emotion,' she read aloud, 'have been known to burn to death. The unleashed energies consume their bodies and they are lost in the fire.'

She closed the book and grabbed her bag from the table. As she began to put the books in the bag, a fragment of some other voice flitted by her ear. Her rage had almost gone, the last vestiges of the pulsing power fading away but managing to carry this last note to her. She paused, looking at the door. Something was out there. Something like the knowledge contained in the books. She frowned, hand on the last book, which she suddenly realised was the one full of dark magic. She pulled her hand back with a yelp and gave it a suspicious glare. She was almost sure it hissed at her as she stalked deliberately past it without a backward glance.

Opening the door, Sophine made her way down the corridor, following the lingering trace of the knowledge fragment. Before long she found herself in her old classroom. The desks were just as she'd known them, students' books lying around on the tables and some cloaks left behind. One desk, bizarrely, had a shoe on it.

'Are you in here?' Sophine asked the empty air, glancing up at the night sky through the windows. The smell of parchment and ink combined with the scent of teenage bodies to give that familiar classroom musk; the desks were unremarkable. And yet…

She closed her eyes again, letting the image of Balderwin ignite her emotional fuel and raise her consciousness. The now-familiar thrum of angry power blazed through her body and she listened for the scraps of knowledge as she had with the books. Motes of light seemed to swirl around her, just beyond vision, more in her mind than truly seen; gradually she began to see the classroom before her even through her closed eyes, an image with a peculiar yellow sheen as though filtered through a stained-glass window.

'Show me,' she said.

A man was sitting on the floor, his back to her. He was muttering something she could not hear. The desks and chairs were pushed to one side of the room, leaving him an empty space around where he sat, the carpet rolled up. He had drawn something on the floorboards before him – a symbol of some kind, with three jagged shapes sticking out of it that looked to be pointing at something. Sophine moved around him, watching the lines of energy flowing around the man and into the symbol, infusing it with his will. The man, who she could now see with a dull sense of grim anger was the scarred priest from the tavern, was grimacing with the effort of the endeavour. The designs of the symbol were collecting the energy, forcing it into tight turns and delaying its dissipation. As she stared, she understood; this was a complex and forbidden spell. It would take effect after the scarred priest had gone, following the lines of the symbol and up those jagged shapes…

She pulled back and opened her eyes, sudden fear robbing her of the rage she was using. The power and the vision vanished. She stared at the places where the jagged shapes were pointing.

'Thaniel, Rigel…' the shapes were pointing at the desks where they typically sat 'And me.'

She let out a short, mirthless laugh.

'You weren't targeting us,' she said. 'We just sat in the wrong chairs.'

She dropped her bag and rummaged through the books, trying to drift through them as she had before but finding it maddeningly hard to concentrate. She couldn't summon rage; fear was coursing through her and banishing anything else. Finally she found a page with the same symbol and one glance at the introduction was all she needed.

'Oh no,' she breathed. 'No, no *no.*'

***

185

Amir Barten tugged at his collar as he trudged towards the private audience room beneath the Senate Building. It was hot down here, and damp. He was just figuring out what to say to Ariene Gloriana when something slammed him hard against the dank stone wall. A familiar face leered into his, the reek of a stinking robe and hideous breath suddenly filling his nose.

'You ruined everything Barten,' hissed the mad non-priest. 'I had her in my grasp and you interfered again.' Something hard and cold pressed against his stomach; Barten could feel its razor edge through his fine silk shirt.

'Are you insane?' he barked, just about managing to put something other than fear into his voice. He dropped his tone to a whisper.

'What did you expect me to do? Let your band of marauding citizens tear her apart?'

The leering priest smiled coldly and pressed the blade harder against his belly.

'If that had happened,' Barten gasped desperately, 'the Senate would have been accused of murder.'

The blade receded a little. A flicker of doubt crossed the ugly face.

'Think about it Kahin. The Senate just ordered her to be brought for questioning. It didn't pass any motions against her or her mage or—'

Kahin leaned in again. 'And who's fault is that? You hijacked the debate to let her off the hook.'

'But—'

'You miss the point, my lord,' Kahin said flatly, staring into his eyes. 'It was the *mage* I wanted. I needed the Senate riled up so that the *people* would be riled up. Then the attack would have some legitimacy when it all went wrong.'

'What do you mean?'

'The mage is compromised, Barten. He's a slave to his emotions. He can't help but use powers that are forbidden. So when we came for his mistress…'

Barten understood. Ariene hadn't been the target, not really. Not until she began to associate with the young mage who'd saved her life, who apparently Kahin had somehow set up to fall victim to youthful folly. His hatred for the vile priest deepened a notch.

'Perhaps he's not as compromised as you thought. The Travellers arrived before me; they were the ones who stopped your mob, not me.'

'Your Travellers! You sent word to that monster of a woman and—'

'No! They'd never have listened to me. Think about it, Kahin, they belong to House Gloriana.'

Kahin did not drop his gaze, though the ghost of uncertainty still flickered within his dark eyes. He stepped back a pace, still holding the wickedly curved blade in one calloused hand, glaring at Amir through narrowed eyes.

Amir tried not to let his relief show as he straightened his shirt.

'Kahin,' he said, 'I suggested to the Senate that The Sacred Circle should see to the matter of sending for Ariene, didn't I? I had every intention of letting you have her. Ariene must have expected trouble the moment she was summoned to the Senate and got word out to the Travellers before your mob was even assembled.'

'How could she know?' growled Kahin, his blade still held ready.

'Her mage,' suggested Barten, 'or maybe just long experience in politics. Don't underestimate her in that regard, Kahin. She's been playing these games far longer than you or I, it isn't surprising she anticipates our moves.'

'Our moves?' snarled the scarred priest. 'You expect me to forget you arrived with an army to stop me?'

'I suspected you would do something rash, so I sent word to Portgate for an escort just in case. I didn't think murdering a respected member of the Senate would advance His Benevolence's cause. Especially when the priests had been given the task of presenting the Senate's decision to the Lady.'

Kahin was silent, glaring at him. With evident reluctance, he sheathed the blade.

'You're a fool, Barten. If that mage had started throwing fireballs at citizens it would all have been over. Lucky for you it was the Travellers who ruined His Benevolence's ascension.'

'Not ruined, just delayed.'

Kahin turned away, his fists clenching and unclenching by his side. Amir watched him apprehensively.

'You've made your move, Kahin. Now I need to clean up the mess. The Lady is awaiting her questioning, so if you'll excuse me.'

Kahin turned back with a vehement shake of the head.

'Oh no. I'm going to be right there with you. She's not going anywhere, she—'

'Forget it. You are not a member of the Senate, so you aren't entitled to question her. Besides, that room is full of other Senators by now I assure you. She isn't a prisoner, and will have to walk out of here unmolested.'

Barten greatly enjoyed the look of dismay on his unpleasant compatriot's gnarled face.

'If we hold her, we could draw the mage out when he comes to rescue...'

'Not acceptable. She has to be afforded all dignity. We have to be patient, Kahin; Ariene has won this round. Find someone else to kidnap.'

The instant he said the words he regretted it. Kahin's face changed from dismay to serpentine cunning, and he nodded thoughtfully.

Oh no, thought Amir. *What have I done?*

***

Rigel wrinkled his nose at the smell of blood and peeled back the bandage around the man's torso. He winced and put it back again. The gash beneath was large, not bleeding so much now but the lumpy skin around it suggested serious bone problems. The man had been hit hard with Skylock's hammer so Rigel was amazed he was even breathing. It had caved in most of his left side and something, probably the ground, had ripped an ugly tear across his back. The man was young, not much older than Rigel himself. He lay breathing shallowly with an unpleasant rattle in his chest, his skin grey and cold. Rigel knew he was dying.

'Don't die,' Rigel whispered at the man. 'Please don't die.'

He couldn't shake the memory of the sudden hush of the crowd, the strange way they'd simply walked off or run away. He'd never seen anything like it before, but one suspicion nagged at him and wouldn't let go: those people had not been in control of themselves. Which meant…

'It wasn't your fault,' he said sadly, bitterly regretting the terrible wound the over-eager Overseer had dealt him. How many others had died, he wondered? Senselessly killed for nothing, merely puppets manipulated by some unseen enemy and let go the moment Ariene was beyond reach.

Misery welled up inside him, the kind of existential hollowness he'd felt on the bridge with Ariene and back in the quarry facing the bleakness of his future. He let it come, feeling tears forming at the corner of his eyes. Then he felt it.

The warm feeling, tingling up his spine, spreading to his limbs, settling in his stomach. A hot pulse of energy, just like he'd felt before. Rigel gasped, letting it fill him, trying to suppress the elation he felt as it did so in case he ruined it.

He turned his eyes on the dying man, seeing those silvery strands running through his body just like Ariene's. The pulsing light of his heart was dangerously faint, a large chunk of the web broken and dark, the dim glow in the latticework of his brain darkening as the catastrophic breakage leaked silvery essence out into the shadowy world beyond.

Rigel reached out, remembering how he had done it with Ariene, and touched the man's head. He let his consciousness drift, flowing through the failing traceries of the silver network, reinforcing it and reinvigorating it. He hovered over the massive crater in the web, willing it to repair itself, forging new connections and empowering misaligned strands to link back up with their original moorings. The energy was like a hot current flowing through his mind, blinding him to all else…

190

Someone was banging on the door. Rigel's eyes flew open and he fell back, gasping, torn from his work as the energy stuttered, failed, died. The feeling of despair and misery was gone, replaced with shock and the simple, mundane question of who was at the door.

'No!' he cried, scrabbling to his feet and peering anxiously at the blood-stained bandages wrapped around the young man. The patient was breathing more steadily now, the hideous death-rattle was gone and colour had returned to his skin. Rigel's hands shook as he lifted the bandage and looked beneath. He collapsed back into his chair, exhaling hard in utter relief. He ran a hand through his unruly hair.

The banging came again.

'What?' he shouted irritably. He'd brought the Overseer's hammer-victim to Balderwin's estate a few minutes before, as Ariene had commanded, and had simply laid him down on the sofa in the ground floor reception room whilst he ran for bandages. He hadn't tried to move him since.

Rigel stood up, wondering idly where the servants had gone. Sophine's peculiar little army of waifs and children with dangerous eyes were supposed to work here, weren't they?

He made his way to the front door as the banging came again, and pulled it open.

Outside, all was dark, the lights of the city shining prettily on the river. Sophine and Thaniel stood in the doorway, Thaniel looking confused and Sophine looking murderous.

'Took you long enough,' she said as she shouldered past him. Thaniel followed, giving his friend an apologetic shrug.

'Don't you have keys?' Rigel asked, closing the door and locking it. 'This is your house now.'

'I...forgot them,' Sophine said evasively.

Rigel raised an eyebrow.

'Alright fine. I didn't think I'd need them,' she admitted.

'You used a portal?'

She nodded.

'Where'd you go?'

'Hilda's,' she hefted a heavy looking bag and went to the dining room. They followed after her, and she dumped the bag on the table. 'I went to get the rest of Thomas's books.'

The young man in the reception room groaned. Sophine froze. 'What was that?'

'You...missed a lot,' Rigel said. He went to sit at the table, cradling his head in one hand. 'There's a guy in there.'

'What guy?'

'He got hit with a hammer.'

'A big one,' Thaniel put in.

'But he's ok now,' Rigel finished. He waggled his fingers in the air. 'I fixed him.'

Sophine stared at him.

'I think you'd better start at the beginning.'

Rigel told the tale of the evening, about how the Senate had voted to hold a hearing against Ariene and then sent for her to present herself. He told her how a mob of angry citizens somehow got word of the proceedings, and decided to take matters into their own hands, leading to a confrontation at Ariene's.

'You don't sound like you believe that,' Sophine said, 'about the mob deciding to attack Ariene.'

Thaniel snorted a laugh and Rigel shook his head.

'I don't. The scarred priest was there. He said something weird...What was it, Than?'

'He was waiting for us.'

'Yeah, waiting for us before they could begin. And then the crowd went nuts.'

Sophine went slowly to the window and looked out. Her skin looked incredibly pale in the moonlight, her eyes almost black.

'That scarred priest is a mage,' she said eventually. Rigel and Thaniel didn't reply, just stared at her.

'I saw an after-image of him, at Hilda's. That's why I came back.'

Thaniel crossed his arms.

'That's why you turned up at Orswell's and spirited me away through that horrible portal?'

She nodded.

'We all needed to be here. But I think you two already figured it out from what you said.'

Rigel frowned.

'Maybe, but I wasn't sure. Influencing a mind is hard work, never mind *controlling* one. Let alone controlling *hundreds* of them.'

'It wasn't mind-influencing like we know it, Rigel,' she said heavily, sitting down opposite him and sighing. 'He used a spell.'

'A spell? Like, as in, a pre-purge witchcraft spell?'

Sophine indicated the books on the table with a languid gesture.

'All there in ink and parchment. Spells, curses. Necromancy. Conjuring. It's all real.'

'And this scarred priest mage man knows how to do it?' Thaniel raised an eyebrow and leant back in his chair, arms still crossed.

'He knows enough,' Sophine said. 'He cast a spell at Hilda's.'

'It's not possible, Soph,' Rigel insisted. 'If a mage was learning about that sort of thing, they'd—'

'They'd what? Be expelled? Publicly shamed? Executed?' Thaniel shook his head.

'The guild would want to cover up,' he said grimly. 'They'd never admit publicly that one of us was into that sort of thing. It could start a whole new purge.'

'Exactly,' said Sophine. 'I think he was kicked out, and now he's made a deal with The Sacred Circle.'

'What kind of deal?'

'What's he been doing recently, Than?'

'Stirring up trouble for mages,' Rigel said. 'Trying to get Ariene censured for witchcraft, blaming mages for murders...'

Sophine nodded. 'And who was behind the purge in the old days?'

No one answered. Everyone knew the dark history of the church, before its rebrand as The Sacred Circle.

Eventually Rigel spoke up. 'What was the spell he cast?'

Sophine didn't answer at first, her hesitation doing nothing to make Rigel feel better.

'It was a spell to increase a mage's connection to his or her emotions. An old spell teachers used to use to enhance the abilities of students that found it hard to connect to their feelings.'

'That's weird,' said Thaniel. 'Why cast a spell like that in The Barbican? Mages don't use emotions.'

194

'Because…' Sophine hesitated again. 'We're taught to avoid emotions so we can tap into nice, easily controlled abilities and do inoffensive things like building and healing and crop growing or fortune telling. All of that is manipulating *existing* energy streams all around us and most mages spend nice quiet lives doing just that. Ever wonder why?'

'Not before today,' Thaniel said grumpily.

'Because the mages of the past used emotion to connect with the energy *inside* them. And emotion is powerful; it can kill you if you don't control it properly. The book talked about mages burning from the inside out when they lost control, because it's something that actually *generates* energy all on its own. But with proper training, the mages in the old days had access to far more power than we can tap just through dreamily feeling the connections between outside things. And the abilities it opens up: portals, conjuring, spells…Things that come from creating new energy – those are what led to the purge. So to modern mages, emotion is forbidden. It says so in the Charter.'

Rigel laughed bitterly.

'So unhinging some apprentice kids…'

'*Teenage* apprentice kids,' added Thaniel, frowning down at the table. 'Emotional ones.'

'And then making the city hostile to mages…'

'Uncontrolled emotional powers,' nodded Sophine. 'Like in the tavern. Like Balderwin. Your time slowing and your healing on Ariene when she was practically dead.'

'Me fixing the ruined wall,' said Thaniel. 'I couldn't do it. It was impossible. The wall had been crumbling for decades, it had almost no residual energy left. Until Eric appeared and I got all…flustered. Emotional. Then it just rebuilt itself with a flick of my fingers.'

Rigel looked at him.

'You also threw one of those maniacs into a wall during the tavern attack.'

'Well yes, but I prefer the wall story.'

Sophine nodded and pulled a book towards her.

'We've been set up,' she said, leafing through the first one. Her tone hardened into a growl. 'And now we need to fight back.'

Chapter Eleven

Asterheim's Noble Quarter was, in places, sorely misnamed. With the majority of the larger noble estates tucked away against the city walls or along the river, much of the rest was given over to those amenities all residential areas needed. Being merely a short walk from the harbour and the mighty Portgate Castle which sat alongside it, it also catered for the needs of soldiers and sailors and all manner of travellers eager to see the grand manses of the nobility of Asterheim.

Alongside the crowded roads, brothels sat unashamedly next to taverns and herbalists' shops, tailors and cobblers competed for trade within spitting distance of the blacksmiths and armourers. A confused mass of trades and vocations, all with their own noises and smells and, naturally, waste products, lined the once-cobbled roads. The area had grown so fast and without direction that the original layout of the streets had been irreparably changed. The nobles themselves tended to follow the roads around the city walls, if not on them, or travel by river. Anything to avoid the providers of the very services that they relied upon, and the filthy streets between them that were bustling with foreigners and soldiers and merchants.

Thaniel was trudging slowly through a particularly busy square situated at the intersection of four streets. Once, the square had been little more than a few stalls sitting at the crossroads yelling about their produce. It had since expanded, more and more merchants joining and jostling for position, some establishing a permanent presence and their rivals then doing the same. Of the four roads leading in, no trace could now be seen anywhere for hundreds of metres, until they re-emerged on the other side of the sprawling market mass.

One had to have a good sense of direction to end up in the right place on the other side, weaving between the shops and stalls and thieves and prostitutes, with a hand clamped tight over any valuables.

Through the chaos, Thaniel caught sight of a familiar face. Eric sat on an upturned barrel by a crude wooden bar, behind which a tender was dispensing a thick brown ale to a group of cheering sailors. Eric looked thoroughly miserable, and not a little drunk. He blinked sadly into his tankard and took a deep swallow, sloshing some of the drink on his expensive-looking blue shirt. Thaniel shouldered his way through the sailors to reach him. Eric looked up and stared at him in some amazement.

'You're here!' he said excitedly, a grin finally replacing his slack-eyed stare.

'I'm here,' Thaniel agreed, peering at him. 'How long have you been sitting there?'

'Since I gave up searching,' Eric said in a sulky tone, his expression turning accusatory. 'I've been wandering around this reeking mess for hours.'

Thaniel glanced around them. The sun was shining, the mood of the crowd seemed jovial enough. It did, however, reek. Sweating people in old or dirty clothes, sailors and soldiers off duty and drunk. Rotting produce cast away in the street. It all came together in a glorious stink.

'Searching for me?'

Eric snorted and took another swig of his drink. 'Who else?'

'Did Orswell send you?'

'Yes,' Eric said, a little too briskly. 'You disappeared and no one knew where you were.'

'I didn't realise he kept such a close eye on us.'

Eric didn't reply, signalling the barman for another drink and indicating another barrel. Thaniel sat down; it was hideously uncomfortable. All un-sanded wood and hard edges. He took the proffered tankard with a forced smile.

'You alright to get this one?' Eric said, looking at him hopefully. Thaniel paused with his drink halfway to his lips.

'I don't have any money,' he said quietly, throwing a glance at the barman who hastily looked away.

'Me neither,' Eric said with a grin, 'but I told him I was waiting for Lord Orswell's mage. Seems content to let me drink for free.'

'Content to have Lord Orswell owe him you mean,' Thaniel said, smiling at the barman and making a toasting gesture. The barman smiled and nodded back. 'We'd better not make a habit of this or things could get nasty.'

'It's fine this once.'

'Maybe.'

They drank in silence for a while. Finally Eric looked at him with a warm smile that made Thaniel's stomach flutter.

'I'm glad you're alright.'

'I'm glad you came to find me.'

'Orswell sent me.'

'No he didn't.'

Eric smiled shyly.

'No. He didn't. Where did you go though? We were…I was…worried you'd been kidnapped or killed or something. You vanished last night, no one saw you leave and then you didn't come home.'

Thaniel thought for a moment. There was nothing he could say about Ariene or Sophine that he could tell Eric, well meaning though he was.

'I was at The Barbican over in the guild quarter. I needed to find some things out.'

'About the wall?'

'The wall?'

Eric nodded. 'When you fixed the wall, it was like nothing I'd ever seen. Our master was astonished.'

'*Astonished* was he?'

'Astonished,' Eric laughed and took a deep drink.

Thaniel laughed with him. 'Sure, yes. I went to read up on how to astonish people.'

Eric put his tankard down and stared at Thaniel for a moment.

Then he leaned over and kissed him.

***

Watery sunlight streamed in through the narrow windows of the even narrower corridor, high up on the third floor of the Balderwin estate. Dust swirled and drifted in the light, like glittering flecks of gold. The corridor ran around three of the four sides of the building, a service passage for servants with sheer flights of stairs at various points to enable staff to vanish and reappear on the other side of the house without walking through the plushily decorated expensive rooms below, or bumping into Lord Balderwin.

Sophine trod carefully along the corridor, walking as lightly as she could to avoid making any noise. It was maddeningly hard to keep her mind in the appropriate state to maintain the complicated spell she was trying to learn whilst concentrating on where she put her feet. Rage was something she had thought she knew, but using it was much more difficult than letting it use her. She could still summon the anger using the image of Balderwin, but the emotion was somehow weaker now. A memory of rage rather than pure anger; it was almost as though she was feeling it in a detached academic way instead of with the visceral hate she'd felt before. The energy it produced was getting smaller each time she used it. And dissipating sooner.

Something moved behind her, something flitting between the beams of light. Sophine tried to turn, but she was too slow. Something slammed into the energy barrier she was struggling to keep around her and shattered it, throwing her attacker back. Sophine staggered, a hand flying to her head as sudden pain lanced through it. The spell had been difficult, requiring her to pass a portion of her will into the air around her body and keep it there, endlessly circling her, endlessly repeating that she shall not be touched, she shall *not* be touched...

To have something so inextricably linked to her own mind smashed so abruptly was like a physical blow, and she felt a flare of anger at herself for having walked right into the trap. A shadow moved suddenly to her right and she gripped the rush of anger and used it to spirit herself five feet to the left. The portal was poorly made and purely emotional, the exact kind of magic the book warned about, but her destination had been simple: beyond the reach of Misty's knife.

The blade slashed through the space she'd occupied seconds before and Sophine turned to run. Adrenaline and panic had replaced her controlled anger and she had no time to rise into the peaceful serenity required for conventional mage abilities. She ran, stumbling in the gloomy corridor, and felt a savage kick from behind. She fell sprawling on the ground and as she tried to rise, Misty's grinning face came at her, illuminated for a moment amongst the swirling dust motes.

Sophine knocked her back with a primal yell of anger, a pathetic telekinetic shunt, barely strong enough to gain her a moment's space. Misty's face contorted in a comical look of surprise but she quickly recovered enough to fling her knife straight at Sophine.

Looking back, Sophine was able to recognise that it was the sudden look of shock on Misty's young face that had given her the control to rise above the emotions and slow the knife. Levitation, one of the simplest uses of the world's interconnected energies, was not difficult for a mage in control of her mind. The knife slowed and stopped inches from her face, turned, and flew back to the wide-eyed Misty. It hovered, point first, at the girl's throat.

Sophine let it drop. Misty stared at her, the thin waif's chest rising and falling rapidly with the exertion of the short battle. Sophine dropped to the ground, suddenly exhausted. She ran a hand through her thick, sweat-soaked hair and shook her head.

'You nearly had me,' she said. Misty scooped up her knife and threw it in the air, end over end, catching it again deftly by the handle and sheathing it in a smooth motion.

'Nearly. Can you teach me that trick?' Sophine grimaced and nodded.

'Sure. It should only take a few years.'

'Years?' Misty pulled a face.

'I started when I was years younger than you. Takes a long time, and even then it isn't perfect. I almost didn't stop that blade.'

'Hardly a blade. It's blunt.'

'You didn't tell me it was blunt.' Misty shrugged.

'Didn't want you to think I was going easy.'

'I didn't. At all. I hurt just about everywhere. My head feels like it's splitting in half.'

Misty helped her up, and they made their way towards the stairs.

'I need to get to The Barbican,' Sophine said wearily. 'If it's this hard to protect ourselves from attack, then we need to practise.'

'You still think they're in danger?'

'I think we're all in danger, Mist. And we can't all handle ourselves like you can.'

***

The route from the Senate Building to House Gloriana's estate was a pleasant walk on a day like this, through the markets and shop-lined streets of the noble quarter. Being a little further from the harbour and Portgate Castle than the likes of the Orswell grounds, this area was quieter and generally catered for a more sober crowd of people. Lady Gloriana had insisted on walking, the better to show her complete lack of concern following her interrogation. Rigel walked beside her, having decided to escort her home despite being told to stay out of sight.

'I'd have been quite safe on my own, Rigel,' Ariene was saying, leaning easily on his arm. She looked tired and a little shaken. Dark circles showed under her eyes and her cheeks looked more hollow than usual. She had not slept well in the private chamber at the Senate Building, it was clear to see.

'But you could have brought me something to wear,' she muttered as she pulled her travelling cloak around her, a shapeless thing of dull grey material. Next to her brown and utilitarian riding clothes, she didn't look at all like the Lady of House Gloriana. She'd been in the midst of fleeing when the mob had attacked, and had gone straight from there to the Senate with Lord Barten.

'Sorry my lady,' Rigel smiled, 'I didn't think you'd want to draw attention.'

'I am a Senator and Lady of a great house, Rigel. I always want to draw attention.'

'Noted, ma'am.'

'Don't call me that,' she said absently, gazing around at the market stalls. 'Still, a degree of anonymity might be a good thing, mightn't it?'

'It might, my lady.'

'Oh do stop with the formality. No one knows me here, as you just pointed out. I'm now younger than most people think I am and dressed for the road. I could be just about anyone, a well-travelled woman stepping out with a dashing young man.'

'Dashing?'

'Yes, dashing. Why must the young take everything so seriously?'

He smiled. 'Just not sure if it's a compliment.'

'Well don't take it personally. At my age, anyone with a few less wrinkles and who can walk unaided is positively irresistible.'

Rigel chuckled politely, painfully aware that they were dancing around the subject of the interrogation. After a moment or two of silence she glanced at him.

'I didn't say anything you know.'

'I know.'

'About you, Sophine, Thaniel. I simply said you were my mage and it was all above board.'

He nodded.

'Did they ask about your…health?'

'No, curiously enough. Lord Barten did the talking, as was his right. And Amir is many things but a pawn of The Sacred Circle he is not, as it turns out. They may want to see me strung up from the nearest rafter, but he doesn't. If nothing else, he knows he needs me to agree to an orderly transition of power, one that benefits him, before I'm unceremoniously knocked off my perch.'

She chuckled.

'All the more reason, of course, not to agree to any such transition. Strange though.'

Rigel's ears pricked at that.

'What's strange?'

'There was a priest in there with us for a while.' Rigel felt a stab of cold in his guts.

'Ugly man, scar? Wearing a robe that looked like it needed a wash?'

'No,' she said.

Rigel exhaled in relief.

'No, I wouldn't say that,' she continued. 'Hideous man, with a scar, wearing a robe that looked like it needed burning. Quite different.'

Rigel stopped and looked at her.

'I'm serious, Ariene. That man is dangerous.'

She smiled and touched his face.

'Like I said, dear. The young are always serious.'

He stared at her. She sighed and took his arm again, guiding him along.

'I know he's dangerous, Rigel. I saw him in the Senate whilst Barten's lackey failed to make a case against me and I saw him again out of my window last night. I just don't know why he's dangerous or what he's up to.'

'I think I do.'

'Really?'

'He's trying to start a war against mages in this city. He was at Hilda's, casting forbidden spells on students to make them dangerous. Sophine found out.'

'She's a clever girl, that one,' Ariene muttered, frowning hard. Rigel glanced at her.

'He was also the one who forced those people into a mob to attack your house. The man we brought to Balderwin's said he remembered nothing after having his dinner that night and the silver lines in his brain had fragments of someone else's willpower woven throughout them…'

Ariene looked at him with a strange expression.

206

'I think he plans to start a full uprising against mages, somehow,' he said hastily, not wanting to even try to explain the silvery-lines comment. 'Goading us in the tavern was his first try.'

Ariene looked grim.

'Not his first. Someone has been working to get the conversation going against mages for some time; it's only now that I realise how it's all connected. So this priest is the one…'

'It can't just be him.'

'True. Barten is involved somehow too. Strange that Amir is working with him though, it doesn't make sense.'

'You said the priest was there for only part of the time you were being questioned.'

Ariene looked at him, quizzically.

'What did you say before he left?'

She frowned, about to reply, when a loud crashing noise cut through the general hubbub of the market crowd. Screams and shouting followed, rippling through the market as a cloud of black smoke began to rise into the air. People started running, pushing and shoving in their haste to get away from whatever was happening. Shopkeepers started shrieking for water, to stop the fire they were convinced was starting.

Rigel and Ariene hurried towards the cloud of smoke, heading in the opposite direction to most of the frightened citizens.

A shop was ablaze, thick black smoke billowing up into the air with a peculiar gusto, as though propelled from beneath by some force. A crowd had gathered before the shop, a sturdy looking place of heavy wood standing three stories high and fitted with good windows, which now splintered and shattered in the heat.

Rigel pulled Ariene back as she tried to reach the building.

'Look!' he pointed, having to shout to make himself heard.

The crowd was making no move to assist, they merely stood screaming at the blaze. Some waved their arms, others had clenched fists, their eyes wide with fury.

Someone burst from the doorway, clutching rolls of parchment, some of which were smoked and crisped. Others were actually on fire. The man threw them on the ground and started stamping on them, calling to the crowd to fetch water from the river before he realised the peculiar stillness that had overcome them. The figure straightened, looking at the mob, realisation dawning on his face. He was a bearded man in his fifties, his red tunic of decent material marking him out as a reasonably wealthy merchant.

As one, the crowd began screaming. Rigel jumped, and felt Ariene beside him do the same. The merchant, to his credit, did not wait. He ran, shouldering his way through the suddenly enraged crowd and scrabbling free of their clutches. The maddened mob gave chase, no more than an arm's length behind him.

'He's a mage!' Ariene called, shaking Rigel from his horror-induced stupor. The words resonated within his head. It was a lynch mob. Just like the one that came for Ariene.

He felt sick; everywhere he went, violence and madness seemed to follow him like some inescapable shadow stalking his every move. Panic warred with despair inside him and he reacted without thought, trying to grab Ariene and make for the safety of the mansion.

Ariene was like iron. Unyielding. Unmoving. The noise around him, the scream of the crowd, the crackle of splintering wood as the mage's shop was destroyed, all was dulled and echoing as though from far away.

'No, no not now!' Rigel yelled through choked sobs, his anguish serving merely to fuel the unwanted power spilling through him and slowing time still further. The crowd was nearly motionless; the mage who had stumbled moments before fell painfully slowly to the ground, the gleeful shriek of the man closest behind him a distant howl. The outstretched fingers of the shrieking man reached hungrily for his victim, moving no more than inches each second. Rigel threw up his hands in frustration; what was the point of this ability if he couldn't affect anything? All he could do was watch it all happening in excruciating detail, helpless to do anything about it.

In irritation, he turned his thoughts inward, desperately searching for the source of the infuriatingly mercurial power. He was dimly aware of the emotion within him, the sick feeling of helplessness and the guilt that surrounded it. He reached for it, determined to turn it to his own purposes for once.

Something gleamed out of the corner of his eye, dragging him back to the outside world. The motionless statuary of the crowd was glowing.

Silvery strands of filament light within each individual body pulsed brightly, all connections in harmony with one another. Unlike Ariene and the man from the previous mob, whose web of silver light had been damaged, these were whole and beautiful. Images of souls rendered in glittering capillaries. But there was something else too. Something malignant.

A dark link of spidery shadow connected each person in the crowd, wrapped insidiously around their minds and suborning their will to that of something else. He watched it gleam and flex, in constant motion, as if the webs to which it linked continuously rippled and shook beneath its grip.

Rigel gritted his teeth and tried to follow the dark shadow, over the heads of the crowd. It bucked, resisting his touch, and the doubtful pit in Rigel's stomach increased, threatening his tenuous hold on his barely controlled powers. A single thin strand of something dark and wispy lifted up and away, stretching back over the street to a house on the other side and disappearing into a window.

Rigel made a desperate gasping sound and tried to direct his rapidly failing energy into the thin black link between the spellcaster and the crowd. The link shivered and writhed, but Rigel held on, near-panic lending him some measure of control for a moment.

'Come on,' he half-whimpered. 'Come on, please…'

The ethereal link twisted and writhed a moment more, and Rigel screamed with desperate concentration.

'Do what I want for once!' he yelled through tears of anger.

To his shock and sudden horror, the spidery link snapped with an unearthly howl, and by his side Ariene stumbled and fell.

He caught her, his limbs so weak and wobbly with the effort he almost dropped her. All at once the crowd stopped yelling. At the front of the crowd, the mage picked himself up and ran on, oblivious to the change in his fortunes. A grey-haired woman in a pink shawl who moments before had been baying for blood turned and frowned at her surroundings, rubbing at her temples.

At the same time, an agonised wailing echoed from a window on the other side of the street, a dreadful sound ghastly enough to chill the blood. The woman with the pink shawl had gone pale, looking around at her former compatriots, muttering and pointing.

'What was that?' Ariene breathed, clutching at him and peering in the direction of the horrible scream. Rigel found he knew the answer without having to think.

'Kahin,' Rigel spat, giving the distant window one last furious glance. He turned away to regard the blazing fire, wanting so badly to calm his mind and reach for the serenity to redirect the heat energy away, but knowing that he could not. Snapping that link had been luck; he'd had almost no control at all.

With resigned apprehension, Rigel stretched his arm towards the building, closing his eyes and willing himself to do what he should have been able to do so easily. What Sophine or even Thaniel could almost certainly have done. The calm did not come, as he'd known it would not; no power rose to do his bidding. He watched helplessly as the mage's shop was blackened and splintered, consumed in the fires of ignorance. As its roof finally groaned and caved in, releasing clouds of filthy smoke and burning ash into the air, the familiar shades of misery and self-loathing once more took up malign residence in the back of his mind. He felt Ariene's grip on his arm tighten.

The grey-haired woman in the pink shawl was staring at him with flat, unfriendly eyes. Even with Kahin's spell broken, the crowd simmered with resentment and mistrust. Silence had fallen, but for the crackle and snap of burning timber.

'I think we should leave,' Ariene muttered, 'these people have no love of mages.'

'They don't know I'm—'

She smiled thinly.

'Put your arm down, dear.'

211

Rigel hissed a curse and dropped his arm, keeping his eyes down as they made their way through the watchful crowd. He could feel them staring, their hostility coming off them in unspoken waves.

'This city is primed to explode,' Ariene said as they cleared the street and made their way towards her estate.

***

The reception room in the Heart of Asterheim was in fact a series of rooms that had been merged, somewhat crudely, into a single chamber. The brickwork was scratched and uneven where walls had been removed to extend the space into what now seemed to serve as a kind of throne-room. A number of small carpets had been dragged together to run the length of the improvised audience chamber, though they were all of such different design that it ruined the intended effect. Lord Amir Barten had to suppress an amused smile as he was shown in by a shuffling priest in a gold robe. By his side, the silent representative of the Mortuary Guild appeared not to notice, his heavily lidded eyes peering disinterestedly out from a hollow-cheeked face ringed by a long white beard. The man had met him outside the cathedral, coincidentally seeking an audience with His Benevolence at the same time. He hadn't said why, merely exchanged minor courtesies in a dull, lifeless voice which seemed entirely appropriate to his chosen vocation.

Up near the end of the chamber, under the large stained-glass window which showed a great serpent devouring its own tail amidst fire and light, sat a wooden high-backed armchair. The man perched upon the chair fidgeted, his leg bouncing up and down nervously and his fingers tapping out an uneven rhythm on the chair's unadorned arms. A ring tapped against the wood maddeningly erratically, setting Amir's teeth on edge.

Barten and his silent companion came to a halt a respectful distance from the chair, and Amir bowed politely. This was his first meeting with His Benevolence Lyoris Mountebank, High Priest of The Sacred Circle. He was not particularly impressed, and more than a little surprised.

The highest-ranking priest in Asterheim, indeed in Astregoth itself, was a thin man in his twenties, with a mop of unruly black hair and hard, calculating eyes. He was pale and gaunt, as though he hadn't eaten for some time, and he radiated a nervous energy that made Barten feel uneasy. Lyoris wore a dark jerkin over a light shirt, his black trousers disappearing into worn-looking boots. He looked far more like a scholar than a priest, with neither sceptre nor mitre nor any hint of gold ornamentation. He didn't even have an ouroboros symbol anywhere on him.

Amir studied the man for a moment, mastering his thoughts lest they show on his face. Mountebank held his gaze, watching him carefully with a hint of a smile twitching at the corner of a thin-lipped mouth. His eyes seemed unusually large, light brown orbs glistening in the colourful light filtering through the glass.

'Your Benevolence,' Amir said finally, giving the man a smile. Mountebank returned it, and held up a scrawny hand, ring first. Barten hesitated a moment, but took the hand and let his lips lightly brush the large green gem sticking ostentatiously out of the ring. The priest held the hand out to the Mortuary Guild representative, but when the man made no move to take it, smoothly withdrew it and grinned at them both.

'Welcome, my friends,' Lyoris said in a nasal, reedy voice. 'It has been *so* long since I had new visitors.' His left foot was tapping rapidly against the floor, but mercifully the ring had stopped for the moment.

'To what do I owe the pleasure?' Lyoris's left eye twitched twice in quick succession.

He held a hand up to it, as though to calm the dancing nerves with a soothing touch. His right eye glanced at the Mortuary Guild representative.

The silent man drew himself up, his wrinkled face scrunching still further as he peered at the High Priest. His thick white beard seemed almost to bristle.

'I have come to ask you to censure one of your priests,' the elderly representative said bluntly in a heavy, tired voice. 'He assaulted one of my workers and demanded administrative processes be *disregarded*,' he said the word with venom, as though horrified at the mere idea of due process not being followed, and paused to slowly shake his head. 'These processes are *necessary* for the correct functioning of our office. He did this, sir, at knife point and claimed to do so with *your* authority.' He was breathing heavily now, as though emotionally overcome. He straightened up again with visible effort.

'What do you have to—?'

He paused, bowing his head and taking another deep breath. 'To say for yourself?' Lyoris smiled blandly, though his eyes were hard.

'It doesn't much matter,' he said conversationally. 'You won't remember any of this.'

'I won't…remember?' The older man blinked. He took another shuddering breath.

'No. I should thank you really. You'll be bringing me and my ally here together. Very good of you. Selfless. Praise the Circle.' Lyoris let out a peculiar giggle.

The old man turned to glance at Barten as though seeing him for the first time, then crashed heavily to the floor. Amir jumped back, horrified, but Lyoris merely raised a hand. At once, three golden-robed priests leapt forward from their posts lining the room and dragged the representative away across the mismatched carpets. Barten looked at Lyoris, who simply held up his ring.

'Don't worry, my lord,' he said mildly. 'You aren't in any danger.'

'Danger? What did…?' Amir looked at the ring. 'He didn't kiss the ring?'

'That's right, he didn't. And now he's asleep. All hail The Sacred Circle.' Lyoris gave a thin smile that looked far more like a mocking grimace.

'I don't…follow.'

Lyoris looked at him for a moment, as though weighing his words. 'Can I trust you, Amir?'

'As much as I can trust you.'

The young man grinned, his right hand slapping the chair's arm three times in quick succession.

'Indeed, indeed. We're in this together after all. Too close to the end now to play games I suppose. Ah, Kahin!' This last was directed at the scarred priest who had made his way into the audience chamber unnoticed. He was standing a few paces away, looking pale and

215

ill. At Lyoris's call he approached, his hand rising to his forehead. He winced as he knelt.

'My lord,' Kahin mumbled, kissing his master's ring and standing back.

Lyoris let out a short laugh, his gaze darting all around Kahin's body as he leant forward in his wooden chair.

'What *happened* to you, man?'

'Spell, lord. A spell was broken whilst I was attached to it.'

'Tut, tut, Kahin,' said Lyoris mockingly, wagging his finger and smiling widely. 'Spells are forbidden, aren't they? Naughty! Plus, you never were much of a mage were you?'

'No, my lord.'

'Which is why you're mine now.'

'Yes, my lord.'

'Never mind, Kahin, off you go. Stand over there by the window and see if the light does you any good.' He flapped a pale, long-fingered hand at the stained-glass window and turned back to Amir as Kahin trudged wordlessly to face the window.

'Poor Kassi. He was a mage, you know.'

'I suspected.'

'Yes, yes. Not a very good one though. Not a very good student. Always trying to push, trying to do forbidden things.' Lyoris frowned in mock-consternation. 'That's why he ended up at the monastery, just couldn't resist, and then he got found out. Out on his ear, he was. A useful talent relegated to being a monk, offering cheap tricks to people who couldn't afford the real thing.'

'You speak as though it wasn't chance.'

Lyoris leaned forward with a gleam in his eye; his foot stopped tapping.

'Oh it wasn't. Not a bit. There's no end to the things one can bring about if one knows the right combinations to use.'

'Combinations?'

'That's why he wanted the monastery to be one of the targets, of course. Erase his shameful past. He wants to be a priest, you know.'

'I noticed.'

'Only has the one robe, poor thing.'

'Noticed that too.'

Lyoris laughed aloud and clapped his hands, rocking back in his chair. He flapped one arm in Kahin's general direction.

'How could you not!' he cried between laughs. His guffawing continued, not affected in the least by the fact that Barten was staring at him in bemused silence. Eventually he calmed down enough to continue speaking.

'And now of course, he's hurt himself trying to use spells when alchemy works just as well, if not better,' Lyoris paused. 'Well, better in fact, if we're being truthful. And we must be truthful, mustn't we, my lord?' He made the sign of The Circle with his fingers and gave Barten a serious look. Just as quickly he was grinning again.

'Alchemy,' repeated Barten, thinking about the Mortuary Representative. His eyes flicked to the ring on the High Priest's finger. Lyoris stopped grinning and was suddenly still, poised, his eyes staring. An image of a spider in its lair leapt suddenly to Barten's mind.

'Ah, you understand I see,' Lyoris said softly. 'Yes alchemy, my lord. Combinations of various chemicals. Herbs, liquids. Things harvested from other things: living, dead. There is a whole world of mysterious compounds and mixtures that can have quite the most incredible effects. And…we can trust one another, can't we?'

Barten smiled thinly.

'We already covered that, Your Benevolence.'

'And so we did. I merely wanted to repeat it because I do *so* value discretion.' Lyoris's eyes were hard, his face still and pale in jarring contrast to his jovial tone.

'We have been partners in this plan to take power for some time, Your Benevolence. I think it is too late to suffer a lack of discretion.'

Lyoris watched him a moment longer, utterly motionless. Utterly expressionless. Despite being twice the man's age, twice his weight and probably twice the fighter in any school of combat, Barten felt a flush of cold fear.

'I agree,' the High Priest said softly. He flopped back into his chair, once more grinning. His feet started tapping again. He held up his ring again, speaking fast in a jittery tone. 'The ring you see, it's an antidote to something you've been breathing in since you arrived. An insurance policy to avoid any hostile interactions. Impressive, no?'

Barten did not move, watching the madman on the makeshift throne with careful eyes. 'Very,' he said.

'A useful way to climb the ladder,' Lyoris giggled. 'I am quite the student of alchemy. My former master despaired of me, however. Didn't share my vision, or my affinity with the way things mix. I can almost…see the way things work to create effects. My own personal touch of magic. Perhaps I should have been a mage, what do you think?'

'Perhaps,' Barten said carefully.

'Oh I can't tell you how good it is to talk about these things with someone who hasn't been...' he leaned forward, putting his hand against his mouth and whispering conspiratorially, 'over-exposed. Makes them all a bit dull!'

He leaned back and laughed.

'Well after my career in alchemy ended so abruptly...he threw me out. I'm over it, don't worry...I had to find my own way and after I stumbled on a way to get people to, let's say, *like* me, I was set. And here I am, High Priest of The Sacred Circle. Not bad is it?'

'Not bad at all.'

'But not enough, of course. Not nearly enough. Which is what this is all about.'

'I...yes.'

Lyoris leaned forward again, all humour gone from his eyes. He clicked his fingers at Kahin, who immediately turned and came to stand beside his master.

'When the time comes, the Senators will never choose one of their own to lead. They could never trust a rival to be Echelarch. You know this; it is why you agreed to help me in the first place. They will elect me, but you must follow my lead. Kassi has told me how your interference led to Ariene Gloriana being both free and alive...'

'I was trying to gain her guilds so we'd have the votes in the Senate. If you'd just killed her off it would have caused chaos rather than—'

Lyoris cut him off with a dismissive wave of the hand.

'I don't want to discuss it. You are to follow Kahin's lead from now on. My lead. Understand?'

Barten bristled at the tone, but he was enough of a realist to know he had no cards to play in this particular moment.

'I understand,' he said.

'Good. This has been a long plan in the making. Remember the strangely burned bodies? That was a compound of my own making, quite hideous on contact with the skin. Gloriana's poisoning too, which is why I now have a personal stake in the downfall of that mage of hers. It should have been perfect and he just appears out of nowhere and,' he waggled his fingers, '*poof!* She's better again.' Lyoris slumped back into his seat, angrily staring at his boots like a frustrated child.

'Goading him into making a large public display of mage wrongdoing is never going to work, Lyoris. Kahin already tried…'

'Oh I think he will, we've made sure he can't help himself and now we know the name of his tutor, don't we, Kahin?'

Kahin nodded.

'And anyway that isn't the whole plan, my dear Amir,' The High Priest was smiling again, eyes wide with ambition. 'You aren't seeing the big picture. The Senate is primed, thanks to you. The people are primed, thanks to Kahin. There are whispers everywhere of witchcraft. All it needs is a suitable demonstration and the city will explode. If you get on board and take Kahin's lead from now on, you'll see. The mages will bring their downfall on their own heads, and despite your bungling of the Gloriana guilds we *will* all sweep into power. She's weaker politically than ever; she won't be able to stop what's coming. You will be the greatest lord ever to hold office in this city, second only to me. And we will remake the world.'

'Remake it how?'

Lyoris smiled broadly and shook a finger at him.

'Now now, let's not build the world until we own the land beneath it. I'll forgive your meddling with the Lady Gloriana since it sounds like it was all a big misunderstanding. Fancy getting the Senate all riled up and then just letting her go.' He wagged his finger playfully and made a tutting sound.

'Now, get out.'

Lyoris sat back and waved a long-fingered hand at him. Barten hesitated, caught somewhere between indignance and relief. He wanted to make some threat, some parting remark to show he wasn't some vassal, but found he could not summon the will to do so.

With all the dignity he could muster, Lord Amir Barten turned to the door.

Chapter Twelve

Creating light was one of the simplest tasks a novice mage learned at The Barbican, and Sophine did it almost without thinking. To reach out for the energy in the world around her and cause it, with a small mental tweak, to change state and become visible was as natural as breathing. She held up a hand and directed the pale silvery glow around the tunnel she was following, smiling to herself as she took another turn, utterly confident of the correct direction. Rigel, Thaniel and Sophine had used the tunnels many times, most recently to visit the quarry. Although they didn't know where all of them went, they knew perfectly well how to reach The Barbican from the street beyond.

The tunnel was damp and stuffy, the air close and humid, smelling faintly of rotting creatures. The murmuring sound of soft, moth-like things writhing unseen in deep dark crevices kept her from pausing too long in any one place. The walls were covered in unpleasant mould and the pale roots of plants that had forced their way in from the outside. Sophine's boots splashed in the murky water that had collected on the cracked brick floor.

Up ahead, a glimmer of light began to gleam on the walls. Sophine dismissed her light and slowed her pace. The tunnel abruptly ended at a short ladder which led up into a damp cold room at the back of the novices' quarters, which was reached through a ragged hole in the wall. Long ago, someone had placed a wardrobe against the hole to stop the draught. By the time Sophine had joined Hilda's, the foetid moisture from the tunnel had eaten away at the wood of the wardrobe and left a ragged hole. She could still recall the joy of discovery that she'd felt the day she realised she could fit through that hole and enter a hidden room all of her own. It hadn't been long before the three of them had found the tunnels, and they had used them ever since.

Sophine squeezed her way into the wardrobe and carefully opened the door. She grimaced guiltily at the light snores of the young novices in the beds around her, wondering if she was doing the right thing.

Making her way through the dormitories to the corridors, she shifted the weight of the heavy bag on her shoulder. She'd spent as much time as she'd dared reading and re-reading the spell she'd seen the scarred priest use, making some adjustments to the designs and symbols he'd used to channel his complicated intentions. Her intentions were much simpler, but she was still terrified of getting it wrong. Her mind kept drifting back to the warning in the book about uncontrolled emotional powers and how mages had been known to burn in the fires of their own rage. She shuddered.

The great hall was just ahead; Sophine paused at the heavy wooden door and listened carefully for any sound. When none came, she slowly pushed the door open and slipped inside.

The great hall of Hilda's Barbican was nothing more than an audience chamber capable of seating maybe a hundred students, though it had never held even a third of that in Sophine's time. The worn wooden chairs were piled up in stacks at either side of the hall, between the purely ornamental brick pillars that stretched to the ceiling, hung with banners and pictures drawn by the students. Large windows overlooked the hall, showing only a few faint stars peering through the thick cloud of the night sky. Sophine flicked her hand and threw a ball of silvery light into the air as she crossed the familiar flagstones, pausing in the middle of the hall. At the opposite end of the room stood the wooden stage where the masters would sit whilst the rector spoke to the assembled students. She looked at it for a long moment, remembering the many times she'd sat here quietly fuming about her fate. Doors to either side of the stage stood open, the darkness beyond leading to other parts of The Barbican: the masters' offices and classrooms.

Sophine shrugged the bag off her shoulder and sat down cross legged on the floor, putting the book down beside her and flipping to the now heavily annotated page. Within a few moments she was ready, the candles arranged in an asymmetrical pattern and the chalk design on the floor looking as close as she could get to the pattern she'd finally settled upon. She traced it one last time with her eyes.

'This is insane,' she muttered, following the lines of the diagram. 'Totally insane...'

Even so, it had to be done. Her hope was that this would help her fellow mages overcome their natural inclination to ignore emotion whilst also allowing them to access it safely, but now she came to it, her resolve was wavering.

'We don't have a choice,' she said to herself, not for the first time. 'This is our only chance.' She wondered why she couldn't quite believe it, a small voice inside her whispering that she was doing this because she *wanted* to. That she'd turned the corner and become one of the dangerous mages the book warned about, a Darkling. One of the unhinged magicians that had brought about the purge and plunged the world into a dark theocracy for decades afterwards…

She ignored the voice.

Conjuring Lord Balderwin's sneering face – this time next to Misty's innocent one – was just about enough to access her rage and hate. The anger uncoiled within her like a snake from an opened basket, rising to spit its venom into the world. She directed the energy slowly, muttering her spell, turning her words into instructions that bound the motes of swirling power into specific and complex forms…

'What are you doing?' asked a voice. Sophine looked around, startled, knocking over one of the candles and losing her grip on the mental strands of the complicated weave of the spell. Her rage vanished, replaced with panic and alarm. Traces of energy flared into visible light and danced around the chalk; burrowing inside it, suffusing it…

'No, no *no!*' she cried, trying to rub at the chalk in a purely instinctive act of desperation. She sat back, staring, her mouth open. Then she looked round angrily.

Four small children were watching her, novices of no more than eight or nine. They wore pyjamas embroidered with the crest of Hilda's Barbican. She glanced at the door, which was open a crack; she hadn't seen or heard them enter.

'What are you doing in here?' she spluttered, making shooing motions with her hands. 'Go back to bed.'

'You woke us up,' said one of the kids, a bright-eyed boy with thick red hair sticking up from his head at crazy angles.

'We weren't really asleep,' said another. This one was smaller, a blond-haired girl with piercing eyes.

'Where did you come from?' the third asked, shortly followed by the red-haired boy asking what she was doing again. She hesitated, unsure how to answer.

'Are you a burglar?' asked the girl with the piercing eyes.

Sophine exhaled, not quite a laugh. She shook her head.

'No I'm not a burglar. Now go back to bed, please.' She turned her eyes to look at the symbol on the floor. Parts of it were glowing, briefly flaring with light and fading only for other parts to light up. She stared at it in mounting panic.

'We can help you,' said the third child, the youngest from the look of him. He puffed his little chest out. 'We're going to be sages.'

'Mages,' said the girl.

'Sages,' repeated the boy, '*sages*.' He frowned. The girl rolled her eyes.

Sophine ignored them, blowing out the candles and giving the chalk symbol another desperate rub. The chalk flared and burst as she touched it, the energies within protesting at the interruption of the instructions they had been given. She could feel the spiralling escalation of the spell and suddenly knew with grim certainty that she should have left it alone. The power she'd managed to pour into it was flowing in a disordered circuit now, following its own path. She stared a moment longer, horrible foreboding and guilt pulsing like ice in her veins.

She stood up and ushered the kids away from the spitting design. Little sparks and flashes were coming off the edges of the symbol where she'd broken it, and she looked away.

'What is that?' the girl asked, as Sophine gently pushed her away.

'It's nothing,' Sophine said. 'You need to come with me now, we'll go this—'

There was a crash, off in the darkness to the right of the stage. Someone was yelling, and someone else yelling back. Sophine tightened her grip on the kids and pushed them towards the door.

'Back to bed all of you, close your doors and don't open them for anyone except your masters.'

The youngest boy started to cry. Sophine felt a flash of guilt, but the yelling behind them was getting louder. She pulled the little girl towards her.

'Look after him, ok?' The girl nodded fiercely. 'Now go.'

The red-haired boy and the fierce-eyed girl shepherded the other kids away as Sophine turned and ran for the corridor beyond the stage.

By lucky chance she caught sight of a gleam of silver as the little ball of light she'd conjured flashed on a blade. She leapt back, cold focus descending as the knife buried itself in the wooden pillar by her head. She reached out a hand, her anger acting as an extension of her body as her hastily conjured force gripped the man lurking in the shadows and flung him bodily across the length of the hall. He crashed to the flagstones and lay in a crumpled heap.

Sophine was already moving, sprinting into the darkness and pulling her ball of light behind her.

Up ahead, four men were struggling with a fifth, wrestling him through a hole in the walls as he struggled and screamed. One of the men turned, and Sophine felt her hatred rise as she recognised the scarred priest. He flung something at her, something that shattered on the ground by her feet, with such speed that she barely had time to jump back. She ignored it, gathering her strength and summoning her power…but then she was sitting down. Her head was spinning. Her stomach was roiling. She saw fragments of glass by her hands, strange mist before her eyes. Her vision was failing.

Sophine looked up with an effort of will; as though through water, she saw the scarred priest snarl and duck through the hole in the wall, dragging the other man along behind him.

Just before her eyes closed and her head slumped to her chest, Sophine saw the man's face.

It was Master Thomas.

***

Somewhere far away someone was calling him. A voice he didn't recognise, using words he couldn't understand. But they were meant for him, their meaning directed at him. He rose up towards them, through the murky haze surrounding him, ascending like a drowning man kicking desperately for the surface…

Thomas opened his bleary eyes and looked around him. Through a watery fog he could make out four dark walls, a desk in the corner with a candle burning on it, and a chair before him. Someone was sitting there. A shape in the golden robe of a priest. He blinked, clearing the vision before him. His head hurt and he groaned. The light from the candle was at once too bright and also far too dim to let him see anything clearly.

'What's your name?' repeated the man in the golden robe. He had an unpleasant voice, and a less pleasant face, the flickering light throwing the ragged tear across his jaw into stark relief and shrouding his eyes in shadow.

'Ashkey. Thomas Ashkey,' he mumbled, his throat dry and scratchy. The left side of his face throbbed; it was both oddly numb and acutely painful at the same time. He supposed it was swollen.

'You are a master at The Barbican.' The man wasn't asking. Thomas nodded, then instantly regretted the motion. Hot pain lanced through his brain, like it was sloshing about in his skull. He groaned again.

'Answer me,' said the man.

'A master, yes. I tutor students.'

'Student mages.'

Thomas wasn't sure that was a question, so he simply groaned again and prodded the inside of his cheek with his tongue. It was definitely swollen, he could feel the tissue all bunched up. On instinct he tried to calm his mind, to rise into a state of serenity in order to syphon a bit of energy from the outside world into healing him. Serenity, however, wouldn't come.

'Don't bother,' said the golden-robed man with obvious relish. 'We're in Stonegate Castle.'

Thomas frowned. He knew of no reason why that should make any difference. He didn't reply.

The ugly man leaned forward on his chair, peering at him. He looked slightly nonplussed.

'The castle is the oldest in Asterheim,' he said, a little irritably, 'and a few of its oldest rooms still hold powerful wards from before the purge. This room is as close to a sanctuary from your kind as it's possible to get. Do you feel cut off? I do.'

Thomas blinked at the man and decided to try again. He calmed his mind and reached out for the energies around him; they were there, but just beyond reach. As though the stone of the walls absorbed them and kept them away from his probing mind.

'Interesting,' he said thickly, an academic part of his mind that hadn't quite grasped his predicament noted that he should come back and learn more later.

'Who…?' he began, before thinking better of it. 'Why am I here?'

'Think of yourself as a cog, Master Thomas. In a very big wheel.'

'You mean a machine?'

'No, a wheel.'

Thomas blinked.

'But isn't a cog a little round wheel…?' he asked.

'A cog is one of the teeth on the little wheels, so—'

'So it fits in a machine—'

'No! It's a cog on a wheel!'

'You said *in* a wheel though…'

'Enough!' shouted the golden-robed priest. He stood up and paced around for a moment, clenching and unclenching his fists. 'How did you ever teach anyone anything you…you pedant?'

'I've been called worse.'

'I've no doubt.'

The priest stomped back to his chair and sat down with a sigh. He peered at Thomas with a curious look.

'Tell me about Rigel.'

'Rigel? What about him?'

'Did he murder the messenger on the road to Ceresheim?'

Thomas laughed out loud, quite forgetting where he was. The laughter made his head thump harder, and he leaned forward, rapidly gasping shallow snatches of breath. It was only then that he realised his hands were tied behind his back.

'Rigel couldn't murder anyone,' he said, realising he was slurring his words but unable to do anything about it. 'He was a barely adequate student at best, a bit shy and depressed. Not the sort to take any kind of action over anything let alone murder someone far outside the walls. I don't remember him ever leaving the city for anything, not even visiting his parents. *Especially* not that, in fact.'

'The messenger was killed by forbidden sorcery.'

Thomas felt a grin flash unbidden across his face. 'Sounds unlikely.'

'It's not.'

'Well then, it can't have been Rigel.' Thomas chuckled and shook his aching head. 'Poor Rigel. Still, he ended up with a patron didn't he, lucky lad. I was worried about him.' His vision swam and he felt a wave of nausea. He sat back in his chair.

'Are you going to keep me here?' he asked, the words starting to meld into one another.

'No,' said the priest flatly.

'So I can go?'

'No.'

Thomas tried to process this, breathing heavily. His thoughts were slow and thick. 'So what happens now…?'

He could hear the smile in the other man's voice. 'Now you get *rescued.*'

***

231

One of the very few perks of being widowed was that one no longer had to share a bedroom. To have a private space all to herself which not even servants entered after dark had over the years become, to Ariene Gloriana, a source of great comfort. And never more so than now; with her revitalised body carrying not a single ache, she was free to truly enjoy her own company.

Or at least she had been until moments before.

A great storm of black lightning exploded into being, shattering the tranquillity of her bedchamber. The very air itself ripped apart with a howling shriek as the storm peeled back the unfathomable forces that held the mortal world together. Wind from nowhere blew gustily around the room, throwing her papers and books into the air and crashing them against the walls. Her candles sputtered and died in the gale and her carefully pinned hair came loose, streaming around her as though she stood on the bow of a ship during a storm. The black lightning spread, opening up a vast yawning darkness at its centre which swelled to approximately three times the size of a person before vanishing just as suddenly as it had come. The wind died. The lightning was gone.

Sophine, Rigel and Thaniel stood where it had been.

Ariene closed the book she'd been reading and just about managed to hold onto during the storm, several pages of which had been ripped out by the violence of the portal. Torn paper floated forlornly on the remnants of the ghastly wind before settling lazily to the floor with soft scrunching sounds.

'You could have just knocked,' she said, replacing the ruined book carefully on a small table by her legs. Sophine reached out towards the candles and reignited them with a motion of her hand.

Thaniel turned and threw up noisily into a plant pot.

Ariene sighed. 'Will it be *every* time, dear?'

Thaniel tried to answer, but stuck his head in the pot again and heaved. She looked away with a heavy sigh.

Rigel had gone to sit on her bed, looking shaken. He held onto the bedpost as though afraid he would fall, but at least he didn't look likely to vomit on her duvet. Sophine meanwhile looked grim, sitting at the desk in the corner of the room.

'You're getting good at those,' Ariene remarked pointedly to Sophine. The girl glanced at her.

'We were careful,' she said. 'No one saw.' Ariene chose not to reply and made a half-hearted attempt to smooth her hair down.

'Sooner or later Orswell will notice that Thaniel keeps vanishing.'

'He already did,' said Thaniel distractedly, now free of the plant pot but wandering haltingly around the room looking for a place to put it. Ariene eyed it with distaste.

'Darcy!' she shouted. Thaniel looked mortified as the girl arrived to take the pot.

Ariene smiled.

'Thank you dear, that'll be all for now.'

Darcy wrinkled her nose but departed with all the dignity she could summon. Lady Gloriana turned to Sophine.

'So, what can I do for you three? I assume this isn't a social call; it must be midnight by now.'

Sophine stood up and went to the window, staring grimly out at the starless night. 'They've taken Master Thomas,' she said quietly.

'What?' cried Rigel, half-rising from his seat before gripping the bedpost and sitting back down with a wince. 'What do you mean "taken"?'

'And who's they?' asked Thaniel.

'I think I can guess,' said Ariene dryly.

Sophine nodded. 'I was at The Barbican, I saw that scarred priest.'

'Kahin,' said Thaniel. 'His name's Kahin.'

'He and some others got to Thomas in his room, dragged him away. I couldn't stop them. I tried...'

She shook her head bitterly and stared out of the window.

Rigel managed to rise to his feet this time, and came over to her. He placed a tentative hand on her shoulder.

'You didn't...you know...' He held his fingers up and opened them slowly.

She scowled at him.

'No I didn't. I didn't do anything. He threw something at me, some kind of glass bottle. It was a drug, knocked me out.'

Ariene was on her feet, pacing.

'A drug as a weapon, that's quite specialist. Seems he's learned some new tricks.'

'Maybe not so new,' Rigel said pointedly, looking at her. 'Someone got Orswell's brother that poison.'

Ariene nodded thoughtfully and went to her closet. She rifled through Senate dresses and blouses and jackets.

'What are you doing?' Rigel asked. She turned and looked at him.

'I'm not about to go riding to the rescue of your tutor dressed in my nightgown, Rigel Wheatley.' She held up a finger as he

234

started to speak. 'And I don't want to hear anything about it being too dangerous or whatnot. I am considerably older and wiser than the three of you put together, and I will be coming.'

'It's dangerous,' he said, a tad peevishly.

'You know, if I close my eyes and concentrate,' she said, 'I can almost hear your voice bouncing around in my blood saying 'you will live'. It's most disconcerting. I have a suspicion that I will be a lot harder to kill than anyone else in this city, and that's including Overseer Skylock.'

Rigel was silent, staring at her. She turned away.

'Can you create a portal to a person, dear,' she called to Sophine over one shoulder, 'or must it be a place?'

'I'm not sure,' Sophine admitted, still looking angrily out the window. 'It's all about emotion, so I think I can just aim for him personally...'

'That won't work,' said a deep male voice from the doorway. Ariene turned, clutching a riding shirt to her chest.

Darcy poked her head around the imposing form of Lord Barten. 'Lord Barten here to see you, my lady.'

Ariene didn't look at her, merely held Barten's dark gaze. 'Yes, thank you dear,' she said. Darcy vanished.

'I think you could do with new staff, Lady Gloriana,' Barten remarked with a half-smile.

'Not at all, Amir. We can thank her for this little ice breaker. When guests arrive uninvited it's always nice to have something to chat about. Now would you mind turning your back whilst I dress?'

Barten bowed and turned around. Ariene flashed warning eyes at the three mages and nodded at them to make a retreat through the back door.

'Don't dismiss the magelings, Ariene,' said Barten, without looking round. 'They will want to hear what I have to say.'

She shrugged the shirt on and grabbed some riding trousers, noticing as she did so that the three mages had not moved.

'Young people,' she muttered, pulling the trousers on. 'Right, I'm dressed. What do you want, Amir?'

'You can't trust in magic to get to your tutor,' he said, approaching a pace or two with half-raised hands. He looked like a man unaccustomed to imploring trying to implore. It was almost comical.

'And why is that?'

'He's being held in Stonegate Castle in the eastern walls. The cell is warded somehow, I saw Kahin taunting your Master Thomas about it.'

'Why tell us this?'

'Because I want you to think before you act. Why would they hold him there unless they knew you'd try to come for him?'

Rigel stepped forward.

'So you're saying they took him to what, goad us into rescuing him? And then made it impossible for us to rescue him. That makes no sense.'

Amir bowed his head, and Ariene was old enough to recognise an adult trying hard not to condescend a touchy teenager. Barten rose a notch or two in her estimation for that.

'They took him because he was your tutor, yes. And they're holding him where you can't reach him so you will try a more…direct method. One that will see you caught or worse.'

'Why do you care?'

'Let's just say I'm afraid of what might happen if things go badly wrong.' Ariene sighed, a faint smile on her lips.

'Still holding your cards so close, Amir.'

'Forgive me, Ariene, but you would never trust me if I didn't.'

'I can't trust you when you do. I wonder how we were supposed to find out where he was being held if not for you coming to tell us.'

He gave her a sad smile.

'You'd find out soon enough, perhaps under less pleasant circumstances for your master,' he said. He turned back to Rigel.

'You're being lured into a trap, and you can either trust me or not. But Ariene knows me well enough to know that I am involved in the wider game,' he looked at Ariene.

'That wasn't in doubt,' she said, a touch bitterly.

'And that I want to win,' he added.

'Again, not in doubt.'

'Then trust that what I am doing is for my own interests, not that of that vile lunatic priest who took your tutor. Our interests are no longer aligned, as you saw from the near-catastrophe with that mob.'

Rigel looked at her, confused. She nodded.

'It's true enough. I think they shared interests once, but Amir's aims are political. This feels more personal, like that mob. Like the poison.'

Barten nodded.

'Here's what I want,' he said, crossing his arms, 'I want that man out of the castle, and I want the situation de-escalated whilst I think of a way to turn it to my advantage which, I might add, I believe to be the city's advantage at this point.'

237

'Saving all of us now, are you Amir?' said Ariene. 'I hope it's not too little too late.'

He looked at her, but did not reply. He turned for the door and paused before walking through.

'I'm still Castellan of the Battlemasons so I have authority at the Castle. I will order the guard changed in three hours,' he said without looking back. 'I'll delay the replacements for an hour. You will have that time to get in and grab your master. He will be ready to go. Don't be late.' Then he was gone, stomping away down the hallway.

On the little table near where he'd been standing was a rolled-up piece of paper.

Ariene crossed to it.

It was a map of Stonegate Castle.

Chapter Thirteen

'Give me your hand!' screamed Sophine, leaning down as far as she could for Thaniel, who clung white-faced to the single piece of rope that was still attached to the battlements, the only remainder of the ladder they'd brought. Rigel, shivering on the walkway along the night-shrouded battlements, looked behind them. The shouts of men and the clang of steel from beyond the guardhouse fifty metres away were getting louder.

Only hours earlier, the plan had seemed so simple. Rigel had been tasked with slowing time so they could get close to the castle walls without being spotted. Thaniel would then use his gift for levitation to hook their rope-ladder (courtesy of Ariene's stable-boy, who did not explain why he had it; Ariene had given him a look and promised to discuss it later) over the battlements and they'd be up on the walls in – literally – no time. No one was willing to chance Thaniel actually levitating them over the walls, and even Thaniel had looked relieved about that. Once inside, they'd use the window of time Barten had given them to sneak to the room where Master Thomas was being held, then Sophine would blast a way through the storeroom wall on the northern side. That wall was thin and weak, and led straight on to the street. They'd be away long before anyone noticed the hole.

All very simple.

It had not worked out that way.

'Grab him!' Rigel cried, unnecessarily. Sophine heaved on the rope instead, shouting at Rigel to help her. He ran over and pulled on the rope, managing to drag Thaniel a few more inches up the wall. He held on as Sophine leaned back over and this time Thaniel made a grab for her wrist. She yelped and cursed; Rigel let go of the rope and grabbed her instead. He heaved. Thaniel appeared over the battlements and crashed heavily to the stone floor, whimpering in terror and relief. Sophine slapped at him for a mad moment, cursing him for a fool.

The door to the guardroom burst open, and the pathway atop the walls was suddenly filled with running soldiers. Thaniel was on his feet, eyes wide, shaking in primal horror.

Rigel tried to usher them the other way towards the other guard tower standing silent and apparently abandoned about thirty metres to their right. Getting inside was their only hope.

The guards were almost on them when Thaniel shrieked and flung his arm in their direction as he turned to run. Five guards were lifted bodily off their feet and thrown backwards in the air. One of them screamed hideously as he fell over the walls and vanished over the other side. The three friends slammed through the guardhouse door and Sophine gestured to the wall with a cry of anguish, which crumbled and collapsed to seal the entrance. She stood panting, half-formed words spilling from her lips in a torrent of incomprehensible nonsense. Thaniel sat hugging his knees, shaking his head. His hands were red and raw, badly burned from clinging desperately to a rope. Rigel backed slowly away from the collapsed stone, covering his mouth with his shirt against the rising cloud of dust and rubble.

'I'm so sorry,' he said again. 'I'm so, so sorry.'

Sophine looked over at him, and something about his appearance seemed to shake her from the horror she was reliving. She came over and gave him a hug. When she pulled back, she looked into his eyes.

'You tried, Rigel. You really tried. It was…bad luck.'

Rigel grimaced. Luck wasn't the problem; it was his innate inability to do anything useful at any time. They had been halfway up the rope-ladder when Rigel had felt his control slipping. Time had started to force its way back in. The noises of the castle at night, the distant laugh of soldiers, the clang of weapons and the murmur of low voices had started to drift back through the silence, getting louder and clearer with every second. The more he concentrated on holding it, the faster it seemed to slip, until they were simply climbing up a castle wall at night in full view of any guard who happened to be looking. And then, one had.

Whether Lord Barten had made good on his promise to delay the guard rotation, they did not know, but the soldiers posted outside the gates were still on duty. It was one of those dutiful souls who had casually glanced up at the sky, and noticed three people scaling the castle.

He'd shouted, he'd run, he'd banged on the doors to raise an alarm. His companion, armed with a bow, had taken a shot at them and missed. Sophine and Rigel had both made it over the wall when he fired a second, which hit the ladder and caused it to unravel, leaving Thaniel clinging for dear life to a single rope.

'Open up in there!' someone shouted from the other side of the collapsed wall.

Thaniel snorted and looked up, a silly smile on his face. 'Someone doesn't know how walls work,' he said.

Rigel laughed, in spite of himself. Sophine crossed to the other side of the guard tower, a space only a few metres wide but with a trapdoor leading down to the ground and a door out to the other wall.

'Do we head down or along?' she asked, looking at Rigel.

He unfolded the map and ran his finger along the line that designated the wall they'd scaled.

'The room where Master Thomas is being held is on the other side, so maybe we should head along the walls and drop down at the next tower.'

Thaniel stood up and shook his head.

'They'll see us, Rige. I think our first aim should be to disappear.'

He nodded.

'What do you suggest?'

They both stared at him.

'Really? Time dilation again? Because that worked so well last time.'

'There's less pressure this time, though,' said Thaniel, wincing as he prodded his blistered hands.

'Just hold it long enough for us to cross the courtyard,' added Sophine, looking out of the narrow guard room window. The courtyard was an approximate square of open ground in the centre of the castle walls, presumably where parades and formations were held. There was no way to cross it without being seen unless Rigel could pull off his party trick.

'*Just*,' repeated Rigel bitterly.

'It's either that or we have to get around the walls, or work our way room by room on the lower floors,' she said, shaking her head. 'If we're going to get Thomas, I think that's our only play.'

'Ugh, fine,' Rigel said, throwing his hands up. 'But I think–'

'That we're doomed and the whole plan is a disaster and everything everywhere is bleak and awful?'

'I...maybe?'

'Hold onto that, that's your energy reserve. I have my rage, Thaniel has his frankly sickening crush on Eric and you have your boundless reserves of existential despair thanks to your coldblooded parents.'

'I hate you.'

'No, hate's mine. You stick with despair.'

Rigel managed a thin smile and turned away. It was the easiest thing in the world to let go of his false positivity and slide back into the bleakness he usually carried around with him. He felt it return, a faint image of his half-remembered mother's face floating somewhere in the bleakness. He lingered on the sadness for a moment, letting it stew, then willing it to become something more. Heat kindled within his stomach; vibrations echoed up through his feet. He gasped as the warm tingling rose up and filled him, like a coiled spring needing release...

'Open the door,' he said. Thaniel heaved the trapdoor up and flung it aside. Rigel released the feeling, channelling it through his mind and focusing on time. The trapdoor slowed to a stop, inches from the floor.

'Go!' shouted Rigel, an irrational fear that he'd frozen his friends as well as the guards, threatening to break his concentration. But then Sophine started moving and relief took the place of fear. Rigel grunted with effort of keeping both from ruining the flow of power. Thaniel followed Sophine, dropping down to the ladder under the trapdoor and climbing swiftly down. Rigel was right behind him, feeling like he was carrying a goldfish bowl and trying not to spill it as he held on with most of his focus to the despair that usually came so naturally to him. The blurred image of a woman's face tugged at the corners of his mind.

They made their way through the lower level of the guard tower and out into the open air. The courtyard stretched before them, hundreds of metres of open ground overlooked on all sides by the tall castle walls. Up on those walls were armoured figures, frozen in the act of running to the site of the ruined tower door, brandishing spears and swords. Everything was illuminated by the braziers burning every few metres around the outside of the courtyard. The moonless sky would give some cover in the centre, but not much; the place was almost obscenely well lit.

Rigel felt fear jostling for control, knocking up against his energy reserves and threatening to extinguish them.

'Run,' he said. 'Run, run, run!'

They ran. The distant voices and clangs of armoured figures remained muted, as though very far away or heard through murky water. Rigel wanted so badly to close his eyes, to pause and stoke the energy reserves, but panic was creeping in and the voices were getting louder.

Not far now...ten metres...five...

Rigel slammed the door closed behind him and collapsed against it, nearly sobbing with relief as the world returned to normal.

'Well done, Rige,' said Thaniel, puffing a little but otherwise not looking like he'd been in any way exercised by the run. Sophine, however, looked terrible. She paced, gasping for breath and holding her side.

'I feel sick,' she said between snatched breaths. 'You never said we had to run *that* far.'

Rigel couldn't speak for a moment, the combination of exhaustion and relief robbing him of all faculties but breathing and shaking.

'Where are we?' asked Thaniel, plucking the map from Rigel's belt and peering at it.

'Here,' said Sophine, pointing. 'This is some kind of storeroom,' she glanced around at the empty shelves and cases that filled the otherwise bare room. 'Guess they need some supplies.'

'Leads to the corridor that runs the length of the wall,' said Thaniel, 'and the room Barten marked is…here.'

'A straight run from here,' Sophine said with a grin. 'All the guards will be on the other side of the castle looking for us so we have an advantage. We get in, grab Master Thomas and make our way back along this corridor,' she pointed at the map, 'and out.'

'Easy,' smiled Rigel, getting shakily to his feet. 'Let's go.'

Sophine was right, there was not a soul left in this service corridor. Every guard seemed to have been drawn away; a quick glance out of the window had shown them a line of men forming across the courtyard, facing back the way they'd come. They apparently hoped to seal off the exits and pen them in.

They made their way along the empty hall, their footsteps echoing off the heavy, bare stone. The door marked by Barten was up ahead. Thaniel looked at them questioningly, and they nodded. He closed his eyes and thrust a hand out.

The door slammed off its hinges and crashed loudly to the floor, tearing a huge chunk of stone out of the wall with it as the very large metal locking mechanism attached to it ripped its way free. Someone inside yelped.

'What kind of imbeciles are you?' boomed a second voice. They hurried inside and found Amir Barten standing in the corner of an unadorned room lit by a number of candles, many of which had now blown out thanks to Thaniel's dramatic entrance. Master Thomas sat on a chair by a desk, drinking something from a tankard and looking thoroughly confused.

The left side of his face was swollen and red, and he blinked at them with one good eye.

'You could have just knocked, morons,' hissed Barten, moving to the door and peering out.

'They're all on the other side,' said Sophine. 'Our plan didn't work out very well.'

'I ordered the guard changed like I said, why didn't you just—'

'We tried! The guards at the gate still saw us.'

'You came over the wall in full view of the gate guards?'

'Well, we...'

'There are two other walls accessible from inside the city,' Barten said through gritted teeth. 'Did you not think those might be a better bet?'

'Do you think,' said Master Thomas thickly, slurring his words horribly, 'that we could be moving along? I assume this is a rescue.'

246

'It is,' said Thaniel.

'Well then. Let's get going shall we?'

'Oh I don't think so,' drawled another familiar voice. Barten turned, horror dawning on his face, but not fast enough. Kahin's blade thrust up under his armour, expertly placed between the plates to strike him in the lower back. Barten froze, his mouth open in a silent scream. Kahin leaned in close.

'Lyoris thanks you for your service,' he hissed. 'I'll make sure you—'

Whatever he was planning to make sure of was drowned in Thaniel's scream of anger.

The young mage threw his hand out, blasting Kahin off his feet to slam heavily against the stone wall of the little room. The scarred priest landed in a crumpled heap and did not rise. Barten fell to his knees, his mouth opening and closing in wide-eyed disbelief.

'Go,' he managed to gasp, looking at the four of them. 'Get out...'

He toppled onto his side, blood spreading in an expanding pool beneath him.

Rigel knelt on wobbly legs, desperately summoning the power to see the silver strands as he had twice before. Thaniel grabbed at him.

'We have to go, Rige! We can't stay!'

'Rigel come on!' shouted Sophine.

For once, it was actually working to his command. The network began to resolve itself, tiny lines and glistening webs tracing their way over the man's prone form. But slowly, too slowly.

'Rigel!' shouted Thaniel again. 'Guards are coming!'

They had no time. Rigel exhaled hard in frustration.

'Live!' he barked, focusing what little energy he had left on the gaping hole he could just about make out in Barten's body-web. It glimmered once, twice, in response, tiny strands of silver tentatively reaching across the breakage. A seal began to form, but not enough.

'Dammit!' he shouted, letting himself be pulled up by his arm and stumbling after Thaniel.

Behind them, the shouts of men and heavy footsteps confirmed what Thaniel had seen. They didn't have much time. They turned a corner and caught sight of Sophine, a few metres down the next corridor, waving frantically.

'Stop!' someone shouted, something heavy and metallic clattering to the floor behind them; a thrown spear, Rigel assumed. He almost couldn't run anymore.

Thaniel threw him through the next doorway, turning immediately to slam it closed and heaving a wooden storage cabinet across it to bar entry. Sophine was standing at the far wall, hands raised, eyes closed.

'We took a wrong turn,' slurred Master Thomas dreamily. 'We're trapped.' He didn't sound at all concerned.

'Nope,' said Rigel, indicating Sophine. Thomas blinked at him and turned, just as the lower block of bricks in the wall simply imploded. The upper level buckled, bracing against the sudden loss of its lower support, a long crack snaking its way up the wall and spreading like forking lightning through the castle.

'Better go,' said Sophine. 'That doesn't look stable.'

Master Thomas said nothing, but his good eye locked on Rigel's. He held his gaze for a moment and then ducked under the wall. Rigel turned to wave Thaniel through. His friend shook his head, a look of concentration on his face.

248

'No, after you, Rige. I'm sort of keeping the wall up, here.'

Rigel raised his eyebrows and ducked under, followed by Sophine. Thaniel came through just after, and with a sigh of relief, turned to the wall and made a curious gesture with his hands. The wall shuddered and appeared to almost flex, flowing organically back together as the dust from the implosion and bits of rubble rose to take their places again. Within moments the hole was gone, repaired completely.

Thaniel turned with a grin. 'How's that?' he asked.

'Impressive,' said Rigel, and meant it. 'Really impressive.'

'Erm, excuse me,' said Sophine mock-seriously, 'did you not see me dissolve the wall?'

'Well yes. That was impressive too.'

'*Thank* you.'

Master Thomas turned away, limping slowly towards the city under the lightening sky.

***

Ariene had no need of a cane any longer, but she'd been reliant on it for so long that it almost made her feel vulnerable to leave it behind. Her knuckles still cracked as she kneaded her hands on the enamel pommel, but now the sensation was satisfying rather than painful.

She looked around at the other Senators in the white tiers around her, wondering who knew why they'd been called to this emergency session by the Speaker. The messenger had told her it was about Lord Barten; he appeared to have been attacked, but the hapless boy hadn't known how badly. For that reason, she'd worn a respectful black dress in place of the usual blue, something elegant with lace sleeves, and her hair was pinned up behind her head. Other Senators and lords of the greater houses whispered and gestured; none of them appeared to be any better prepared than she was.

That, at least, was something.

Ariene turned her head, stretching out an ache in her neck which she blamed squarely on young Sophine's late-night visit. She'd had no word from the three youngsters since, and was almost certain that this session was about their attempt to rescue their tutor. She closed her eyes and focused her thoughts; she would need all her skill to deflect what she suspected was coming, if the rescue had gone awry.

A hushed murmur swept through the assembled Senators and the worthies of the city up in their red seats, and Ariene turned to see what had caused the commotion.

A man had entered the Senate Building, slowly walking down the steps towards the white tiers. He wore an elaborate golden cloak, chased with silver filigree and embroidered with signs of the Ouroboros, with its hood drawn up to conceal his face. As the silence fell, the man reached up and lowered the hood to reveal a stern young face framed in black hair held back by a thin gold circlet. He removed the cloak in one smooth motion and handed it smartly to a man behind him, revealing the simple golden robes of a Sacred Circle priest beneath. Then he continued his procession to the white tiers, taking his seat silently without acknowledging anyone else. The man with the cloak went to sit quietly in the red tiers.

Ariene narrowed her eyes. The unexpected arrival of the one Senator who never attended, the one she had never even seen in the flesh, was an unwelcome development. His Benevolence, the High Priest of The Sacred Circle, Lyoris Mountebank himself had come.

And based on his theatrical first impressions, Ariene disliked him immensely. As she stared, the surprisingly young man seemed to sense her scrutiny. He turned his head slightly to look at her, and his eyes gleamed with a sudden mirth, as though showing through a tightly controlled mask of composure. His foot began to tap rapidly against the floor. Then the moment was gone, and his face returned to an expression of studied piety.

A terrible sinking feeling settled into Ariene's stomach. This could not end well.

The Speaker stood up from his chair and made his way to the dais, dressed in a sombre dark jerkin and shirt. He held his hands up for quiet until the murmuring died away, before clasping them in front of his chest and wringing them nervously.

'My lords, Senators and representatives of Asterheim,' he began, his voice shaky and his eyes darting around the room, 'we have been called for an emergency session to give you grave news. Last night, there was an assault on the great castle of the Stonegate from within the city. Three soldiers were killed and one of the towers brought to ruin. I'm told the repairs will take months but…worst of all, Lord Amir Barten, head of House Barten and patron of many significant guilds was himself attacked and lies on the point of death in the Priory of the Sisters of Ourob. I will now defer to the Abess…' he trailed off, gesturing to the elderly lady who sat amongst the assembled Senators in the red and white habit of a Sacred Sister.

251

She stood brusquely, scowling at the Speaker with her chin jutting up pugnaciously.

'I would caution the Speaker against unnecessarily theatrical descriptions of the patient's condition,' she spat. Ariene concealed a smile; the two of them had never been friends, but she admired the other woman's venom.

'Lord Barten is not at the *point of death*,' she continued. 'It is quite within our considerable expertise to care for him. However,' she paused, looking down as though to collect her thoughts, 'he has suffered a grievous injury. A blade, most likely a short knife or dagger, has penetrated his lower back and caused considerable damage. It is a miracle that his kidney and liver were not punctured, indeed judging from the angle of the wound I am astounded that they were not. Had they been, he would almost certainly have died by now. In the event, our mages confirm he is healing, and that they can do no more for him; he must survive on his own and shows every sign that he will.'

'Can he return to his duties, sister?' someone called. She whipped around with a snarl and fixed the man with a glare.

'Of course not, you fool. He will be incapacitated for some time, as I said it is quite remarkable that he is healing at all. Ordinarily such injuries are beyond even mages to fix.'

'That is unacceptable,' called a youthful Senator who practically sprang to his feet. 'House Barten's interests are vital to the continued running of this city. They control the Battlemasons, let's not forget. We cannot have Asterheim's military leaderless during a time of crisis.'

Ariene got to her feet and turned to the Senator. She did not recognise him, which marked him out as a lesser son of a lesser house, much like the Speaker. His clothes were well tailored and his eyes eager with the gleam of ambition.

'The Battlemasons have a clear command hierarchy, Senator,' she said in ringing tones designed to hammer their way into every ear in the hall. 'The simple incapacity of Lord Barten will make no difference to their day-to-day activities.'

'A power vacuum, my lady, is a dangerous thing in such a guild.'

She recognised him at last. Lord Cromantis's youngest. He'd served in the Battlemasons for a time, if she remembered correctly, which explained his excitement about possibly leading them. She intended to shut him down.

'And what do you think they'll do, Senator? Rampage through the streets? Nonsense. They will remain in their castles and man the walls, and wait as they have these last decades.'

The young man stared murderously at her.

'They need leadership,' he insisted. Ariene moved in for the kill.

'And who will lead them? You?' she asked, leading him to it. 'What experience do you have of such things?'

He smiled triumphantly. 'I have been a soldier! I commanded—'

Ariene cut him off with a devastating smile.

'We have had soldiers commanding soldiers before, Senator. It rarely ends well.'

'I'm not a soldier now…' the upstart said, flustered.

Ariene turned from him dismissively, taking in the whole chamber with her final words.

'If leadership is needed, let it be a politician with the experience and will to countermand the worst impulses of the soldiery.'

There was a murmur of assent that left the poor young Senator entirely deflated. He slumped, defeated, into his chair.

Lord Cromantis himself rose next, perhaps seeking to deflect attention from his son's clumsy attempt to wrest authority for himself. A large-bellied man dressed in simple dark clothes, save for a heavy silver chain studded with jewels, Cromantis had never wanted much beyond his few guild holdings which included the vital Grooms and Farriers. Ariene had always thought he looked a bit like a horse himself.

'May I ask the Speaker, what befell the Castle?'

The Speaker hurried back to the dais and haltingly deferred to the Commander of Stonegate castle. Not being a Senator or an officer of sufficient rank, he was seated in the red tiers amongst the priests and guild officers. He stood now, and made his way to the dais at the Speaker's invitation to stand, in full plate and mail armour, holding his helmet in the crook of one arm. His scabbard, at least, was empty in deference to the august assembly.

'The Castle was attacked, sirs, by three individuals.'

'Preposterous!' someone called. 'Three? Three people caused such damage and nearly managed to assassinate Lord Barten?'

The Commander was not moved. 'Three,' he repeated. 'They came over the wall, and were spotted by my men. They were unarmed, as far as we could tell.' This he added in a grave and poignant tone. The Senators drew a collective breath as many of them realised what this meant.

'Mages,' someone whispered, and the whisper took hold. Soon the word was hissing around the room.

'Indeed,' said the officer stiffly. 'We believe they were mages.'

Ariene rose to her feet on a tide of adrenaline and shouted above the rising clamour. 'Commander!' she called. 'Was it dark last night?'

254

The rising tide of voices receded a little as Senators turned to look quizzically at her.

The officer frowned.

'It was, my lady.'

'As I recall, the moon wasn't even out.'

'No, my lady.'

'And when your men spotted them in this dark, lightless night, where were they?'

The man hesitated.

'Some way up the wall, my lady.'

'I've been to Stonegate, sir,' Ariene said, almost conversationally now that the noise had died down. 'It is a very impressive castle.'

'Thank you, lady.'

'With very high walls.'

'I…Yes, Lady.'

'So then. How sure are you that your men saw the correct number of people high up on the walls on this dark night, and how sure are they that they saw what weapons they were or were not carrying?'

The officer paused for a moment, then stared at her straight in the eye.

'Lady, I was on the wall last night,' he growled. 'I saw them with my own eyes. Three of them, unarmed. Not ten metres away. And then, five of my men were thrown into the air. One fell to his death over the wall. Two more smashed their heads against the stone. And then a tower that has stood for centuries collapsed with no fire or steel set against it. It was magic. I would stake my life on it.'

Ariene stood for a moment in the sudden tense silence, her mind blazing, searching for a way to bring this back under control. Slowly, she lowered her eyes and sank back into her chair.

'Oh you fools,' she whispered to herself. 'You stupid, stupid fools.'

The room was in commotion, shouts and accusations flying back and forth over the heads of the raging Senators. Words like 'charter' and 'traitors' were being thrown around, and Ariene felt a sudden instinctive need to leave. She was patron of The Guild of Mages, and had been accused once already. She glanced around, catching sight of the Speaker talking rapidly with the High Priest; that made her mind up. It was time to go.

As she began to rise, the Speaker ran to the dais and screamed for calm. She glanced at him, wondering if she could escape before he restored order, but the Senators seemed eager to heed him and the noise quickly abated. Ariene sank back into her seat, her heart pounding with trepidation. She cracked her knuckles as she gripped her cane.

'My lords,' said the Speaker, somewhat breathlessly, 'a proposal has been put to me which I am sure will see this matter resolved. By the grace of The Circle, His Benevolence Lyoris Mountebank has attended the Senate today and has agreed to accept the burden of censuring The Guild of Mages for the actions of its unlicensed students at The Barbican and their lawless tutors.'

'Unacceptable!' shouted Ariene, quite without thinking. She was on her feet before she knew it. 'I am the patron of that guild, so I should be—'

'You have been attainted once already for failure to keep the mages in line!' thundered Lord Cromantis, who seemed to not have forgiven her for making a fool of his son. 'I would urge you to stay out of this, Lady Gloriana!'

Ariene stared at him, desperation bleeding into despair. She dropped her gaze, slumping back into her chair and closing her eyes.

Lyoris slowly stood from his seat and made his stately way to the dais, glancing at her as he went. His eyes gleamed again with peculiar mirth, and she was certain no one else noticed the way his fingers tapped erratically against his sides. He stepped past the frantic Speaker, who scurried back to his seat, and turned to face the audience.

'My lords!' he called out in a peculiarly nasal voice. He held his hands up, long pale fingers forming the shape of The Circle. 'As you know I do not often take my seat. I leave the running of the mortal realm to you, the worthy nobles and officers of our city. My concerns are *spiritual*.' He put his hand over his heart and smiled. To Ariene, it was a sardonic, patronising grin, but no one else seemed to notice.

'If you trust me to take this action for you, then I will gladly accept the burden.' He smiled sadly, sighing deeply. 'Alas however, my priests are no match for unrestrained mages.'

'Take the Battlemasons!' someone shouted.

Lord Cromantis rose again. 'Lord Barten's guilds need leadership, Your Benevolence. Being not a political creature, you are perhaps best placed to hold them.'

Murmurs of ascent swept through the room as Senators who would not trust one another with a single new guild saw in the suggestion a way to keep their own power. Mountebank was an outsider, a nobody; perfect for the job. Ariene itched to say something against it, but she knew they would shout her down at best.

'And with the Battlemasons,' mused Lyoris, theatrically putting his finger to his chin, 'I could confront the mages of The Barbican and exact the will of the Senate…'

'Please, Your Benevolence,' called a young woman dripping in jewels and furs, 'it is the will of The Circle!'

'Ah,' said Lyoris with a broad smile, 'but in this place, it is the will of the Senate that matters.'

The Speaker jumped up as if on cue.

'All in favour of granting His Benevolence stewardship of the House Barten guilds?' The roar left no room for doubt.

'And all in favour of requesting His Benevolence to confront The Barbican?'

Ariene was halfway to the door before the approving shouts began to abate.

Chapter Fourteen

The walls enclosing the heavy form of The Barbican stood some ten or so metres high, wrought in rough stone and wide enough for two people abreast. It had been expanded over the years, with a parapet wall at about chest height with crenelations at regular intervals. Hilda and those who had come after her had gone as far as they dared to make the mages' safe haven defendable without provoking the more suspicious members of the Senate, but even now it was hardly an impregnable fortress.

As soon as word had reached her that the Senate was debating the disaster at Stonegate Castle, Sophine had known what was coming. Someone would be coming for them, and she had no intention of being taken. She, Rigel and Thaniel had fled to Hilda's and decided to hide there. What they hadn't expected was the sight that greeted them as the night fell and the rain began to pelt the stones.

The three of them were on the walls, leaning over to watch the sunset, when Rigel straightened and tugged at their sleeves.

'Look…' he said softly.

From every street that led away into the city there came a stream of people. Some holding torches, others hefting tools. Amongst them, in loose collections of fifty men here or a hundred there, marched Battlemasons in steel plate and mail armour, carrying spears and bows and swords. The crowd was strangely silent, not a single voice raised in song or challenge.

Only the heavy trudging of armoured feet and the splatter of rain could be heard.

'Their faces…' Thaniel pointed at the crowd. 'They look like they're sleepwalking.'

And so they did. Sophine gazed at the enormous mob, professional soldiers and common citizens walking in unhurried silence. Their faces were slack, their eyes locked on the night-shrouded walls of Hilda's Barbican with a dull malice.

'Kahin,' she breathed. There, leading the slow-moving army, was the scarred priest himself. His face alone was not slack, his eyes gleamed with anticipation; his smile broad and vicious.

'I thought he was dead,' said Thaniel. Sophine shook her head.

Below them, in the courtyard leading from the main gates in the wall to The Barbican's main entrance, five or six people were running. Sophine knew them all. The other tutors, masters, and the rector in her red robes and long white hair. They bustled and exchanged frantic whispers as they hurried to meet the crowd outside. Behind them came a loose group of students, kids as young as seven or eight clinging to the legs of the older ones.

The rector and her assistants opened the gate and half-ran to the crowd, identifying Kahin as the leader from his position standing before the gate.

'What is the meaning of this?' demanded the rector, an elderly woman but no less commanding for it. Most people would have shrunk back from her controlled fury; Kahin merely snarled.

'You are to dismiss your witches, old woman,' he said, 'by order of His Benevolence Lyoris Mountebank of The Sacred Circle.'

The rector looked over the assembled army and fixed Kahin with a glare that would have cowed a saner man.

'Mountebank has no authority here,' she declared. 'I answer only to—'

The rector jerked back with a yelp, and Sophine let out a short sharp cry that wasn't quite a scream. The rector stumbled away, hands pressed to her stomach, and Kahin looked up at them and smiled hideously. His blade glinted red in the dying sunlight. The other masters stood, dumbfounded for a moment before turning to run, but they were too late.

Arrows thudded into their backs and pierced their chests, dropping them instantly. The crowd began to surge forward.

Thaniel, to his credit, flung out an arm and swung the heavy gates closed with a motion of his outstretched hand.

'Seal it!' he cried, shouting down to the students standing in frozen horror amidst the wailing of the youngsters. Several of them ran to the huge wheel with its heavy chain and began to lower the portcullis with ponderous turns of the great spokes.

The archers standing with Kahin drew their arrows and notched them. The priest was pointing at their spot on the wall.

'Rigel!' screamed Sophine, backing up and throwing her arms over her face as the archers let fly.

The arrows slowed, but didn't stop. They'd already crossed half the short distance. Sophine saw the lethal points flying at her, twenty sharp promises of death not quite held back by the unreliable power of Rigel's hastily conjured spell.

'Sophine!' Rigel called beside her, 'I can't hold them!'

The children down below were muted now, but their horrified cries still rang in her ears. The murder of the rector and the masters still played before her eyes. And the grin, the evil smile on the scarred face of the man who had haunted her and her friends for so long...

She had no need of Balderwin now. Rage exploded within her, righteous and powerful, a searing heat that demanded to be let free. She recalled the book's warning at the dangers of uncontrolled emotion and tried to pull her mind back from the brink. Her skin felt hot, unbearably hot, it hissed as the rain hit it...

She screamed and flung the power away from her, throwing it as raw energy into the darkening night and channelling all her denial, all her hate, all her rage into forcing it to spread itself over The Barbican like a vast, unwieldy blanket of burning heat.

To Rigel, Sophine's spell looked like a glimmering bubble of glistening gold. It seemed to shimmer into existence for a moment, between them and the approaching arrows and stretching the entire length of the wall, before fading from sight just as quickly.

Sophine stood for a moment with arms outstretched before falling to the ground, her skin steaming. Rigel lost his grip on his power and screamed as the arrows flew straight at them. Their deadly points slammed heavily into Sophine's invisible barrier and clattered away. He blinked at the space where they'd been for a moment, almost giddy with relief. Above him, a few inches over his head, rain pelted against an invisible screen with a dull, muted sound.

And below, the surging crowd reached the barrier and struck at it with maddened cries.

Rigel knelt by Sophine and brushed the hair back from her face, she opened her eyes and looked at him.

'We're alive,' she said. He nodded.

'How long will the barrier hold?' he asked.

'I don't know,' she said, climbing to her feet, 'it's not something I've read up on.'

'Thaniel!' Rigel cried, leaning over the wall to the courtyard, where Thaniel was trying to point people to the great hall. 'There's a shield, get up here!'

Thaniel looked up and nodded, turning to face the hysterical crowd of novices and apprentices. He started directing the older mages to the wall.

'Rigel,' said Sophine softly, looking out over the parapet. The army was a howling mass of bodies, thrashing and screaming beyond the invisible barrier. Kahin was gone. 'They'll break through,' she said dispassionately.

He nodded.

'We need to get everyone out.'

'You take the kids,' she said, watching the four or five older apprentices heading bravely to the walls, concentrating as they levitated chunks of rock and bits of wood. 'I need to warn the older mages.'

'Warn them about what?'

'I...tried to cast a spell here. The spell Kahin used. They could be in danger if they don't know.'

Rigel said nothing, merely looked at her for long moments. Eventually he nodded. 'They're in danger anyway. At least this way they have a chance.'

Her shoulders sagged, a rush of relief replacing a guilt she hadn't realised she'd been feeling.

'I'll meet you back here when the others are safe.'

There was a crash, and the gate shook. Sophine winced and put a hand to her head.

Someone below was trying to smash a large hammer through the gates, and that last blow had pierced her barrier to hit the wood. The next blow was deflected, and the man grunted in animal rage.

'We don't have long,' she said, as the man smacked his hammer against her barrier again. He was joined by another assailant, and another. Arrows continued to clatter uselessly against the shimmering veil, but not all were deflected. Sophine danced back as one zipped past her head, a reaction that would certainly not have saved her had the arrow been on target.

Rigel hurried away, bounding down the steps to the courtyard. Thaniel ran up to him, his hair in disarray.

'I'm taking the kids into the tunnels,' Rigel shouted. Thaniel nodded and pointed at the great hall.

'I sent some of the apprentices to gather everyone not on the walls in there,' he said.

Rigel nodded and clapped him on the shoulder. He turned to run.

'Need help?' called Thaniel. Rigel turned and pointed to the gate.

'Sophine thinks the barrier can't hold. When it's down, you need to hold the gates; she'll be weak.'

Thaniel nodded and ran off. Rigel made his way to the great hall.

***

Five tutors and maybe thirty or so students of various ages milled fearfully around the great hall. Rigel came to a halt and tried to count them, nodding at the three or four apprentices from the year below his own, who he vaguely knew. What he would have given to have the other three classmates from his own year-group, he thought ruefully. They'd been good mages, but they were gone. They'd all had their patronage in hand before him, so they'd gone at the last Patronage Day to start their careers. He wondered if they'd be alright...

'Is this everyone?' he asked. Madam Raftopolis, an older lady in a green dress with long dark hair, nodded. Three smaller kids were huddled around her skirts, and she looked at him bleakly.

'We checked the dorms, this is everyone,' she said. Her voice was admirably firm, though she must have been terrified. Her specialism was crops; she could gently persuade plants to grow many times their natural speed and use far less water to do it. It filled Rigel with anger to think of such a gentle soul sheltering here whilst a baying mob tried to smash its way towards her. He shoved the thought aside and made a quick assessment. They were too far from the dormitories now; it was too risky to herd everyone across the courtyard with the chance of Sophine's shield failing at any moment.

'Come with me,' he said, heading towards the corridor that led to the masters' offices.

265

The passage that led to the quarry was that way, hidden behind a partially collapsed wall in another forgotten corner of the crumbling building. It led through the city walls straight to the quarry; from there they could decide what to do.

They hadn't gone more than a few metres when a familiar sound echoed through the corridor behind them, just out of sight around the corner. It was the rasping, tearing sound of the portals Sophine used, but Sophine was on the walls…

'Go, go!' he yelled, pushing and shoving the refugees ahead of him and heading back.

'Where do we go?' Madam Raftopolis cried, frantically grabbing the youngest children and dragging them along as they screamed.

'Wait by Master Thomas's office,' he called, turning to run back.

The ripping, thunderous sound stopped abruptly and Kahin stepped into view, grinning his vile grin. Flickers of dark lightning snaked around his filthy robe.

'His Benevolence Lyoris Mountebank wishes to thank you,' the scarred priest said, waving his bloodied knife at Rigel. 'Without you none of this could have happened.'

Rigel backed up a step, his mind purely focused on buying time. Behind him, the tutors and children disappeared.

'He could have just asked,' he replied.

The priest inclined his head, still smiling. The blade danced from one hand to the other.

'After tonight there will be no need of you however, or your friends.'

'We'll leave,' Rigel said. 'We'll just go…'

The priest shook his head, taking another step towards him. Rigel stepped back again.

'I wish I could believe that,' Kahin said with mock-sincerity. 'Unfortunately, I can't take that chance.'

He flipped the knife up and caught it by its blade.

'You happen to be both the thorn in my master's side and the key to his ascension. Poetic, isn't it? But your song ends here; what comes next is too delicate to allow for your meddling in it.'

Rigel had started to reply when the priest sprang like a coiled snake, his arm flipping out with lightning speed. The knife somehow buried itself in the wall by his head, jutting out at an impossible angle considering it had been thrown directly at his face. Rigel jumped back, woefully too late, as Kahin straightened and looked puzzled. Then the priest flew forwards as something heavy smashed into his back, throwing him three metres to land in a heap against the carpeted ground.

Thaniel stood where the priest had been moments before. 'No time tricks, Rige?'

Rigel blinked at his friend, at the knife, at the priest lying once more crumpled on the floor.

'I didn't have time…' he said weakly.

'There's an irony in there somewhere,' said Thaniel, obviously very pleased with himself. 'Should we…kill him?'

Rigel shook his head vehemently. Thaniel looked relieved. 'Ok good. Let's tie him up then.'

***

The shield was failing, spots of rain pattering to the heavy stone around Sophine. She could feel it almost like a dull ache in her mind, slowly easing as the power she'd unleashed faded. There were eight or nine mages, most her age or younger and only a couple of masters, standing on the walls with her, throwing rocks and lifting the besieging ladders back from the walls using simple levitation. It was nowhere near enough; the crowd was hundreds strong at least, led by Battlemasons in full armour. The young mages shouted and yelled, some of them crying in their fear and anger as they tried anything they could to make a difference. She glanced at them, one hand to her forehead.

'I can't hold it,' she called. 'I'm going to drop it just to the gates, get ready…'

They nodded, some of the older mages starting to usher the younger teenagers towards the stairs.

Sophine concentrated, reaching out for the thinning threads of the shield and collapsing them down to cover the gates. The relief was immense and she sagged slightly, holding herself against the parapet while her strength returned. An arrow clanged against the stone and she flinched back; running for the steps as the crowd realised the shield was gone and started hurling projectiles with renewed vigour.

There was a scream from one of the tutors, flailing and cursing with an arrow through her shoulder. The youngster next to her bellowed in rage and gestured with his hands, as though to lift something else and throw it over the side. He shrieked as a brilliant flash of lightning instead arced from his outstretched fingers to explode amongst the figures below, followed by another and another as the teenager screamed in uncontrolled fury and terror. His eyes were wide, transfixed on his hands, his expression one of utter horror as he unleashed torrents of unchecked energy channelled straight from his abused nerves.

'Stop!' Sophine shouted, trying to run to the boy but ducking back as arrows flicked and flew overhead. 'Stop! You have to stop!'

Her broken spell was doing its terrible work well. The boy was joined by another, shrieking in rage and hurling fire in burning balls into the ranks of silent besiegers. Energies long forbidden and long suppressed, unlocked by her foolhardy decision to release them, reached out for the untrained minds of the emotionally compromised teenagers. Three of them, four; arcs of crackling purple energy ripped through ranks of soldiers, evaporating them where they stood. Armour clattered, empty, to the ground. The mages screamed, a terrible sound at once pleading and horrified, unable to stem the flow of the terrible powers that Sophine's spell had unlocked.

Sophine dragged herself closer against the sudden gale, shrieking at them to stop and wincing against the glare of brilliant light and flashes of impossible colours that hurt her mind to look at. The crash of thunder and screams of the tormented mages flooded her senses. Her guilt and fear robbed her of any power she might have had to stop it.

Howling wind slammed into clusters of torch-bearing citizens, hurling them up and over the heads of their fellows as unrestrained emotion took hold and channelled raw destructive power through hapless students.

The boy with fire pouring in a terrifying wave from his hands was struck through the chest by an arrow. His scream became one of agony and he whirled around, flames flowing like liquid over the battlements around him, before he was suddenly consumed in swirling flames and fell from the wall to land in a burning mass against the portcullis. Sorcerous fire continued to flicker and dance, reaching hungrily for the wood of the gates through the iron bars. Within seconds they were ablaze. The screams of a master caught in the flames as the boy had spun around pierced the air before dying away. The fires consuming his burning husk were quickly extinguished by the pelting rain, but he was already dead.

The first boy was still channelling bright white lightning through his outstretched arms as Sophine ran to him, his mouth open in a terrible scream. Arcs of lightning flickered and sparked off his teeth, lighting his skull from within. Just as Sophine reached him, his hair began to smoke; she slammed into him bodily and knocked him down to the stone floor. The lightning flickered and vanished, but as Sophine tried to check his unconscious form she hissed and jerked back. His skin was fiercely hot, steaming as the rain touched it. The other two apprentices, one conjuring the terrible wind and the one glowing with a deadly purple energy, were up ahead, still screaming in the clutches of their respective emotions. Sophine felt a horrified sickness as she shouted at them to stop; they weren't more than twelve years old.

Sophine tried to settle her mind, still crouched by the body of the lightning-mage, and reached out to touch their raging spirits. They sensed her probing and looked around, not seeming to see her at first but then somehow focusing, using her mind as a lifeline to calm the terrible floods of energy pouring through them. They stepped away from the parapet, staring in horror at their hands. The dread powers they had conjured sputtered and died away, the ghastly purple light vanishing with an almost audible hiss.

270

The master with the arrow in her shoulder joined her, grabbing at the unconscious boy's clothes and hauling him away from the edge wall. Sophine gestured at the two youngsters.

'We have to get them down,' she cried. 'Help me get them to the tunnels!'

'What tunnels?' the master shouted back over the rising thrum of the rain.

'I'll show you, come on!'

They dragged the unconscious boy down the steps and were halfway across the courtyard when Sophine collapsed. A spasm of pain ripped through her head and she knew with grim certainty that the shield was broken.

'Run!' she shouted, unable to rise as the ripples of the broken spell reverberated through her body. 'Storeroom, behind Master Thomas's office. Pile of rubble…There's a passage…'

The master nodded and heaved the boy onto her shoulder with surprising strength.

She and the two traumatised students turned and vanished into the great hall just as the wooden gates exploded; the burning mage's body had finally released the last of the energy that had consumed it. The force detonated the great doors and tore the portcullis clear away, sending it flying across the courtyard to clatter finally to a stop on the flagstones.

There was a pause as the crowd outside regarded the hole in the defences. And then with a hideous keening wail, Kahin's makeshift army erupted into a bloodthirsty horde.

Waving torches, pikes, swords, hammers, hundreds of maddened individuals ran for the gates screaming incoherently and baying for blood.

Sophine saw them coming, and found she could not move.

***

Rigel turned back once he was sure the tutors and kids were sure of the way, re-joining Thaniel in the corridor that led from the Great Hall to the courtyard.

'Ok they're away,' he panted. 'We should—'

'Thaniel!' cried an unfamiliar voice. Thaniel turned, a look of sick horror creeping over his face.

'Eric?' he said in disbelief as a young man with dark hair came running towards them. 'What are you doing here?'

'I came to find you,' said the newcomer. 'I was in the dorms when someone came to bring the mages to the hall and then everything went crazy so I went—'

'I'm so sorry,' interrupted Thaniel, pulling Eric into a fierce hug. Tears were forming at the corners of his eyes. 'I'm so sorry. I told you I came here last time I vanished, didn't I? Oh Circle, I'm so sorry…'

'What's happening?' Eric asked, sniffing against Thaniel's chest.

'He has to get out, Than,' Rigel said. 'We don't have time…'

'I know,' said Thaniel, straightening up and gripping Eric by the shoulders. He started to speak, but Rigel had a sudden thought and interrupted.

'Eric,' he said, 'if you want to help us, there's something you can do.'

Thaniel looked at him suspiciously, his hands tightening on Eric's shaking shoulders.

Outside, the roar of the crowd and the crash of heavy things against stone and wood suddenly became much louder. The shield had failed. Rigel felt a flutter of terror and pushed it down.

'You need to get word to Lord Barten at the Priory,' he said. 'He and Lady Gloriana need to get to the Senate.'

'The Senate?' Thaniel almost laughed. 'Rigel what are you—?'

'Just hear me out,' Rigel insisted.

The key to my master's ascension, sneered the memory of Kahin inside his mind.

'This is all deliberate,' he said. 'The attack, it's all designed to do something in the Senate. Someone is making a grab for power. Lord Barten isn't behind it, so he and Ariene need to be warned if word hasn't reached them, and I'm guessing whoever is behind all this won't want them there when they make their move.'

Someone outside was screaming, a horrible howl echoing up the corridors. Brief glimpses of white-blue light lit up the walls by the Great Hall's open doors, as though a lightning storm raged outside.

Eric was nodding, fear warring with determination on his face. He looked at Thaniel. 'I can do that,' he said.

'We have to get to Sophine,' Thaniel said. 'She can get him there.'

Rigel was about to reply when a master with an arrow through her shoulder came running into the hall, hefting an unconscious boy and followed by two students, both of whom were wide-eyed and sobbing. He recognised the unconscious boy as Alakis, the twelve-year-old from the undercroft, the one who had been levitating stones in a distant time that couldn't possibly have been just a week ago.

'Are you the last?' asked Rigel, ushering them along. The master nodded, her face set and grim.

'Except the girl,' she said tightly.

'Head to Master Thomas's office,' Rigel said. 'There's a tunnel—'

'I know,' the master replied, hurrying away with the two students. Rigel watched them go and turned back, just as something enormous exploded outside, shaking the building. Thaniel, Eric and Rigel all ran outside, and paused in sudden terror at the sight.

Sophine knelt alone in the rain, her shoulders slumped, her hair lank. The Barbican's great gates lay in ruins not far from her, the portcullis warped and twisted a few feet away, prongs of ruined steel pointing jaggedly up at the dark sky. Hundreds of screaming men and women were pouring through the destroyed gateway, jumping over fallen stone and waving their weapons in mindless savagery.

'Sophine!' Rigel shrieked, but she didn't turn. The first marauding lunatic, a heavy man in steel armour hefting a hammer as large as himself, was feet from Sophine, spittle on his beard and his pupils like pin-pricks in the white orbs of his eyes. He swung the hammer, and Rigel screamed, throwing out his hand desperately and trying to freeze time, but the power would not come.

Sophine jerked backwards, her body flopping like a marionette being pulled by strings. She flew like a ragdoll across the courtyard and into Thaniel's arms. He staggered and exhaled sharply, almost dropping her, but then turned smartly.

'Come on!' he yelled, shaking Rigel from his terror induced stupor. They ran back inside the Great Hall and Thaniel almost tossed Sophine at him. Rigel fumbled the catch and collapsed holding her, just managing to keep her head from banging against the floor. Thaniel made a sweeping gesture with his arm, grunting with effort as though swinging something heavy. The roof of the hall cracked and some of it collapsed, falling heavily to the ground and blocking the passage they'd entered by. A great cloud of dust exploded upward, obscuring the view of shattered stone and piles of rubble. Silence fell, broken only by the groan and snap of protesting stone as the rest of the structure began to move and crack under the sudden loss of support.

'We have to go,' said Rigel gently, helping Sophine to her feet. She looked around in bleary-eyed confusion, her gaze unfocused and her lips moving in silent commentary.

Thaniel was still, staring with his back to them at the wall.

Rigel looked around, and realised what Thaniel was thinking. 'Thaniel,' he said softly. 'We have to go…'

His friend didn't answer, just continued to stare at the wall.

'He was out there,' he said eventually, his voice a ghostly whisper. 'He was out there when the roof came down.'

Rigel shook his head, though Thaniel couldn't see it. 'He wasn't. I didn't see him run in.'

'I left him,' Thaniel choked, his shoulders spasming. 'Out there. With *them*.'

'There was nothing you could do,' Rigel said, sharing a look with Sophine. 'We all had to run, and I didn't see…'

'I saw,' Sophine said. Her voice was strong, confident. Thaniel turned around.

'I saw him running,' she said, avoiding Rigel's eyes, 'but he wasn't running this way. He headed for the walls.' She smiled. 'Smart, really.'

Thaniel was staring at her with a heartbreakingly hopeful expression. 'Smart?' he asked.

'The crowds were coming here. To the hall, or to the dorms. Or the studios. Heading for anywhere that mages might be. They weren't going to the walls. He'll slip by them easily enough.'

'If they catch him…'

'They won't,' added Rigel. 'He's a clever guy.'

Thaniel digested this for a moment, before taking a shuddering breath and pushing his filthy hair back away from his face.

'Yeah. He'll be ok,' he said with a shaky smile. 'Let's go.'

Chapter Fifteen

An orange haze lingered over the darkness across the river, the light of flame on rising smoke. A distant roar carried with it the clang of steel and the heavy crack of burning stone.

Something terrible had happened, and Ariene had a pretty good idea of what.

She shivered, pulling her threadbare shawl tighter across her shoulders. There had been no word from the young mages she had almost come to think of as her children, not since the botched rescue. Had they gone to the Barbican? Were they caught up in the madness there?

Ariene kept her eyes on the light, as though she might hear them or see them and know they were safe. If she turned from the open window, if she stopped worrying, her worst fears could yet be realised. She felt something warm and wet moving slowly down her cheek, but refused to wipe it away, tightening her grip on the shawl instead.

Behind her, Darcy opened the door and came bustling through into the darkness of the unlit room.

'My lady,' she called uncertainly, repeating it again when she caught sight of Ariene's unmoving form silhouetted against the glowing sky.

'What is it, dear?' Ariene had to force life into the words, her throat uncharacteristically choked.

'Lord Barten is here, my lady. He's waiting downstairs.' Ariene turned at that.

'Barten is here?' Anger, her reliable old companion, rose to banish the fear gnawing at her bones. 'This was all for him,' she said bitterly, gesturing at the burning night, 'but he's well enough to come here now?'

Darcy was unmoved by her outburst, as ever. She nodded and made ushering gestures at her.

'He's very ill, my lady, but he says it's urgent...'

Ariene scowled but allowed herself to be flapped towards the door, muttering about Darcy's lack of ability to tell a man 'no' and how it would come back to bite her one day. She kept it up all the way down the stairs but the muttering died on her lips when she entered the reception room.

Barten half-lay on the couch, looking very pale. His shirt was half unbuttoned and his boots unfastened; he looked like someone had tried ineffectively to dress him and then given it up as a bad job before throwing him into a carriage. His skin gleamed with clammy sweat.

'Amir,' she whispered, realising she'd never seen him looking so dishevelled and vulnerable. Her heart began to beat faster and a terrible chill crept into her bones as she realised what that might mean.

'Lady Gloriana,' he managed, giving her a weak smile. A young man appeared through the door behind her, holding a cup of something which Barten took and drank greedily. The young man was

278

dark haired, handsome, and had a haunted look to him that looked out of place on such a pleasant face.

'Who are you?' she asked, conscious that she was deliberately focusing on the less distressing question first. The young man bowed smoothly.

'Eric, Lady Gloriana. I'm an apprentice to Lord Orswell.' She stared at him for a moment before it came to her.

'Thaniel's Eric?'

The youngster looked at his feet, but not quite fast enough to cover a smile. She ignored it.

'What happened?' she asked bluntly. The smile vanished.

'We got separated, my lady. At Hilda's. He told me to get to Lord Barten and tell him what was happening. I don't quite understand how, but the…people…attacking the Barbican just ignored me.'

'Sorcery,' put in Barten with a growl. 'They'd been bewitched, I'd wager. Unless Lyoris has found a way to refine his toxins even further.'

She glanced at Amir, filing that little piece of information away for later. She returned her attention to Eric.

'How bad was it?'

'Bad, my lady. Several mages were killed, and lots of soldiers too.'

'My soldiers,' spat Barten, before wincing and holding his side.

'They were tearing the place apart,' added Eric. 'Some of them were hammering at the walls as I ran away. Others setting fires. It was terrible.'

'And Thaniel?'

'He sealed himself and the others in the great hall. They were evacuating mages through there so I imagine they all got out. The crowd weren't thinking, they were just...berserk. So I doubt any of them figured out where the mages went.'

Ariene crossed the room and sank into a soft armchair. Relief swelled up inside her and she basked in it for a moment, allowing herself the pleasure of knowing her newly adopted children and their friends were probably alright. Terrible sadness followed in its wake at the thought of those who had died, and the suspicion of what might be coming next...

'Why come here, Amir?'

Barten shifted his weight and swung his legs off the couch to bring him to a seated position. He patted his side.

'I should be dead, Ariene. Your mage did what he could at Stonegate and he's the only reason I'm alive. But I know the plan was for me to be killed. Kahin did it.'

She sucked in a breath and sat bolt upright. 'I should have known.'

Amir smiled mirthlessly.

'I guess we aren't allies anymore. I was used. Probably seemed poetic to him to blame my death on your mages.'

'Then I'm glad you're alive.' He shook his head.

'Didn't matter in the end. The attack was enough. Look what Lyoris managed to do with it.'

'He took your guilds and attacked The Barbican,' Ariene said, following the thought through. 'But why?'

Amir looked at her for a moment, his expression grim. Then she knew.

'The murders. The tavern. My censure. All this talk of witch-craft and now Lyoris is the darling of the Senate...'

He nodded.

'And now the good people of the city have been attacked by forbidden magic.' Ariene glanced at Eric. The boy nodded.

'Some of the mages did things they didn't mean to. Throwing fire and lightning from the walls...'

She closed her eyes and sank back into the chair. She could see it all unfolding. A second Purge.

'The Senate has been called for an emergency meeting,' Amir said darkly. 'I take it you didn't receive a summons.'

Ariene exhaled, not quite a laugh. She shook her head.

'Me neither,' he said, nodding at Eric. 'If I hadn't been told by this fellow what had happened at the Barbican, I wouldn't have suspected. But I did, and my spies confirm it. They'll be starting soon.'

'I don't think I'd want to be there, Amir. Frightened fools screaming about what they don't understand.'

He regarded her for a moment and sighed, rising to his feet with a pained expression. 'It's you who doesn't understand, Ariene.'

She looked at him sharply.

'Lyoris has done this for one reason alone.'

'To start a religious purge in the name of his precious Circle?' He shook his head.

'Lyoris isn't religious. Not at all. His aspirations are earthly, I assure you.' Something she'd said to Rigel came back to her in a flash of sudden clarity.

Neither, that one is a puppeteer... 'Earthly? You mean...'

He nodded.

'He will use this to appoint himself Echelarch.'

'You can't be serious!'

'It's what he's been working towards this whole time. And enough Senators are thoroughly his to make it happen. The rest see him as an apolitical nothing at worst. At best, a hero in a time of crisis. They don't know how dangerous he is.'

Ariene was pacing. She hadn't even realised that she'd risen from her chair. She felt sick. She felt angry. She could sense the world shifting around her, as though she stood on rapidly thinning ice beneath which lurked unseen shark-like creatures with black hearts and no souls, their dark eyes gleaming and razor-edged teeth bared. Without even thinking she stepped up to Barten and slapped him hard across the face. It stung her hand, but she barely felt it. Barten, to his credit, flinched but said nothing, avoiding her eyes.

She stared at him, her stinging hand throbbing in time with her rapid breaths.

'You've destroyed it all, Amir,' she said, her voice barely above a whisper. 'Our world is coming apart and it's all your fault.'

He looked back at her sharply, some of his old fire lighting his eyes.

'If you'd done as I asked and planned for your succession, I could have secured the votes Mountebank needed without this violence…' he trailed off, the words dying as though even he couldn't bring himself to defend what he'd done.

She raised an unimpressed eyebrow.

He stepped away and sighed. 'It seems so very foolish now. I just thought…what harm in having a deluded priest think he's going to be a king for a while? With his backing I'd have gained your guilds and those of some others, and when it came time to raise the issue of restoring the Echelarchy…well. I'd just change my mind and what could he do? I'd be the most powerful Senator in Asterheim by then and he'd still be nothing but leader of a band of fanatics. But I was deceived. I couldn't have known what he really was or what he was planning.'

Again, a hint that there was something even darker to the High Priest that Amir had yet to divulge. She took a shuddering breath and decided to leave it for the time being. She pulled the shawl from her shoulders and tossed it aside.

'Well,' she said, 'now we do. Darcy!'

She hadn't realised the poor girl had been standing awkwardly in the corner the whole time until she jumped at the sudden shout. Ariene managed to summon a weak smile for her.

'Get my Senate dress, would you dear?'

'But you said it was a trip hazard—'

'Don't remind an old woman of her foibles, dear. It isn't polite.'

Darcy rolled her eyes and bustled away. Eric was left hovering alone in the corner.

Ariene clicked a finger at him.

'Help me, would you Eric?' The young man hurried forward and she took his arm, calling back over her shoulder to Amir.

'Let's go, my lord, and do what we can to clean up your mess.'

***

The boy with the scolded hands was named Alakis. He had told Sophine only after a lot of crooning words and gentle hugs. The apprentice had said he was thirteen, but he was almost certainly younger. He had followed the older mages to the wall because his older brother had been amongst them. The brother had not survived.

Alakis was the one who had thrown the lightning from his hands, and the raw, red flesh around his fingers and palms suggested he had been very close to being consumed by the energies he'd channelled. Sophine found she couldn't let him go, needing to hold him and soothe him with a fierce determination she knew on some level was more about guilt than compassion, but no less real for that.

The other mages who had escaped the sacking of Hilda's Barbican were each dealing with their ordeal in their own way. The four remaining masters sat in a group talking in low voices on chunks of rock, with the exception of Madam Raftopolis, who stood apart staring at the moon. Master Thomas was there, his swollen face keeping him from saying much. From time to time he looked up, glancing at Sophine and looking for Rigel and Thaniel, as though keeping tabs on them. His expression was maddeningly neutral.

At the last count, there had been a total of twenty-four novices and apprentices. The youngest were around eight years old, the oldest no more than fourteen. They milled around in small groups, and Sophine assumed they were naturally gravitating towards their own classmates. The two or three others who had given in to their terrible powers seemed to have coped better than Alakis, one of the girls insisting she didn't remember hurling deadly purple energies at the besieging Battlemasons. The hollow look to her eyes suggested otherwise, but Sophine hadn't pressed her.

The quarry was cold and barren, the moonlight gleaming on the mirrored surface of the lake. Behind them, not far beyond the walls, the crackle of burning wood and the occasional crunch of falling stone could still be heard as Hilda's Barbican slowly died. No one had pursued them, and from the sounds of it, the army sent against them had simply disbanded.

She looked up, tightening her grip on the sobbing Alakis as a group of four boys from the older class stepped towards her.

'What did you do?' asked one, bluntly. His expression was hard to read in the moonlight but his tone was bitter.

'Excuse me?' she replied.

'You did something,' another one said. 'You knew something about what was happening on the walls. No one else knew.' He turned and pointed at the group of masters, who had risen to their feet and were watching them. 'They didn't know.'

'So how did you know?' the first one asked. Silence fell across the abandoned quarry as even the hushed whispers of the traumatised kids fell away. Heads turned to look at her.

Sophine stood, gently steadying Alakis as she did so. She was cold, the breeze pushing at her thin jacket. She tugged at it, trying to pull it closer.

'I knew because...' she began, casting her glance across the assembled refugees. She could almost hear her heart slamming itself against her ribs, as though desperate to be free of her guilty body.

Rigel stepped up behind the apprentices.

'She knew because she saw the spell being cast,' he said loudly. The apprentices turned, some showing a flicker of fear on their young faces that irritated her; to her mind, she was by far the more dangerous of the two of them.

'Sophine saw a vision of the priest, Kahin, the one who led that army to the Barbican. She saw him casting a spell to unhinge students. He was a mage.'

Master Thomas had stepped closer.

'I knew it,' he said, slurring a little as though his brain still hadn't worked out his tongue was a few times too big. 'He knew too much about mages to be a priest.'

Rigel nodded, avoiding Sophine's eyes as he continued his not-quite-a-lie tale.

'The spell acts like an intoxicant. Lowers your inhibitions and connects you with your emotions like pre-purge mages. But we aren't trained for it, and that's what happens.' He spread his hands helplessly.

'You could have warned us,' said the ringleader of the apprentices, a stocky boy with messy brown hair. His tone was still bitter, but the accusation had gone from it. He now looked miserable rather than angry.

Rigel nodded.

'We tried,' he said. 'I wish we'd had more time.'

'We have even less now,' added Madam Raftopolis, pointing out over the quarry and down to the valley below. In the distance, torches were moving, spreading out from a large chunk of black that had to be Easterly Castle. Some miles away down the road leading from the East Gate of Asterheim, Easterly was the bastion that guarded the approach from the east of Astregoth, the city of Terminheim and the mountainous region that provided most of that city's industry, known as the Stone Belt.

'If they're mobilising now, they were given orders before the attack,' said Master Thomas. 'We can't flee that way.'

'You can guarantee that Westerley and the Halifort in the south both had the same orders,' added a master that Sophine hadn't ever properly met, a wizened woman with long tumbling locks of blonde hair and a rake-thin physique. She had been the one with the arrow through her shoulder, before someone had healed the wound for her. 'There will be no exit that way either.'

Some of the children began to cry, and Thaniel started to gather them up and talk to them in soothing tones. Sophine looked away; she felt like crying herself.

Rigel had gone to sit on his own, perched on a large chunk of weathered quarry stone.

He spoke up now, his voice low and hard.

'We couldn't leave anyway,' he said. They looked at him, some quizzically. Sophine sat down on the ground; she knew what was coming. She picked up a stone and flicked it at the lake.

'Kahin said this was all part of a bigger plan,' said Rigel, gazing out at the torches of the patrols moving onto the roads and passes leading from Asterheim. 'A plan that starts by targeting Hilda's. It's a purge.'

There were some gasps, as those few either too young or too foolish to have grasped the danger finally understood.

'The city's full of mages. We can't just leave,' Rigel continued. 'We have to get back in, help organise the other mages and get out together.'

'How?' asked one of the older kids. Rigel shook his head.

'I don't know. But we have allies. We have safe places. I say we go back in—' Three or four people started shouting objections, but Sophine leapt to her feet.

'Quiet! This is the only way and you know it.'

They glared at her, and Rigel continued.

'We go back in. We hide in a safe house,' he met Sophine's eyes and she nodded. It would be Balderwin's. Where else?

'We come up with a plan, and spread word to the other mages of the city. We all go together.'

'There are hundreds of other mages,' someone protested. 'How can hundreds of people leave a city without attracting attention?'

Rigel hesitated. He glanced at Sophine but she was stumped too. There was simply no way…

'A ship,' said a weak voice. Sophine looked around. Alakis was staring up at her, his hands tucked into his armpits, but his eyes were alert and clear. 'A ship has lots of people.'

Rigel let out a short bark of a laugh and actually clapped his hands together. 'A ship!' he cried. 'The Great Harbour! You're a genius, kid.'

He looked back at the huddled group of displaced mages and grinned broadly. 'We'll all get out by ship. It's not like we have to go far, just away from here.'

Sophine's heart lifted to see them smile again, as they dared to believe they might be alright after all.

She hoped her face didn't show how little she believed it herself.

***

If anything, Elmira Valette's ponytail was even more savage this time. Ariene's own hair almost ached at the sight, but Valette seemed not to notice. She paced the dais in front of the Senators, her swirling green dress bathed in the moonlight streaming through the high windows and the burning torches hastily put out for the emergency session. Behind her, sitting innocently under its shimmering purple veil, sat the object to which Ariene's eyes kept returning. The object that this entire charade was being played out to win: the Echelarch's long-forgotten throne.

'I have a witness to present to you, my lords,' said Valette, turning abruptly and allowing her long gown to flap dramatically around her, 'an honest woman who saw the horrors inflicted on the good soldiers of the Battlemasons by the vile witches of the Guild of Mages!'

There were some incoherent shouts of protest, but they were drowned by the murmuring of the fearful Senators. A plump woman with red cheeks was led to the dais by the Speaker, her dirty overalls suggesting she was not only a cook of some kind but one that had abruptly been dragged to the Senate in the middle of preparing something messy. She looked fearfully around, her hands clasped before her round belly. Ariene's heart went out to her.

'Tell us, mistress Godwin,' Valette said, not even looking at the witness. 'Tell us what you saw!' With that she strode down the dais and sat in her white tiered seat. Ariene wondered at that. She nudged Barten.

'Isn't she one of yours?' she asked. Amir nodded slowly.

'Once, she was,' he said between clenched teeth. 'It seems she's found herself a new employer.'

'She's sitting in the white tiers,' Ariene said.

'A generous new employer.'

'Generous enough to be able to buy her Senatorial rank?'

Barten looked at her. 'I don't know if buying had anything to do with it. Lyoris has methods of getting what he wants.'

Ariene fell silent at that. It was the third time Amir had suggested something malign about Lyoris besides his ambition. She frowned and turned back to the dais, where Valette was making gestures at the witness, urging her to speak.

'I were…I was…' began the woman hesitantly, pushing locks of lank, sweaty hair away from her face. 'I saw the crowd come past my house. Me and my husband were going to bed see, it was an early start because the bread comes at dawn and we—'

'Please try to stay focused, Ms Godwin,' said Valette. The woman swallowed and shuffled her feet.

'The crowd come past, 'undreds of them. All with swords and hammers and whatnot.'

'What did the mages do?' probed Valette. 'What did you see that frightened you?'

'Fire,' said the woman, her eyes wide saucers. 'There was fire coming down off the wall. I sees it and says to my husband, I says, where's that coming from? And he says they have treb-sheys in castles and vats of boiling oil, for defence like, but I says to him,' she paused and took a deep breath, 'I says to him no, this ain't a castle ye old fool. Because it ain't, is it?'

When no one replied to this apparently non-rhetorical question, the witness pressed on.

'I says it ain't a castle and they ain't no treb-sheys. And then I sees it.'

'What did you see?' asked Valette.

'A boy. On the wall. He was making the fire with his hands.'

Lord Aresbrook, Ariene's old ally, rose to his feet with the aid of two men on either side of him. He coughed aloud to gain the Speaker's attention, but when the Speaker waved at him to sit down he simply began to speak, his voice loud and strident despite his infirmity.

'May I ask the lady if the night is dark tonight?'

'It is,' said the woman, nodding effusively in agreement.

'And the fire was coming over the wall, to flare up amongst the crowd I presume?'

'Oh yes sir,' she said, still nodding.

'Then how was it you could see this boy, madam? In the dark, we do not see beyond the brightest point of light. Or at least that has been my experience. Perhaps you have exceptional eyesight?'

The woman shook her head vigorously. 'Oh no sir,' she said. 'I sees him because the one next to him were flinging lightning from his hands. Like a tropical storm it was, forks of lightning flying from his hands, bright as day. I could see everything.'

Aresbrook sank back to his seat, his expression one of shock.

Valette was on her feet, ushering the woman away and replacing her with a soldier who stood just as awkwardly in his plate armour. He was an older man, with a wiry grey beard and pinched eyes in a wrinkled face.

'This is Captain Berenswood of the Battlemasons,' Valette said.

The man began to speak, directing his words at the young woman as though he'd said them many times before.

'I don't remember anything of the—'

She shushed him and paced to the other side of the dais, whipping her ponytail around as she turned back to face him.

'How many of your soldiers died last night, sir?'

The man blinked at her for a moment and peered up at the ceiling.

'Fifty-three confirmed dead, my lady,' he said, 'as of this morning. About twice that injured. Some are missing. We found only their armour.'

The gasps of the Senators reverberated around the chamber. Even Ariene took a breath at that terrible statement.

Valette waved the man away.

'There is no doubt,' she yelled, as the captain trudged heavily up the stairs in his armour and the Senators fell into a frightened mumbling, 'no doubt that the secretive mages of the Barbican have breached the Charter to which their guild is bound. They have turned on the citizens of this city, turned away from honour, turned on you! Who can stop them if the Battlemasons cannot?'

'Traitors!' yelled someone in the crowd. Others began to angrily shout. Beside Ariene, Barten rose painfully to his feet and bellowed as loudly as he could over the rising noise. He leaned heavily on the seat in front.

'My lords!' he shouted with a pained expression, as the clamour began to fade a little. 'The Battlemasons were taken from me! I am their rightful Lord and patron. I am confident that in my hands they would have—'

'In your hands the Battlemasons failed to stop a mob attacking the Lady Gloriana!' Viscount Roach yelled at him. Ariene winced; such an unhelpful comment from such a well-meaning source.

'You've done nothing whilst the mages plotted against us!' shouted another. 'What use are you, Barten?'

Ariene could see the looks on the faces of the Senators and know them for what they were. These were rivals with long histories of secret grudges finally sensing the shift in the balance of power. The House of Barten was weak, and they would not see it return to greatness.

'You fools,' she whispered to herself, 'you poor fools.'

Valette had whipped herself into a frenzy, shouting and yelling and baiting the crowd. She finally held her hands out for attention and, when she had it, launched into what Ariene was sure was a well-rehearsed speech, somehow managing to make herself heard over the feverish swell of frightened voices.

'Senators of Asterheim! Too long have we been at odds! We sit in this house and vote and scheme, who amongst us has not been so busy vying for power against our rivals that we turned a blind eye to the realities around us?'

Senators were watching her intently now, the general noise starting to recede.

'We have brought this calamity on ourselves through our paralysis and failure of leadership! Dominated by those with more guilds,' she turned to look pointedly at Barten and Ariene, 'who seek nothing but their own advancement at the expense of those for whom they presume to speak.'

Ariene began to rise to her feet, but the cluster of Senators in the rows behind her shouted at her to sit. She turned to stare at the suddenly hostile faces, realising that the same expressions were repeated all around her. Summoning all the dignity she could, sank back to her seat. She glanced at Amir, who offered her a sad smile.

'And now we are undone!' screamed Valette. 'A brave volunteer steps forward to bring the light of reason and truth to the suspicions we have and what happens?' She gestured to where Lyoris Mountebank sat, head bowed, as though with the shame of failure.

'The mages reveal their evil intent at last!' she cried. 'But what can be done with a handful of borrowed guilds, held by a man whose commitment is to us all and not to his personal power? Your Benevolence!'

Lyoris raised his head on cue and looked, nobly, at Valette. A tear ran down his cheek.

'We failed you!' Valette cried. 'We asked you to protect us without a shield! We demanded justice but gave you no sword!'

She paused for effect, and the Senate paused with her.

'We gave you responsibility without power! And I say we must do so now! The shroud must be lifted!'

There were roars of approval and shouts of protest, as chaos descended. Senators fell into private arguments with one another, clusters of allies screamed imprecations at others. Mountebank rose slowly to his feet and walked, at a measured and stately pace, to the dais just as he had the last time.

He reached the dais and rested one hand on the covered arm of the shrouded throne, his head bowed as though in contemplation. Hush fell across the chamber as the full symbolic meaning of the act hit home with the assembled Senators. None had dared touch the throne in centuries.

Lyoris lifted his head to the great windows above, letting the moonlight fall on his face and gleam from his golden robes.

'I was called as a priest,' he said at last, his words echoing in the now-silent chamber. 'My destiny was to safeguard the souls of our people.'

Ariene could see his body shaking with the urge to tap his feet. His fingers danced a tiny rhythm on the chair.

Valette stepped forward, demure and delicate in her green shimmering dress, her hair golden as his robes in the pale light.

'Will you safeguard our city, too, Your Benevolence?' she asked him softly. Ariene scowled at the contrivance; the pleading beauty and the resistant, brooding hero. The Senate was intoxicated by it; none moved. No one spoke.

Lyoris held Valette's gaze for a moment, then closing his eyes gave a shallow, reluctant nod.

The chamber erupted in a chorus of approval; rivalries and protests apparently forgotten, swallowed by the drama so artfully constructed for them.

Ariene helped Amir limp his way out, ignored by the jubilant Senators.

'Long live the Echelarch!' someone shouted. The chilling chant was taken up and followed the two unlikely allies as they left a Senate radically changed from the one they'd entered.

Chapter Sixteen

With a ghastly tearing sound that scratched at the mind and sucked at the soul, reality peeled back once more. A rip formed in the air just above the ground, a swelling black void forcing its way into existence while a wind conjured from nothing began to blow. Arcing forks of black lightning snaked out to snatch at the abused folds of the world and a hideous howl like the echoing cry of some unearthly being reverberated in the grand hallway of Lord Balderwin's estate. The dark orb, inky and lightless, stretched and quivered for a moment against the pressure of reality pushing back against it, and then was gone. The hallway, cleared of all loose objects by this point, returned to normal.

Sophine turned to check the three passengers had made the trip. All three stood quivering and pale, one of them with the tell-tale clammy skin she'd come to recognise. She pointed at the heavy urn a few feet away, the one sturdy enough not to fall over in the brief wind and which had been placed there for just this purpose. The master lurched at it and buried his head inside, making retching noises. Sophine looked at Madam Raftopolis and the wizened blonde master she didn't know.

'You alright?' she asked.

They nodded. Madam Raftopolis managed a smile. 'You have to teach me that one,' she said shakily. 'Where did you learn it?'

'I didn't,' Sophine replied with a wry smile. 'But I can show you.'

'You made it!' said Master Thomas through his swollen face, arriving via a doorway by the foot of the great stairs leading from the hall to the upper floors. 'We're all back here in the kitchen.' He sounded almost giddy with relief, and glanced at Sophine.

'Is that the last?'

She nodded, running a hand through her long dark hair. 'That's all,' she sighed. 'Seven trips. I'm exhausted.'

'Rest, dear,' said Ariene, coming down the stairs in her blue Senate dress, followed by Rigel. 'We all need to leave anyway.'

Master Thomas seemed a little crestfallen at that, but said nothing.

Misty appeared from behind the master, still thin as a rake but looking far healthier than last time Sophine had seen her. The girl had grown, or perhaps it was merely her posture, and her stride was strong and determined. She wore a modest dress of grey material which nevertheless made her look somehow regal, even though a knife was belted at her side.

Sophine smiled warmly to see her, and Misty nodded back.

'If you'll follow me,' Misty said to the new arrivals, 'I'll show you to your rooms.'

'We have rooms?' asked the vomiting master.

'This is a very big house, sir,' said Ariene. 'There are rooms enough for everyone. There are rules though. No lights after dark, and don't go near the windows. You're all refugees and you're not to leave this house; if you're caught or seen, we're all done for.'

297

The mages nodded and cast grateful glances at Sophine as they were led upstairs by Misty.

'Thaniel's already left,' Ariene said, coming to place a hand on Sophine's shoulder. 'Back to Orswell's. Rigel and I will be heading back to my estate now. We'll meet here again tonight. I'm sorry to have to leave you in charge here, dear, but I don't see that we have a choice.'

Sophine nodded. 'What will you do?'

'I need to be at the Senate this morning, once I've changed and refreshed myself. I need to make some kind of show of being on board with this disaster or I'll find I'm too closely guarded to be of any help.'

Rigel made a growling sound in his throat.

'I can't believe it's all been about this,' he said, stomping to the windows. 'Murder, poison. The thing in the tavern. Master Thomas,' he gestured at his former tutor, who grimaced and nodded. 'Everything. And now The Barbican is dust and the mages are fugitives. All so this man can be Echelarch?'

'And he won't stop there,' said Thomas with some difficulty. 'No one fights that hard to take power without making sure they'll keep it.'

Ariene nodded.

'All the more reason to keep up appearances. Until we're ready, we can't draw attention to ourselves. I just hope I still have the authority to help by tonight.'

Sophine swallowed and tried a weak smile.

'If we work fast, we'll be alright. I can't hide twenty-four kids and five masters here for long anyway.'

Ariene returned the smile and headed for the door, before turning back briefly.

'You couldn't, you know...'

'I'm sorry,' said Sophine, 'I'm so tired.'

'Thought I'd ask,' Ariene sighed. 'Such a convenient way to travel.' Her eyes drifted to the abandoned urn. She wrinkled her nose. 'Even if some don't quite appreciate it.'

Sophine laughed.

'Goodbye, dear,' Ariene said, taking Rigel's arm and opening the door. Bright morning sunlight lit up the hall.

'See you tonight, Sophine,' Rigel said over his shoulder, but she was already halfway up the stairs, her thoughts on nothing more than sleep.

***

Thaniel collapsed on his bed at the Orswell estate and tried to master his swirling thoughts.

His room was large and airy, with broad windows that allowed the bright morning sun to flood the chamber with achingly brilliant light. He groaned and put one arm over his eyes. One thing he didn't have was curtains.

Everything ached; his legs, his arms, his head. He'd been awake all night after the battle at Hilda's Barbican, been frozen half to death in the quarry and suffered the stomach-wrenching horror of transportation via portal. All he wanted was sleep, and to believe that somehow the rise of the dangerously unhinged High Priest as the new Echelarch did not mean he would have to leave all this behind. But the thought wouldn't leave him alone. He couldn't stay. Not when being a mage, the thing he'd worked so hard to become, was suddenly so very dangerous. Deadly even.

The door opened and closed.

'Thaniel!' Eric's voice banished all thoughts of the future and his fears. He sat up, blinking happily in the light and held his arms out. Eric ran to him and returned the embrace, and they sat there on the bed for a moment in silence, locked to one another.

'Ariene told me you were ok,' Thaniel sniffed with a short laugh, 'but I couldn't quite believe it. I kept seeing you at Hilda's, and then the stone came down...'

'I'm ok,' Eric said, muffled against his chest, 'I was ok. They left me alone.'

'I'm so sorry,' Thaniel said into his hair. It smelled like home.

'You don't need to be sorry. You were saving all those people.'

Thaniel nodded, though Eric couldn't see. The moment stretched, and Thaniel realised he never wanted it to end. And following that thought came the bleakness again.

'I'm going to have to leave,' he said eventually.

'I know,' said Eric.

'I don't want to.'

Eric sniffed.

'I know,' he squeaked.

Thaniel closed his eyes. He could feel Eric's body shuddering, his ribs jerking as he sobbed against him.

'Come with me,' Thaniel said. Eric pulled back and stood up, looking at him through tearful eyes.

'I...I can't.'

'I mean it. Come with me.'

'Than, don't...Where will we go? All I know is here.'

'Wherever we end up. What does it matter?'

Eric wiped his eyes and shook his head, looking down at Thaniel.

'I'm nothing, Than. I'm not a mage. I'm not *anything*. Not even a tailor or a baker. I'm dead weight. If I'm here I'm safe. I've…I've got a life. But out there,' he gestured at the window, 'I'm nobody.'

'You're not nobody to me.'

Eric started to sob again though he was clearly trying not to. He wiped tears away angrily.

'You mean it, don't you? You'd take me even though I have nothing to offer.'

'You do. And yes, I do. And yes, I would.'

Eric hesitated for a moment, still not quite holding back tears.

'You're a fool,' he smiled through his sobs, but he let Thaniel reach out and draw him closer.

As his arms wrapped around Eric's waist, Thaniel gestured to the door. It locked itself.

***

Lyoris looked like he hadn't slept. His already pale face was gaunt, and his eyes were shadowed. He sat in his golden priesthood robes in a chair positioned just in front of the still-shrouded throne, and looked extremely ill at ease. His feet tapped endlessly against the floor and his eyes darted around the room as though seeing conspirators in every corner.

'I wish to be affirmed at once!' he shrilled again, with a small slap of the hand against the chair's arms. Again he seemed to bite his lip, visibly straining to hold himself back, and smiled a broad unconvincing smile that looked far more like a grimace.

'My apologies, my lords,' he said a little more calmly. 'It is simply that with every passing hour I feel the dreadful risk we are all facing rising ever higher. I am told that no mages were taken from The Barbican. None.' His composure slipped again and he flinched violently as he repeated the word.

'None!'

No one replied.

'They could be anywhere!' The Echelarch-elect cried. 'I must have the power to deal with them and I must have it now. Why can we not hold the affirmation vote now? I understand the Senate has rules, and I recognise that this is a huge change to our way of life but this…this is…this is a *crisis*…and *I can't do anything until you affirm me!*' These last words were delivered as a near-shriek. In the stone-cold silence of the chamber, the Echelarch's echoing voice seemed to border on the hysterical.

'Your Grace, if I may,' said Lord Barten, rising to his feet and making deliberate use of the Echelarch's title even though Lyoris had yet to be affirmed and under normal circumstances would not have any power at all just yet. It went some way towards soothing the poisonous wretch and he gestured lazily for Barten to speak. Amir bowed low and continued.

'I have received word, Your Grace, that Ceresheim in particular is not…Well, they are disappointed that they were not consulted in the decision to restore the Echelarchy. I fear that the same sentiments may be held in Terminheim and other smaller cities across Astregoth.'

'What do I care for them?' replied Lyoris sulkily.

302

'Without the support of the other major cities, Your Grace, Asterheim cannot survive.'

'They don't support me? Are they traitors then, Lord Barten?'

'They merely express concern, Your Grace. In particular because the throne was given by acclamation and the final vote to make it official is so soon. The affirmation vote should be held in a few days, to allow their delegates time to attend…'

'Oh should it, now?' cried Lyoris petulantly.

'So they say, Your Grace,' Barten said smoothly, with a bow.

'And how did you come to know this, Barten? I was only acclaimed yesterday! No one can ride that fast between here and there without killing a herd of horses or sprouting wings.'

'The Messengers' Guild employs mages, Your Grace,' said Barten, ignoring the snarl that curled Lyoris's lip. 'They are capable of communicating over great distances with their colleagues in the Messengers' Guilds in other cities.'

'You might advise them as their patron, Lord Barten, to invest in horses.' Lyoris's tone was icy.

'Yes, Your Grace.'

'Very well. Three days then. We will hold the affirmation vote in three days.'

Lyoris leapt to his feet and made as though to leave, but someone called from the white seats and he turned back, irritably.

'What?'

'May we ask, Your Grace, what you plan to do about the mages in the city?'

'Given how fast word travels, Senator, no you may not. I wouldn't want my plans known by the common citizens before I leave this building.' He scowled first at the speaker and then at Barten, who averted his eyes in a deliberate show of submission.

'We're being asked, Your Grace. Our guilds use mages, or even employ them. Our citizens are asking…'

'Enough!' shouted Lyoris, his thin body trembling with restrained emotion. He hesitated for a moment and then began to speak, but Barten couldn't tell if he was begrudgingly divulging information or literally making it up on the spot.

'I imagine that when the time comes,' the Echelarch-elect said with forced deliberation, 'mages will be asked to turn themselves in for questioning. If they have nothing to hide, then they have nothing to fear. The Travellers have branches all over the city. I shall instruct them to conduct the assessments and—'

'By The Circle you will not,' said a deep, powerful voice. Lyoris appeared to turn even paler, if such a thing were possible, and his trembling stopped. He stared, unmoving like a coiled serpent, at the woman who had dared to speak.

Overseer Skylock, head of the military wing of the Travellers, had risen from her rarely occupied seat in the red tiers and stood, arms crossed over her considerable chest, glaring at the new lord of Astregoth. She wore a white civilian robe that, though generously cut, utterly failed to hide her enormously muscled arms.

'We will not act as some gang of thugs for you or anyone else to use against our own people,' she said.

Lyoris pointed an angry finger at her, his other hand clenched tightly at his side. 'You are not a Senator, Overseer, you have no right to speak!' he roared.

'I have as much right as anyone,' she sneered, 'or have you not usurped our entire system by declaring yourself Echelarch? Who has any rights anymore?'

'I was acclaimed!'

Skylock turned her head and spat on the Senate floor.

'Acclaim that, you whelp. Until you're affirmed and the throne we've done so well without these last centuries is restored, you're no Echelarch.' She turned and marched to the stairs, other Senators ducking aside to avoid her massive arms.

'Arrest her!' shrieked Lyoris. Skylock stopped and turned to him in some surprise; other Senators also seemed caught off guard. Until this moment, none of them had ever known a Senator to be censured by the will of a single man, still less arrested. And with the Echelarch not yet affirmed, the power balance was still uncertain. Barten tensed, trying to sense which way it could go, before subsiding in disappointment as Battlemasons appeared in the doorway, blades drawn.

Skylock turned her forceful glare on the soldiers and appeared to weigh up the odds before glancing back at the silent assembly.

'You've made a terrible mistake,' she growled at them, before being led away at sword point.

The Senators looked at one another, but none dared meet the eyes of the furious Echelarch-elect. More soldiers filed into the room as the Overseer was taken out. Barten watched them a moment before glancing back at Lyoris and nearly jumping in surprise to see that the poisonous toad was watching him intently. Barten offered him a respectful nod of the head.

Lyoris scowled and stalked away into the chambers behind the Senate audience room. Barten exhaled slowly.

***

The wine in Rigel's cup was acrid and sour, but apparently that was what it was supposed to taste like. Misty had said it had come from a very expensive merchant, though she hadn't said if she'd actually paid for it, and Rigel had stared at it dubiously as the golden liquid flowed into his glass. It did, however, have a peculiarly moreish aftertaste that kept him reaching for his glass.

'Easy there,' said Thaniel with a weak smile. 'Could be a long night.'

He was right; the air felt strangely heavy and tense as they waited for everyone to arrive. Ariene had spent the day with the Senators, doing what she could to figure out what the new Echelarch might do next and how it might affect their fledgling plans. Rigel just hoped she hadn't been arrested on sight; she hadn't made a friend of Lyoris the High Priest, so there was every chance Lyoris the Echelarch would want her where he could see her.

Down the hall, visible through the doorway to Lord Balderwin's gloriously furnished dining room, the front doors opened to admit Lady Gloriana. A swirl of cold night air entered with Ariene, bringing with it the first few dropped leaves of Autumn. The candles on the table flickered in the short gust of air. Rigel took a swallow of wine and caught Thaniel's eye. Ariene did not look happy.

She stomped into the dining room and threw her expensively laced silk gloves carelessly onto the table.

'Skylock was arrested,' she said without preamble, pouring herself a large glass of wine from a pewter jug. She swirled the liquid in the glass once and then downed it. She poured another.

Rigel was horrified.

'Arrested? Who could possibly—'

'Lyoris has guards. He already held the Battlemasons from when Barten was stabbed, so even though he hasn't been affirmed he already has the means to enforce his will.' She took another swig of wine.

'It's all madness out there. No one knows what to do with an Echelarch and now he has military force to back him up. We haven't had one for so long that no one knows what rights we're supposed to have or how far his authority extends...'

'My lady,' said Rigel, 'surely he only has the authority we let him have.'

'Exactly,' she muttered. 'That's what I've been trying to tell people all day. By the rules of the Senate, he is no Echelarch until the affirmation. But they won't listen. They're all more afraid of one of *us*, their political rivals, rising to replace the Echelarch now we've restored the throne, than they are of Lyoris himself. They still don't see the threat, even though Skylock was arrested *in the Senate* just for speaking against him.'

'Any word on his plans for mages?' asked Sophine, looking darkly at Ariene from her corner of the candlelit table.

'Nothing good. He didn't want to discuss it, and when he tried to give us a bland, reasonable answer to mollify us, what he came out with was barbaric.'

'Barbaric?'

'That mages should turn themselves in to the Travellers for questioning. All of them.'

'That's insane!' said Thaniel with a disbelieving laugh.

'And that's what he thought we'd swallow *for the time being*,' Ariene growled. 'I have absolutely no doubt his real plans are far worse.'

'So we're still getting out?' asked the wizened rake-thin master, from where she stood in the shadows. Her shoulder was still too painful from the arrow to sit comfortably on the high-backed seats, though thanks to Rigel it was mostly healed.

'We have no choice,' said Ariene, taking a smaller gulp of wine. 'The city won't be safe for mages when Lyoris's power is settled.'

'Or anyone else,' added Rigel. Ariene looked at him for a moment, candlelight dancing in her hard eyes. Then she nodded.

'It galls me that we will have to lose you, dear,' she said, 'but you need to leave. It's down to the Senators to handle Mountebank.'

'I could stay...'

'No, Rigel. The others will need you. All of you,' her eyes swept round to take in Sophine and Thaniel. They nodded.

The moment stretched.

'So,' said Madam Raftopolis, helping herself to wine, 'by ship, we said?'

Ariene sighed deeply and closed her eyes.

'Yes, by ship. I am still a Senator, and I still have influence. More than that, I have money. I can charter a ship big enough to take you, the mages, and the others.'

'That's a lot of people.'

'I have a lot of money.'

Madam Raftopolis nodded and glanced around the room, perhaps forgetting that this was not Ariene's house. She sipped her drink.

'We don't have any way to contact the other mages,' put in Sophine. 'We don't know where they live…'

Thaniel stood up and leant forward with his palms on the table. Rigel suppressed a smile; Thaniel's face was flushed with the wine and he was clearly feeling his theatrical side just now.

'Lord Orswell is patron of the Citizenry Guild,' he said, overly seriously. 'If anyone has access to those records, they do.'

'So how do we get them?' asked Sophine with a raised eyebrow.

'I'll get them. Eric and I will go and get them, and get messages to everyone to be ready to leave on…on…' He paused and looked at Ariene.

'When are we doing this?'

Ariene was about to answer when Lord Barten strode through the door and sat at the table.

'Three days,' he said, running his hands over his bald head. 'We have tomorrow and the day after. Then the ship needs to sail, on the day of the affirmation vote, when the Senate is too busy to notice.'

Thaniel nodded grimly.

'So we get the records tomorrow, get the messages out the next day. That's not a lot of time for people to get ready.'

'It'll have to be enough,' said Ariene.

'More than you know,' Barten said, with a pointed look at her. Ariene sat back and returned the look sourly. She gulped some wine, sloshing some on her sleeves.

'Why, what now?'

'As the *former* Castellan of the Battlemasons, I still have a few friends there. They've received orders, this afternoon, to take all known mages into custody at midday on the day of the vote. Around the very time Lyoris becomes Echelarch, in fact.'

In the silence that greeted this horrific development, Barten reached over and claimed one of the pewter jugs. He winced a little, and Rigel realised he was still suffering from his wound. Rigel stared at him dumbly as he poured a generous measure of the golden liquid into his glass.

'All of them?' breathed Thaniel; it was not quite a question. Barten nodded without looking up. He sat back and adjusted his sleeves before taking a sip.

'All of them,' he repeated.

'On what grounds though?' Sophine asked. Barten barked a mirthless laugh.

'On the grounds that he'll be the Echelarch, and that he's a complete psychopath.' He chuckled again before shaking his head. 'He's afraid of mages; he knows what they can do and he knows that besides the Battlemasons and Travellers, both of which have already been dealt with, they're the only group in this city that has the actual ability to oppose him.'

'The Senate will oppose him,' said Ariene stiffly.

'Only when they find out,' said Amir, 'which they won't until after they affirm him.'

'If they even last that long,' said Rigel. Barten looked at him with a raised eyebrow and a brief puff of forced amusement.

'What?' Rigel said darkly, taking a sip of wine. 'You think he'll want to keep the Senate around once he's crowned? If he's arresting healers and builders and truth-seekers, just because they *could* oppose him *if* they tapped into the powers they've spent their entire lives suppressing, why not arrest Senators who could oppose him far more easily?'

Ariene nodded heavily and rose from her seat in a swirl of silk.

'You should have been a politician, Rigel,' she said pensively, swilling the wine in her glass as she paced the room. 'He's right, Amir. You know he is.'

Barten leaned forward and placed his glass on the table. He stared at it for a while.

'Even if that's so,' he said eventually, running his hands over his head again, 'he won't make a move until the affirmation vote. We should focus on getting the mages out. This young man's idea about the Citizenry Guild is sound, so I think we should do that.'

'Agreed,' said Ariene, still pacing thoughtfully.

'And in the meantime, you and young Rigel go to charter the ship.'

'There's something missing,' said Master Thomas, his voice less slurred now he'd healed somewhat. He came forward to stand in the circle of candlelight and clasped his hands before him, as though presenting to a panel made up of Senators and his former students.

'The Battlemasons will already be in the city if they're heading to arrest everyone by midday. If the ship is leaving on affirmation day—'

'Which it is,' said Barten, 'because the Senate will be distracted and so will everyone else...'

'And we don't have the time to organise it any faster,' put in Ariene, still pacing.

'-then we need to do something to disrupt the soldiers,' finished Master Thomas as though no one had interrupted him. 'Otherwise there's a good chance people will run into soldiers on the way to the boat.'

'Ship,' said Sophine quietly.

Outside, it began to rain. Fat spots of water spattered against the floor-length windows, the tapping sound filling the silence left by Master Thomas's brief but portentous words.

'Ceresheim,' Barten said suddenly, rising to his feet and gasping at the sudden pain in his back. He grasped the unfortunate Ariene by the shoulders as she happened to be closest to his chair. She blinked at him in confusion.

'I told the Senate today that Ceresheim was opposed to the restoration of the Echelarchy,' he said, walking briskly around the table to stand by the window. 'I was there once. Had a miserable time. Rained all week. Grain Belt and all that.' He tapped an expensive looking ring against the glass.

Thaniel caught Rigel's eye and raised an eyebrow. Rigel shrugged helplessly; he had no idea what Barten was driving at either.

'Which one of you is the best at...' Barten wiggled his fingers in the air, 'complicated things?'

'You mean subtle magic? Spells?' asked Master Thomas, a little indignantly.

'Maybe,' said Barten. 'I'm thinking...conjuring. Making things look like they're there when they aren't.'

'Difficult,' said Madam Raftopolis. 'Very difficult. The kind of sorcery that needs an enormous amount of energy that you just can't get from the natural world. I've heard stories about before the purge when people did that sort of thing...'

'Stories where?' asked Sophine quietly. Madam Raftopolis looked sheepish for a moment, but drew herself up straight.

'Thomas has some books,' she said, 'old grimoires and spell-books from before the purge. I took a look through once or twice.'

'I have those books,' said Sophine. 'I've used them. They're not stories. If the kind of sorcery Lord Barten is talking about is in there, I can perform it.'

Madam Raftopolis looked somewhere between impressed and offended, and not at all sure how to respond. She simply looked at Sophine with a frown, opening and closing her mouth like a fish.

'I can do it,' Sophine said, turning to Barten. 'What were you thinking?'

'An army,' said the handsome lord with the dark skin, pointing out of the window in the vague direction of the distant city walls. 'An army appearing on the southern horizon on the morning of the affirmation vote. A reason for the Battlemasons to deploy outside the walls, drain their resources. Fewer soldiers on less important missions like gathering up mages or guarding the harbour.'

Sophine nodded soberly.

'I'd better find my books,' she said. 'But this time I've got three days. Recently I've had a lot less time to learn forbidden spells.' She smiled sweetly at Madam Raftopolis, who appeared to have a sudden attack of professional idealism.

'Just who is your patron, young lady?' she demanded.

'Lila,' Master Thomas said gently. 'I don't think that's relevant anymore.' Raftopolis glared at him for a moment, before giving a self-effacing smile and nodding.

'Yeah, that ship's sailed,' joked Thaniel with a grin. Rigel winced. No one returned the grin. Thaniel looked down at the table and seemed to suddenly develop a fascination for the grooves in the wood.

'So that's settled then,' Ariene said. 'Lord Barten will stoke the fears of Ceresheim's displeasure in the Senate. Rigel and I will charter a boat once we have an idea of numbers. Thaniel will take Eric, go to the Citizenry Guild, get the information and send the message out to the mages. Meanwhile Sophine will be learning her illusion spells and be ready to draw out the army on the day.'

Everyone nodded, a feeling of sudden positivity growing in the room despite the thrashing rain which was now pelting the windows heavily.

'One other thing,' said Barten, looking closely at Rigel and Thaniel. 'You two are like your friend, aren't you?' He nodded at Sophine. They exchanged a look.

'How do you mean, sir?'

'I mean, you can perform those kinds of spells.'

Thaniel and Rigel both started to answer, talking over one another to express their hesitant denials.

'Gentlemen,' Barten said, holding out a hand for quiet with the easy confidence of a man used to command. They fell silent. 'I know you healed Ariene and elevated her from – forgive me my lady – ancient decrepitude to the formidable woman she now is.'

Ariene snorted and sipped some wine.

'I know you healed me and defeated the fallen mage Kahin at the Stonegate. I know you somehow rescued a school full of mages from him and an army of Battlemasons.'

'That was mostly Sophine,' Thaniel mumbled. Barten's hand flexed a little and he went quiet again.

'Kahin did something to you three. Something that enabled you to use this kind of power and I can see you're uncomfortable with it.'

Rigel grimaced.

'It's a curse, sir. It doesn't do what I want it to do…'

Barten ignored him and continued.

'Well, this plan is going to demand a lot of us all. I suggest you take what you've been given and use it. Your friend has developed into a powerful mage, a woman capable of any number of powers and who would quite rightly fill the hearts of those like our new Echelarch with fear. Learn from her, and stop with the snivelling lack of confidence. Do so before affirmation day.'

'Yes, sir,' said Thaniel meekly. Rigel simply stared at the table.

'Alright then,' he said, coming around the table to where Ariene now sat. 'Get some sleep. I need to get home before I'm missed. As does Ariene. My lady?'

'Lord Barten,' Ariene smiled up at him, rising smoothly to take his arm and giving him an appreciative look.

'Formidable,' she said teasingly. He smiled and led her away. Rigel's eyes followed them out, then he looked suddenly at Thaniel.

'You don't think…' he nodded in the direction they'd gone.

Thaniel's eyes went wide.

Chapter Seventeen

On presenting their credentials as apprentices of Lord Orswell's, Thaniel and Eric had been taken to a reading room at the Citizenry Guild, complete with plush chairs and heavy tables, well-lit by stacks of candles and candelabra as well as the daylight pouring through the window.

Books lined the room on heavy wooden shelves, though they all looked ancient, heavy and entirely unappealing. One quick glance at a volume on one of the shelves had made Thaniel regret his curiosity.

'Lesser Lineages: A Genealogical Study of the Tertiary Houses of Asterheim. Volume Six. Oh wow,' he looked along the shelf, 'it runs to twenty or so volumes.'

Eric looked vaguely ill at the thought.

'Someone sat and wrote that,' he said. 'Can you imagine?'

'I cannot,' said Thaniel, running a hand over the rough grey covers. 'What do you suppose this is made of…?'

Eric pulled a face.

'We might not want to know.'

Thaniel pulled his fingers back as though stung.

The heavy wooden door swung open and a man in his mid-twenties walked in carrying a box of books. He was heavy-set and smiley, with a mop of artfully arranged blonde hair and well-fitted clothes. He looked nothing like the kind of person Thaniel had expected the terminally dull Citizenry Guild to attract. He plonked the box on the table and stood back with a smile, pushing his hair back over his ears.

'There you are,' he said proudly. 'Will there be anything else?'

'No, that's all, thank you,' said Eric, pulling out one of the seats and sitting down. The junior smiled again and turned to leave with a flourish that made Thaniel smile.

'He's one of Orswell's lost souls, isn't he?' Thaniel said, picking up one of the books they'd been given.

Eric didn't even look up from the book he'd taken off the top.

'What gave him away?' he said in a tone dripping with sarcasm. 'This is no good, it lists mage licence applications but only up to three years ago.'

'This one too. Though it has some from two years ago.'

Eric frowned.

'So are the old ones all still current or...?'

Thaniel sighed and scratched his head, peering at the books as though they might offer some insight.

'Could you sit down?' asked Eric, 'you're making me nervous the way you're hovering like that.'

'No,' said Thaniel, flipping a page.

'Why not?'

'Maybe I like you nervous.'

Eric made a sound somewhere between a snort and a laugh and reached for another book, but discarded it quickly as a piece of paper slipped out of it. He picked it up and the colour drained from his face.

'Thaniel…'

'What's that?'

'List of Mages: Names and Whereabouts (Copy),' Eric read flatly. 'This was written only a few days ago, look at the ink. You can still smell it.' He held the paper out to Thaniel.

Thaniel took it slowly.

'Copy,' he repeated thoughtfully. Eric nodded.

'Someone already did the work for us, and they made a copy.' Their eyes met.

'Mountebank?' Eric asked.

'Has to be. This is bad,' Thaniel replied heavily.

'So someone already has a list of the mages…'

'Must be the Battlemasons,' sighed Thaniel. 'He's going to just have us all rounded up…'

'Don't think about it,' said Eric. 'We have a job to do. We need to get the warning out before the Battlemasons use their list.'

'Which we can, thanks to Mountebank,' Thaniel added. 'Let's get to it.'

***

The Great Harbour of Asterheim was a vast expanse of water, partially formed by a natural outcrop of rock jutting into the sea in a gentle curve. The rest had been constructed by Stonesmiths and mages many centuries before, a great wide circle of stone leading to the Western Ocean. A fortress was perched on the southern side; the Sea Gate, it was called. It housed the chambers and mechanisms that kept the enormous chain taut across the mouth of the harbour anytime the Senate or harbour officials of sufficient rank ordered it closed. In theory, this also ensured that ships berthed in Asterheim paid the taxes due on their cargo before leaving. The chain was so thick and heavy that a single person had no chance of lifting one of the links alone, and the sheer size of the winch mechanism necessitated that Sea Gate be built around it. The chain had not been raised for many long years however, and Sea Gate had fallen over time into considerable disrepair.

Around the harbour were piers and berths for ships of all sizes, merchants selling materials and spices and all kinds of other people selling all kinds of other things, including themselves. Thaniel's eyes bulged at the sight of a particularly well built, and particularly nude, merchant of this latter variety. Eric gave him a shove, but his gaze was glued to the man too. Ariene rolled her eyes.

'Keep your heads clear, gentlemen,' she said, as they approached the ramshackle wooden building with the word 'Harbourmaster' written above it in large letters. All around them, crowds of people yelled and called, carrying boxes and crates and swigging drinks from various kinds of bottles. The smell of fish and salt hung heavily in the air, and the water gleamed in the afternoon sun. Ships bobbed and swayed, naked figures reclining on some of them, enjoying the sunlight.

'I like it here,' said Thaniel, looking around in fascination.

'I bet you do,' murmured Eric.

'Hush,' said Ariene, marching into the Harbourmaster's hut and approaching the desk set up at the end of the room. A heavy-set man with only half an ear on his left side peered up at her. He, too, smelled of fish and other, less palatable, aromas.

'Can I help you, my lady?' he asked, peering with unusual intensity at her. His voice was deep and thick, as though each word had to fight its way out past something unspeakably unpleasant, and his remaining teeth were brown. Ariene fought to keep a neutral expression.

The apparent Harbourmaster's right hand reached for a piece of paper sitting on a stack of others. He glanced at it and threw it aside, leaning over to rifle through more before sitting back with another one and placing it on the desk before him.

'I would like to charter a ship,' said Ariene. 'I am Lady Ariene Gloriana…of House Gloriana,' she added, unsure if this fellow would know just how important she really was.

'As it happens, we have a number of cargo ships in, my lady,' he said gruffly with a bright smile, scanning the piece of paper with evident difficulty. His lips moved as he read, his head inches from the paper. The way he said 'ships' made her think of congealed offal.

'That's excellent.'

'I imagine any number of them would be happy to take you,' he said, still scanning the paper. 'I even have some leaving today.'

'It won't be until—'

'Ah!' the man cried, sitting upright. Ariene tried not to shrink back from the smells emanating from the man's open mouth.

'Gloriana?' he asked, though it sounded more like 'oreeana'.

'Gloriana, yes,' she replied.

'Sorry, my lady. Orders from the Echelarch.'

Eh-shlark…

'What orders?'

'No travel for persons on this list. Came through from Citizenry just today.'

'That's preposterous!' she cried. 'I am a Senator! Scion of one of the greatest Houses in Asterheim!'

The man smiled at her, prodding the paper with one thick finger. 'Postrus it might be, Lady. But the paper says Gloriana.'

A cold hand reached up inside her and slowly closed its clammy fingers around her heart. She struggled to keep her composure.

'There must be something you can...' she said, but the way the man's smile widened further and his eyes gleamed made her trail off.

'Sorry, *Lady*.'

She held the Harbourmaster's gaze a moment longer, outrage and helplessness stealing her thoughts and clogging up her tongue. Words formed and died in her mouth. She saw the hopes of all the innocent souls she'd set out to save burning in her mind's eye, ashes of guilt settling on the bones of her ruined plans.

'Lady Gloriana,' said a familiar voice behind her. Ariene froze, trying in vain to master her emotions as Lord Orswell stepped up behind her. She turned slowly, looking up at him but not trusting herself to speak. She adjusted her travellers' cloak absently. Next to her, Thaniel and Eric stood in open-mouthed silence, their hands linked unconsciously as they looked at the ruin of everything.

Lord Orswell, patron of the Citizenry Guild, looked from Ariene to his apprentice and his mage. A small smile flickered at the corner of his mouth. Behind him stood three decidedly *unsmiling* armed men.

'If you would be so good, Eric and Thaniel, to wait for me outside, I will meet you shortly.' His eyes flashed to Ariene's again, just briefly, a look full of meaning that she didn't quite catch.

321

'My lady,' he said, sweeping past her with the dismissive courtesy so characteristic of him. His retainers stared at her with open hostility.

She didn't dare look back, merely ushered Thaniel and Eric from the building and hurried them to a spot a few metres away on the pier. She tripped on her gown, barely noticing as Thaniel reached out to steady her. She tugged the material away from her feet and stumbled on, her mind a blank haze of grey despair and cold fear. Fishing boats bobbed on the water just near where they stood, and beyond in the distance the great Western Ocean glittered beyond the mouth of the shimmering harbour. It all looked so incongruously peaceful and ordered. Ariene had never hated a sight more in her life.

'What just happened?' Thaniel was asking, stalking around with his hands rubbing at his hair. Eric just stood and stared at the water; his pale, wide-eyed stare of disbelief mirroring perfectly how Ariene was feeling.

'He saw us,' Thaniel said. 'He was right *behind* us…'

'And is, again,' said Lord Orswell lightly. Thaniel whipped around with a yelp, moving unconsciously to stand near Eric, who to his credit stood silently staring at his master. Orswell gave him a small smile.

'Can we assist you at all, Lord Orswell?' asked Ariene, having recovered some of her dignity. Her hands absently toyed with the folds of her dress, lifting and tugging, lifting and tugging. He held up a hand and shook his head.

'Ariene,' he said softly, 'I think here, now, we can dispense with the playacting. I think it's high time we talked.'

'About poison?' she spat without thinking, dimly aware she was now knotting the material of her dress in her hands.

'About ships,' he replied, glancing away at the large vessels berthed at the furthest ends of the piers, where the water was deepest. The cold hand around Ariene's heart tightened its grip and she gasped involuntarily. Thaniel's hand gripped Eric's. Orswell held Ariene's gaze for a moment.

'I know all about it, Ariene. Everything. I know you planted this one in my household,' he nodded his head in Thaniel's direction without breaking eye contact with her. 'I know these two went looking for the names and addresses of the mages in this city. And I am not so stupid that I can't figure out why.'

She tilted her head, her jaw rising defiantly.

'And so. You finally picked a side. Well played, Orswell. I did wonder whether your brother did it all by himself but —'

'He did,' interrupted Orswell, with a flicker of annoyance. 'Don't lump me in with that fool. I never much liked him, as I told Thaniel the first day we met, and I had nothing to do with the poisoning. And you're right. I have picked a side, though not the one you mean.'

The hand around her heart stopped squeezing for a moment, hope daring to flicker like a candle spluttering in a stiff breeze.

'Why are you here, Orlond?'

'To hire a ship, of course.' He smiled.

Eric spluttered something that was somewhere between a cough and a laugh.

'To hire a ship,' he repeated in disbelief. Orswell smiled again, as though having done so once, he now couldn't stop.

Ariene tried to keep her voice level and even as she replied.

323

'I think, my lord, that it might be helpful if you explained…for the sake of my nerves.'

Orswell looked back at her and his smile faded. He paused a moment, looking away out to sea as he gathered his thoughts.

'It's a fact of life in this city,' he said quietly, hesitantly, as though voicing thoughts long since held under guard. He stopped and swallowed, furrowing his brow. Behind him, his few household retainers looked aside and shuffled their feet.

'It's a fact that all others see when they look at people like me…like us,' he nodded at the two boys, 'is our so-called *perversions*. No don't,' he said as Ariene made to offer a protest. 'Don't deny it. Priests have sneered at me and Senators have laughed at me all my life; so I kept a low profile and denied myself the only things I've ever wanted. All to avoid giving anyone cause to destroy me and my house. At first I did that for myself, and later to protect my boys.' He glanced at Ariene, as though unsure how much she knew.

'You mean your apprentices,' she said. He nodded.

'Them, and the others who I've fostered over the years. The lost ones. The ones who work in the Citizenry Guild, living their underground lives together and sharing what happiness there is for them in this place. They're the ones who told me what you two were up to.' He looked at Thaniel and Eric.

'I guess we should have realised,' muttered Thaniel.

'Eric should have, certainly,' agreed Orswell. 'He was a spy himself.'

Eric stiffened by Thaniel's side. Thaniel looked at him sharply.

'Don't look so shocked; you were a spy too,' said Orswell. Thaniel began to splutter a denial but Ariene waved a hand at him; now was not the time for that.

'Eric wouldn't do it,' said Orswell, 'just like you wouldn't spy for Lady Gloriana. That's when I took a closer interest in you two, and in a way that's why I'm here now. It's certainly the only reason you're still alive. So don't blame him.'

'How did you know?' asked Ariene lightly, as though discussing someone's thoughts on the latest weather patterns.

Orswell laughed, wagging a finger at Ariene.

'You've done your time in the arena, Lady Gloriana, and you're one of the best players the Senate has, but even you have your blind spots. Ask Thaniel how I knew he was a spy.' He turned to look at Thaniel, who offered him an apologetic smile. 'How about it, Thaniel? Knowing me as you do now, does Ariene's plan to plant you in my household sound remotely plausible? On the very day of my brother's murder, another lost soul stumbles into my path who turns out to be my brother's mage…'

He shook his head ruefully and fixed Ariene with a look.

'Did you really think a man of my years and experience would somehow not see the politics and intrigue I've lived with every day of my life, just because you flashed a well-toned backside at me through a pair of wet breeches?'

'I'm sorry, Orlond. It was politics.'

'It was prejudice,' he said gently. 'And it nearly cost Thaniel his life.'

Ariene looked away, conceding the point.

'That too, perhaps, yes.'

Orswell sighed and made an ushering motion with his hands. 'We should get going, we're attracting attention.'

Ariene stood her ground.

'A moment, Orlond. This ship…'

325

'Ah yes,' he said, smiling again. 'I heard that the boys were looking up mages, and after the disaster at Hilda's Barbican I realised they must be planning to get them out. Because they deserve better than to live under threat of persecution. But I also knew that because you haven't been playing along with the Echelarch you're on a no-travel list.' He grimaced. 'Citizenry has some benefits. But I could have guessed when you weren't invited to *the* social occasion of the century.'

Ariene frowned at that, a small alarm ringing in her mind that she couldn't quite place.

'Social occasion?'

'Don't worry,' he said wryly. 'It was painful. Lyrois threw a party over at the Cathedral, of all places, invited his supporters and snubbed everyone else. He's even more peculiar up close. He told us he'd made his own wine and insisted we all toast his health and stared at us whilst we did. I made my excuses and left, but not before I swiped one of his wine bottles.' He shrugged. 'A small protest but sometimes the small ones are all we have.'

'Indeed,' said Ariene, confused.

'Anyway,' continued Orswell, 'I want better for my boys. Like you do for the mages. I should have wanted better for myself, but I didn't have the strength to reach for it until Thaniel and Eric showed me what life *should* be like. So when I realised your plan wasn't going to work, because Lyoris blacklisted you, I decided to charter the ship myself. So we'll all be coming with you. My apprentices, and any of the Citizenry boys who want a free life. I know your mages have ways of getting about,' he cast a sideways glance at Thaniel, who gave a shaky smile, 'so I suggest you join us by those arcane means rather than wandering through the city when the time comes. It isn't safe.'

Ariene tried to reply, but emotion had choked her throat. She took Orlond's arm and let him lead her towards the city, feeling like a woman saved from drowning by a dolphin that she'd taken for a shark.

***

'So how did it go today?' asked Ariene, looking over her glass at Amir. He leaned back in his chair, unconsciously adjusting position to ease the pain in his back, and stared off into the night. The stars stared back, cold and white and distant in a black sky. Ariene shivered.

It had been a long, difficult day. Orswell's change of allegiance had thrown her more than she cared to admit, and now the plan was looking desperate. A band of waifs and orphans collected over Orswell's lifetime was planning to board the ship at the same time as the city mages. Meanwhile her name was on a no-travel list so she wasn't even in control of the ship. It was all slipping away from her, and if they failed, she was sure her name would be on other lists before long. If it wasn't already. She shuddered.

Now she was at Barten's residence, having decided it was too risky to go back to Balderwin's and not wanting to be on her own. They sat on a balcony outside one of the upstairs reception rooms. Behind them, beyond the open balcony doors, a roaring fire burned in the hearth. It was just about countering the icy chill of the night air, though it was a close contest.

Barten sighed and ran a hand over his bald head.

327

'Not well. The Senators are terrified to say anything and Lyoris hasn't been seen. Seems like he's planning to reappear only on the date of the senate vote affirming him. I couldn't find anyone willing to talk openly about his vision for the future or what our place might be in it.'

She sipped her wine, unsurprised by the information.

'Well,' she sighed, 'he's put me on a list. He's handed out lists of mages to the Battlemasons. He's probably got other lists and everyone knows it. They're all too stuck in their own worlds to realise it's happening to everyone. If they did, perhaps they could fight back, but for now...'

She trailed off.

'They don't know what to do,' Barten said, with a touch of bitterness. 'The Senate always worked on rules. We all knew what was and wasn't done.'

Ariene snorted.

'Like poison.'

Amir gave her a look.

'Come on, Ariene. We all played the game. Even you did.'

She pursed her lips but didn't contest the point. She'd done her share, it was true.

'But the rules were respected,' said Barten, staring off once more into the night, 'and now here's this man, changing everything to suit himself, gathering more and more power to him. He doesn't know about the rules. He doesn't care about the rules.'

'And you helped him,' Ariene said. She shook her head and took a deep drink.

'And I helped him,' said Barten heavily. 'That's the point I'm making though. I just thought it was the same game. Politics. Put pressure on your rivals, increase your power. I didn't know what he was really planning until I was already involved, and by then I had no way out.'

'You were helping him become Echelarch, Amir. You knew.'

'Oh please. I was using a priest with no power and a little influence to help me increase my own. He was delusional, and he had virtually no chance of becoming Echelarch, but my part of his plan was just to get rid of House Gloriana. How could I refuse that?'

'Oh how indeed?' she muttered darkly, taking a deep swallow of wine.

'Don't be bitter. We'd always been rivals, and you had no successor. Why shouldn't your guilds have gone to me?'

'Because you're the kind of man who would ally himself with a psychotic priest and only realise he's not to be trusted when he gets a knife in his back. I would never have let you have my guilds. The moment you associated with The Circle, I could never have allowed it. The Guild of Mages under a patron controlled by priests? Never.'

Amir glared at her, the rivalry that had formed their entire relationship for years burning bright again for a moment. Then it was gone, and he grimaced. She smiled softly to herself as he ran a hand over his head again.

'That's the point though, Ariene. He played us all. Small steps, each time with a heavy dose of rationalisation; *this is more to my benefit than not, and he's still no threat so...why not...?*'

'Are we sure he's a threat now?'

Amir looked at her with eyebrows raised. 'To mages, he is,' he said flatly.

'Not just them. I mean everyone else. Orswell wants his…apprentices…out because he knows what The Circle thinks of men like them, and it's already bad enough in this city. The mages want to get out for more obvious reasons. But how do we know he's a threat to anyone else? The Senate might come to its senses and get rid of him.'

Barten barked a short, bitter laugh. 'Oh, he's a threat.'

Ariene put her glass down firmly.

'That's the fourth time you've hinted at that, Amir. What do you know?' He held her gaze for a moment, the starlight dancing in his eyes.

'I know that Lyoris is an alchemist,' he said quietly.

'An alchemist?'

Barten nodded grimly, pouring himself more wine and offering her a refill. She waved it away, peering at him intently.

'He's an alchemist who poisoned his way into the priesthood,' said Barten, sitting back with his glass and swilling the liquid. 'He controls them all with chemicals he mixes himself. Sometimes with the help of that blasted priest mage, Kahin.'

She changed her mind and reached for the wine bottle. She poured a generous glass as Barten told her all about the demonstration in the Cathedral, where the Mortuary Guild worker was dragged out after not receiving the antidote…

'That's it,' Ariene said in dawning disgust. 'That's what the party was about.'

'Party?'

She stood up from the table, moving to stand by the balcony railing. The cold air tugged at her dress, but for once she wasn't thinking about her feet, and the chill creeping up over her skin was nothing to do with the night.

'Orswell said the strangest thing today,' she said, swilling her drink round its glass contemplatively.

'Oh?'

'He said he'd been invited to a private party with Lyoris, for him and the rest of the loyal senators. He made them toast his health with a wine he made himself.'

'Interesting. So if Orswell is still breathing…'

'Then it wasn't poisoned. But if Lyoris was only hosting Senators he thinks are loyal, then he wouldn't be poisoning *them*…'

'He's poisoning everyone else,' finished Amir. 'He's going to poison the Senate at the vote of affirmation and only his supporters will survive because they drank the antidote.'

Ariene tightened her grip on the rail, giving in to a rare moment of introspection as she stared at the night sky.

'How did we get here?' she mused, shaking her head. 'How could we have been so *blind*? When we tore the last Echelarch from his throne all those centuries ago, we should have finished the job. But instead we carried on with this ridiculous pretence that an absent monarch was the fount of all power, everyone tiptoeing around playing the politics by the *rules*,' she glanced accusingly at Barten, 'and hoping the flimsy structures we built on a purple veil wouldn't fall down around our ears.'

She laughed at the absurdity of it all.

'And because we didn't fix the system when we should have, all it took was someone with the will and opportunity to break the rules and we're right back where we started: with a tyrant in charge and a population in fear.'

Amir stood, wincing a little at the lingering pain from his wound, and came to join her. Together they looked at the inky outline of the mountains, their jagged peaks reaching like desperate hands for the starlit sky.

'We can't let this happen, Ariene.'

She clenched her teeth.

'No. No we can't.' She took another sip and drew her arm back with a snarl of rage. Amir calmly took the glass from her hand before she could hurl it over the balcony, and downed the rest of the wine.

'We'll think of something,' he said.

***

Sophine sighed and pinched the bridge of her nose, wondering why Rigel couldn't conjure a portal to save his life. Her realisation that her jacket was far too thin had come way too late, and now she was beginning to shiver.

'It's too cold for this,' she muttered to herself. Raising her voice she called to Rigel who was standing a few metres away under one of the trees that obscured this particular part of Balderwin's estate from spying eyes.

'This really shouldn't be this hard,' she called impatiently.

'I'm trying!' he shouted back.

'Try harder,' yelled Thaniel from the other side of the garden. 'It's cold!'

'You do it then!' Rigel called back.

'I'm not the one who needs to get Ariene on a boat, Rigel! Concentrate!'

Whatever Rigel muttered to himself in reply was lost in the swirl of leaves rustling in the wind.

'Remember what I said,' Sophine called, trying to inject some positivity into her tone but coming off as sarcastic. 'Tap into your overblown sense of melodramatic despair…'

Rigel's reply was obscene. Sophine sighed.

'Think about how Mountebank is going to kill us all,' shouted Thaniel. 'That's pretty bleak!'

'Shut up!' Rigel said in alarm. 'You never know who might be listening…'

'That's it!' called Sophine. 'Use that!'

'Thaniel being a moron?'

'Use your fear of getting caught and everything falling apart!'

Rigel didn't respond, and from what Sophine could tell, he seemed to be making frantic gestures as though trying to physically open a door. Her heart sank, but tried to keep the expression of disappointment from her face; Rigel was in shadow but she was lit up by the stars.

'Oh this is impossible,' Rigel said, sounding defeated. 'I'm never going to…'

Reality rippled and tore as a ragged hole appeared in the air, a dreadful sound like tearing meat and cracking bones accompanying the sudden wind and arcing black lightning. Something very much like a scream, sounding desperate and somehow hungry, echoed through the garden. Sophine was suddenly certain, completely and utterly sure, that something from somewhere beyond their world had seen the tear in the fabric of eternity and was lurching its hideous way towards it.

'Jump, Rigel!' she shouted.

The hole vanished, only to burst open again next to Thaniel. Again the echoing wail reverberated through her mind as much as the air; this time closer. Rigel fell through the hole, arcs of black light flashing across his body and vanishing into the grass as it closed. The wail faded, though she could have sworn it ended on a note of frustration. She shivered again and trudged towards the boys, who were whooping and cheering across the garden.

Thaniel had managed, just about, to conjure the shield she'd accidentally formed at The Barbican earlier on. He had seemed very sure he could do it again, though Sophine had her doubts. The most important thing was that the boys could get themselves out of danger, so she supposed they could use Rigel's portals to escape instead of using a shield if they had to. Besides, Rigel could also manipulate time though he seemed frustratingly unable to do it when he actually wanted to.

'Nice work,' she said as she approached them.

'Did you hear that scream?' They looked at her blankly.

'The scream through the portal,' she said. Neither of them gave any indication they knew what she meant. Thaniel shrugged. 'It was different being on this side,' she added. 'I could hear it better...'

Rigel was blinking at her.

'Okay, okay. Just...don't use it if you don't have to. I think it's forbidden for a reason.'

Thaniel grimaced. 'It certainly is. Makes me feel terrible.' He eyed Rigel. 'You seem ok though.'

Then he jumped back as Rigel bent double and vomited on Balderwin's immaculate garden. 'Hey what the—' yelled Thaniel.

The vomiting Rigel shimmered and vanished as Sophine began to laugh.

'Surprise!' she yelled. Thaniel looked to his side and saw Rigel staring in fascination at the spot where the fake had stood. They locked eyes, and Rigel began to laugh.

'Amazing!' he said, his eyes gleaming in the starlight. '*Amazing!* That was incredible!'

'Thank you,' she said. 'I spent all day on it. Not easy. Not at all. While you were off dealing with the ship I was trying to figure it all out. It's so much more than just emotion, you've got to channel it in these awkward ways. Holding images of what you want to see, what you want *other* people to see, and *which* other people…the right level of detail…it's crazy.'

'Sounds worse than portals,' said Rigel.

'Much worse,' she agreed.

'So you're still the best,' he said, with a mocking smile.

'But of course,' she flicked her hair with a grin.

'Well, as long as that's clear.'

Chapter Eighteen

It was affirmation day for the new Echelarch of Asterheim. Or would be when the sun slipped over the horizon. Sophine glanced at the rapidly lightening sky to the east of her spot on the city walls, and felt her heart pounding in her chest. From where she stood, just to the side of the great Fishergate, she could stare out to the south towards the looming shadow of Westerly Castle only a few miles away. Not far beyond, the road stretching from Fishergate down to the south vanished into a forest. It was from there she planned to make her army of light and confusion appear; there was nowhere else that could plausibly hide an army from sight so the choice had been made for her.

Sophine pulled her long fur-lined coat tight around her. She felt terribly exposed, not just because of the chill morning wind blowing along and over the high walls of Asterheim, but also because she was certain to be discovered before long. The thought had plagued her since she'd managed to get herself here unseen; someone would find her and that would be it. The plan would be ruined. And it would all have been for nothing…

The first rays of brilliant sunlight streamed over the horizon. The signal was given, such as it was. Barten had arranged the Senate to be in session from dawn and Rigel would have the mages ready to move an hour later, by which time, if Sophine did her job well, chaos ought to have consumed the city. Thaniel was helping his master arrange for his apprentices to escape; they'd start moving once the sun was up.

It was time. She pulled the coat tighter, more afraid than she had ever been.

'It's alright, dear,' said Ariene, coming up alongside her, linking an arm through hers. 'If you can't do it, no one will blame you.'

Sophine bit back a cutting response, feeling heat rise in her cheeks. She tried to shrug off the arm, but Ariene held on.

'They shouldn't have given you this job,' the older woman said with scorn dripping from her words. 'Some girl who never even got a patron could never have amounted to anything…'

Sophine threw off the Senator's arm and whipped around in sudden blazing rage. 'How dare you—?'

Ariene was smiling blandly. She gestured at the lightening forest, now coming into focus. Sophine hesitated, feeling the familiar fires of rage stoking the power within her. She glared at Ariene a moment longer, then turned away. She looked out, past Westerly Castle as the sunlight traced its way slowly down the fortress, from the great turrets to the high stone walls, gradually bathing the slumbering world in brilliant light.

'Balderwin would have been too good for you,' continued Ariene, viciously. 'Even such a low, monstrous beast of a man wouldn't take you…'

Sophine felt something rising from her stomach like a dragon spreading its wings, its neck uncoiling, burning heat flowing up her neck as it unleashed its fiery breath and flooded her mind with dazzling energy. She gasped, recalling the images she'd spent the night creating with Ariene. Men in armour marching with a heavy tread. Banners bearing the triple diamond banner of Ceresheim flapping in the morning breeze. Hundreds of cavalry, their horses heavy with protective shielding and carrying their masters' lances in packs strapped to their sides. A moving ocean of military might to instil panic and fear in all but the most battle-hardened soldier.

The energy within her flitted and coiled around the images she wanted, refusing to take shape, too bright and powerful to be tamed. It began to bite at her, tearing at her flesh. On a distant, physical level, Sophine felt her skin starting to burn; she gasped, struggling to resist the urge to let go of the painful energy.

'Control it, Sophine,' Ariene said, using the same tone of stern instruction used by the masters, so familiar to her after years at Hilda's that she obeyed without conscious thought. The energy lashed and writhed, but began to take form. The heat prickling her skin receded, and she opened her eyes, reaching out a hand to the distant forest. The burning energy, fuelled by her rage and given form through her will, caused barely a ripple in the visible air as it leapt the distance from her outstretched fingers to the trees, but once there, it did as she commanded.

A mist began to rise, obscuring the first lines of the great boughs of the forest. Through the pale wisps marched the vaguest impression of an army, still-formless shades gradually becoming solid, forming into glittering plate mail and shining swords brightly catching the morning light. Sophine winced a little; the illusion was not perfect. The sun had yet to reach the shadows beneath the trees and so her conjured soldiers gleamed all on their own. There was nothing else for it, she couldn't revise the images now. She pushed on, channelling more and more energy through the tight confines of her prepared images. More and more soldiers emerged from the misty trees, advancing into the light so that they at least looked more realistic.

There were shouts, the lookouts on the walls noticing the spectres and calling out to their fellows in disbelief. Men began to run, the clamour began to rise. Someone started blowing a horn, which made a dreadful wailing sound. More soldiers began to run about on the walls, passing behind Ariene and Sophine without pausing to question why they were there.

'I think that's far enough, dear,' said Ariene softly.

Sophine shook her head. 'I still have some more to bring up,' she said.

'The front lines are clearly within sight of Westerly Castle,' the Senator replied. 'We don't want them too close or someone will notice they all have the same face.'

'They don't all have the same face,' Sophine said, uncertainly.

'Are you sure?'

'No.'

'Then, it's far enough.'

Sophine nodded and had her illusions pause. The flow of energy receded, now just needing a steady stream of concentration to maintain them. She exhaled heavily, not realising how difficult it had been to create them until now.

'How long can you hold them?'

'I'm...not sure. It's not difficult, but I'll tire eventually.'

'Excuse me, ladies,' someone said behind them. Sophine turned, and looked up into the face of a young soldier peering out of a heavy helmet. 'What are you doing here?' he asked, looking around with a clank of ill-fitting armour.

'We came to see the view,' said Ariene. 'I am Lady Ariene Gloriana.'

The soldier was wrong-footed. He took a clattering step back and glanced around.

'You…you are?'

'Yes, dear. And thank you for volunteering your services.'

'I…What?'

'We were told by the Castellan that someone would be coming to provide an escort,' Ariene continued smoothly. 'I presume you are he?'

The young soldier stammered, shifting noisily from foot to foot in agitation.

'We're very grateful,' said Ariene, turning away. 'Please ensure we don't come to any harm and make sure no one else bothers us.'

'I…Yes, madam.'

The soldier stood dumbly behind them for a moment, before apparently deciding to accept his new posting and drawing himself up to attention.

Sophine kept her eyes on the ghost army as another soldier came running up and exchanged words with their new protector, who whispered frantically back using words like 'Senator' and 'protective duty'. The other soldier ran on, his armoured feet clanking against the stone.

Sophine released a shaky breath and concentrated.

***

Walking in four groups went some way to making the mages less conspicuous, but Rigel still bit his lip every time he looked back to check on them as they walked the distance to the docks from the Balderwin estate. He felt horribly exposed; each group had only one or two adults and a number of children, so at first glance they could be taken for families. But families with travelling cloaks and hoods up, carrying bags and heading out of the Noble Quarter...

It was an unusual sight to say the least.

Rigel wore high boots and dark trousers, with a red jacket over a shirt. He wanted to look like the kind of person who might not be local, heading to the docks to catch a ship back to wherever he was from, and certainly not the often-scruffy mage in the service of Lady Gloriana. He was not at all sure he'd pulled it off, and kept tugging at the jacket. Lord Balderwin's wardrobe had by now been significantly depleted.

'Hey,' he called as they turned a corner onto a lane which ran through some parkland, 'hoods down ok? We look way too shifty with them up.'

There were some nods of agreement, some mutterings of darker comments. He turned back. The short lane opened out into the heavily built-up area near the docks. Portgate castle loomed ahead, housing the barracks for the Battlemasons charged with the security of the port and a number of other civilian offices concerned with travel and commerce through the Western Ocean. Rigel eyed it with suspicion and not a little fear, as though the castle itself were watching them.

They turned down a commercial street, heading round to the southern end of the harbour where their ship was berthed. Rigel could barely think over the pounding of his heart and the adrenaline throbbing through his body. Up ahead, a man and woman laden with travel bags hurried out of a shop. The man dropped a bag as he fiddled with a key, only to be bashed on the shoulder by the woman who clearly felt their priorities lay elsewhere. The man looked around, and Rigel followed his gaze to see Battlemason soldiers trudging heavily in their direction looking at a sheet of paper. The man dropped the key and bag and ran with the woman to the other side of the street, where they vanished into a crowd. The soldiers arrived at the shop and pushed their way in, emerging a few moments later and shrugging at one another as one pointed to the dropped bag and keys. They looked around for a moment before moving on.

'Mages?' asked Master Thomas, appearing at Rigel's side and making him jump. He hadn't realised he'd stopped to watch.

Rigel nodded and pointed to the sign outside the shop.

'I thought they weren't starting until midday,' said Madam Raftopolis from behind them.

'Let's go,' said Rigel, not wanting to think about how many mages may have already been rounded up. Behind him, the refugees hurried along, the crowded street at least masking the procession.

Up ahead, at the end of the street, the ground turned wooden as the harbour began.

The smell of salt water and fish began to permeate the air. Rigel's heart leapt as he saw ships on the water, wondering which one might be theirs...

'Young man,' said a familiar voice. Rigel turned to see Lord Orswell smiling at him. He tried to smile back. Orswell nodded at a huge vessel berthed some way away down a long stretching pier.

'That's the one,' he said with a smile. 'Needed a big ship for everyone so, unfortunately, it's a bit of a walk.'

The ship was like a small galleon. Long and wide, its sides surprisingly high out of the water, with a figurehead of an implausibly large-breasted woman whose modesty was preserved, barely, by swathes of long red hair. Three enormous masts of heavy wood held furled sails which Rigel was sure would look glorious when the ship got underway. It looked like it could hold hundreds of people.

Rigel found he couldn't reply, simply making choking sounds as sudden emotion robbed him of speech and dignity. Off to his left, the two mages from the shop arrived, milling around wondering where to go.

'Ruinously expensive to hire,' said Orswell blandly, ignoring Rigel's barely suppressed sobbing, for which he was absurdly grateful. 'But how else is a Senator to travel?'

Rigel managed a laugh at that, and peered at their unexpected benefactor.

Orswell wore a splendid tunic of yellow and white silk, almost like he was competing with the sun for dazzling brightness. He looked happy, his normally sallow cheeks flushed with excitement. He'd oiled his beard and trimmed his hair. He clapped Rigel on the back.

'My apprentices are already on board, for the most part. A few dregs are still arriving. But they all have their travel licences courtesy of the Citizenry Guild so I can't foresee any issues with our getting underway long before the affirmation vote gets going.'

Rigel's blood turned to ice in his veins. 'Travel licences?'

Orswell looked at him sharply.

***

Lord Amir Barten was pleased to note that His Grace the Echelarch-Elect was, to put it lightly, very upset. Lyoris paced up and down on the dais at the centre of the Senate, his fists clenching and unclenching by his sides. He wore his simple dark clothes and looked like a scrawny scholar, having been called to the Senate far earlier than he'd intended to arrive due to Barten's emergency summons. His face was red and his hair unkempt.

'This is completely unacceptable!' he yelled, for perhaps the fourth time, the words sounding increasingly petulant the more he repeated them. He paced on, his fingers lingering over the arm of the throne he had yet to sit in. He paused there for a moment, his body quivering. Then he shook, visibly jumping as though startled, and paced away.

'Who called this session?' he asked the silent assembly of Senators.

Barten rose to his feet, rubbing absently at his side. He couldn't reach the spot where the knife had penetrated his back, but somehow he couldn't help trying.

'I called the session, Your Grace,' he said in a grave tone. Lyoris whipped around and fixed him with one of his peculiar, emotionless stares. It was like looking at a snake.

'You, Lord Barten?'

'Sir, there is grave news from Westerly Castle and has been confirmed by Fishergate within the last hour.'

Lyoris continued to stare, motionless, before finally turning away and waving at him to continue.

'There are reports of soldiers amassing in the forests beyond Westerly, sir.'

'Amassing?'

344

'Forming. Lines of them.'

Lyoris frowned as though struggling to comprehend. 'What do you mean, Lord Barten? Speak plainly.' Amir smiled and bowed his head politely.

'As you wish, Your Grace. Ceresheim has sent an army to our walls.'

There was a sudden commotion as Senators began to shout and talk over one another, demanding explanations and shouting imprecations. Lyoris stood silently, staring up at the high vaulted ceiling.

'Lord Barten!' someone shouted. Amir turned and located the shouter. It was Lord Cromantis, father of the youngster who had tried to take control of his guilds, or so he'd been told. He almost wished the boy had been given them; it would have saved a lot of trouble.

Holding his arms out for quiet, Amir gestured at Cromantis. The shouting subsided a little.

'How certain are you of this, my lord? Do we have any idea of the enemy's strength?'

The enemy, thought Barten, *is standing on the dais, my lord. Behold his strength for yourself…*

The words danced on the edge of his tongue, daring him to give voice to them. He bit them back, with some considerable difficulty.

'A few hundred heavy horse, my lord, and perhaps double that of pikemen. The rest are Battlemasons and most likely some auxiliaries from the city. We can't be sure as, so far, they have not advanced far from the treeline.'

'Keeping their numbers hidden,' said Cromantis darkly. 'They expect us to give battle?'

345

'That would be my analysis, my lord. They are waiting to see how we respond before they reveal their strength.'

'Have they issued any demands?' asked the richly dressed young woman sitting by the elderly Lord Aresbrook. She wore a gown of shimmering green silk and emeralds dangled from her ears amidst thick red hair. Barten inclined his head to her and averted his eyes in case he lost his train of thought down the front of her bodice.

'So far nothing, Lady Aresbrook.'

'Then the first question is what should we demand of them,' the young lady said fiercely. 'Namely to remove themselves from our territory or face the consequences.'

'And what consequences would those be?' asked Lord Cromantis in such a condescending tone that Amir winced. Lady Aresbrook rose smartly to her feet and fixed Cromantis with a glare.

'That we will destroy them and send their bones back to Ceresheim in small wooden boxes, or something of that nature, I should think.'

'A difficult message to give, my lady,' said Barten, sensing an opportunity, 'since our Battlemasons are presently wandering the streets.'

'What?'

'No order has been given—'

The lady threw her hands up in the air and shouted. 'Then give the order, Barten, you're Castellan—'

'My lady, I am not,' said Barten softly. 'The Echelarch-Elect is the Castellan of the Battlemasons, as indeed he is overlord of all other guilds. Including yours.'

The same stunned expression settled onto Lady Aresbrook's and Lord Cromantis' faces. It was clear that in the moment, both had forgotten the new Echelarch entirely, falling back on the old methods of crisis resolution. As one, they all turned to the dais where Lyoris stood in shivering rage, his face almost puce. Lady Aresbrook sank slowly into her seat. Lord Cromantis remained standing for a moment, before his son pulled him down.

'My lord,' Amir began, but was cut off by Lyoris's unhinged bellow of rage.

'Enough!' the Echelarch-Elect cried, actually stamping his feet. Barten was too stunned to laugh. 'Ceresheim comes to my walls on the day of my affirmation as Ecehlarch and you, the Lords of this city, forget your places and start yelling and squabbling like children!'

No one replied.

'I will handle this myself! I will…!' he groped for words. 'I will smash them!'

Barten rose to his feet. 'My lord,' he began.

'Your *Grace*!' screamed Lyoris. 'I am your Echelarch!'

'Your Grace,' repeated Barten with devastating smoothness and calm, 'you must send the Battlemasons out immediately. Recall them from their…errands.'

'Just what are these errands Lord Barten is so deliberately highlighting for us, *Your Grace*?' asked Lord Aresbrook from his wheeled chair.

'They are seeing to matters of security and need to—'

'Matters of security!' laughed Lady Aresbrook, rising once more in a rustle of silk. 'I should think the army on the doorstep is of some relevance to security, *Your Grace*, or am I mistaken?'

'We did say mages were a threat,' said Barten blandly, as though defending his Echelarch.

'Mages? They're rounding up mages?' asked Lady Aresbrook.

'I believe so…'

'How did you know that, Barten?!' demanded Lyoris.

'I still have some friends at the office of the Castellan, Your Grace, they informed me.'

'Traitors! I shall have them—'

'Perhaps the Battlemasons should be redeployed, Your Grace?' said Lord Cromantis, cutting through the rant. Lyoris paused, his scrawny chest heaving as he gulped in air. His red face was sweating and he dabbed at it with a golden handkerchief.

'Yes,' he muttered. 'Yes of course.' He clicked his fingers and a priest ran forward.

'Give orders for the Battlemasons to meet the threat beyond. The Travellers can handle security inside the city.'

'But Your Grace,' replied the priest, 'the Travellers haven't received the list of—'

'I don't care!' shouted Lyoris, backhanding the man across the mouth and sending him scurrying away. 'Just do it!'

'In the meantime, my lords, Your Grace,' said Barten, taking in the entire assembly, 'we should discuss what terms we could offer to placate Ceresheim and what would not be appropriate…'

The murmuring began again and one by one, Senators rose to offer their thoughts.

Amir turned to look at the dais, a fleeting glance. Lyoris was sitting on the stone floor by the throne, one hand tracing the wood of the chair he so sorely wanted to possess with erratically tapping fingers. His eyes stared off into the distance, wide and twitching.

Good, good, Amir thought, *just need to delay this charade a little longer…*

***

Orswell was rigid with panic.

'You mean to tell me no one here has a licence to travel?' he hissed through clenched teeth, darting fearful glances at the bands of patrolling Battlemasons wandering idly up and down the wooden piers or standing in small groups outside the various offices and merchant shops.

'I didn't...We didn't...' Rigel fumbled for an answer, his stomach a roiling mess of icy fear. He glanced away at the ship, swaying gently in the deep water at the end of the pier. It was so close...just a short run away.

'Rigel,' Thaniel said quietly, nodding a head behind him. Rigel turned to look.

The sizeable group of milling citizens was now beginning to attract attention. Some few hundred people were gathered on the jetty, huddled in their travelling cloaks and hefting bags. This in itself was not unusual for a busy dock, but their shared looks of fear and furtive glances at the guards made them stand out a mile. As Rigel watched, a bored looking soldier with a halberd propped up against some boxes next to him narrowed his eyes and straightened. The woman who had peeped round at him hid her face and tried to shuffle through the crowd. The soldier took a step forward, hesitated, then made his way towards the Harbourmaster's office with a look of determination that Rigel did not like at all.

'If we don't do something right now, everything's ruined,' said Rigel in a hurried whisper to Orswell. The Senator glared at him, pinching the bridge of his nose.

349

'Dammit,' he muttered, and turned to address the officer in charge of the line of soldiers blocking access to the main pier. The officer, a grim, thin-looking man with a cruel scar and one good eye, peered up at him from where he sat languidly on a damp-looking box. His armour was battered and his trousers ripped. Wisps of unkempt white hair hung down over his face.

'You there,' said Orswell, his voice surprisingly steady, 'move these men back, I need to get my retainers on board.'

The officer's good eye narrowed.

'Your *retainers* are already aboard, Lord Orswell,' he drawled. 'They boarded an hour ago as I recall. Those Traveller boys just finished loading their bags.' He jutted his chin in the vague direction of some manual labourers who sat glumly by the side of the water.

'Don't travel light, your *retainers*,' the man continued, spitting a blob of something vile onto the wooden pier. 'Probably best,' he smiled unpleasantly, 'think I'd want out too if I were, you know, a *retainer*.'

Some of the men nearest the officer chuckled but it sounded forced. Most of them just shuffled their feet, avoiding Orswell's eyes.

'The ship I hired,' said Orswell evenly, indicating it with a wave of his hand, 'can accommodate far more than the few who boarded earlier. I was merely waiting for the others to arrive.'

'They have licences?'

'I gave you all the licences the first time round. You've seen them already.'

The officer digested this a moment, and leaned back on his box to peer at the gathering crowd.

'I see families there. Old men. Women. You telling me those are retainers too? Just what might you be up to?' he asked, sliding off his box with a sinuous grace that belied his scruffy appearance 'My *lord*?' he added insolently.

Orswell held his gaze for a moment, before opening his mouth to speak just as a peculiar sound filled the air that made him, and everyone else, pause. It was the deep, droning sound of a war-horn, blasting from somewhere to the south. Rigel could feel it reverberating in his chest, could almost see it rippling on the softly surging water of the harbour. Before long another horn, this time much closer, joined the cacophony. Thaniel was saying something, but Rigel missed it. He leaned closer and yelled.

'What?'

'Portgate!' shouted Thaniel, pointing at the military stronghold to the east of the harbour, where the Battlemasons had their barracks and armouries. 'Other...must...been Shieldgate!'

The horns faded into echoing silence, and for a brief moment everything paused. Soldiers looked at one another, faces slack and disbelieving. Somewhere, a seagull cawed inquisitively.

Then the spell broke and chaos reigned. Everywhere, sergeants and lieutenants ran to find their units and barked at them to move. Outside the harbourmaster's office there seemed to be some disagreement between two apparently high ranking Battlemason officers over what the horns signified; the first, a younger man wearing a golden sash across his armour and elaborate pauldrons, was gesturing at the other, an older man with far less ostentation but whose crossed arms radiated an undeniable air of authority. The older man, having listened to the hysterical imprecations of the junior for as long as he evidently felt appropriate, knocked the boy out

351

with a well-timed fist and left him sprawled on the pier as he strode away yelling orders. Within moments, every Battlemason was making a hasty retreat away from the harbour. Rigel couldn't help but pump a fist jubilantly in the air.

'Sophine did it,' he said, and Orswell gave him a brief smile.

'Let's go,' he yelled at the milling crowd of mages. Their expressions of terror and confusion suddenly became bright smiles and hopeful cries, as they gathered their bags and ushered the children to hurry.

Rigel turned to head to the boat, and came face to face with the unpleasant spitting officer. He and his men had remained in place, the officer snarling at the commotion and the soldiers wide-eyed and hesitant.

'Don't you have orders?' said Orswell, making to brush past him. The wiry little man held out an arm.

'You think I don't know a diversion when I see one?' he snarled unpleasantly. 'A pack of filthy wretches without licences just happens to show up and the horns blow for the first time in decades?'

'You're being called to the walls,' Rigel spat angrily, 'there's an army out there...'

'And how do you know that, whelp?'

Rigel gaped at him, struggling to think of an answer.

'Something ain't right,' snarled the officer, 'and none of you are getting on that boat.' He gestured to his men.

'Take them,' he growled, drawing his sword with a speed that shocked Rigel; before he could blink Orswell was being forced to his knees, a blade at his throat. The other soldiers were coming forward, brandishing their spears and swords; their faces showed none of the confusion of a few moments ago. This was what they knew, after all.

'No!' yelled Thaniel, thrusting out an arm on reflex and blasting three of them up and away. One splashed into the water with a horrified cry and sank immediately to the bottom.

The officer was yelling, struggling with Orswell who was trying to free himself. More of the soldiers were rushing them, Thaniel forcing them back with his signature telekinetic blasts.

'Rigel!' he shouted. 'Get them on the ship!'

Rigel shook himself and gestured behind him to the oncoming crowd.

'Move it, come on!' he shouted, ushering them along. 'Leave your bags, just run!'

Some of the departing Battlemasons had heard the commotion and had turned, heading their way at a full run. Desperate, Rigel tried to summon the shield Sophine had shown them, but his adrenaline-soaked system was stopping him from reaching his power. Panic blotted out everything.

A small boy of four or five was walking in a dazed circle, his cheeks wet with tears as he called for his father. The crowd was rushing by, paying no heed; somewhere in there, the child's family must have been swept away. Rigel leapt forward and grabbed him, pulling him close and running along with the rest as the boy shrieked and wailed in his arms. He passed Thaniel, who seemed to be in some kind of standoff with the remaining soldiers, who were warily pointing their weapons at him but not coming any closer. The evil-looking officer had vanished, and so had Orswell.

'Thaniel! We have to go!' Rigel shouted over the bawling child's screams.

'You go!' Thaniel called back, glancing towards the back of the crowd where the Battlemasons had almost caught up. He grunted and threw a blast at them, knocking the front rank down into the next, but the force was weaker than before. Thaniel looked strained; he wouldn't be able to repel another assault if the Battlemasons came at him again.

Rigel hesitated, and looked at the child crying miserably for his father. The boy's little fingers clutched his tunic, his whole body juddering with the force of his terrible fear. His hopelessness. Despair. Just like the emptiness inside him whenever he tried to picture his mother's face.

There…

Rigel felt the stirrings of heat within him and kept his eyes and thoughts on the poor boy. His need to protect seemed to stoke the fire inside, swirling and building the energy of emotion, dispelling the paralysis of adrenaline.

'It's alright,' he whispered to the child, 'just hold on…'

For the first time, Rigel deliberately reached out with his mind, forcing the flow of time to buck and heave, crashing like a wave against his resolve and gathering like a growing weight on the other side of the temporary barrier he had placed between the mages and the rest of the world. He gasped with the sudden feeling of opposition, staggering a little as though physically bowed by the pressure of time trying to smash back through. He gripped the child as tightly as he dared, not really knowing how to hold another tiny person without hurting them.

The boy had stopped crying. He looked around now with bright, wet eyes, as though seeing for the first time. All around them things had simply stopped. Birds hung, motionless in mid-flight. Ships, caught mid-sway, seemed oddly off-balance. Soldiers no longer yelled. Only the pattering of desperate feet on the wooden boards of the pier made any sound at all.

The boy was staring in fascination at a gull, caught in a deep swoop not three metres away. Then he seemed to remember what he was doing and peered at the running crowd of mages and their families.

'Where's Daddy gone?' he asked as he looked around, his frowning curiosity so strangely adult that it made Rigel laugh.

'He's alright?' asked Thaniel, coming to stand by them. The boy looked at him.

'Daddy's on the ship,' the child said with a decisive nod. For emphasis, he turned to point a tiny finger at the motionless boat.

'Yes, he is,' Rigel agreed, not knowing what else to say. 'Can you go with—?'

A young man came running through the crowd, yelling incoherently, and seemed to get even more hysterical at the sight of the boy in Rigel's arms. He ran towards them, arms flailing, his travelling cloak flapping around him.

'Connor!' he cried in half-relief and half-anger, grabbing the boy from Rigel without even appearing to see him. The man turned to run for the ship, smothering the child in kisses between choked sobs.

'He's ok,' Rigel called after them weakly. He looked at Thaniel. 'He's ok, right?'

Thaniel shrugged.

'You're holding this well,' he remarked, bizarrely casually, nodding to the mid-flight bird.

'I can feel it, pushing in on my head,' Rigel said, tapping his forehead. 'It's strange...'

'They're almost aboard,' Thaniel said. Rigel looked up. The last of the mages and their families were clambering up the gang planks. 'Should we get their bags? How long do we have?'

Some of the running mages had done as Rigel suggested and left luggage littered around. Rigel put a hand to his head and closed his eyes.

'Not long,' he said with a wince. 'But let's grab what we can.'

'Where's Orswell?' asked Thaniel.

Rigel shook his head bleakly. Thaniel let out a bark of frustration and kicked a nearby crate, which did not move. He yelped fiercely and fell over, clutching his foot.

'It's like kicking stone!'

Rigel shook his head and allowed himself a smile.

'What did you expect? Come on.'

When time snapped back into place, it seemed to the confused Battlemasons that the crowd of people had simply vanished before their eyes. Only the few remaining soldiers who had been facing off against Thaniel had any idea where they had probably gone, but they collectively decided that discretion was the better part of valour and slunk away in search of their cruel-faced officer.

On the ship, Eric and Thaniel embraced fiercely as Rigel walked to the prow of the ship. He breathed a heavy sigh of relief as swarms of soldiers failed to materialise on the pier and normality appeared to return to the docks. Behind him, families reunited and wept with joy as they were led away into the cargo areas below decks by the sailors. It hadn't gone smoothly, but the first part of the plan was done. It was time to implement part two.

He bit his lip.

Chapter Nineteen

In one of the lowest rooms of the Seagate Castle, the great seaward fortress of Asterheim Harbour, resided the winch mechanism for the Great Asterheim Harbour Chain. A vast wood-and-steel wheel with man-sized spokes, reinforced with bands of iron, connected to a huge cylinder around which the massive chain could be wound, link by ponderous link, as the ship-shattering line of thick metal was slowly raised above the surface of the water to bar entry for any vessel. Any fleet or navy trying to breach the city's defences through the harbour would find itself stuck, floundering, turning in on itself as Asterheim's own naval strength was brought to bear on their flanks. The Seagate itself housed tower after tower filled with deadly slits from which archers could rain flames on such a stranded fleet.

To raise the barrier, another heavier and no less impressive chain had to be unwound. This one connected to a counterweight, suspended on the walls of the Seagate, held in place by its own vast machinery. A lever in the winch room could drop the counter, unwinding its own heavier chain and in so doing, raise the barrier.

In theory, it was a glorious place. Vital to the defence of the city and, by extension, of the country. Proud, ancient, necessary.

To the guards stationed here however, it was a tedious prison of damp stone and chilly draughts. Almost never used, the great winch sat immobile and rusting. Some of them darkly wondered, on the many endless nights of winch-duty, whether the wheel could even raise the chain at all, or even if the chain itself had not by now rusted away to the point of uselessness. As far as anyone alive knew, a ship could simply sail straight through it, smashing the ancient links like rotted wood. There were those who had placed bets on the likely state of the chain if and when it was eventually raised, some of whom had died without ever seeing the outcome of their wager. Thus it had become known as the Dead Man's Wager, the pot increasing as each departing contestant left their share to a successor who added his own.

It was, to his shame, thought of the wager that filled the second soldier's head when the stinking priest with the scarred jaw strode in and casually broke the first soldier's neck with a gesture. Jumping back in horrified alarm, he nodded frantically and leapt to obey the murderer's demands, wrapping his numb hands around the thick lever that operated the counterweight. Under normal circumstances pulling the lever without cause was punishable by death, but at least there would be a trial of some sort. It didn't look like the crazy man in the gold outfit would be quite so reasonable if he *didn't* obey. The soldier pulled the lever, straining against ancient mechanisms that protested at his temerity, that he should have the gall to disturb them after so very long. He heaved and pulled, lending his whole body weight to it, and something deep beneath his feet clanked heavily. The lever moved.

Somewhere outside, the vast counterweight of solid iron dropped at lightning speed into the water and sank instantly beneath the waves. The winch mechanism gave an alarming clang as the first great chain was suddenly pulled taught, and then slowly began to turn, the huge spokes rotating inch by inch at first and then faster and faster as the vast forces began to find their equilibrium. The counterweight, so carefully made to be just about heavy enough to drag the Great Chain at a steady pace from its resting place on the seabed, sank lower and lower, slowly turning the cylinder until, like a leviathan of legend, the Great Chain rose up.

The soldier stepped back, turning fearful eyes at the strange man in the dirty gold robes, who smiled back with a grin like death himself and raised a gnarled hand.

The soldier's last thought was that he might have won the Dead Man's Wager.

***

The captain had cast them off, the ship moving with surprising speed from its berth.

Rigel had never been on a ship, or a boat of any size for that matter, and he was at once exhilarated and terrified. The idea that nothing was beneath them but water, endless and cold and filled with murky things with teeth and scales…

'Rigel!' Thaniel's cry was filled with anguish. He was pointing over the railing, towards the walls of the harbour rising proudly out of the sea. Rigel looked, but couldn't see what his friend was pointing at.

'It's Orswell!'

Rigel squinted, and just about made out the figures marching along the wall towards the Seagate Castle. One of them was wearing something very bright, possibly yellow.

Orswell.

'What can we do?' Rigel looked at Thaniel. He gave a helpless shrug.

'Friend of yours?' asked a gruff voice. They turned to regard the captain, a swarthy man of middle years, wearing a peculiarly ostentatious red military coat with medals sewn on the breast. He was quite clearly not a military man, with his rotten teeth and hideously tangled beard, which made Rigel wonder just what had happened to the naval officer whose coat he was wearing.

'I recognise him,' the captain continued, 'he was the one came to see me when he had his permits. Reckon he's my client.'

'Client?' said Rigel.

'Aye. Customer. Client. The one who paid me.' The captain turned his blue-eyed stare on Rigel. 'You ain't.'

'He told you the plan,' Thaniel said. 'He trusted you to see it through?'

'Paid me, lad. Not trusted.' The captain laughed a single, loud hoot of laughter.

'But you were paid—' began Rigel.

'I ain't gonna throw you overboard, lad,' snarled the captain with a wave of his hand, 'but seems to me that fellow paid a lot of money to get you and yours out of this stinking cesspit of a city.' He nodded at the distant figures trudging towards Seagate Castle. 'Seems to me, you owe him.'

'We weren't going to leave him,' Thaniel said, without much conviction. He met Rigel's eyes.

361

'You know what we are, captain?' Rigel said, looking back at the rugged sailor. 'You know why we're running?'

'Aye. Told me. Don't sit right with me what they're doing, neither. I've had many a mage on my crew, keeps the storms off for one thing.'

'Alright then, tell your men not to panic when we do this...'

When reality peeled back and sent black lightning sparking from the stones of the old walkway atop the harbour wall, the mean-faced officer yelped and jumped back, shouting and swearing to any god he could name. A swollen orb of darkness materialised before his eyes, growing in size so fast he began to hop and fumble for his sword, making whining noises and letting go of the chain he'd been holding to secure the prisoner. Unearthly wind blew, threatening to throw him from the wall and making his moth-eaten trousers flap wildly.

Thaniel stepped through the portal, a little pale but otherwise in control of his stomach, for which he was very grateful. He stood, outlined in howling unreality, wreathed in flashing darkness and fixed the officer with a stare.

'I'll be taking the prisoner from here,' he said over the scream of the howling wind.

The officer, having finally managed to draw his sword, dropped it and ran. Thaniel let him go, suppressing the urge to flick him over the wall.

'My Lord Orswell,' he called, holding out his hand to the prisoner, 'your ship awaits.'

Rigel sat gasping on the deck of the ship as Thaniel stepped back through with Orswell. The portal collapsed and vanished, the wind dying and leaving tendrils of dark lightning sparking on the deck.

Thaniel helped him up, peering into his face. 'Are you alright?'

Rigel tried to nod, but he was tired. So very tired. 'I'm not as good at this as Sophine,' he said.

'Speaking of,' said Thaniel nervously. 'It's time to get her and Ariene on the—'

'Full stop lads!' yelled the captain suddenly. 'Stop! Backwater now! Backwater! And if your backs don't break I'll break them for you! Pull!'

Rigel ran to the prow of the boat, using the rail for support as the ship lurched underfoot, the oarsmen changing direction as abruptly as they could. Up ahead, just past the looming vastness of the Seagate Castle, the Great Chain was rising. Piece by ponderous piece, it emerged from beneath the rolling depths, streaming with water, stretching link by link across the mouth of the harbour. One moment the middle of the heavy iron barrier remained submerged, the next it too was rising, slowly and inexorably, to form a straight line taut across their exit route.

'We're sitting ducks, lads!' yelled the captain, looking strangely excited about it. His eyes gleamed and he rested one hand upon the hilt of the old sword belted at his side. 'Someone don't want us leaving! Har!' His beard quivered and his 'borrowed' navy coat flapped.

Rigel eyed him, wondering just how sane the man was.

'We have to get Ariene,' said Thaniel by his side. Rigel scoffed a scornful breath of laughter.

'And bring her here to what, die with us?'

'Sophine's with her,' he replied. He nodded at the chain. 'She can take care of that.'

'I can take care of that,' muttered Rigel, sliding to the deck and rubbing at his forehead. Thaniel looked at him dubiously.

'Okay okay,' said Rigel. Thaniel closed his eyes and adopted his comical 'concentration' face.

Rigel looked up at the captain.

'Captain!' he yelled, interrupting the man's ranting mid-flow and making him turn half-crazed eyes on himself. 'We have to keep clear of the Castle,' he said, nodding at the imposing form of Seagate with all its archery-slits and who knew what else. 'They'll have ways of taking out ships...'

The captain muttered and growled and stormed about yelling orders at his men, and slowly the ship began to turn laboriously away from the looming threat of Seagate.

***

The lightning-wreathed hole in reality faded and died, leaving Sophine alone on the walls trying to process what she'd seen through Thaniel's portal. The chain had been raised, for the first time in who knew how long. She knew what that meant. She hadn't even needed to hear Thaniel's frantic attempts to explain. So after pushing Ariene through the portal, she'd leapt back before it closed. She had one more task to accomplish before they could leave; she just hoped she was up to the challenge.

The soldier who had been protecting her and Ariene for the last few hours was stuttering and blinking, both terrified and amazed by what he'd just seen.

'You're...you're...'

'A mage,' she said blandly, watching as the spectral army she'd created faded and vanished. She wished she could see the looks on the faces of the Battlemasons deploying in formation just beyond the city walls. Curiously, from what she could tell, none had left Westerley Castle, though it was possible they had done so on the southern side beyond her sight. Either way, to see the officers' bewilderment as the enemy blew away like sand on a windy beach would have been priceless.

The effort of maintaining the illusion once it had been conjured had proved mercifully low. Sophine had been able to keep it in place whilst sitting and standing, even chatting to Ariene at some points. Perhaps she did have the strength for what was coming after all.

'That was...' stuttered the soldier.

'You can go,' Sophine said, waving dismissively at him and wondering if she'd picked that up from Ariene. 'Dear,' she added with a half-smile.

She needed to concentrate; making a portal to somewhere you didn't know was tricky. The sort of portal magic the more advanced book had mentioned; the very one that warned against using them at all. She'd only done it once, the very first time when she'd ambushed the messengers to keep Rigel and Thaniel from being expelled. So very long ago, when such things had mattered so much.

Sophine collected her thoughts, focusing instead on what she thought she knew of the great chain. It was big, made of iron – everyone knew that. It had to have some kind of winch, maybe some soldiers guarding it...

'I'm coming with you,' said a voice like a thin blade behind her. Sophine turned sharply, and almost laughed aloud at the sight of Misty. The girl was as thin as ever, but dressed in leather and mail she couldn't have taken from Balderwin. Two knives were belted at her left hip, a third on the right.

'What are you doing here?' said Sophine, surprised but not at all unhappy to see her.

'My place is with you,' said Misty simply. 'I owe you my life; I wasn't about to let you do this alone.'

'How long have you been here?'

'As long as you have. Ariene was right about you needing a protector, she just didn't know you already had one.'

Sophine smiled and shook her head.

'We need to get to the Seagate,' she said, as a rising clamour of panic started to filter through the men on the walls. Soldiers were running, bells clanging. Someone was blowing yet another horn that had some form of military significance. She looked around, men were brandishing swords and running into the city.

'Idiots,' she muttered.

'They don't know it was an illusion,' said Misty. Sophine nodded.

'They think the enemy's transported itself inside the walls.'

'We need to go,' said Misty, loosening the right-hand knife in its sheath.

'I'm struggling to visualise Seagate…'

'Visualise harder.'

Sophine sighed heavily and turned away. *A winch, a room, a castle, a soldier, near the sea, near Rigel…*

That would have to do. Summoning Balderwin's leering face, Sophine tore reality open once again.

***

Lord Barten made his way up the steps to the great doors. Senators on either side raged and shouted, others sat slumped in their chairs wondering what had happened to their world. Lyoris himself had just departed into the chamber at the back of the room to prepare for the affirmation vote.

Barten had no intention of staying for *that*, if indeed that was the real reason for the Echelarch-Elect removing himself at a time like this. Though Barten had been sure Lyoris would never dare act against the Senate before he had been affirmed and consolidated his power, things had become so heated and so out of control that he no longer trusted the former High Priest to be rational. If indeed he ever had been. With Lyoris disappearing, he had decided he'd stalled long enough; if the mages weren't away now then it was too late. The Senators needed to be evacuated; there was no need to actually affirm the lunatic before doing so.

His hand-picked men, Battlemasons who were loyal to him alone, awaited his signal just beyond the Senate Building. They'd get everyone out fast, and then when Lyoris's plan was exposed, that would be the end of—

'Sorry my lord,' said a muffled voice from within a heavy steel helmet that was suddenly inches from Barten's own face. Amir blinked.

'No one in or out,' said the Battlemason. Next to him, his companion shifted position with a clank of heavy armour, hands crossed on the pommel of a drawn sword. Amir stepped back and took in the sight with dawning horror; there were six of them, forming a ring of steel across the doors. He looked away and down; other exits were similarly blocked.

He stepped back as though in a daze, wandering three steps down towards the dais before he noticed the missing columns. Some of the decorative pillars around the edge of the Senate Building were gone, small stumps all that remained. Small stumps with incongruous little holes cut in them. Little holes through which tiny wisps of greenish vapour were escaping.

Ariene had been right. They were all going to die in here.

'Oh no,' he said aloud in a detached, mellifluous voice, unnoticed by any of the bellowing Senators. He sank slowly to the floor, sitting on the steps as dreadful realisation swept over him.

'Oh no.'

***

They'd appeared in a badly lit corridor, smelling of damp and salt and rotting fish. The flame from the torches on the wall flickered pathetically in a chill breeze. Sophine had gestured to Misty to stay close, but the shadows were so thick she couldn't be sure the girl was even with her as she turned another corner and headed towards what looked like the outline of a doorway to a better-lit room.

'It has to be Seagate,' she muttered to herself, yet again, trying to make herself believe she hadn't transported them half-way around the world. It was like nowhere else she'd ever been; everything about the smell and the damp suggested it was near the sea, but that was all she could be sure about. It could just as easily be a lighthouse somewhere in the Western Ocean, or a fortress along the craggy south coast where the fishermen had beards so long that they wrapped themselves in them to keep warm against the icy winds.

She opened the door and stepped into the well-lit room. Something pushed her hard from behind, knocking her over to lie sprawling on the stone floor just as something fast and wickedly sharp buried itself in the doorframe where her head had been seconds before, with a thick sound of splitting wood. Sophine rolled to her feet, her eyes widening in horror and fury as Kahin stepped into view, gesturing to his knife which flew back to his hand.

'I've been waiting,' he said, flicking the knife from hand to hand. 'I thought the other one would come. The boy. But you'll do.' If the fact that he'd missed her bothered him, he gave no sign. He threw the knife again, viper-fast, but Sophine was ready this time and spun away from the flickering blade to throw a blast of telekinetic force at the deranged priest-mage. He gestured with his left hand, deflecting the blast and making a curious sign with his right. Sophine's throat constricted, but she twisted aside and vanished into a poorly made portal like the one she'd used against Misty, reappearing only a metre away, but it was enough to shake the spell loose.

Kahin straightened up, a flicker of doubt crossing his disfigured face. He took a pace to his right, and Sophine matched him, circling slowly, only then realising where they were.

Behind the psychotic priest stood a massive wheel mechanism, a vast cylinder around which was tightly wound the vast links of an enormous chain, straining under the weight of their own immensity. To the right of the huge cylinder, another chain strained taut and vanished through the floor. Sophine was no engineer, but she knew a counterweight when she saw one.

She allowed herself a thin smile. She'd made it after all.

Kahin's lips were moving, his hands twitching in a series of intricate gestures, the meaning of which escaped her. Instinct made her dive to the right, a sizzling ball of blue light missing her by inches. A smell like acrid burning filled the room as the ghostly light evaporated the stone behind her, just as she slammed into the floor and felt something in her chest snap. She gasped, trying to reach for her anger but finding only fear. Kahin grinned a lunatic smile and raised both hands.

And then Misty was there. A blur; a shape; a thin waif so easily ignored and so very, very deadly. She seemed to flicker into existence, Kahin's eyes only darting to notice her when she was already too close. He yelped as she flitted by, a phantom in the shadows cast by the enormous wheel, and suddenly two knives were protruding from his filthy golden robe, now stained with blood. He stepped back, blinking in disbelief, the words of his spell dying on his lips. He leaned against the great spokes of the wheel, gasping.

Sophine raised her hand, cold hate settling over her with all the dread power she knew it could grant. With a grim smile she unfolded her fingers. The links of the counterweight chain parted like the petals of a dying flower and snapped, releasing the Chain with a terrible suddenness that tore the whole cylinder and wheel mechanism from the floor and ripped it through the stone wall with an explosion of masonry and dust. Kahin was instantly crushed beneath the cylinder, smeared across the ragged remains of the floor and torn apart as it pulled him along. The Great Chain plummeted heavily to the seabed, never to rise again. A salty wind began to blow through the gaping hole in the wall.

Sophine stood slowly, the stench of human insides and salty fish-air made her want to retch. She stretched out a hand to Misty, and gathered the girl to her. They stood for long moments, not speaking, glorying in being alive as the waves churned beyond the broken wall, far beneath them.

Chapter Twenty

Thaniel had just been about to ask Rigel for the fifteenth time whether he thought Sophine was ok when the harbour-facing wall of the Seagate exploded. With a sound like the thunderous crash of gods colliding, the tower from which the chain protruded burst open in a great detonation of massive stone blocks, throwing vast chunks of rock and pieces of rubble far across the water. Something impossibly heavy ripped its way through the wall and smashed into the sea, tossing spray metres into the air and sending waves rippling across the harbour. Fishing boats and larger vessels alike bobbed and swayed in the sudden unexpected swells.

'Heads down, lads!' shouted the Captain, cackling madly at the sight. Crew and the few mages who had ventured up on deck scattered, hands futilely held over their heads, everyone apparently morbidly certain that to stay where they were invited a chunk of stone to smash them to pieces, and that a flimsy pair of hands might help them avoid their otherwise inevitable doom.

Rigel considered this with a peculiar dispassion, staring up at the ragged tear in the wall in which he was certain Sophine had died. He floated on a bed of cold detached guilt, seeing nothing but her final moments. Exploded by some terrible power she had unleashed to save them all. Destroying the chain had taken all her strength, made her give up her life for—

'Sophine!' shouted Thaniel, running past him to the stern. Rigel blinked.

He turned, frowning. Sophine was standing with Misty, smiling and hugging Thaniel.

Then Thaniel was in front of him again, waving and talking, putting his hands on his shoulders.

And shaking. Hard.

'Hey!' Rigel said, pulling away. 'What the hell are you doing?'

'Sophine's alright, Rige,' Thaniel said in the tone typically adopted by parents of very small or very stupid children. 'She's ok.'

'She...' Rigel sniffed, wiping away a tear that seemed to have formed and realising it was one of many. His voice choked and he couldn't speak, so instead he walked forward and hugged Sophine as she reached him.

'I thought you died,' he said, not caring how squeaky and high his voice was.

'I nearly did,' she said, pulling back and entirely ignoring the snivelling mess Rigel had become. 'Kahin was there.'

Thaniel's jaw opened comically wide and he gaped at her before recovering his wits. 'That's impossible,' he said. 'I blasted him...'

'He survived,' she said blandly. 'Again. But he won't survive this time.'

'What happened?'

'He got...smeared. There was a lot of him left on the floor.'

'And the wall,' added Misty.

'And the chain,' Sophine said with a nod.

'Plus I stabbed him, so...' said Misty, shrugging.

'She did,' smiled Sophine, taking the girl's hand delicately and looking at her with such intensity that Rigel looked away, gruffly swiping at his nose.

Ariene stepped up onto the deck and made her way over, holding her skirts up to daintily step over chips of stone and larger chunks that were scattered across the deck. She embraced Sophine and stood facing them all, her face grim. Behind her, Orswell had appeared, carrying a box that clinked as he moved.

'I'm afraid we don't have time to celebrate yet, dears,' Ariene said bluntly. 'Now that the refugees are safe, I have to return to the city. The Senate, the people, our entire way of life is in danger. It is entirely likely that I am going to my death, but I've faced that once and it wasn't particularly bothersome.' She smiled at Rigel. 'I won't ask you to come with me, because if I fail then you will be stranded and alone in a hostile city remade in the image of that vile priest who, if he hasn't already killed half the Senate, will shortly do so. Those who he does not kill will live in fear. And everything we hold dear will be dead. There will be no place for mages, and even you can't hope to fight a whole city. I ask only that you get me back there, let me confront him, and—'

'Save it, Ariene,' said Thaniel with a wry smile. 'You know we're coming with you.' By his side, Eric stiffened, muttering urgently. Thaniel turned and muttered back, holding his hands gently to Eric's suddenly sobbing face. Rigel looked at Ariene uncertainly.

'Even if we do go, I don't think we could possibly hope to—'

She cut him off with a gesture and gave him a hard, appraising look.

'Enough Rigel. We could. And will.' She moved closer, speaking in a low voice only meant for him. 'Your parents didn't believe in you, I know that. I know you haven't believed in yourself ever since. But listen to me, Rigel. You've saved me. You've saved these mages. You have it in you to save everyone in this city. They didn't believe in you, but I do, and so should you. Do you understand?'

Rigel's eyes glimmered with unshed tears, and this time he didn't try to swipe them away. He nodded, haltingly at first and then with a renewed vigour, as though something inside him had finally clicked.

'Okay,' he breathed heavily with a jerky smile. 'Let's go save *everything*.'

'I had a feeling you'd say that,' said Orswell from behind them, hefting his box. 'In here are three bottles of wine. I said I swiped one.' He grimaced, not quite a smile. 'I actually swiped three; we all have our petty amusements. Whatever Lyoris is planning, Ariene tells me it will involve poison and we deduced that the antidote was in his wine. Take them, and maybe they can help anyone he's already dosed.'

'Young man,' Ariene called, interrupting Eric and Thaniel's hushed conversation. Eric looked at her bitterly. 'The danger is only mine...Mostly. I am the one who will be denouncing the Echelarch to his face in the hope of persuading the Senate to grow a backbone and stand up for our way of life. These three will be there only to help me, and they will leave the moment I see things becoming dangerous.'

Rigel started to protest, but Ariene's stare stilled his tongue.

Eric was listening to her with a tenuous hope on his face that Rigel couldn't look at for long.

'I assure you, Thaniel will be back on this ship once we have done what we can. We all know how these three can get around; I'll make sure they leave before things get bumpy.'

Eric reluctantly released Thaniel's hand. Slowly, he made his way to the side of the ship and looked out over the water, watching the ruined tower of the Seagate drifting by.

'Very well then,' said Ariene. 'Let's go and see if Asterheim can still be saved.' Sophine gestured at the air, and reality ripped once more.

***

A palpable sense of panic had gripped the city. Everywhere they looked, Battlemasons ran frantically in all directions, units of twenty or so men chasing phantoms that had yet to appear and yelling at people to get inside and lock their doors. People fled before them, overturning merchant stalls and scattering goods on the cobbled streets.

Unfortunately, the arrival of a ghastly orb of black lightning in the expansive courtyard outside the Senate did little to quell the rising sense of chaos. As soon as they materialised, Ariene could see armed men charging at them from various points, yelling war cries and levelling spears.

She swayed on her feet, one hand on her stomach. The sense of disorientation was horrific. To step from a gently swaying boat to the solid ground of the Senate courtyard through a swirling vortex of images and sound was enough to make her want to lie down for at least a week. Sadly, as ever, the men in her life had other demands on her time, and these ones were fear-crazed soldiers pointing spears at her.

'Oh Circle save us, Circle save us,' Sophine was panting. Ariene waved a hand at her irritably and hushed the girl, stepping forward and holding her head as high as she could with her stomach in such knots.

'Battlemasons!' she cried in the ringing tones she'd used many a time to great effect within the Senate and out of it. That, and the imperious look on her face, were the only cards she had to play. But Lady Ariene Gloriana had played many times, and she knew the game better than most. She stood staring at the oncoming soldiers, chin tilted up, forcing her beating heart to calm itself through pure effort of will.

'Stand ready!' she yelled, as though she were their commander and this was a parade day. The effrontery of it was sublime, the audacity outrageous, but she knew soldiers. Panic and disorder were not their strong suit. A good leader and a set of orders was preferable any time of day you care to mention and, in her experience, at night too.

The front lines faltered as men looked at her, looked at one another, tried to remember just where their loyalties actually lay. Some stopped, others slowed. All seemed confused. Ariene saw the moment and seized it in an uncompromising grip.

'Battlemasons of Asterheim,' she called, letting her voice drop to a deeper note, a stentorian commanding note. 'We face a terrible threat. Not from Ceresheim; you've seen that they have gone. No! The threat is in there!' she pointed to the Senate Building. Some soldiers turned to look, others just frowned.

'I am Lady Gloriana, Senator of Astherheim and patron of many guilds,' she continued. 'I have come to free this city from the shackles of tyranny. Who will follow me?'

A young officer stepped forward, leaning on his spear. He saluted, with one hand across his chest and head slightly inclined.

'Lady Gloriana, the city is in chaos, what can we do?'

'Escort me to the Senate, Captain, and I will do the rest.'

Just what she was going to do with a Battlemason entourage she had no idea, but it was better than being skewered on a spear.

'It's Junior Sub-Lieutenant actually, ma'am…'

'*Captain*,' she repeated deliberately, looking him right in the eyes, 'lead on.' The young man could barely contain himself; his chest puffed out and his grin looked like it might split his face in half.

'Follow me, men!' he called grandiosely, and trotted off to the Senate with his unit at his armoured heels. She let them get a few paces ahead and followed, gesturing to the mages.

'What are we going to do with them?' Rigel asked in a whisper as he caught up with her.

She shrugged.

'They can give out the wine,' she said.

***

The yelling within the chamber had continued to rage so continuously that Barten was no longer able to really hear it. No voices called out to him, nothing distinctive was said. He vaguely wondered if he was dying, trapped in a chamber slowly filling with a poison that might kill him in an hour, three hours, three days, whatever the whim of the mad alchemist had been when he devised it...

It could only have been moments since he had wandered in a defeated daze back up to the helmed soldiers guarding the doors and slumped by their feet, but it felt far longer. His limbs were heavy and his head felt too big. He was fairly sure he was sitting on someone's foot, but the soldier was either too dumb or too unsure about the current state of politics and the balance of authority to do anything about it. A dim recess of his mind informed him that, yes, this was not normal behaviour and, yes, he was probably being poisoned. His legs ached and he wanted to rest.

A new sound cut through the din, a banging of something quite faint accompanied by a familiar voice, calling him from far away.

'There it is,' he muttered. 'I really *am* dying now.'

'Open this door!' yelled the voice. Barten frowned. Why would he be hearing Ariene Gloriana's voice, of all people? Wasn't she on a ship half a world away by now?

He blinked, and the world came into sharper vision for a moment. Senators' voices became more distinct, and he saw more than a few others slumped in their chairs like himself, exhausted, looking pale...

'How dare you keep a Senator out of the chamber!' Ariene yelled through the door. The banging came again, and this time he recognised it for what it was. He lurched to his feet, swaying against the faceless soldier who caught him and steadied him.

'Are you alright, sir?' asked the helmet. He tried not to laugh in the man's face and instead summoned what strength he had left and yelled back through the door.

'Ariene!'

'Amir!'

'Don't come in,' he called, not liking the slur to his voice.

'What?'

'Poison!'

'Amir! Amir what—?'

'Get out, Ariene, just get out!'

Lady Gloriana's reply was too faint to hear, and Amir was slipping down, sliding back down to the cool stone floor. He was hot, just needed to rest his head a moment on the cold, cold stone.

***

'We're too late,' Ariene growled, a note of hysteria entering her voice as she thumped a small fist against the heavy wooden doors. She glared up at the carved heroes endlessly posing overhead who, as ever, did very little to help.

'What do we do?' asked Thaniel, hovering anxiously behind her. Ariene was silent for a moment, then looked at each of them in turn.

'Rigel, you stay here. Your greatest ability is healing, you did it for me.'

Rigel started to reply, his face worried. She felt a flash of anger and gestured for quiet. 'Enough with the snivelling Rigel. You are a superlative healer when you have to be so put those fears away and be who you are. Now, I want you to use everything you have to counteract the effects of whatever foul pestilence that wretch has released in that room.'

Rigel nodded dumbly. She held his gaze for a moment, as if measuring him, then beckoned to the newly minted Captain of the

Battlemasons. He trotted over eagerly, his cheeks still flushed with his sudden change of fortunes.

'Pick five of your best,' she said to him. 'Protect this mage as though your life depended on it.'

He saluted smartly and, with only a slight askance glance at Rigel, ran off to pick his men.

'Thaniel, you come with me,' Ariene continued.

'Where?'

'We're going to the holding cells. There will be people there, political prisoners and friends, who don't stand a chance unless we free them. Your gift is those vicious blasts of force, so I want you to open cells with it.'

'I can also heal buildings,' he said, a little peevishly. She smiled at him.

'If we need it, I'll let you know,' she said, moving on to Sophine. Thaniel shuffled his feet and felt Rigel's eyes on him.

'I heal buildings,' Rigel mimicked quietly.

'Shut up,' he mumbled.

'Sophine, dear, you're on your own. I'm sure the boys don't mind me saying you're the most powerful.'

'We don't,' sighed Rigel, rolling his eyes.

'I need you to destroy the source of the poison. It will be under the chamber, in the vaults below the building. They haven't been used for anything in centuries, except storage, but beware. It's like a labyrinth down there.'

Sophine nodded, her dark eyes alight with purpose. She flicked her hair past her shoulders.

Ariene touched each of them on the shoulder and without another word, marched away. Thaniel hurried to catch up.

381

Rigel turned to the great wooden doors and knelt on the cold stone before them. His Battlemason honour guard formed up around him in a ring of metal, facing out, weapons ready. He closed his eyes, as much to shut out the uninspiring sight of soldiers' backsides as to concentrate.

'This is the end of everything,' he muttered to himself, hoping to reach the bleak despair he knew had generated his power before. 'The Senators are dying. The Echelarch is a monster. If I can't do this, it's over…'

Nothing. Either he was too wired or it was too artificial. He tried to conjure his mother's face, the blurry vision that normally slipped into his brain like a sliver of hot iron, carrying with it all the guilt and sadness of the terrible disappointment she must have felt towards him to have sent him away. It didn't come. Instead, to his surprise there was another face, strong and proud, framed by thick greying hair.

They didn't believe in you, but I do…

There it was. Gradual at first. A glimmer of heat, like an overturned coal that flares suddenly into new life. Slowly rising, the heat swelled up, becoming bright behind his eyes, a strange radiance he could sense but not see.

He held Ariene's face in his mind, her pride in him pouring like golden light into a void he had never known existed somewhere deep and dark inside him.

Enough snivelling…

…be who you are…

The power was strong, the force of it thrumming like a furnace in his belly.

'Show me,' he whispered through his astonishment, trying to adjust to this new source of energy. A soldier looked round at him curiously. 'Show me the life-webs...'

A tiny mote of silver appeared before his eyes, gleaming dully against the black that had replaced his sight. It grew, gathering form, lengthening, twisting, looping back on itself. Slowly at first, then faster and faster still, it traced the form of a person a few metres away, lying on its side with its head to the floor. The glittering web of the body came into focus, many thousands of interlinking strands flickering with silver life, the clusters of light around the heart and brain pulsing in arhythmic, erratic flashes. And beyond the complex web, another began to resolve itself, glittery silver threads rapidly forming the shape of another person, this one moving and gesturing. Another, just beyond, still and unmoving as the first. More, and still more. A vast room full of them.

Rigel gasped as the vision moved closer and shifted to appear below him, as though he were flying through a black room filled with hundreds of silver-wire figures, all of them pulsing with light but many of them fading and dull.

'Show me,' Rigel said to the darkness, his voice a faint whisper like a ghost drifting through a dream. 'Show me...'

Swirls of green began to flicker into focus, squirming and writhing as though trying to avoid his gaze, seeming to stay just out of sight as he moved his eyes towards them.

'No,' he whispered, reaching down inside himself further and letting the fire within him burn brighter, 'show me...'

The green was visible now. Interlinking with some of the figures, invading them. Infiltrating them. Tying itself slowly around the strands of ghost-light. But there were so many figures. Too many networks to focus on at once. The green light was everywhere at once; Rigel tried to draw back to see it all, but he bobbed weakly, unable to rise.

'More power,' he muttered, opening up his emotions to release more energy. A dim memory of a warning threatened to rise to the front of his conscious mind and he pushed it firmly away. The heat washed over him, intense and thrilling. He rose higher, riding the wave of power and gasping at the sheer delight of wielding it. The green was everywhere, he could see it all now, twisting and writhing within some bodies, rebuffed and shut out of others. It was within his power, all he had to do was reach out and wrench it from them. He stretched out a hand, closing it tight and feeling the rippling green almost squealing in his grip–

'Sir!' someone was shouting at him. Rigel rocked on his knees and gasped, trying to open his eyes. The vision collapsed. Pain wracked his body and he toppled over, shrieking as an intense burning sensation washed over him. There was a foul smell in the air, like burning hair...

It went dark, as someone threw something over him and thumped him hard through it. He moaned in pain.

'It's out,' the voice was saying. 'I think he's ok...'

Rigel sat up and tore the quick-thinking soldier's cloak from his body. His skin was red and raw in places, angry burns along his arms and the back of his hands. He hissed as he looked at it.

The young captain reached out a hand to help him up.

'Are you alright sir?' he asked, looking him up and down with something between revulsion and pity.

Rigel nodded and fell back to his knees, trying not to look at his shaking, blistered arms.

'I have to try again,' he slurred. 'I have to try...'

***

The dank lower floor of the Senate Building housed the cells, rough-cut holes in the stone with heavy iron bars, they were the kinds of places where one could be conveniently forgotten. As Ariene had predicted, they were heaving with prisoners, not all of whom were still alive. People cried out and thrust hands through the bars, pleading and begging.

Ariene moved along the walkway, heading for the prison officer's quarters, steadfastly refusing to speak to anyone before she'd dealt with the guards and had the chance to actually make a difference.

As she passed one cell, however, a voice cut through the rabble. 'Ariene!'

She turned and gasped at the sight. Overseer Skylock was no less massive for her short imprisonment, but lines showed in her face that hadn't been there before and her skin was pale and sweaty.

'Skylock,' Ariene ran to the cell and put her hands through the bar. Skylock grimaced and raised her hands, with great effort since they were weighted down with an enormous pair of shackles.

'What did they do?' Ariene asked, in spite of herself.

'Nothing,' Skylock rasped. 'That's the problem. Nothing, for days. I think they want me to die here.'

'Not today Skylock. And not tonight.'

'So ask me tomorrow?' finished the Overseer with a small smile. Ariene nodded. 'Thaniel,' she said softly.

By her side, the blonde mage reached out a hand and clenched his fist. The shackles warped and snapped, falling with a heavy clang to the stone floor. Skylock instinctively massaged her abused wrists and rose to her feet, the crack of her unkinking spine was like a snapping branch.

'Get them all out, Thaniel,' said Ariene. 'And if anyone comes round that corner, blast them.'

'Yes, ma'am,' replied Thaniel with a grim nod.

'We're getting you out of here, Skylock,' Ariene said. The Overseer shook her bald head.

'No, Ariene,' she growled, 'I'm not leaving.'

'You're not?'

'Not without that weasel's head.'

The door snapped open under the force of Thaniel's power, and swung heavily inward on rusted hinges.

The Overseer stepped out and stretched, her face a mask of grim rage.

***

Ariene had been right about the level beneath the Senate Building. Entering by a disused passage, Sophine had tentatively descended, conjuring a ball of light which made her think of the wall passages they'd all played in as kids. It was damp, dark, and extremely claustrophobic.

She'd made her way steadily, the twists and turns not nearly as labyrinthine as Ariene had suggested. A few storage rooms had stood to either side of the corridors, full of mouldering clothes and rotting furniture. Sophine had checked them all nonetheless, being not at all sure how far she needed to go until she was beneath the audience chamber.

Sophine turned a corner and instantly jerked back, extinguishing her light with a thought. Up ahead, the corridor was lit by a steady green glow. She peered round carefully, remembering how Kahin had nearly taken her head off with a thrown knife. Someone was down there, moving about in front of the light source, making the green flicker. Whoever it was had not seen her.

Sophine stepped out and moved quietly down the corridor, picking out the details of the chamber beyond in the peculiar light. The passage opened out into a large room, long and wide, at the centre of which stood a table with something on it. To the side was another table, with a bowl of some glowing green substance that was creating the steady light. Sophine peered at the device on the larger table. It was a long glass tube, like an enormous tankard, filled with a liquid that bubbled and hissed. A figure standing by the table was carefully adding something to the liquid, making it bubble and boil all the more. The figure jumped back as the liquid almost frothed up to the top, but it did not overflow. The air above the tankard seemed to ripple, as though whatever was in the tankard was hot like stone on a summer's day. The apparatus was placed just beneath a small hole in the ceiling.

'You've come to stop me, haven't you?' said a voice. It was a high-pitched, unsteady voice, and the speaker punctuated it with a short, derisive laugh. The figure placed a bag on the table and turned, dusting his hands off. He was a young man, his pale skin gleaming green in the peculiar illumination. He seemed unable to keep still, jerking and twitching as he regarded her, his interlaced fingers wiggling.

'It looks like I'm already too late,' she said, moving slowly forward. She eyed the tankard; she could probably just knock it aside, but she didn't know what might happen if she did. It could explode, bring the building down. She'd heard stories about accidents in alchemists' workshops and this looked like a decidedly unstable compound to say the least.

'Oh, no, no,' said the man, turning aside to regard the liquid bubbling in the tube. 'Not too late, no. Not yet.'

'And...who are you?' she asked, moving steadily closer. The man moved aside, keeping his distance from her. She wondered if he was some menial, sent to do his master's bidding. Something about him rang alarm bells within her but she couldn't be sure why, in fact her thoughts were being strangely slow. She blinked and focused on the tube, dimly aware of the thin man moving away, going around behind her.

'Oh me?' the man laughed a rasping, high-pitched titter of a laugh that set her teeth on edge. 'I'm the man with the plan. The visionary.'

'You work with Mountebank?' she asked, reaching out to touch the tube. The liquid within seethed and she jerked back.

'Careful now,' said the weedy man in his reedy voice. 'Handle with care!' He giggled.

'Is this safe to touch?' she asked, peering at the tube. 'How do I get it out of here?' She glanced around the room and realised it wasn't in fact a room at all. Passages like the one she'd entered by stretched off in front and to the left, down to other little corners lit by green glows.

Four corners. Four tubes. This was a square of access corridors beneath the chamber.

'To get it out now would be quite impossible,' said the little man with what sounded like genuine regret. 'A careful mix in a contained environment like this and the result is quite toxic, oh my yes! But toxic in a *controlled* way. People won't just keel over and die, no no nothing so crude. They won't realise they're corpses until sometime this evening when they're safely away from here! Best not to fiddle in case they all choke to death.' He tittered again, and she heard a peculiar tapping she couldn't place until she realised he was dancing a little jig behind her. She tried to turn, but her thoughts were gummy and her body was sluggish. She stumbled, falling against the table, and the little man jerked forward to catch her.

'Stupid girl!' he growled, the jovial trickster gone and replaced in an instant by a raging lunatic. He flung her to the side, and she yelped as whatever had been cracked in her chest during the fight with Kahin jarred against the stone. She rolled over, trying to rise, the thought that this was Lyoris Mountebank himself finally forcing its way through her addled senses. She kept her eyes on him as she got her feet underneath her, but he was too busy carefully adjusting the tube to notice her. Or so she thought until she reached him.

With a smooth motion, he turned and expressionlessly pressed something cold against her stomach. She suddenly felt light-headed, dizzy, and something was wet on her hands as she touched where he'd pushed her.

Sophine stumbled a few paces and collapsed, gasping.

'I think,' she mumbled, her thoughts scattered into fragments of conflicting voices, 'I think I've been stabbed.'

The wiry man turned at that and came to crouch alongside her.

'You know,' he said with a frown, tapping a finger against his lips, 'I think you might be right…'

A large shadow detached itself from the wall with feline grace and enclosed the Echelarch-Elect's head between mighty, vengeful hands.

'Acclaim this, Your Grace,' growled Overseer Skylock, and twisted the Echelarch's neck in one sudden motion, snapping his spine with a sound like a cracking whip that echoed loudly in the ghostly chamber. His limp body fell heavily to the cold stone floor, lifeless.

'Thaniel,' Ariene said from behind the massive Overseer, 'it's all up to you now. Burn it, burn it all.'

***

The green threads were writhing and resisting, twisting and tearing out of his grip as he pulled them inexorably out of the bodies of the dying Senators. Rigel could feel the heat burning within him, wanting desperately to rise up and consume him, but he held on to his control and forced it back. His mind hung above the black chamber, pulling on the green, seeing some of the dull grey webs beginning to spark to silvery life again, but it was hard. So hard. There were so many, so much pestilence and infection, and the power to burn it away was so very close and tempting…

The ground shook, throwing him to the side and scattering the soldiers standing around him.

Something cracked overhead, a chunk of marble falling to shatter by his feet amidst a drift of falling dust. He stood up, his heart sinking at the thought that once again he'd failed to complete his task. The ground shook again, sending more cracks snaking across the marble and stone of the Senate Building.

'Sophine,' he breathed, taking a step towards the passage to the underground just as Ariene and Overseer Skylock exited at a dead run. The hugely muscled Overseer was carrying Sophine, who moaned and clutched her stomach…

'Rigel!' Ariene shouted at him as he ran to them. She pointed back the way she'd come. 'Thaniel!' she cried.

Rigel hesitated, torn between Sophine and his friend. 'Go!' Ariene yelled. 'She'll be fine!'

Not knowing what else to do, Rigel ran across the quaking ground to the door they'd used and plunged down into the darkness. Up ahead, flames were flowing like liquid, billowing and surging down the corridors. A figure stood silhouetted against the bright orange and yellow, hands outstretched, screaming.

'Thaniel!' Rigel shouted, holding his hands up against the heat and trying to reach his friend.

Thaniel stopped screaming, but he didn't turn, didn't lower his hands.

'Thaniel, stop!'

Fire poured from Thaniel in torrents, cracking walls, destroying stone. The ground quaked again and an ominous creaking came from overhead.

'I can't! It won't stop!' Thaniel managed to shriek, his screams becoming sobs of terror as the flame continued to pour from him, cascading in unchecked fury like water from a broken dam.

Rigel tried to inch closer but the heat was too intense. As he turned his head away from the terrible fire, he noticed a chunk of stone that had fallen from one of the rapidly spreading cracks in the tunnel wall. He bent and picked it up, a memory of the day in the quarry before this had all started bobbing to the front of his mind. The three of them, throwing rocks into the lake and talking about the future. He smiled, in spite of himself, a peculiar sense of calm washing over him.

He opened his palm and let the rock rise to hover above it. Then he glanced at Thaniel, and with a nudge of will smacked it into his friend's head. Thaniel yelped and dropped to the floor, the last gouts of flame sputtering and dying. Rigel ran to him and heaved his friend to his shoulders. The corridor shook and creaked, rivulets of dust and stone spilling from cracks breaking through the walls like the jagged arcs of lightning.

Rigel ran as best he could through the corridors, hefting the unconscious form of Thaniel. They burst from the disused doorway and joined the panicked surge of people running from the Senate Building. Someone had let the Senators out, and most of them seemed well enough to run. Lord Barten was a few metres away, looking horribly ill but still managing to shout for order while Ariene's pet soldiers penned in the Senators. The newly promoted Captain was trying to make them all drink from Orswell's wine bottles and from the frustrated look on his face was not having an easy time of it.

'Rigel,' Ariene said from somewhere behind him. He turned, gently easing Thaniel down to the ground.

'He's not burned?' Ariene asked, peering at Thaniel with surprise. Rigel shrugged, the pain of his own burns returning in a searing flash.

'Sophine needs healing,' Ariene said. Rigel felt panic rise within him.

'I thought you said she'd be fine!' Ariene was unmoved.

'And she will be,' she said evenly, 'when you heal her.'

Rigel stared at Ariene for a moment.

'It was for the city,' she said softly.

He snorted, not quite a laugh. 'Politicians,' he muttered.

***

Rigel was still healing Sophine and himself, head bowed and eyes closed, when the Senate Building finally collapsed into a smouldering ruin. Thaniel's sorcerous fires continued to burn, melting superheated stone and reaching up to blacken the jagged remains of the pillars that had supported the once-beautiful roof. They stood staring at the broken husk of the Senate Building, as the smoke rose into the clear sky.

'Pretty impressive fire,' Rigel said eventually.

Thaniel nodded. 'Thanks.'

'You going to heal it?'

'Heal it?'

'*I heal buildings*,' Rigel mewled in a mocking voice. Thaniel hit him on the shoulder.

'Maybe soon,' said Ariene from behind them. 'But not yet. We need to work out what it's going to be first.'

'I wasn't being serious,' Rigel said quietly. Ariene ignored him and carried on as though he hadn't spoken.

'This time, we're going to do it right. No purple veils over disused thrones, no pretending the past isn't gone.'

They nodded.

'Time for a new start,' said Sophine.

'But first,' said Thaniel, peering up at the column of smoke, 'we have a ship to catch.'

Acknowledgements

In many ways, *The Shrouded Throne* represents my frustration with the world we find ourselves in post 2016, and celebrates the idea that even in these dark days there's hope for change. But I couldn't have written it alone.

I have to start with a big thanks to Rowan at Vulpine, for making this book a reality. I know the original draft had so many errors you nearly went mad editing it, but thanks for sticking with me.

To my friends, many of whom have served as unwitting inspiration for the characters or their names, thanks for existing and enabling me to steal your various attributes. Since none of the characters are based on me, for once, I needed you to feed my bibliovampiric creative process. Consider yourselves immortalised.

But the biggest thank you is to my husband. I have zero confidence in a writing project when I start, and his encouragement and support even from page one means a huge amount to me.

Steven D. Jackson is a British novelist, who lives on the South Coast with his husband and son. You can find him on Facebook, on Twitter at @SDJackson85 or Instagram at @steven_d_jackson.

If blogs are still a thing when you're reading this, then he has one at sdjackson.blogspot.com.